The Last Dance

Danielle and Friends
Book Two

Nick J. Mercorella

Creative Consultant: Deb Rhodes
Cover by: Gabrielle Mercorella
Author Photo Credit: Eileen Escarda
Editor: Bridget Hutchinson

ISBN: 978-0692626665
ASIN: B01AXOB5LO

Acknowledgements

I have a number of women in my life. A daughter and daughter-in-law, four step-daughters and a step-daughter-in-law. Between them, they have given me six grand-daughters, and I lost count of how many great-grand-daughters. A kid sister, sister-in-law and a number of nieces.

For the most part, they are all strong, confident women. I use their strength to portray the strong female characters in my books. I thank them for that and for being a vital part of my life.

Again I have to thank Deb Rhodes for her thoughtful input. These stories would be very different without her honest critic.

Deb, right on as usual.

Thank you Gabby for the perfect cover.

Eileen, I never looked so good. Thanks for that!

Bridget, I promise to be more careful in the future.

And, thanks to those of you who have taken the time to read this book. You are the reason I do this.

To the women in my life!

I love you all!

Table of Contents

The
Last
Dance

Prologue

Evelyn sighed as the maitre'd walked away after seating us. I concurred. He was very good looking and charming. Although I was with three very lovely ladies, I always got the lion's share of attention because I was the only one who possessed a naked left ring finger. My sister Elizabeth, who had just turned forty, and my two sisters-in-law, both in their mid-thirties were definitely head turners. I was sure I could hold my own with them, but, as I said, I had an advantage. I was single!

Sandra, my Brother Ed's wife, looking at the back of the retreating maitre'd said, "Catherine, I don't know whether to envy you or feel sorry for you."

I gave her one of my, what does that mean looks.

"It must be wonderful to be free to date any good looking man that comes along, but I'm not sure how that kind of freedom could compare to what I have with your brother and the boys."

She had an excellent point. I loved my life, but I did sometimes envy what Beth, Sandra, and Evelyn had. Loving husbands, great children and they always seemed very content with their lives.

"It's nice. But it's not all it seems."

"Bull," Evelyn answered, "You know darn well you could have a date with that guy before we left the restaurant tonight! What man wouldn't want a date with a tall, blond, blue-eyed beauty with a figure most women would sell their souls for?"

She was probably right. I never had trouble getting a date when I wanted one, and the maitre'd in question did seem interested, but it truly wasn't always as fabulous as it seemed.

"Maybe, but, I'm on a hiatus. I decided to take some time off. My last date didn't turn out too well."

I got inquiring looks from all three of them, but I wasn't about to ruin our monthly sister's night out with a sad story. I made light of my comment and as always, we had a good time together.

But I did give some thought to my life. I was thirty-three years old. I had a very comfortable two bedroom apartment that was my oasis away from the world. I drove a mid-sized car that was less than a year old. I loved my job and the people I worked with.

I made enough money to allow me a comfortable if not

extravagant lifestyle. And, as Evelyn intimated, I always seemed to have a date when I wanted one. There was only one love affair in my life, and that was many, many years ago and ended in disaster. Since then, I had a few brief romances and a few short-lived affairs but had never gotten serious with a man.

I was not free with my virtue, and I choose the men I sleep with very carefully. And, never on a first date. Well...almost never. There had been a few occasions, including Jamey, the last man I dated.

His was good looking and charming, but it was our first date, and there was something about him that made me uncomfortable. I was having a good time with him, and the discomfort I felt wasn't a serious problem, but there was no chance we would share a bed that night. But, I did wind up in a hotel room with him that very night. I'm still not sure why, and I'm not all too clear on what happened in that room, but when I woke up the next morning with the mother of all headaches, I also felt used and just a little ashamed.

That's when I decided to take a little time off from the wonderful world of men and reevaluate the criteria I used to determine who I would date. I didn't expect it to last this long. It had been two months since that night with Jamey, and I still felt no need to rush back onto the playing field.

When the maitre'd passed our table again, I naturally glanced in his direction. I wasn't the only one. But my attention was drawn to the man he was escorting to a table. He was probably the most gorgeous man I had ever laid eyes on. Tall and handsome. He had a confident air about him, and the girl with him was exactly what you would expect to be with such a man. She was spectacular.

Now that is something I would break a few rules for!

Little did I know the changes that were about to take place in my life would be controlled by this very man. My job, my life, my entire future would be affected by this man, and I would be the one to initiate it all.

Chapter 1 - The New Boss

We rotated the restaurants where we met for our monthly night with the girls, and we wouldn't be back to De Giorgio's for a while, so playing up to the good looking maitre'd and getting him to ask me out would have to wait. The next month we met on Wednesday as usual, but the month after that I had to ask the girls to switch to a Tuesday or Thursday.

My boss was retiring, and the guys in the Sales Department decided to take him out to dinner. John had done such an excellent job for the company that the Dillman brothers were throwing a big retirement bash for him on Friday, but we wanted to do something special for him, and Wednesday was the only night we all had free.

We were all very sad. John was a good man, and we had flourished under his leadership. We would miss him. After the party on Friday, we probably wouldn't see him very often. He promised to stay in touch, but we knew his wife had plans for an extended vacation.

We had done so well with John at the helm, the company expanded and built a new factory. It was three times the size of the original unit, and it was up to us to bring in the orders to keep the production lines rolling.

In spite of our sadness at John's departure, Friday's party was a blast. John was seated at the head table with the Dillman brothers and another man. A very good looking man. I had a feeling I had seen him before, but we were having so much fun I didn't give it much thought. The entire sales team sat together, and we reminisced about our time together.

Sara, who was John's Administrative Assistant, brought her husband, Peter. Ted, our most experienced salesman, brought a very classy lady as his date. Tim brought his wife, Emily and Artie our most junior salesman brought a sweet young girl. I was with a gentleman I had dated a couple of times over the course of two or three months. He was pushing for more of a relationship, but I wasn't that into him, and this would probably be our last date.

Move up or move out! Isn't that what they say?

The five of us gossiped about Ted's date. Not his usual fare. Ted was the lady's man of the office, and he changed girlfriends as

3

often as men changed their socks. And most of his dates were not what you would consider classy. But, this one was different. Constance was lovely, bright and charming. We agreed among ourselves that Ted was attempting to change his image. We all felt he was in line for John's job, and he was trying to show the Dillman brothers that he was cleaning up his act.

I liked the people I worked with. I even liked Ted in spite of the fact he wouldn't accept my constant turndowns for a date. I did have a rule against inter-office dating. It wasn't a set in stone, never to be broken rule, but I knew it wasn't a good idea, and there wasn't anyone in the company interesting enough to make me break that particular rule.

But, Ted never stopped trying. When I moved over from accounting to do the specifications package for the sales department, Ted's advances became more low-key and sincere. You might even say more respectful. But, I still had no interest. The party went along, and I think we all had a good time. We all said our goodbyes to John when it broke up.

When my date brought me home, I knew he was ready to ask for more or end the relationship.

"Catherine, we've had four dates over two months. I really like you, and I'd like to see you more often."

"I like you too, but I'm not in a good place right now, and a relationship is not something I'm into at the moment."

There were more words between us and when he left, I knew he wouldn't call again. I spent some time thinking about what I had told him. It was true. Ever since my break-up with Bobby, I have never dated the same man twice in a row. I knew that someday I would have to change my attitude, but I still had trouble trusting men to the point where I was willing to give my heart away. I put it out of my mind and went to bed.

Monday morning we walked into the office leaderless. It would be strange without John here. There was a message waiting for me. The Dillman Brothers had called a meeting in our conference room for eleven o'clock, and the entire sales department was to attend.

I was the second to arrive. Sara was already there setting out pads, pencils, water glasses and such. When the three salesmen walked in Ted sat down next to me as usual. He never stopped trying. We talked about Friday's party and how strange it was going to be with John gone. Eleven o'clock on the dot, Both Dillman brothers walked in. They had another man with them.

Paul and Patrick Dillman were very friendly and outgoing people. They both asked if we had a good time at the party and, as usual, were very congenial. They both had a way of being extremely friendly and still upholding the dividing line between employer and employee. I liked them both. They were good people to work for.

Paul, the senior Dillman, and CEO of Dillman Brother's Manufacturing took his place at the head of the conference table. Patrick, the COO, took the seat to his right as usual. The third man, the man I saw with them at the party Friday night was offered the seat to Paul's left, the place usually occupied by John. With a look, Mr. Dillman asked for quiet.

"People, meet Marco Antonelli. I cannot tell you how lucky we are to have this man as our new SVP of Sales. I expect great things from you now that Marc is in charge."

That announcement was our first shock. The man he was replacing wasn't even a Vice President, much less a Senior Vice President.

Marco Antonelli seemed to be in his mid-thirties, looked to be in excellent shape and was extremely good looking. I had the same feeling I had Friday night. I knew I had met, or at least seen this man before. He's not the type of man you could forget. I took a good look at him, and finally realized it was the man I had seen at De Giorgio's Restaurant a couple of months ago when I was with Beth, Sandra, and Evelyn. He was the handsome man with the light brown, wavy hair and killer eyes. I also remembered the gorgeous woman that was with him.

I could imagine Ted's response to the announcement. This new guy was going to be competition when it came to attracting the ladies. Tim and Artie seemed to take the announcement with a wait and see attitude.

After Mr. Dillman left, Mr. Antonelli gave a little speech.

"I intend to spend the first couple of weeks getting to know what you do here at Dillman Bros. and getting to know you individually. Until I have a handle on things, please continue doing what you have always done."

The first week we hardly had any contact with him. He spent his time in his office going over reports, upstairs on the Executive Floor or with the Production Manager. The only contact I had with my new boss was a friendly, "Good Morning, Ms. Jensen," as we passed in the corridor.

Gino, the Production Manager, whose sister was Administrative Assistant to one of the Dillman Brothers gave us our second shock concerning Mr. Antonelli.

"I heard they gave this Antonelli guy a one-year contract at a salary of a million dollars."

That was an outrageous amount of money for a Sales Manager, and everyone wondered what kind of magic this man possessed.

The second and third week he interviewed each of us individually. He devoted almost an entire day to each of us. My turn came on Wednesday of week three.

"I prefer to be called Marc. This is going to be a team effort, and I'm just another member of the team. Would you mind if I called you Catherine instead of Ms. Jensen?"

That was OK with me, and I sensed my new boss was a gentleman.

Marc was not only great looking, but he was also classy and elegant. He carried himself with an air of confidence and authority. And I guessed that under the suits he always wore, was a great body. I wasn't the only one who noticed.

Sara, who was happily married, never missed a chance to gaze at Marc when he wasn't looking. Susan, my primary contact with the Design Department, also found it difficult to avoid looking at our new boss. The other girls in the Design Department were always finding excuses to come over to our area when Marc was in the office. This man was a magnet for women, but he seemed disinterested.

His questions for me were direct and to the point.

"Exactly what is it you do for the Sales Department?"

"The products we produce are very detailed and complicated and require exact specifications. These specs have to be included in the contracts we have with our customers, in great detail, and they have to be sent to the production floor in perfect order. I'm the one who takes the design sheets puts together the Specification Package in additional to doing some secretarial work."

Our meeting didn't last long, and I wondered where I would fit into his plans for the department.

Marc also spent time talking to the people in the Design Department. Thursday he spent most of the day upstairs on the Executive Floor and the rest of it with the designers. The only one he seemed to spend any real time with was Susan Cunningham.

Susan was with the Design Department and she and I frequently consulted on the various specifications our customers required. Susan was a beautiful, and charming girl and all of the single men in the office were taking turns making a run at her. Although Susan was a shy girl, it was obvious she had a thing for Artie. Everyone knew that Artie was more than interested, but he too was very shy and never made a move. I'm not sure if anyone else noticed, but I thought:

If you don't do something soon, Artie, Marc is going to steal her away from you.

Friday morning we all got an email stating there would be a sales meeting at ten o'clock in the Conference Room.

When I arrived, Tim and Artie were already there. Ted was the last of the salesman to arrive and sat next to me as usual. When Marc arrived, he sat at the head of the conference table and began by asking us if we wanted coffee or something before we got started. Marc always seemed to have a container of coffee in his hand. When we were all settled, he made a formal statement.

"It is my practice to record this type of meeting. Sara will transcribe the notes, and you will all get a copy. I have found this is very helpful later on when we discuss various aspects of the meeting. So, if there are no objections, we can begin."

Hearing no objections, Marc started by telling us he had spent most of yesterday with the CEO and the other Senior VPs.

"I told them under the circumstances, you guys were doing an excellent job, and I believe what I told them is true. The Sales Department had done so well the company decided to increase their production facilities. Now that we have four times the capacity, we need four times the orders. But your contracts are so complicated you guys don't have the time to pursue the new business needed.

"The solution is simple. Four times the capacity means four times the number of salesmen required to fill that capacity."

Marc looked around the room to gauge our attention.

"I have a different solution, and I wanted your input if it seems practical. My plan has three main components, and I suspect you will not be happy with the first two. This is completely radical, but before you shoot me down, I'm asking you to take a week and give it serious thought. Then, if you don't like it, come back to me individually or as a group and tell me why. Maybe together we can find a way to adjust it."

After he gave us a minute to contemplate what he had just said, he spelled it out for us.

Radical didn't begin to describe his plan.

Chapter 2 – The Plan

Marc handed us each a couple of sheets of paper.

"The type of customers we deal with now are too small to fill the new plant. We have to find larger companies with bigger needs. I've compiled a list of the companies we should go after."

After giving us a minute to look over the list, Marc continued.

"Impressive list, isn't it? These people are not the one hundred thousand to one million dollar type of orders we are used to. These people can generate orders between one million to one hundred million dollars."

Tim was the first to speak.

"I'd love to sell to these people, Marc, but we're seen as too small to handle their business."

"Not anymore, we have quadrupled our capacity."

Artie told Marc, "True, but they don't know that."

"Then we'll have to tell them."

I think Ted spoke for everyone.

"Marc, we'd all love a chance to sell to these companies, but there is no way we can even get an appointment with them. Our reputation as an excellent but small company precedes us. How do we get in to see these people?"

Marc smiled. A cat that swallowed the canary smile.

"Through the back door."

That got questioning looks from everyone, including me.

What was he proposing, we lie in wait for these people at the back door of their office and force them to listen?

When the answer came, it was beautifully simple and incredibly complex.

"Let me explain. In the column next to the names of potential customers is another name and in the third column is yet another name. For instance, next to the potential client, Carter Aviation, is the name Tony Paterson and next to his name is Danielle Palmer. Tony Paterson will get you an appointment with James Carter of Carter Aviation."

"And why would Tony Paterson be willing to get me an

appointment with Carter Aviation?" Ted asked.

"Because, Danielle Palmer will ask him to."

Before anyone had a chance to question that response, Marc held up his hand.

"There are one hundred and fifty names in the first column. Those are potential customers. The second column has forty-nine names. These forty-nine people have good business and/or personal relations with the names in the first column. Good enough to get you an appointment with the people you need to see.

"The third column has six names on it. These six people have a business and/or personal relations with the people on the second sheet. They will introduce you to the people on the second sheet."

Marc paused and gave us time to attempt to understand what he was saying. When he got nothing but questioning looks, he explained.

"You will meet the people in column three. We will have dinner with them. They already know why we need their assistance. You will like these people. They are all personal friends of mine, they are all very friendly people, and they are more than willing to help."

Another pause. This time, Marc looked at each of us individually trying to gauge our reaction and understanding. Seeing nothing but confusion, he explained.

"Here's how it will work. When Danielle Palmer was with Deltron Motors, she came up with a gadget for diesel trucks that revolutionized the trucking industry. She sold that device to Paterson Trucking. Paterson spent forty-seven million dollars to equip his entire fleet with this LNG/Diesel thing. It has resulted in a fuel cost savings to Paterson of over fifteen percent. With fifteen thousand trucks on the road, you can imagine the savings.

"Because of these savings, Paterson Trucking has taken on many new clients, and Carter Aviation is one of them. Paterson has reduced Carter Aviation's land freight costs by over twelve percent."

Marc looked at the four of us again.

"As you can imagine, Carter Aviation loves Paterson Trucking and Paterson Trucking loves Danielle Palmer, and Danielle Palmer is a friend of mine and soon will be a friend of the Dillman Bros. Sales Department. Questions?"

Of course, there when tons of questions and while the boys were getting them answered, I looked over the names on the third column.

Nick Amonti: I knew the name. He was the CEO of NAS Financial Group, a company with assets of over a billion dollars. His own personal net worth was rated at close to that figure.

Danielle Palmer: Anyone who watched the news or read a newspaper five or six years ago knew her name. She had developed a gadget for diesel engines that was truly revolutionary.

Terrance Daniels: The only thing I knew about him was Danielle's Industries produced some of the best kitchen equipment in the world, both for domestic and professional use. I have a few of his gadgets in my kitchen.

Stacy Geer: Every woman in the world knows who Stacy Geer is. She's the hottest Woman's Fashioner designer around and has been for years.

Harry and Angela Combs: I didn't recognize those names at all, but being in the company of the other four, they must be heavy hitters too.

And Marc had said they were personal friends of his, and they would be willing to do this for us.

There is a lot more to Marco Antonelli then any of us realized.

When things quieted down, Marc continued.

"You three are much too valuable to spend most of your time on small companies and renewal orders. I know they require your expertise and Catherine's Spec Package, but for the most part, they are just reorders.

"I want each of you to have an assistant. Their function will be to handle the reorders. You will still be in charge of the account, but you will not have to spend as much time going over contracts, which in the end only have minor changes.

"We have very talented people here at Dillman. You know most of them and their capabilities. I want each of you to pick someone you feel you can work with and give me their name. If I agree, we will both talk to them about the new position."

Ted immediately said, "Good idea Marc, I'll take Catherine."

Marc looked at Ted. After a long contemplative moment, he asked, "Am I missing something here, gentlemen?"

Getting no response, he continued with more questions.

"When was the last time any of you signed a contract without Catherine's Spec Package? Could you even sign a contract without the Spec Package? Are you willing to give up Catherine's work and use her as an order clerk?"

11

Well someone really does appreciate what I do around here. I could learn to like my new boss, outsider or not.

Again, getting no response, he continued.

"Listen, guys, this is really going to take a team effort. You three seem to get along fine. I've checked you sales records and over the course of the past three years you have all earned approximately the same amount of commissions. That's important to note because part two of the plan requires that you consider becoming a real team, one for all and all for one."

Once again, he gave us a minute to absorb that statement.

"I would like you to agree to an adjustment in your employment contract with Dillman. It will be temporary until we see how it works out. I am suggesting we pool the sales commissions, and each of you draw a quarter of the pool, with the other quarter distributed among your assistants."

This time, a much longer pause while the guys thought over what Marc had just proposed. As promised, it was radical.

"Don't think too much about it until I finish. I don't expect an answer for a week. Talk it over among yourselves and I will be available if you have any questions. I think to implement the rest of my idea we have to be available to help each other, and shared reward will make it easier to give up the time necessary. How about a break for lunch?"

Marc left the room, and the guys talked about what Marc had said while we all munched on deli sandwiches. When I made a trip to the little girl's room, I again noticed Marc was talking to Susan. When the meeting continued, it became very interesting indeed.

"Before we continue, I need to tell you something. My contract with Dillman Brothers is for one year. It will not be renewed under any circumstances. And, since I am being paid very well for my service, I have instructed the people upstairs that there will be no Sales Managers cut out of your commissions. For the remaining eleven months of my contract, there will be no deduction for me from your commission checks."

Even if we didn't increase sales and only continued to get the sales we were used to, it meant Marc was giving up over two hundred thousand dollars in commissions. Even if Gino was right and the company was paying Marc a million dollars that was a lot of money to give away.

How to win friends and influence people. If Marc thinks that this move will have a positive effect on the three salesmen...he might be right!

12

The meeting ended a little after four. Marc asked me to stay behind.

"Need a potty break?" he asked, "I need a cup of coffee. Why don't you meet me in the break room?"

When I got to the break room, Marc was sitting at a table with his container of coffee, looking very thoughtful. He stood up as I approached his table.

Truly a gentleman.

After we were seated, he seemed unsure of himself. This was odd. One thing I had noticed since he was first introduced to us was this was a man who was very sure of himself. He always seemed to know exactly who he was, what he was doing and where he was headed. The beginning of the conversation surprised me.

"Catherine, you aren't obligated to answer this, but it could be significant to what I have outlined today."

"Fire away," I said.

"I know this is none of my business, and I could probably get into a lot of trouble for asking you this, but I'd really like to know the answer."

He hesitated, seeming unsure if he should continue.

"Is there something personal going on between you and Ted?"

"Wow! That really is personal. Why does it matter?"

"Catherine, what I outlined today is really radical, and the only way it will work is if the four of you believe in it. Believe in me.

"Salesmen don't like anyone to fool around with their commission checks. I've asked them to share their commissions, not only with each other but also with their new assistants. I need them to trust me for them to be willing to do that.

"I also have plans for you that will require them to trust you more, and a personal relationship with Ted would most likely get in the way of what we have to do."

Marc looked at me. Directly into my eyes. What he said next gave me more insight into the man who was my boss.

"Catherine, you must believe I am an honest and honorable man. I have no vested interest in Dillman Brothers. I agreed to take this position for a year. I get paid either way. If we fail, it doesn't cost me anything. If we succeed, I don't gain anything. I will not extend my contract under any circumstances. I have my own business to run. I took this job as a favor to a friend, and I would like to succeed because I would like to succeed. That's just the way I am!"

Before I had a chance to answer, Marc looked at his watch.

"It's quitting time, but I'd like to continue our conversation. Are you free this evening? Would you have dinner with me?"

I didn't know how to answer that.

Was it an order? He was my boss, and this was a business.

Marc must have guessed what I was thinking.

"It's an invitation, not an obligation. We can continue this on Monday. But I would like to tell you what I have in mind and give you the weekend to think about it."

I agreed, and after we closed up our offices, we met in the parking lot. Marc suggested we take one car. He said I could pick up my car after dinner, so I agreed to go with him.

I learned a lot about my new boss that night and a lot about the man, Marc Antonelli.

Chapter 3 – Dinner with the Boss

The conversation in the car was casual. Mostly small talk. The restaurant was very nice, and I noticed unusually quiet. Marc mentioned he often held business meetings here because it was so quiet. After we had our drinks and had ordered dinner, he returned to business.

"I'm sorry if you feel I was out of line with that question."

"It's OK, Marc. It just surprised me."

Well, girl, it's decision time. Are you going to trust this man or not?

"Marc, trusting you without actually knowing you is asking for quite a lot. But for some reason, I do. So, the answer to your question is no. Ted has tried to get me to date him since the day I started at Dillman, but I have this thing about interoffice relationships, and when I realized Ted was the skirt chaser he is, I was glad I turned him down. But, he keeps trying."

"Is that going to be a problem?"

"No! When it's time for business, Ted is all business. He's romantic pursuits have never interfered with his work. He's extremely good at what he does. We all expected he would be given the Head Salesman job, and it was a surprise when you were named instead."

"Any hard feelings?"

"A few grumbles at first, but I think they have a wait and see attitude now."

"What did you think of my plan?"

"Very ambitious. Do you really believe that we can get orders from the people on your list?"

"If we don't, Dillman Bros. will lose their new factory."

My next question was as personal as the one he asked me.

"Are you really good friends with the people on the third list?"

"Yes, I am,"

"They're all very rich. Does that mean you're rich too?"

"That's a very personal question," he answered.

"More personal than if I was having an affair with Ted."

It was a couple of minutes before I got an answer.

"OK Catherine, here's the deal. I need you to trust me. I need you to be completely open and honest with me. So, I will trust you and be completely open and frank with you."

"Sounds fair," I replied.

"Yes, Catherine. I am what you would consider rich. Not in Nick Amonti's class, but I can hold my own against Terry Daniels and Harry Combs. Is that important?"

"Then why did you take a job as Sales Manager for Dillman Bros. It doesn't make sense."

"Excellent point. It reinforces my opinion of you."

"And what is that?"

"That you are an intelligent lady and the perfect person to help me implement the plan I put forward this afternoon."

"I appreciate the compliment, but it doesn't answer my question."

"The truth is, I am doing this as a personal favor to Nick Amonti. And before you ask, Nick's interest is NAS Financial Group financed the expansion, and he wants to see the company fill the plant so he doesn't have to foreclose on the mortgage. Nick is a very smart businessman, but not all of his deals work out the way he planned. He can take the financial hit if this doesn't work, but it's against his nature."

"Why would you give up a year of your life to help Nick Amonti?"

"That, dear lady, is an excellent question. The answer is very long and complicated, and I will be happy to tell you about it at another time. The short version is I owe this man, and I am doing the kind of thing he would do for me if I asked him.

"Nick Amonti, The man worth over a billion dollars would take a job as a vice president in another company?"

"He's gone further than that. Some years ago, Nick was scouting for a vice president for his business. He had someone in mind, but he only knew them by reputation. Since NAS Financial Group is a family business, all key positions are held by family members, Nick wanted to be sure this person's personality would fit in. When a position opened up in her office, Nick took a position as Administrative Assistant to this department director. He held that job for over six months, if I remember right."

"Did he hire her?"

"No. When he got to know her, he realized she needed a job that offered her a challenge. The job Nick had in mind would be boring. He thought he could offer her enough to get her to make the move, but he was sure she wouldn't be happy there. So he went in another direction."

"I don't believe it!"

"It's true."

But, I did believe him. I was sure I would believe anything this man told me. He was so sincere.

"I can tell you more stories about him and why I'm doing this, but tonight, we need to talk about Dillman Bros. and your part in the plan. OK?"

I hope you're right about him, Catherine.

"You're the boss!"

"Yes," he said firmly, "I am the boss. But that only means I have the final say on anything that goes on. I need to be seen as just another member of the team. I will be out trying to help the salesmen with whatever is necessary. I need to be trusted by the entire team to make this work. I can't afford to appear to be above them."

"That's not going to be easy."

"I am well aware of that. It's why I need your help. It's obvious the guys respect you. They not only appreciate your work, but they respect you as a person. I don't want you to influence their decisions, but I would like you to get them to take my proposal seriously and give it serious thought before making up their minds. It's important they are all in agreement with what I have outlined."

I don't know why, I hardly knew him, but I had complete faith in this man. He seemed so genuine. Not only did I feel he could be trusted, but I felt his idea would work if given a chance.

"OK, Marc. I'm on your side. What do you need me to do?"

"What I need you to do first is trust me. I've told you about why I'm here and what I get out of this so you know I'm in this for the benefit of Dillman Brothers and no other reason. I run my own business. Nick Amonti is my partner. When he asked me to do this, I couldn't say no. The reason he asked me is he believes I am the man for the job. I don't want to let him down."

"Marc, I said I'm on your side. What can I do?"

"Catherine, I need you to babysit Ted, Tim, and Artie. I don't want you to influence their decisions, but I need you to let them know I am an honest man who can be trusted. I need them to have the confidence to come to me and openly discuss any disagreements they

17

have with me or the plan. I need them to believe I am a team member, and it truly is one for all and all for one. That's not going to be easy, but you're the only person they respect enough to listen to. And, second, I need you to tell me if there is a problem that they won't come to me with."

"I won't spy on them for you."

"I don't want you to spy for me. If there is a problem, encourage them to come to me with it. Make them believe I will listen. If that doesn't work, I'll have to go to them. But, I can't go to them if I don't know what the problem is. Fair?"

"Sounds fair?"

"There are a couple of other things we have to discuss tonight. What I told you about Nick Amonti and me has to stay between us. I trust it will remain our little secret. You can't even tell the rest of the team."

"Why?"

"Because, if word got out how far Nick was willing to go to keep one of his mortgages from being foreclosed, it would make it impossible for him to do business. There are a lot of hustlers out there, and it would be easy for them to borrow money from Nick and then rely on him to run their business for them. It could ruin him."

"OK, our secret."

"Next," he said, "I want more respect for the team. Our guys are not just salesmen. They are analysts. As of next week, we will be the Client Analysis Department. It signifies what we actually do. And the guys' title will be Client Analysts."

"Sounds impressive."

"That's the purpose. It should get us more respect from potential customers and also the rest of the people at Dillman Brothers."

After a short pause and a smile in my direction.

"On the same note, what you do is so important I want more respect for you. You will no longer have secretarial duties, for the team or anyone else. Sara is a pretty sharp gal. As of Monday, she will be responsible for all five of us. I will be in the field a lot, and I have no need for a full-time secretary."

Wow! He really does respect my contribution.

"You may have noticed I have been spending some time with Susan Cunningham."

I wasn't about to tell him I had noticed, so I just said, "I've been

18

too busy to notice much of anything outside my little cubbyhole."

He continued without noticing my little quip.

"She said you two get along pretty well. How true is that?"

"Very true. Susan and I get along just fine. She's a talented girl, and we often confer on the numbers I need for the spec sheets."

"Good. When the new orders start coming in, you'll need help. I've talked to the other members of the Design Department, and we all agree Susan is the right person to complement you. I have spent the better part of the last week feeling her out.

"I think she will not only agree to the transfer, but I think she would welcome it. She will be working under you, and I'm hoping you will mentor her and bring her up to speed as quickly as possible."

Now, an even bigger smile.

"You will be heading the department. As of Monday, you will be promoted to Director of Client Specifications and your salary will be increased to director level. Any questions?"

"Wait a minute. From clerk/secretary to Department Director in one jump. That's a lot to take in, in one gulp!"

"Catherine, no one in the department considers you a clerk or secretary. They know how important you are to them, and I'm sure they will agree with your promotion. When I was upstairs yesterday, that part was the easiest part to sell."

"This will take some getting used to. That's a big responsibility."

"A responsibility you have been carrying out for over three years, successfully. This is just recognition for your work. You are definitely qualified for the position, and I think you'll make a great mentor for Susan."

Then, very sincerely he said, "Catherine, I see big things in your future. You are an intelligent, talented and dedicated lady. You will go far in the corporate world. This is just a stepping stone."

I had nothing to say, and we were both quiet for a while.

The rest of the evening was filled with small talk. I tried to assimilate everything I had heard today and this evening, but it was way too much to think about all at once. And besides, I was having dinner with a very handsome, charming and wealthy gentleman.

Not bad Catherine Jensen, not bad at all!

When Marc dropped me off at my car, he asked if I would call him when I got home.

"Just so I know you got home safe."

"Marc, I'm thirty-three, not thirteen."

"Catherine, I'm old fashioned. I do respect the fact a woman can be independent and take care of herself, but I enjoy being a gentleman and treating women like ladies. Since you had dinner with me tonight and I'm not seeing you home, I'd just like to know you got home safe. OK?"

"OK," I said and took his cell phone number.

On the drive home, and right up until bedtime, Marco Antonelli kept swirling around in my head.

He really is a true gentleman, honest and sincere.

Then I had to admonish myself.

Remember, he's your boss, and even if he wasn't, you know how dangerous office relationships can be.

Oh well, not much of a chance for me anyway. A man with his charm, good looks and money probably has women like the one I saw him with standing in line.

Chapter 4 - The Meeting

Saturday morning, Tim called.

"Catherine, the guys decided to meet and discuss what we heard at the meeting yesterday. Since we all consider you a part of the sales team, we'd like you to come too."

Of course, I agreed. We meet at the Pub. It was one of the local bars that surrounded the office. We often stopped at one of them after work for a beer before heading home. I guess it made us feel closer to socialize out of the office.

I was the last to arrive, and the discussion was already in progress. Overall, they liked Marc's idea of going after bigger orders. They also like the idea of having an assistant to take care of the re-orders. That would surely free up their time, but it would also cost them. Tim was the most vocal.

"I don't mind pooling my commission checks with you guys, but giving twenty-five percent to three people we don't know is a problem for me. I appreciate Marc's decision to drop his cut, but that won't be enough to make up the difference if we don't produce more business."

They knew I had gone to dinner with Marc last night, and they wanted to know what we talked about. They also wanted to know what I thought of our new boss. At first, I wasn't sure what I could tell them. Then I remembered Marc's words, and I decided to trust what he had said.

"Marc has big plans for the department. He's changing the name to the Client Analysis Department, and you three guys will be Client Analysts. He's also promoting me to Director of Client Specifications. He intends to move Susan Cunningham over as my assistant."

That seemed to impress them.

After we had discussed every aspect of the plan, we all gave our opinions. The guys wanted me to go first. I thought back to the conversation I had with Marc last night, and I knew he meant every word. If this plan didn't work, it wouldn't be for lack of trying. But there was no way it could possibly work unless everyone was on board.

"Marc said he's only going to be here for a year. No contract renewal either way. I believe him. I think he is a good and honest man. I'm sure he has complete faith in what he told us.

"But, he knows it can only work if we all agree and we all give it our best shot. Remember he said you guys will pick your assistants. If you three get together and pick three people you all can trust, I see no reason why this can't work. I vote yes!"

They discussion continued for a while and in the end, we all agreed. They would give him the time needed. It was unanimous.

"Remember what he said about the team concept," I told them, "Marc is just a member of the team. If you have a problem or question, you have to let him know. I'm sure he will be open to anything you have to say, and if you don't want to talk to him, you can speak to me, and I'll relay it without telling him who it came from."

I had just put myself on the line with my coworkers and my friends.

I hope I'm right about you, Mr. Antonelli.

Monday morning we all marched into Marc's office as a group and told him our decision. He was pleased. Just before we left his office, he gave me a wink and a smile. It made me feel warm all over.

The rest of that day and the next day were spent moving. Marc thought our office layout was very inefficient. Susan, Sara and I were moved to desks in the Design Department. Marc and the three Client Analysts were moved to offices on the floor below us. That made it difficult to coordinate with them.

The entire corridor where our offices used to be situated was closed off by the Maintenance Department. It was lousy working conditions, but Marc promised it would only be for a month at the most.

This was going to take a while. The guys picked their assistants, and Marc agreed with all three choices. Over the course of the next three weeks, Marc took each of the guys to dinner separately. He allowed them to bring a date, and he was always accompanied by a different woman, so I was told by the guys the next day.

Ted was very graphic as usual about the nature of the women Marc seemed to date.

"They range in age from early twenties to fifties, and they all seemed very attentive to Marc."

I had no reason to care what Marc did with his free time, but I was jealous.

That's so stupid of you, Catherine!

Marc and I had dinner together at least once a week. It was all business, and he was always a gentleman, and I always let him know I got home safely. Marc also took the guys to dinner with the six friends that were listed on the third sheet.

"The sooner you and my friends get to know each other, the sooner we can start going after new business."

I was never invited to meet this group, but I really wasn't in the sales department and had no reason to meet them. Of course, Ted had to comment on the ladies in the group.

"Danielle Palmer is a total knockout. On a scale of one to ten, she's off the chart.

"For a broad in her fifties, Stacy Geer is dynamite. I'd ring her bell anytime she wants. And that Angie isn't bad either."

When I asked Tim and Artie about Ted's comments, Tim said, "The three women in the group were charming and classy. Marc's dates weren't slouches either."

That last comment made me sad, and I didn't know why. Tim also a made comment about Ted's date.

"Ted brought the same girl to the dinners with Marc's friends he had brought to John's Retirement party a couple of months ago."

We had all commented amongst ourselves that Ted was trying to show the Dillman brothers he was cleaning up his act because he was sure he was in line for the Sales Manager's position.

Tim editorialized, "Ted probably didn't want to be embarrassed by his standard dates in front of these people."

He also told me, "The people who were going to help us were very friendly, and seemed very interested in Marc's plan. I think we have a real chance of making this work."

The guys kept up with the re-orders, training their assistants and finding new accounts. These were the usual variety, one hundred thousand to one million dollars.

We weren't quite ready for the bigger guys yet.

Whenever Marc and I had free time, I would tutor him on how the order process worked and how the specification package fit in. Marc realized he couldn't master enough information to actually go out and sell, but he was sure he could get in to see some of the big potential clients and then take one of the guys and me to work the specs and order terms.

On a Monday morning, about six weeks into the new plan, Marc was waiting for us downstairs in the lobby. When we had all arrived, he escorted us to the renovated space where our offices had previously been. It had been transformed.

Marc gave us the tour.

I looked at my office door and noticed the name plate. Catherine Jenson - Director of Client Specifications. I had to smile.

It did look nice, and the increase in pay wasn't bad either.

The setup was not only efficient but very classy. Expensive wood paneled walls, new carpeting, Paintings on the walls. And every office was equipped with upscale furniture. Marc finished the tour.

"I had the office walls facing the corridor made of glass. I think it will give us a feeling of camaraderie if we weren't closed off from each other. There are blinds for private meetings and such, but I prefer them open at all other times."

We spent the better part of a week moving into our new digs and getting organized. The guys loved the new respect they were getting.

On Friday afternoon of the following week, Marc was in my office, and we were going over one of the spec formulas.

Marc was having a difficult time getting the concept. It was evident Marc was very intelligent. He picked up the other parts we had been working on very quickly, but this one seemed to escape him.

It was almost five o'clock, and I casually said, "It's quitting time. How about I buy you dinner tonight?"

He answered immediately.

"Sounds like a plan!"

Chapter 5 – Dinner with the Boss - Part Two

Since it was my treat, I picked the restaurant. It wasn't as quiet as the one Marc had taken me to, but it was quiet enough. We had spent almost an hour going over the problem when Marc suddenly brightened up.

"How stupid of me. I was coming at this from the wrong end. I see it all now."

And, that was the end of business, and before he had a chance to bring up anything else about work I said,

"Marc, can I ask you something personal."

"You can ask," he smiled, "But that doesn't mean I'll answer."

His smile indicated he was in a good mood so I plunged on.

"Why aren't you married?"

That brought on a very surprised look.

"What makes you think I'm not married?"

"That's easy. A guy like you wouldn't take off his wedding ring, and you don't wear one. And from the reports I've been getting from the guys, every time you're out with them, you have a different date with you. What wife would put up with that?"

Marc giggled.

"Very perceptive, but they're not dates, Catherine, they're escorts."

Escorts! This man needs to pay professional escorts? Please don't let him say he's gay!

"No Catherine, not professional escorts. They are ladies who work at my office. I learned from Terry Daniels it's not good policy to date people who work for you and everyone in my office knows it. The single ladies who work for me enjoy going to fancy parties and expensive dinners and they're confident I won't take advantage of the situation, so they are happy to accompany me to business dinners."

That made me feel foolish, but I plunged on anyway.

"That's why they varied so much in age! But, that doesn't answer my original question. Why hasn't some smart woman grabbed onto you?"

"What makes you think a smart woman would want me?"

"Well, let me think… You're charming, a real gentleman, intelligent, wealthy and extremely good looking. Those sound like pretty good reasons to me."

That brought out a genuine laugh from him.

"I was married once. It lasted five years. It was before Nick Amonti invested in my business and I wasn't sure if I was going to make it, or go bankrupt. That made it very hard on the relationship and about ten years ago it ended. I do date. I just never met a woman I would want to spend the rest of my life with. The friends I mentioned all have super relationships, and I want what they have. That would take a very special lady."

"Maybe you're looking in the wrong places."

Catherine Jensen, what's wrong with you? You're talking to your boss. Are you crazy?"

"And just where should I be looking?

"Catherine, you're an idiot. How are you going to get out of this?"

But, in spite of my better judgment, I said, "Maybe you should look closer to home…or work!"

"Ms. Catherine Jensen," he said very seriously, "Are you making a pass at me?"

"Would you mind?"

Now you've done it. How are you going to face him at work on Monday?

"Catherine, I would be flattered."

"In that case, the answer to your question is yes!"

"Catherine, the idea of a personal relationship with you has crossed my mind. I think you are a beautiful, classy, talented, dedicated lady, and I would love to get to know you personally. But the consequences have stopped me from pursuing the idea. Have you thought about those? What about your taboo against office relationships?"

Now you've done it. How are you going to answer that?

"Marc, I don't know what came over me. I don't know why I said that. I really do like you, not only as a boss but as a person, as a man. I can't answer your questions. I haven't given this any thought at all. I just like you, and I like being around you."

"Catherine, when this is all over, and I'm no longer associated with Dillman, if you're still available, I will put a RUSH on you like you've never experienced before."

"That's ten months away. It was difficult enough being near you forty hours a week, but now that I know how you feel, it will be impossible."

Neither of us spoke for a long time. I could sense he was weighing the consequences. It would be a much harder decision for him then it was for me.

When he finally broke the silence, he called for the check. For want of something to say, I reminded him it was my treat tonight. He looked at me for a long moment.

"Catherine, I have no problem with allowing a lady to buy me dinner, but since this is our first official date, it has to be on me!"

That statement brought me back to reality. I hadn't thought this all the way through. I hadn't thought about it at all. I don't know why I said the things I said. I meant them, but I never thought he would feel the same way, and even now I couldn't believe he might agree.

"Exactly what does that mean?"

"It means Ms. Jensen, I formally accept your proposal, but with caveats."

"That sounds ominous."

"It will be difficult. First, and most important, business is business. This stays out of the office. We are not co-workers, I am not only your boss but in charge of eight other people. No show of affection in the office. If we have a tiff or a spat, it gets left downstairs in the lobby.

"Second, it will be impossible to keep this a secret from the team. If questioned, our reply will simply be; "it's not open for discussion." We do not discuss any part of our relationship, or even that we are involved in a relationship, with anyone at Dillman.

"I don't think we'll have any trouble with Tim, Artie or Susan. I'm not too sure about Ted. This can't affect his performance. If it does, the three of us will have to discuss it.

Marc paused and looked deep into my eyes.

"Also, I have always been a one-woman kind of man. To me, a relationship means exclusive, and I will expect the same from you. Can you deal with all that?"

"Marc, I don't want to cause you any trouble, and I don't wish to disrupt the team or your plan. If this will cause any kind of waves, maybe it's not a good idea."

Still looking deep into my eyes, Marc asked, "Catherine, did you mean what you said to me? Do you really have an honest desire to

27

have a personal, maybe romantic relationship with me?"

"Yes, it's all I've been thinking about."

"I have very good friends, Catherine. And I've learned a lot from them. One of the things I've learned is every relationship has problems. The ones that last are the ones where the people involved can solve those problems. I don't know where this will go, but I do want to find out. Okay?"

"Okay," is all I could say!

Marc paid the check, and we left the restaurant. Instead of going back to the office for my car, we drove to Los Olas Blvd. Marc parked the car, and we went into a very nice piano bar. It was called the 88's, and Marc seemed to know everyone there.

While we were walking to an empty table, a lovely young girl made her way over to us. She couldn't have been more than twenty-five. She gave me a very thorough once over and said, "Another relative?"

Marc laughed at the question.

"Not this time, Annie. Catherine, this is Annie. Annie is sort of the unofficial hostess here. Annie, meet Catherine…my… lady."

That got a surprised look from Annie.

"You mean someone has finally got you hog tied?"

"It's a very real possibility," Marc said.

"Well, congratulations, Catherine. Every gal in this place has been trying to get a rope around this critter."

Annie's comment made me feel good.

"Now that I've got him let's see if I can hold on to him."

"Honey, I think you've made an excellent start! Marc, does this mean I can't dance with you anymore?"

"I'll let you know, Annie. Catherine and I haven't discussed the rules yet."

"Honey, it's clear that you've got him. Be a sport. Don't keep him all to yourself. There'll be a lot of broken hearts in here if he doesn't dance with us. Tell her about the Amonti Rule, Marc. She seems like a good gal, she can deal with it."

With that last comment, Annie was gone.

"How many broken hearts," I had to ask as we sat down.

"I honestly don't know. How many women are here tonight?"

That comment earned him a smack on the arm.

"Feisty little wench aren't we?"

"Don't you ever forget it," I told him, "What's the Amonti Rule?"

"Nick and his wife come here often. It's their favorite hang-out."

"We're talking about Nick Amonti, the billionaire, and **this** is his favorite hangout?"

"Yes, Catherine. Don't judge a man by how much money he has. Nick likes to be around good people, and because the owners of this place are careful as to who they let in here, it's usually filled with good people.

"Thursday, Friday, and Saturday they have a combo. Sunday thru Wednesday, just the piano. Between sets, they play classic dance club music over the sound system, but the piano is all about couples dancing."

The piano player started playing a lovely waltz and Marc offered me his hand. He turned out to be a terrific dancer. Why did that surprise me? This man is perfect.

Easy Catherine. Don't get carried away. You know him as your boss. You have no idea what he's like outside the office.

Back at the table, and drinks ordered I commented on how smooth he was on the dance floor.

"If I think I'm good, just wait until you dance with Nick. He's the one who talked me into taking lessons."

"Why would Nick Amonti want to dance with me?"

"Nick dances with everyone in his party. All the ladies love to dance with him. Nick and his wife are very much in love. After six years of marriage, they may be more in love than when it started. That's the kind of relationship I've been dreaming about. They both love to dance, and when they're out, they dance with almost anyone who asks them.

"But they have a rule. The first dance when they arrive and the last dance before they leave, belong to each other. They come here often, and all the regulars know not to ask either of them for a dance until they've danced together first."

"Sounds reasonable. But if they both love to dance so much, why don't they just dance with each other."

Marc gave it some thought before he answered.

"Why do you have steak one day, chicken another day and pasta another day. It's just variety. Dancing is fun and each partner you dance with brings something new into the equation.

"It's perfectly alright for a husband or wife to dance with someone else, as long as they remember who they came with and who they're going home with. The Amonti Rule"

"They sound like very nice people."

"I'm sure you'll like them. And I know they'll love you."

"And just how do you know that?"

"Because, Catherine, they're good people, and they like to be around good people. And Catherine Jensen, you're good people."

"Only one more question," I promised, "What was the comment about another relative?"

Marc got serious before he answered.

"Catherine, the only women I've ever brought here, have been my two sisters."

"No dates?"

"No Catherine. There are special places I like to keep special."

That comment almost made me swoon.

The rest of the night was wonderful. Marc and I danced, and he was good at every dance we did. He did dance with Annie, which earned me a big smile from her, and I danced with two other men, but I made Marc promise I would have the last dance.

"Always," he said.

The ride back to my car was in complete silence and this time, Marc followed me home. He didn't stay. He just wanted to be sure I got home safely. I had a very sleepless night, dreaming about what could be. I knew I was right about this man. Open, honest and honorable, a true gentleman. He was definitely not a player, and he was interested in me.

By the time I finally got to sleep, it must have been after four AM. I slept in late the next morning and was woken by the telephone.

"Catherine, I was hoping to take you someplace quiet today where we could talk. But, I have a business obligation I can't put off."

I was disappointed, and I had a fleeting thought maybe he had a date for tonight he didn't want to break. I tried to sound sincere as I told him I understood, and I felt better when he said, "How about brunch tomorrow?"

"Great," I replied a little too excitedly.

"Pick you up at nine?"

"Isn't that a little early for brunch?"

"The place I have in mind is a bit far from here... Another special place."

That almost made me swoon again.

I agreed to be picked up at nine Sunday morning.

Saturday night, around nine, Marc called. He asked if he was interrupting anything.

"Just folding the laundry and you can interrupt me from that chore anytime you pleased."

"I just wanted to confirm our brunch date."

I told him I'd be ready on time, and that was the end of the conversation. I was happy he called, but I could hear music in the background and a lot of voices. It sounded like he was at a party.

The old feelings started coming back, and I had to fight to keep them from taking hold of me and ruining what I could have with Marc before it ever had a chance.

He's a good man Catherine. Have faith. Don't ruin it with things from the past. He's not Bobby!

Chapter 6 - Brunch

Sunday morning I took my time getting ready. I wore a pretty summer dress with a hem that ended just below mid-thigh. I had noticed in the office Marc paid a lot of attention to my legs, so I added a pair of high heeled sandals to the outfit. I did have nice legs, and I wanted to show them off to their fullest advantage. I took a good look at myself in the mirror, wanting to see what Marc would see.

I stood five foot seven, without shoes, had blue eyes and I was a real blond. I had no complaints about my figure, and I was sure the image looking back at me would please Marc.

Nine o'clock on the button my doorbell rang. I hit the intercom and told Marc I was on my way. When I got to the front door, I was surprised. Marc was wearing a pair of casual slacks and a sports shirt. I had never seen him in anything but a business suit.

Seeing me generated a big smile and a kiss on the check. The drive started in silence. I didn't know what to say. I liked Marc, but I was having trouble getting past the idea he was my boss.

Get a hold of yourself! You started this, don't chicken out now!

Marc broke the silence.

"I missed you yesterday."

"Good. I hope you were miserable all day."

"More miserable than you can imagine!"

That put a smile on my face.

"Catherine, about yesterday."

"That's OK Marc. I understand. You had plans."

"Please let me explain. I have my own company that I have to run while I'm working for Dillman. Saturday is the only day I have to catch up. I start before eight in the morning and sometimes I don't get through until ten or eleven at night. And on some Saturdays, I do work for one of Nick's companies that takes me out of town. I won't be able to see you much on Saturday's until my contract with Dillman is up. But I'll make it up to you on Sunday."

"Mark, you didn't have to explain, but I appreciate that you did. I can deal with it if you can."

"I have no choice. It is what it is. My Saturdays are not my own."

I would deal with it, and right now I didn't want this to ruin our day together.

"Let me guess. We're going someplace romantic, probably on the ocean."

"Good guess. But I'll bet you can't guess where!"

"Too many choices in South Florida. But I'm sure it will be perfect."

"That's what I'm aiming for," he said sweetly.

The rest of the trip was in silence, and when it ended at Fort Lauderdale Executive Airport, I was surprised. The surprise must have been evident because Marc laughed.

"No Catherine. They do have a restaurant here, but it's too far from the ocean."

I kept quiet as Marc helped me out of the car and led me over to a huge airplane. It was as big as the ones you fly commercially. There was a red NAS painted on the tail. We climbed the stairs, and when I saw the interior, I was impressed. It was laid out like a combination living room, office. It was beautiful.

Boy, is this is the way to fly?

A man came aboard after us and Marc introduced him as Jerry, our pilot. After he closed the door, he told us to belt in and get comfortable.

"We'll be leaving in ten minutes."

Then he disappeared into the cockpit.

"The plane belongs to Nick Amonti. Both Nick and his wife are certified pilots and can fly it. When NAS doesn't need it, it's leased out to other people. Nick's niece takes care of that. Nick's friends are allowed to use it anytime it is available. All we have to do is pay for the fuel, and the landing and parking fees."

Two hours later, we were sitting in a very romantic restaurant in Key West, Florida. There was some talk about business, mostly about how the team was taking to his ideas and what they thought of him, but mostly we talked about ourselves.

I told Marc a lot about my life and some about the men I've met. I didn't tell him about Bobby or Jamey. We weren't at a point in our relationship where I was willing to tell this man the most intimate details. Marc responded by telling me about his marriage and his life since his divorce.

"My business was just getting started. I was at a point where I needed funding to bring the company up to its full potential. Since it was a service business, I had very little in the way of hard assets. Raising the needed capital was difficult. Nick Amonti was my last hope. If NAS Financial Group would lend me the money, I knew I would make it.

"After looking at my projections and financials and hearing my ideas, Nick told me a loan was out of the question. There wouldn't be enough cash flow to cover the debt service for a long time. But, Nick offered me a different deal.

"NAS would buy fifty percent of my company for half of what I needed. I would invest that money in the company, and NAS would invest a like amount. I would have the money I needed, and there would be no debt service to worry about."

Mark paused. I think he was trying to determine how interested I was in his story. I smiled, and he continued.

"I was unsure. NAS would own fifty percent of my company and although I don't consider myself an egotist, it was my hard work and sweat that brought the company to that point. I wasn't sure I wanted to share it.

"I made up my mind after reading the Partnership Agreement. There was a clause that stated at any time after the second anniversary of the agreement, at my discretion, I could buy back NAS' fifty percent for half of what the company was worth at the time. If the company went bankrupt, it would be NAS money that would be lost. If it was successful, NAS would make a profit. It seemed fair, and I made the deal."

Another pause, this time, I was sure he was gauging my interest.

"On the second anniversary of our partnership, Nick offered to sell me his share of the company. Business was good, and about to get even better. It would be cheap to buy back the NAS shares, and NAS would realize a profit. It was tempting.

"But, I liked Nick. He was a fair, honest and honorable man. He and his people had also contributed some ideas that helped make the company stronger. I told Nick I wanted to keep him as a partner, but Nick insisted fifty percent was too much. Nick liked the idea of remaining my partner and we finally agreed. I would buy back thirty-five percent of the stock, and Nick would continue to be a fifteen percent partner. We have been good friends ever since. Nick also helped me through the breakup of my marriage."

After brunch, we strolled around Key West, hand in hand. When Marc took me to the beach to watch the sunset, I was completely gone. Our first real kiss was long and passionate. I was definitely in love.

I remembered the very first time I laid eyes on this man and what my thoughts were. Yes, I could break a few rules for this man. I had already broken my 'no consecutive date' rule and my 'no office relationship' rule and I was considering breaking another rule.

When Marc dropped me off at my apartment later that night, I asked him if he wanted to come in for a nightcap.

"Nothing would please me more. But under the circumstances, I think we should take some time. If this doesn't work out, it will be very difficult at work. Let's get to know each other a little better first. I don't think either of us is looking for a fling."

He was right of course. My invitation was pure reflex.

We liked each other, and if I didn't indicate a willingness to bring it to the next level, he might lose interest. That's how men are, but it seems not this man! A kiss on the cheek was all I would get that night, but it was alright.

It was more than alright.

Chapter 7 – Friends

Back at the office, Marc and I played it cool. We would keep our relationship quiet as long as possible. Marc had dinner scheduled with Gino and Rich, the Production and Procurement managers on Monday and with Ben, the VP of Production on Tuesday. I only got to see him at the office.

Wednesday afternoon, Marc popped his head into my office and asked if I liked ice hockey. Not being much of a sports fan, I answered, "Don't know anything about it."

"Well, here's your chance to learn about the game. We're going tonight, straight from here."

That surprised me. Was this an announcement to the team we were dating or was there some other motive? I found out quickly when Artie stopped by my office.

"I hear you're going to meet our benefactors tonight."

"At a hockey game," I replied.

"Could be worse. Could be one of those wrestling matches." And he left giggling to himself.

So, I was going to a hockey game, and I would meet Marc's friends.

I wondered if they knew about our relationship.

When we got to the arena, we didn't head for one of the entrance gates, we went directly to the VIP entrance. I was having difficulty remembering I was dating a rich man. When we arrived at the suite, six people were already there.

Marc introduced me to Nick Amonti, Danielle Palmer, Stacy Geer, Terry Daniels and Harry and Angie Combs. They all seemed like nice people, and the guys were right about the women.

Danielle Palmer, probably mid to late thirties, was absolutely drop dead gorgeous. Stacy Geer was better looking in person than the pictures I had seen of her. Angie Combs, in her mid-sixties, I had been told, could have passed for mid-forties, and she was still a stunning lady.

Marc got a kiss on the check from Danielle and Stacy. But Angie wrapped her arms around his neck and gave him a long kiss on the lips. When she stepped back, holding both of his hands in hers, Marc asked, "When are you going to wise up and dump this old coot,

Angie; you know how long I've been waiting for you."

Angie sighed.

"Marc, if I didn't love the old coot so much, I'd take you up on your offer and then no other woman would ever satisfy you again."

"Don't tease me like that, Angie, you know I dream about you every night."

Harry finally stepped between them.

"That's enough you two before I start to take you seriously."

Everyone laughed. This was apparently a regular thing between Marc and Angie. Nick Amonti turned his attention to me.

"So, you're the lady who managed to tame our maverick? I always knew when the time came it would have to be someone very special."

Well, that answers that question!

"I'm not really sure he can be tamed. I don't even know if I'd like him tamed."

That brought a big smile from everyone.

"You've got yourself a keeper here, Marc."

Marc smiled.

"Working on it."

Knowing these people were aware of the relationship between us made me feel good. These were his friends, and he wasn't ashamed to tell them about me. I was so taken with these people I almost forgot my manners.

"Thank you Mr. Amonti for letting Marc, and I use your beautiful airplane on Sunday."

That got me a strange look from Nick.

"First, Mr. Amonti makes me sound ancient. If you're going to hang around with this guy, you'd better get used to your new friends."

That made me feel even better.

"And, exactly where did Marc take you in my beautiful airplane?"

Marc smiled sheepishly.

"Anton's."

"Really! It's like that, is it?"

Before anyone had a chance to say anything else, a loud horn sounded.

"Game time," Harry said, and the four men headed over to the viewing window. The ladies stayed in the rear of the suite.

"That's the last you'll see of them for the next thirty to forty minutes," Angie said, and all the ladies nodded.

"And don't pay any attention to the arguments. Marc and Nick are originally from New York. They're both Ranger fans. Harry and Terry are Floridians. They route for the Panthers. It will get noisy in here soon. Just hope it's not a close game."

Thinking I had made a terrible mistake by mentioning our trip to Key West, I asked,

"Did I get Marc into trouble about the plane?"

Danielle answered,

"Of course not Catherine. All of Nick's friends can use either aircraft anytime they're available."

"Then why the comment."

"Catherine, I've known Marc since the day of my wedding. In all that time, I have never known him to use one of Nick's aircraft for a date. You must be something really special, so we better get to know each other, because I have a feeling you'll be around a long, long time."

How much better could I feel?

Confirmation of Marc's feelings for me from some of his closest friends. Wow!

Between halves or quarters or whatever they call the breaks they take in a hockey game, the men joined us in the rear of the suite. It was noisy during the game, and Nick and Marc were happy. The Rangers were winning. Terry and Harry kept complaining about the referee and Nick and Marc just laughed.

I noticed something was going on between Stacy and Terry. Also, Nick seemed to be paying a lot of attention to Danielle. I didn't know if Terry or Stacy were married, but Marc had told me Nick Amonti was a very happily married man.

He also said Nick was the most honorable man he had ever known, and Danielle had mentioned she knew Marc since her wedding.

Am I wrong, or is Marc just blind to his friends.

The next quarter started, and the guys were back at it. Florida tied up the score, and the noise from the crowd was deafening. It was pretty noisy inside the booth also, with Harry and Terry jumping up and down.

"Boys and their games," Stacy said, "They never grow up."

When the game was over, Terry and Harry reached into their pockets, and each came out with a hundred dollar bill. They handed the money to Nick and Marc and looked like they had just lost the winning lottery ticket. The Rangers had won.

After the excitement had died down, Harry suggested we all go to the 88's. Everyone agreed, and Danielle asked if I had ever been there.

"Marc took me there on our first official date."

That brought out a big smile from all the ladies and a comment from Danielle.

"A very, very long time!"

There weren't enough seats at the piano, so we sat at a table. As soon as we were all seated, Annie came over. She seemed quite pleased to see us.

"My four favorite men. Get it over with, the nights wasting away!"

All four men got up, and we all headed for the dance floor. My inquisitive look got an immediate response from Marc.

"The Amonti Rule."

After the first dance, Annie grabbed Nick, and the other three men took one of us ladies back to the dance floor. I danced with Harry. We danced with each other's date at least once. Annie danced with all four men, and some of the regulars danced with us also.

Harry was as good a dancer as Marc. Terry was even better, but no one was as good as Nick. We did a waltz together, and it seemed as if we were floating along the floor.

I told Marc,

"All of your friends are superb dancers, but as good as they are, no one quite as good as Nick."

"He's been at it longer. If you think he's good, wait until you dance with Billy!"

"Who's Billy?"

"He's a professional dancer, and he's the instructor that taught the four of us. Just wait until you see Danielle and Billy boogie."

It was a weekday, and we all had work the next day so the night ended early, much too early for me. On the ride back to the office to pick up my car I told Marc how much I liked his friends. He said he

39

was sure they liked me too.

"How could you tell," I asked.

"I know them all a long time. I can tell by the way they treated you. You're one of them now."

"Not nearly in their financial class."

"That will never make a difference to them. None of us were born rich. It's all been the result of hard work. Money is just a tool to them. You would be surprised if you saw their lifestyle. None of us live according to our means."

That made me happy too.

Marc and I were very good at work. I was sure no one suspected. Whenever I had some free time, I continued to teach Marc what the Spec Package was all about. He was very quick and picked it up extremely well.

Susan and I got along great. Her experience in the Design Department was a big help, and she was eager to learn her new responsibilities. The guys were making headway with their assistants, and the Plan seemed to be working.

Marc did finally accept my invitation and making love to him was as wonderful as I had imagined it could be. He was gentle and passionate, and he cared about me. I wasn't disappointed.

Marc again explained why we couldn't be together on Saturdays.

"This will change after I'm done with the Dillman contract."

One Friday night, I asked him if I could go with him.

"I'm interested in what you do outside of Dillman."

"Sure, but you'll be bored to death."

After thinking about it for a minute, he said, "There's no reason for you to get up as early as I have to. When you're ready, you can drive over to my office. Then, when you're utterly bored, you can drive back home."

I arrived around ten in the morning, and Marc had already done a full day's work. He was right about being bored. He was involved in so many meetings with his staff I hardly got to see him at all. He had one of his people give me the twenty-five cent tour and explained exactly what they did.

"We put together, install and maintain Data, Communications and Security Systems. Sort of a one stop shop for corporations needing that kind of service. Since so many things are interconnected these days, a company could hire us to provide them with computer systems, servers, security equipment, telephones and other communications systems. We don't manufacture anything, we put together off the shelf products, find the proper software, install the equipment and offer installation, training, and twenty-four/seven maintenance."

It was an impressive operation. I stayed until around three in the afternoon. It looked like Marc would be at it for many more hours, so I kissed him goodbye and went home. He called around eleven thirty and said he was just wrapping up. We made plans for Sunday, and I went to bed.

After dinner and a show the following Friday night, I stayed at Marc's apartment. I knew he was working on Saturday, as usual, so we got up early. While I showered and dressed, Marc made breakfast. He had said he would be in Miami all day, but I noticed he had his overnight bag packed, and a suit bag was hanging on his closet door.

After breakfast, Marc kissed me goodbye and ushered me out the door. He said he had to shower and leave immediately afterward. On the way out, while passing through the lobby, I thought I saw someone I knew. I didn't recognize her at first, because of the way she was dressed.

She was wearing sweat pants, a warm-up jacket, and sneakers. Her hair was all tucked in under a baseball cap, and she was wearing sunglasses. It seemed she didn't want to be recognized, but I was sure it was Danielle Palmer. She didn't see me, so I kept moving and left the building. Marc called twice that day, and again when he called in the evening, it sounded like he was at a party.

Sunday, when we were together, I casually mentioned I had seen Danielle the previous day, but I didn't say where I saw her. I did say I was surprised at the way she was dressed.

Marc said casually, "She was probably on her way to or coming from a workout class."

I wanted to know more about Danielle Palmer, so I asked Marc some questions, including where her money came from.

"I know about NAS Financial Group and Daniels Industries and every woman knows about Stacy Geer. I know Harry and Angie were business partners in addition to being married, but I'm curious as to why Danielle is considered rich, considering she was just a corporate vice president."

"I only know part of the story. After the LNG/Diesel thing was sold to a couple of small firms and before the Paterson deal, Danielle purchased some Deltron stock, and when Paterson signed that big contract, the stock went through the roof.

"I also know she owns part of a manufacturing company in Georgia. She bought that just before the company was going to declare bankruptcy and when the company turned around, that stock soared also.

"Her brother-in-law handles her investments for her, and he's very good. I have most of my portfolio with him also."

"How do you know Danielle's brother in law?"

"I know the whole family: two sisters, their husbands, a niece and three nephews."

I had heard enough, but Marc wasn't through. Teasingly, he added, "The majority of her money she earned the old fashioned way…she married it!"

I let the matter drop, but that feeling was getting stronger. I was sure I was in love with Marc, and I was pretty sure he was in love with me. But, men think differently than women. Is it possible Marc loves me and still thinks it's alright to fool around? I remembered how Danielle and Nick acted at the hockey game, and when we were at the 88's, she seemed to be more involved with Nick than anyone else. There was something special between them.

Was she involved with Marc also? And, what about his secret Saturday engagements. Was it really work?

Chapter 8 - The Plan in Action

Wednesday morning of the following week, a car picked me up at six o'clock in the morning and brought me to Fort Lauderdale Executive Airport. Marc and Ted were already there. We had a meeting with Carter Aviation set up by Tony Paterson, thanks to a request from Danielle Palmer. Ted was really impressed when he found out we were taking Nick's Amonti's plane to Texas.

Marc told us, "I don't want any delays at the commercial airports, and Nick doesn't mind."

The meeting was with James, "call me Jimbo", Carter, CEO of Carter Aviation, his Procurement Manager, and his Production Manager. We got a tour of the production facilities, and I noticed on one of the production lines, two parts that were being connected together had a large enough gap between them they needed spacers to make up the difference.

This seemed strange, considering I had seen the detail drawings of these two parts and the tolerances called for would make spacers unnecessary. When we broke for lunch, there were too many of us to fit in one car, so James Carter drove his people and Ted, and I went with Marc.

As soon as we were settled in the car, Ted said, "Catherine am I seeing things, or are they actually using titanium spacers to make up for the gap between those two parts?"

"Not only that," I answered, "But they have at least six different sizes because even the gaps aren't even."

Marc perked up.

"Talk to me guys, spell it out for me."

I laid it out for him.

"According to the design specs, there should be no need for any spacers between those two parts, much less the need to have different sizes on hand. It's obvious the tolerances on the specs aren't being met. And those spacers are very expensive. Almost all of the titanium we use in this country is imported, mostly from Russia."

"Could we meet those tolerances?"

"That's why we're known as such a good company. All of our specs are right on," Ted told him.

"Sell that to Carter," Marc told us.

"It wouldn't do us any good. Even if we gave them a product that was spot on, the piece that it's being mated to is still out of spec," Ted told him.

"Push the tolerance angle anyway, and when I get into the conversation, follow my lead."

Lunch was pleasant, and when we got back to the meeting, Ted did what Marc had said. The answer from the Production Manager was what we expected.

"It wouldn't help at all. No matter how close your tolerances are, the other part would still be out of spec."

That's when Marc entered the conversation, and what he said shocked both Ted and me.

"Not if we manufacture both parts."

Jim Carter gave Marc a very skeptical look.

"Marc, I know Dillman Brothers is known for quality work, but it would be difficult for you to keep up with our production needs on one part. How do you expect to keep up with two parts?"

"We have quadrupled our capacity. All of the new production lines have been fully calibrated and tested. We could easily supply you with both parts according to your needs."

Carter's Production Manager was definitely interested.

"How long before you can send us a sample."

I was about to answer him, but Marc cut me off.

"Never!"

That got a surprised look from everyone in the meeting. We all looked to Marc for an explanation.

"We all know samples are handmade. I can send you a sample that has absolutely no tolerance at all. I'm sure the samples you got from your current supplier met the specs perfectly. The proof is in the production runs."

"What do you have in mind," Jim asked, seeming very interested.

After looking at Ted and me, Marc took a deep breath.

"Jim, are you a gambling man?"

"Not as far as my company is concerned, but I do sit at the poker table occasionally."

"How about two to one odds, in your favor?" Marc asked.

"I'm listening," Jim answered.

"I'll bet you one hundred thousand dollars against my two hundred thousand we can meet the specs and tolerances on those plans."

"Still listening," Jim said.

"Jimbo, Tony Paterson said you were an honorable man, and I know Tony is, so I'm going to take a gamble on your word."

After another pause for effect, Marc outlined the deal.

"Right now, you are paying one hundred dollars per piece for each of these parts. I will sell you one thousand pieces of each part for fifty dollars per piece."

Carter's Production Manager said, "You're going to set up two production lines to produce one thousand pieces each? That's going to cost you a small fortune."

"Not if Jim is as honorable as I've been told he is," Marc answered.

"Still listening," Carter said.

Marc got right into the details of his idea, and to say I was totally shocked would be a gross understatement.

"Here's the deal. You pay me fifty dollars each for one thousand pieces of each part. You put them on your production line, but, they must be set up so they are married to each other. If spacers are required during your typical production run, you've saved some money. If our parts mate without spacers, you give us a full order for both parts at one hundred dollars each."

Carter looked at his Production Manager, and then at me.

"Can you do that?"

"Within the tolerances on those Design Drawings, no problem," I told him.

The Production Manager asked me what percentage of rejection I needed. That meant not every part had to be perfect. A certain percentage could be out of spec, and they wouldn't be considered rejections if they could still be used with the spacers. If I told him ten percent, it meant if two hundred parts didn't fall within spec, we would still be considered perfect.

I looked at Marc while trying to do some calculations in my head. I knew our rejection rate was near zero, but I was attempting to judge what Carter and his people would accept. Three percent was the industry average.

Marc was looking at me, waiting for my answer. I could feel him trying to advise me with his eyes.

What does he want me to say?

"ZERO!" I finally answered.

"Deal. You have the word of a Texas Gentleman!"

Marc told Ted to write up the order. I asked for copies of the design drawings. We all had to sign a Non-Disclosure Agreement since the plans were proprietary and the Production Manager and I had to initial both his set and my set of drawings to ensure neither of us made any changes to them.

Marc, Ted and I were left alone while we wrote up the Sales Contract. As soon as everyone else left the room, Ted and I said, almost in unison, "Are you out of your mind?"

Ted took the lead.

"Do you realize how much this is going to cost us? We'll be spending close to a five hundred thousand dollars for a hundred thousand dollar order.

And you, Catherine, zero rejection rate! We'll never get this approved by the guys upstairs!"

"That's my problem," Marc said, "Can we meet those specs?"

"Sure we can," Ted answered, "But, Marc, someone's head is going to roll if we don't get a decent order out of this, and all we have is Carter's word."

"Write up the order and I'll sign it myself!" Marc said.

Ted looked at me for support. He was totally right. This was an enormous gamble, and even if we did get a full order from Carter, if it wasn't for at least one hundred thousand pieces, we'd never make up the original costs.

Considering the cost of the designs, the specs, the patterns, the molds, the production line tooling, and the set-up, it would cost us close to five hundred thousand dollars to produce one piece of each part. Spread that cost over one hundred thousand pieces and the cost is five dollars per piece, plus material and labor. Spread over one thousand pieces, the cost per piece would be five hundred dollars each and we were selling them to Cater Aviation for fifty dollars.

I didn't have anything to add to the argument, and I wanted this to work for Marc's sake, so I smiled at Ted.

"One for all and all for one!"

After a long glance at Marc and me, Ted sat down and wrote up the order. To my surprise, he didn't give it to Marc for his signature.

Ted signed the order himself.

The next day, I brought the design sheets I had taken from Carter's people into our Design Department. Susan and I worked closely with them for a week, and when we had everything right, I wrote up the Production Order. Marc approved it, and I brought it into Gino's office.

Gino didn't have a problem with any part of the order until he got to the number of pieces to be produced.

"Catherine, you've made an error in the size of the production run. You put down one thousand pieces of each part."

"That's it, one thousand pieces each."

The look on his face was one of disbelief. He got up, with the order in his hand and stormed into Marc's office. The discussion was heated and ended with both of them going upstairs.

Gino came down over an hour later, looking miserable. Marc returned about twenty minutes later. He looked frazzled.

"Such a handsome head to have chopped off," I said to him.

That got a smile for me.

"I'm counting on you guys to make sure that doesn't happen."

Ninety days later, two thousand pieces were shipped to Carter Aviation in San Antonio, Texas.

Chapter 9 – The Relationship

Marc turned out to be everything I could want in a man. He was handsome, respectful, charming, gentle and loving. Being rich was a nice added benefit, but he never flaunted his wealth. We dined at very nice restaurants, flew on Nick's plane when it was available, and we did things an ordinary working man couldn't afford, but it was never over the top. He had gotten used to nice things, and he lived his life a bit above other people, but not in an extravagant way.

He was always polite and respectful to other people, no matter what their station in life was. His friends aside from the people I met at the hockey game were all regular people. When his company took off, and he made money, he didn't abandon his old friends.

I met both of his sisters, their husbands and Marc's nieces and nephews. They were all very nice. They seemed happy Marc had someone special in his life. I was told since his divorce, Marc had not taken an interest in a serious relationship, and I got the impression they were glad he had picked me.

My sister, her husband, my two brothers, and their wives all liked Marc, and they too were happy our relationship seemed to be serious. Everything appeared to be perfect.

For my birthday, Marc gave me a diamond bracelet and matching earrings. They were obviously very expensive, and I didn't want to accept them. Marc said everything in life was relative.

"Because of my financial situation, giving you these gifts is no different than one of your brothers giving his wife the same items with smaller stones in line with his economic position."

I guess it made sense in a way, and although I knew they were very expensive, they weren't ostentatious. Marc had exquisite taste, and the pieces seemed to fit me, and you wouldn't realize what they were worth unless you made a concerted effort to look. For Christmas, I got a matching necklace.

We spent birthdays, anniversaries, and holidays with my family or Marc's. We spent a lot of time with our five siblings.

Both Marc's parents and mine were gone, and Marc seemed to be as close to his sisters as I was to my brothers and sister. Both Marc and I were the youngest, and we were both spoiled, Marc by his two older sisters and me by my older brothers.

We tried to keep our relationship as quiet as we could at Dillman, but that was impossible. No one said anything about it, so it didn't become a problem. Our relationship ended at the door to the office and picked up again after work. Of course, after work didn't always mean five o'clock. We both worked late on occasion, and dinners with the team or clients were a regular occurrence.

On average, I'd say we actually dated about three times a week. That was usually dinner alone during the week and all day Sunday. Marc never saw me on Saturday. He had to catch up with his own company, and Saturday was the only time he had. There also was the occasional work Marc did for one of Nick Amonti's companies. He never elaborated, and I never questioned him, but occasionally when he called me on a Saturday night, I could hear he was at a party, and the next day he always seemed exhausted.

I tried to put it out of my mind. I knew I was totally in love with this man, and I didn't want anything to spoil what we had. I was sure Marc's feelings for me were as strong. I also knew our relationship would not progress any further until Marc's contract with Dillman was up.

We did socialize with the people who were helping us, but not as often as we did with Marc's other friends and our families. We danced at the 88's as often as we could manage and that was always fun. I did meet Billy, and he was as good a dancer as Marc said he was. One night we ran into Harry and Angie. Danielle was with them. She said her husband was out of town and wouldn't be home until three AM. Danielle and Billy did boogie that night, and I was amazed at how well they danced together. Danielle could really move. I danced with Harry and Billy, and Marc danced with Annie, Angie, and Danielle. As long as we followed the Amonti Rule, it seemed to be perfectly OK to dance with anyone who pleased us, but I always looked for Marc's approval before accepting an invitation.

Things were going good at work, and I was in love with a good man. The best part was I was sure he was in love with me.

Life was good!

Chapter 10 – The Reward

Marc tried to keep the team focused, but he also thought it was important to keep it fun, so once a month or so, the entire group was treated to a Sunday outing. It did have a wonderful effect on team moral. Everyone was allowed to bring their spouses or dates, and the practice did make the team much closer.

One Sunday it was a picnic in the park. On another Sunday, Marc had chartered a yacht, and we had dinner while cruising the Inter Coastal. On another occasion, we were treated to a Dolphins football game in a Luxury Suite. We always had a blast.

On a Monday morning, a little less than eight months after Marc joined the company. He announced he had signed us up for a seminar in Nashville, Tennessee.

"I've attended this particular seminar before, and it's a lot of fun. It will be three days, Monday thru Wednesday, but we are leaving Friday after work and we'll party in Nashville over the weekend. Spouses and dates will be allowed to join us for the weekend, but they'll be sent home Monday morning."

The next day, I saw Ted run past my office. Two minutes later, Sara called and announced Marc wanted everyone in the conference room immediately. When I arrived, Marc and Ted were having a serious conversation. After everyone was present and seated, including Gino, Rich, and Angelo, Marc said we were waiting for three more people.

We were all surprised when the three more turned out to be both of the Dillman Brothers and Ben Stemmins, the VP of Production. When they had taken seats at the far end of the table, Marc nodded at Ted. Ted stood up and very formally announced.

"Ladies and gentlemen; it gives me great pleasure to tell you a week from Friday, Mr. James Carter of Carter Aviation will be in our office to sign a contract with Dillman Brothers for the manufacture of the two parts we have previously shipped to them. I want to thank you all for the part you have played in this deal."

Gino, still burning from the two thousand piece order asked, "How many this time, another thousand each?"

Ted glanced at Marc. Marc nodded.

"Two hundred and fifty thousand pieces…each!"

The math was simple. Since Marc's plan had been put into effect, the team had been bringing in larger orders. Ten, twelve, even an eighteen million dollar order, but this was fifty million dollars. After the shock had worn off, the conference room was in a frenzy. High fives and congratulations all around. The Dillman Brothers were elated. Gino shook Marc's hand, and the look he gave him was more than an apology.

We had to scramble. We had two and a half days before our trip to Nashville. Since the specs were exactly the same as the previous thousand piece order, we managed to pull it off. The mood around the office was delightful. I was sure the Nashville trip was going to be a celebration.

Friday around lunch time, the conference room started filling up with the teams' spouses and dates. Susan and Artie, who had brought dates to Marcs' other parties, were both solo for this one.

I was sure those two would get to together eventually, but Artie was so shy around Susan he couldn't bring himself to make the move. I considered counseling Susan about taking the lead if she had any hope of a relationship with him, but I had kept it to myself so far. Maybe something will happen this weekend.

At four o'clock, Marc announced,

"That's enough work for today, it's was time to leave. There's a minibus waiting for us in the parking lot."

The three Analysts, their assistants, Susan, Sara, Marc and me plus spouses and dates totaled sixteen in all. The bus took us to Fort Lauderdale Express Airport, and everyone was pleased when we boarded Nick Amonti's big beautiful jet.

Marc explained,

"Nick's plane will take the spouses and dates home Monday morning, and the team will fly home commercially Wednesday night."

The weekend was fun. The Cater Aviation order had put us all in a great mood, and we partied. We stayed together as a group most of the time, but Marc and I did manage to steal some alone time for us. Life was sweet and getting better all the time. We all got up early Monday morning to see the spouses and dates off and then attended our conferences.

I've been to seminars before, and it always amazed me how unorganized the arrangements were. Although we were all registered as a group, our hotel rooms were scattered throughout the hotel, and even though we were all going to attend the same conferences, we were to attend at different times and days.

During the three days, we were there, Marc and I only attended one meeting together. Susan and I attended one together, and Tim and I had one together also. We all met for breakfast and dinner, but the remainder of the days we hardly saw each other.

After sending everyone else home, we were down to ten, and we reserved a table in one of the hotel restaurants for breakfast and dinner. Marc and I managed to steal a few minutes alone before dinner on Monday and on Tuesday we both had early conferences and got back to the hotel before the others.

We had decided under no circumstances would we share a room, even for a few hours, so our together time was in public. I told Marc I wanted to take a swim in the pool before dinner, and he decided to come with me. Knowing Marc wasn't much of a pool person, I asked, teasingly,

"Can't stand to be away from me for even a half hour?"

"You don't think I'd miss a chance to see you in a bikini," he answered.

That comment caught me by surprise.

"Marc, you've seen me completely naked!"

"Not the same thing, my love. You gals will never understand the lure of a partially naked woman. It has to do with imagination and anticipation. That's why men like sexy lingerie and nighties, bare backs, and shoulders, low cut tops, slit skirts and why men prefer stockings to pantyhose."

"And you don't mind when other men look at me like that?"

"Catherine, you are a gorgeous, sexy and sensual women. It doesn't matter what you are wearing, men who see you will want to know what's under the clothes. They will all want to get to know you, have a relationship with you, maybe an affair. There is nothing you can do to change that.

"What they want, doesn't matter to me at all. In fact, it makes me proud you are with me. The only time it might bother me is if they think it's possible. If they feel they can have you, then we have a problem. But, you're such a classy lady, I don't see that happening."

We did go for a swim, and I did wear a bikini, and I was sure everyone at the pool knew who I was with.

No man was ever going to think I was available to anyone except Marco Antonelli.

Chapter 11 - The Incident

Wednesday was getaway day. Marc, Tim, and Artie had an early conference. Brian, George, and Anthony, the assistants had a mid-morning conference. Sara and I had an afternoon meeting, and Ted and Susan didn't have anything scheduled.

Marc and I wouldn't see each other until after five o'clock. He would be on the bus back to the hotel while I was on another bus, going to my conference. Marc had been right. It was a fun conference. All of the speakers and presenters were funny and managed to get their information across in a light hearted manner.

Marc stopped by my room to kiss me good morning before he left for his meeting. I stayed in my room until it was time for my bus to leave. I ran into Ted in the hotel lobby, and he walked me over to the bus station. When we got there, I was informed one of the speakers had canceled, and my conference would be cut short. I would get back at four o'clock instead of five.

I couldn't call Marc because there were no cell phones allowed in the meetings. I was about to send him a text message, but Ted said he'd tell Marc I was getting back early. I didn't give it much thought, and I left for the Conference Center.

When the bus got back to the hotel at four, Ted was waiting for me.

"I've been going over the Carter Aviation contract, and I found a glitch in the specs. I think you, Susan and I could straighten it out relatively quickly."

"Did you tell Marc I would be back early?"

"No one has seen Marc since he got back from the Conference Center. Since Marc doesn't know your meeting was cut short, he probably wouldn't be back until five. By that time, You, Susan and I can straighten out the glitch in the Carter contract and then you and Marc could go for your swim before dinner."

It sounded reasonable, so I agreed. In the elevator, on the way to Susan's room, I wondered where Marc had gone off to. But, I was sure the explanation was understandable. I wasn't going to be around, so he decided to do some sightseeing. But, I wondered why he didn't take at least one of the guys with him.

I started to think about the reaction I got from Marc yesterday when he saw me in my bikini. I was giggling to myself at how I was going to tease him this evening at the pool. Since we boarded the plane Friday afternoon, I had been teasing Marc. Knowing we weren't going to have any alone time together, I took every chance when no one was looking, to rub up against him, allowed my skirt to ride higher up on my thighs than proper and lean over in front of him when I was wearing a scooped neck top. I hadn't considered how much I would be teasing myself in the process. I knew there would be a price to pay for all of this when we got back to my apartment tonight. If my actions were affecting him as much as they were affecting me, it would be a very steep price.

I was looking forward to it!

As we rode the elevator to Susan's floor, Ted was unusually quiet. Not only quiet, but he seemed to be deep in thought as if he were trying to make a decision. He looked nervous as we stepped off the elevator on Susan's floor.

I noticed a Room Service waiter carrying a bottle of champagne and two flutes down the hall. I took notice because the champagne was Marc's favorite: Taittinger Blanc d' Blanc. I was surprised when the waiter stopped in front of Susan's room. Ted and I arrived at the room right behind the waiter.

Ted, still seeming very nervous, suggested, "Maybe this isn't the right time to bother Susan. It looks like she has company and maybe she doesn't want to be disturbed right now."

Ted took my hand and was about to lead me back toward the elevator when the door to Susan's room opened.

It was an entirely unexpected shock to see Marc standing in the doorway. Looking past him, I saw Susan standing at the foot of the bed, wearing a short robe, and I guessed not much on underneath.

I turned and ran back down the hall to the elevator. Ted was right behind me. Luckily the elevator came before Marc caught up with us. The doors closed and the car started moving before he got there. I pushed the button for my floor and heard Ted say, "Maybe it's not as bad as it seems. He wouldn't do that to you in front of the entire team."

I didn't want to hear it, and I shouted, "Shut up, Ted."

The elevator stopped two floors down, and Tim got on. He was on his way to the bar for his usual pre-dinner cocktail. When the car stopped on my floor, I got off with Ted right on my heels. I didn't need Ted taunting me right then, so I did a quick about-face and jumped back into the elevator. The doors closed and left Ted standing on the other side.

Tim gave me an inquisitive look, and trying very hard to hide the hurt I felt, I asked, "Buy a lady a drink."

"For you, Catherine, anytime."

Tim realized something was wrong, but didn't ask any questions. When we got to the bar, I expected Ted and Marc to arrive at any moment, but to my surprise, they never showed. I sat there next to Tim, but I was truly all alone.

How could he do this to me? I loved this man completely. I was planning to spend the rest of my life with him. I thought he was the most honest and honorable man I had ever met. If this man has no honor, does any man? Are they all exactly the same underneath?

My cell phone kept buzzing. I knew it was Marc, and I had no intention of talking to him, so I shut the phone off. After stalling with Tim as long as I could, I made my way back to my room. Luckily for me, neither Marc nor Ted were there. The tears were unstoppable for a long time.

How was I ever going to face him again? I would have to see him every day in the office. I had to travel back to Florida with him on the plane. How could I possibly deal with that? Why did I let this happen to me, again? I was smart enough not to get involved with anyone at the office, yet I allowed myself to fall in love with my boss. Catherine Jensen, you're a fool!

When the door to Susan's room opened, and I saw Marc standing there, my whole world came crashing down. For all these years, I had avoided getting too close to a man because I knew I would always be disappointed in the end. And now that I had taken a chance with someone I believed to be honorable and faithful, all I had done was to prove Bobby was right after all.

After a while, I finally got control of myself. I took a shower and tried to decide what I was going to do. I couldn't face the others, and we were all scheduled to leave on a nine o'clock flight back to Fort Lauderdale. I couldn't do that.

There was a knock on my door, I thought it was Marc trying to explain why he was in Susan's room with her almost naked. I didn't want to talk to him, or hear his excuses, but I wasn't going to let him know just how much he had hurt me. When I opened the door. It wasn't Marc, it was Ted.

He was very understanding. He was not acting like the annoying skirt chasing Ted I knew. He seemed to care. He tried to sooth me.

"Catherine, it won't be good for you to sit in your room alone."

"I can't possibly face Marc and the others at dinner under the circumstances."

"Why don't you and I have dinner here in the room?"

I didn't have the energy to argue with him, so I agreed. Ted never mentioned what we saw, but he understood my reluctance to be with the others.

"Catherine, instead of taking the hotel shuttle to the airport, why don't we grab a cab and get there before everyone else."

"What good would that do? Marc got us all First Class tickets, and I'm seated next to him."

"We'll get to the airport early, and I'll exchange our tickets for coach. I'm sure two economy passengers would be willing to move up to First Class in exchange for their coach seats. When we get to Fort Lauderdale, we can grab another cab from the airport and go straight home. This way, you wouldn't have to ride with the rest of them on the mini bus, or run into them in the company parking lot where our cars are."

It all sounded plausible, and I really didn't want to see anyone tonight, so again, I agreed with his plan. Ted was being very comforting. He was acting like a real friend.

Ted had given me the full rush when I first started at Dillman Brothers Manufacturing. When I was put in charge of the specifications packages for the Sales Department, Ted's advances became more sincere. We were working closely then, and he seemed more respectful of me, but I still had this thing about office relationships, so it still was a no go. We did become good friends, but we shared no more than the same friendship I had with the sales manager and our other two salesmen, Tim and Artie. When Marc and I got together, Ted backed off completely. This was a side of Ted I had never seen.

And it all worked out just the way he planned, except when we boarded the plane, First Class had already been seated and we had to walk past them to get to our seats.

Susan looked directly into my eyes, and I could swear she had been crying. As I passed her aisle seat, she put her hand on my arm. I pulled away and gave her a look.

Don't you dare!

It was the worst flight of my life. It couldn't end fast enough. Ted was as comforting as possible, but there was no way to get the sight of the man I loved in a hotel room with a half-naked woman out of my head. It took all the courage I could muster not to cry out loud.

When we got to Florida, we did as Ted had suggested. I only had a carry on so we didn't have to deal with anyone at Baggage Claim. But, I didn't want to be all alone, so instead of going home, I had Ted drop me off at my sister's house.

The moment she opened the door, Elizabeth knew something was horribly wrong. The floodgates opened again, and the tears came pouring out. She couldn't believe my story. She didn't want to believe it. Marc and I had spent a good deal of time with our families and everyone in my family liked him and thought he was a good guy.

"I'm sure Marc loves you. I don't understand why he'd do such a thing."

"He's a man!" I said, "That's all the reason he needs."

"What Marc have to say?"

"I haven't seen him since it happened."

"Catherine, that's a big mistake. Maybe there's a reasonable explanation."

I told her about all the time Marc spent with Susan when he first joined the company and how I had dismissed it when he made her my assistant. But now, I was sure I was right in the beginning and only fooling myself he could be faithful to one woman.

It was a very long night. I cried myself to sleep and the next morning the car service I called was late, and because Beth and I weren't the same size, the only clothes I had to wear were the ones I had in my carry on from Nashville. From the dew on my car, it was obvious it had been parked in the company lot all night. Ted's car was just as wet.

Although I was late, Ted was waiting for me at the building entrance. He was concerned and said he would be there for me if Marc had anything to say to me. I thanked him for caring, and we rode the elevator to our floor in silence. I didn't want to see Marc at all, but it was inevitable. He was my boss, and our offices were just steps apart.

But, Marc wasn't in the office. Sara said he would be upstairs with the Dillman Brothers most of the day.

It was a relief, but I knew it would only be a short reprieve. I couldn't avoid him for long. Hopefully, by the time I had to face him, I would be in better control of myself.

Ted stopped by my office every half hour or so to check on me. I closed the blinds on my glass wall so I wouldn't have to endure the looks of the team as they passed by my office. I also didn't want Marc to see how upset I was.

I tried to keep busy. We had a number of contracts in various stages of readiness, and there was more than enough work to keep me occupied. It took longer than normal for me to work the numbers because I couldn't concentrate. Susan didn't come to work, and no one had heard from her since the team picked up their cars last night.

Around four o'clock Marc returned to his office. Mr. Dillman was with him, and they called Ted, Tim, and Artie in for a short meeting. Marc left the building immediately after their meeting.

I was glad I had gotten through the first day without a confrontation. But, I knew it wouldn't last. If I didn't want to face Marc, I'd have to quit my job, and I wasn't about to give him that satisfaction.

Around four thirty, Ted stopped by my office.

"Let me take you for a drink before you head home. You need some time to let down before you go home alone."

I really didn't want to be alone right then, so I agreed. Ted had been a rock since this all started yesterday afternoon. Instead of going to one of the regular places we frequented after work, Ted decided to find someplace where we could be sure the other members of the team wouldn't walk in on us. He knew I wasn't ready to face them yet.

We drove to La Chez, a fancy restaurant about twenty minutes from the office. It was very upscale, and the bar was elegant and quiet. We found two seats at the bar and ordered drinks. I had never been to La Chez, and I glanced around the room to take in the ambiance. That's when I got the second surprise in the past two days.

Seated at a table, with a very lovely woman was Marc. They seemed to be engrossed in a very intimate conversation. Ted, noticing my shock looked over to where I was staring.

"Didn't take him long to move on."

His comment didn't make me feel any better. I just stared at the two of them. The lady noticed and said something to Marc. Marc glanced in my direction, frowned and said something to his date.

I was so engrossed at the two of them I didn't notice Ted had placed his hand on my knee and was moving it along my thigh, under my skirt.

The woman with Marc noticed about the same time I did and reported the incident to Marc. I immediately stood up and told Ted we had to go. When we reached the street, I was fuming. I couldn't control my anger, and Ted got the full force of my rage.

It wasn't bad enough the man I was in love with was in bed with a co-worker of mine. It wasn't bad enough my finding him with her mattered so little to him the very next day he was with someone new. But, now Marc and his new lady would think I was being intimate with Ted.

Ted was all apologetic.

"Honest Catherine, I wasn't making a pass. I just wanted to show Marc you could move on too."

I screamed at him.

"That's not your place, Ted. It's my decision what I want Marc to believe."

Just as I was getting to the end of my tirade, a taxi pulled up and let a couple off at the restaurant. Not wanting to deal with Ted any longer, I jumped in the cab. Thinking Ted would follow me to the office where my car was still parked, I decided to stop at my sister's place first.

When I told Beth what happened at the restaurant, she still didn't want to believe it.

"I'm sure Marc is in love with you and all of this must be a misunderstanding."

"If you had been there when Marc opened the hotel room door yesterday or seen him all nice and cozy with this hot blond tonight, you would think differently."

I stayed late, and Beth insisted her husband drive me home. I could have just as well stayed at Beth's that night. There would be no sleep for me. I had to do something.

I wasn't about to quit my job, and Marc would be there for a while. I had only one choice. I had to face Marc and tell him what I thought of him. It would be embarrassing, but necessary. I wouldn't scream or shout or cry. Just straight out tell him what a jerk he is.

You might not scream or shout, but you'll have to work real hard not to cry, Catherine.

Chapter 12 – The Carters

I made an appointment with a car service when I got home so I wouldn't be late to the office again. The dew on my car indicated it was in the parking lot all night again. When I got upstairs, Ted was waiting for me at my office door. He tried to apologize for the incident at the bar last night. I knew my anger was at Marc, and I told Ted to forget about it, and I made him promise to behave himself.

But, it wasn't good enough for Ted. He followed me into my office and apologized over and over again. I knew I was rough on him when we were outside the bar yesterday, but he seemed more contrite than the situation demanded.

"I had no idea you were serious about Marc. I assumed it was just an office fling, and it would be over when Marc's contract was up. I realized by your reaction yesterday you are in love with Marc. Is Marc in love with you?"

"Until the past couple of days, I was certain he was, but now I was sure it was just as you said, an office fling."

Ted was about to say more when Sara poked her head into my office and told him Marc needed him right away.

"Catherine, we have to talk. Don't give up on Marc until we do."

Then he left for Marc's office. Five minutes later, my intercom buzzed. I could tell by the extension it was Marc. I didn't answer it. A minute later it sounded again, and again it was Marc. I ignored it. Then Sara called and said Marc wanted me in his office right away. I told Sara to tell him I was too busy and hung up.

Thirty seconds later, Marc was in my office. He slammed my office door so hard I thought the glass partition was going to shatter. He stormed over to my desk, got as close to it as he could and leaned over so far, his face was just inches from mine. Before I had a chance to say anything, he unleashed a tirade at me.

"We had a deal, remember. Personal stuff gets left downstairs at the lobby door. It doesn't come into the office. This is business. Do you remember, or isn't your word any good?"

I tried to answer him, but he cut me off.

"Don't you dare say anything. I thought you were professional? I thought I could depend on you? Well, I guess that shows how smart I am."

Again I tried to answer him, and again he cut me off.

"Jim Carter is sitting in my office signing the biggest contract this company has ever seen, and he wants to see the gal who put the spec package together. So I suggest, Ms. Jensen, if you don't want to find yourself out on the street, without a job, by the end of today, you pull yourself together and get your ass into my office, right now. And I also suggest you, at least, try to act professionally."

With that, he turned to leave, but he stopped at my office door and turned back to me.

"I'm really disappointed in you Catherine! Really disappointed."

And he was gone.

"What gall. He was disappointed in me! I'm not the one caught with his pants down!"

But he was right. This was business, and I did have to put my personal feelings aside. I pulled myself together as much as was possible and went to Marc's office. Mr. Dillman, Ted, Tim, and Artie were all there, and when I arrived, I got a big smile from Jim Carter. I apologized for being late and made some stupid excuse.

"You're probably working this gal too hard," he told Marc.

"Jim, everyone is working extra hard trying to keep up with the new orders the team is bringing in. I'll probably have to get Catherine some more help soon."

Everyone was in a fantastic mood. A fifty million dollar order doesn't come along often. Dillman had never had anything close to that size.

"If the production runs are as good as the sample run, my Production Manager has three or four other items he wants you to give us quotes on."

That really put everyone in a good mood. Then, I heard a women's voice from the door.

"There you are Good Looking."

I had my back to the door, so I had to turn to see who was there. I couldn't believe what I saw. It was the woman Marc was with at La Chez last night.

"What brass, walking into such an important meeting. Was Marc crazy?"

After glancing around the room, she walked directly over to Marc, put her arms around his neck and gave him a big kiss. When she pulled away, Marc said, "Tell me what I did to deserve that, pretty lady, and I'll make sure I do it again!"

That brought out a big smile from her and a comment from Jim Carter.

"I guess you deserved that, but don't think it's going to become a habit."

Marc frowned, "Story of my life. All I ever get is a taste of the good stuff."

That brought more smiles and a comment from the lady.

"Oh poo, Honey, leave the man alone. He was a splendid company. That will teach you to leave me alone."

Jim, still smiling, asked, "Did I send the fox to guard the henhouse?"

The lady, now frowning replied, "No, darn it, he was a perfect gentleman."

Marc shrugged his shoulders, "You don't fool around with the wife of your best customer!"

That got laughs all around. Everyone but me seemed to know what was going on. But, it was apparent this was the lady Marc was with last night and it was also obvious the fact they were together had something to do with business. I was confused and felt more than a little guilty.

Jim formally introduced his wife, Mary Ellen, to the team and explained.

"I had a meeting here in town yesterday and told Mary Ellen to meet me for a drink at the restaurant bar before our dinner meeting with Marc. The meeting ran longer than expected and knowing Mary Ellen hates to sit at a bar alone, I asked Marc if he would go to La Chez early and keep her company until I arrived."

Looking at me, Jim said, "I'm sure **you** know what it's like for a beautiful woman to be alone at a bar, no matter how fancy the place is! Marc was kind enough to do me this favor."

Marc's reply was typical, "I'll do that kind of favor for you anytime!"

Mary Ellen giggled and said she was hungry and was ready for lunch. Jim invited Marc, Ted and me to join them. I tried to beg off, insisting I had too much work to do, but a look from Mr. Dillman meant I was going.

Mary Ellen said, "You can tell me how you people talked my husband out of fifty million dollars."

And then, looking directly at me, she added, "I'm sure you had a lot to do with it, Catherine. Jimbo never could say no to a beautiful lady."

I knew the comment was meant as a compliment, and it made me blush. So, we all went to lunch. Since Jim and Mary Ellen weren't coming back to the office afterward, Marc took his car. I rode with the Carter's, and Ted went with Marc.

Lunch was pleasant but tense. About thirty minutes after we arrived, I noticed Mary Ellen was running her thumb across the blade of her dinner knife. Jim noticed it too and asked her what was wrong.

"This knife isn't nearly sharp enough."

When Jim inquired, what she wanted to cut. Her answer brought the three of us to attention.

"Not nearly sharp enough to cut the tension at this table."

Marc tried to smile.

"Sorry about that! We've had a rough week. The orders are coming in faster than anyone expected. Jim was right about working Catherine too hard. We have to increase the size of her department. In addition, we spent the first three days of this week at a silly seminar in Nashville, and we're trying to play catch up."

Mary Ellen listened to Marc's explanation. She glanced at Jim, who just shook his head. Looking directly at Marc, she said, "Marc, you know I'm a Texas gal, don't you? Born and bred?"

"And your point?"

"My point is I've been around enough bullshit in my life to recognize it when I hear it."

"Point taken. She's got us, guys. Let's be good so the lady can enjoy her lunch."

And then he laughed. That seemed to break the tension between us and the atmosphere did lighten up. The conversation was mostly about the bet Marc made with Jim back in San Antonio.

Mary Ellen thought he had taken a big gamble, and Marc replied he was absolutely sure we could do it. Mary Ellen asked, "How did you know Jim would keep his end of the bargain?"

Marc replied, "I assumed Jim was a true Texas Gentleman and wouldn't welch on a bet."

That brought smiles all around. Then Marc added, "I also had an ace in the hole!"

That resulted in inquisitive looks from everyone, including me.

Marc let us dwell on that a minute.

"You don't build a company like Carter Aviation from nothing without an astute business sense. I knew when Jim saw that dealing with Dillman would allow him to eliminate those expense titanium spacers he'd have to give us the order."

Everyone at the table knew Marc was right, and it also pointed out what an astute business sense Marc had.

When I excused myself to go to the Ladies Room, Mary Ellen went with me. I wasn't prepared for the conversation that followed, and I really didn't want to talk to her about my problems. But she was determined to tell me what was on her mind, even if I didn't want to hear it. And it didn't matter if I had anything to say, I didn't have any choice but to listen to this born and bred Texas lady.

"I don't know what's going on between the three of you, but I have to tell you what you're doing is not right."

I tried to protest and tell her I wasn't doing anything, but she stopped me.

"I know men, and I'm telling you Marc is a good one. It's clear that he's in love with you. And I'm pretty sure you're in love with him. That was evident by the daggers you were pointing at him last night. I don't know what kind of gamesmanship you two are playing, but it won't help matters."

"I don't understand what you mean by gamesmanship. Marc and I are just boss and employee."

"Catherine, I told you I'm from Texas, and I know bullshit when I hear it. This is none of my business, but I like Marc. He's a good guy, and I know he's hurting. You seem like a great gal, and I know Marc has a lot of respect for you, not only professionally, but as a woman."

"And just how do you know that?" I asked sarcastically

Mary Ellen fumbled in her purse until she found her lipstick before she answered.

"We had a while to talk before Jim showed up. Some of it was about Dillman, the team and Jim's order. And, I'm not sure Marc realized it, but mostly it was about you. He said you were the glue that held it all together. Without your contribution, none of it would be possible. He told me you have a great future in the corporate world if you want it."

"It's nice to be appreciated by your boss, but that's all it is."

Mary Ellen shook her head and turned toward the mirror.

"If you don't care about losing him, it's fine by me, but if you have hopes for a relationship with that man you'd better stop playing Hard Ass and start paying attention to what's right in front of your face."

"What's right in front of my face is the reason I'm in this position."

"I don't understand."

"I'm about to discuss it with the wife of the company's biggest customer."

"Alright, but take a piece of advice from a happily married gal. Throwing another man in his face isn't going to help the situation."

"I don't know what you mean."

"Catherine, what was that all about at the bar last night? You show up at a place where you know he'll be, with another man, and you allow that man to treat you like that in public."

"I didn't know Marc would be there and what you saw between Ted and me wasn't what it looked like."

After painting her lips, she whispered, "That's what Marc said."

I asked what she meant.

"When I saw the way you were staring at Marc I asked him what was going on. He told me you were two people from work, and you were all under a lot of pressure lately.

"I told Marc he was full of it and being the curious person I am, I persisted. I told Marc it was obvious there was something personal between him and you and wasn't it odd she would show up with another man at a place where she knew you would be entertaining another woman. Then when that guy slid his hand under your skirt, I said it was evident where you two were headed."

She continued while fluffing up her hair.

"Marc told me it was a personal matter, and he didn't like to talk about people when they weren't present to hear what was being said about them, but he did say showing up there wasn't something you would do, it was probably Ted's idea.

"He told me, you weren't one of the people who knew he was meeting me here. You were too much of a lady to pull a stunt like that. And as far as the other thing, he said you were too smart to get involved with a womanizer like Ted, but you had too much class to cause a ruckus in a place like this and jumping into bed with a guy just because you were angry with another guy wasn't your style at all. He said he was willing to bet you were outside on the sidewalk right now, giving Ted what for."

I didn't know what to say. But Mary Ellen wasn't finished.

"Catherine, I've known Marc for a total of about six hours. It's not a lot of time, but you can tell an awful lot about a man in a short time. I believe he's an honest man. He's respectful, polite, charming and good looking to boot. He respects you as a woman, and he respects your ability as a professional and I honestly believe he's in love with you. I think it requires a very particular kind of woman for that kind of man to fall in love with, and I know right now he's hurting, and it's because of you. That's an awful lot of man to throw away, honey, and if I were you, I'd give it a lot of serious thought before I did that."

What Mary Ellen said to me is exactly what I had thought about Marc from the beginning, but how does it relate to what I saw in Nashville. I needed to talk to someone about this, but the wife of a customer wasn't the answer. I thanked her for her concern and advice, and we returned to the table.

On the drive back to the office, we were all quiet. Not a word was spoken between us. Even during the elevator trip up to our floor, there wasn't any conversation at all. When we left the elevator, Ted headed for his office. Marc stopped me before I had a chance to enter my office.

"Catherine, I apologize for losing my temper earlier. I'm sorry I raised my voice to you."

I gave him the only reply I could.

"You were absolutely right, Marc. We did have a deal, and I was very unprofessional."

His response hurt.

"Yes, you were. But I still had no right to talk to you in that manner. I'm sorry."

With that, he turned and walked to his office. That was it. I thought about what Mary Ellen had said, "Don't throw the good ones away."

He was a good one, but was he faithful? Could I trust him? Even if she was right about what he had told her about me. Even if he believed everything he said, that didn't mean he still felt it was alright to romance another woman. That's how men are! I've heard that before, and I believed it.

If all men were like that would I be better off alone, or should I just accept the fact all men cheat and just pick the best one available?

Jim didn't seem to have any problem with the way his wife acted toward Marc in the office this morning. Was it he trusted her so completely or was it his way of compensating for his own indiscretions? Was there really such a thing as true love, or was that a fairy tale. Marc had said he had never met a couple more in love than Nick Amonti and his wife, yet the way Nick acted toward Danielle Palmer was much too intimate. What is the answer? Is there an answer?

Maybe, I'll never know.

Chapter 13 - Family

I didn't see Marc for the remainder of the day. Ted stopped by a couple of times, but I wasn't in the mood for more conversation. Mary Ellen's words kept reverberating around in my head.

Until Wednesday afternoon, I was sure Marc was in love with me. Then in an instant, it was all gone. Was I wrong about him before, or was I wrong now. I knew I'd have to talk to him about the incident eventually, but I wanted to wait until I was able to do it without breaking down in tears. That wouldn't solve anything.

Would I ever get to that point?

After work, I stopped at my sister's again. I had to talk to someone, and she was my closest confidant. My two brothers, Ed and Ethan, were there with their families for dinner. Everyone was glad to see me and wanted to know why I was so blue. I didn't mean to bring the entire family into my problem, but Beth had already told them everything I had told her. They were as shocked as Beth was and they all insisted I must be mistaken.

Now that it was out in the open, I decided to tell them the entire story. I related my misgivings about Marc's phone calls on Saturday nights, about his overnight bag and suit bag being packed and ready to go that Saturday morning, about seeing Danielle Palmer, incognito, at Marc's apartment building. Then, I told them about Nashville. I told them about how Marc shouted at me in my office this morning and his apology later on. I even told them about how I felt when I saw him and Mary Ellen together last night. They all wanted to know what Marc had said about these incidents.

"I didn't ask for an explanation."

They were stunned. They all came down on me like a pack of hungry wolves.

"Catherine Jensen," Ed, the oldest scolded, "What's wrong with you? You're obviously in love with this man. Why wouldn't you want to find out the truth? Every one of the incidents you mentioned might have a legitimate reason. Why wouldn't you want to know what that was? Why would you want to live in doubt rather than know for sure?"

"Because I do know. It's obvious. What really hurts is he was so blatant about it."

"You know what?" Ethan asked, "Every one of those incidents could have a perfectly reasonable explanation. Why would you automatically think the worst without finding out for sure?"

"Because," I shouted back at them, "I learned a long time ago that's the way men are. All men are exactly the same. No man can be faithful, and, I've always found that to be true."

"Catherine!" Beth scolded, "Think about what you're saying."

I could see everyone was shocked by my words, but I didn't care. I knew I was right. I had been in love and was totally crushed when I found out the truth. I have never allowed myself to get close enough to a man to have that happen to me again. That was until Marc came along. I had let myself fall in love with him only to find out I had been right all along.

Keith put his hand on Beth's arm to silence her. I could see the looks of disbelief on all their faces. They were dumbfounded by my remarks. Sam, Beth's husband, was the first to speak.

He looked into my eyes and very sincerely asked, "Catherine, there are three men at this table. Does that include us?"

I didn't have an answer. I had never given it any thought. They were family. I never saw them as I see other men.

Ed said, "Answer him, Catherine. Does that include us? Does it include our father?"

"Of course not," I cried, "You're family, you're different."

"We're family," Sam said, "But we're still men first. We have the same instincts, desires, and frailties as every other man. If we're all the same, then you have to include us too!"

That opened the floodgates, and I couldn't control my sobs. Beth helped me up and took me into her bedroom. I couldn't stop crying. I had just accused the four closest men in my life of infidelity.

"What is wrong with you Catherine? They'll never forgive you, and neither will their wives."

Beth stayed with me until I managed to get some sort of control. Ed came in and sat down on the bed next to me. He put his strong hand on my shoulder.

"It's OK Catherine. We know it wasn't meant how it sounded. But Catherine, don't you see how ridiculous your theory is? Don't you see all men aren't the same? Can't you see the difference between us?"

I was totally confused. Ever since that encounter with Bobby, I had held the belief he was right. When I found him with that

69

cheerleader, I knew there was no such thing as a faithful man. I had never considered my father, my brothers, or Beth's husband. They were family, they weren't men.

But, they were, and I was sure they were faithful to their wives and families. But why was I sure? Was it just because they were family and I wanted them to be good honest men? Was it because none of the wives ever acted suspicious? Was it because I just closed my eyes to the possibility?

Why did I separate these four men from all the others?

I dried my eyes as best as I could and returned to the dining room. Everyone was still at the table. I tried to apologize for my remarks, but they wouldn't let me. They said under the circumstances, I had a right to be upset and confused. But, they couldn't understand why I hadn't confronted Marc when these things happened. They were sure he would have an explanation for everything.

"I was afraid he didn't have an explanation that would satisfy me, and that would only make the situation worse."

Again and again, I heard their opinions that Marc was a good man, and they all were sure he was in love with me.

Sam offered, "I always wondered why you never had a serious relationship with a man. Your attitude toward the other men you brought home was always so cavalier I wondered if you would ever find someone to satisfy you. That's why we were all so happy when we met Marc.

"We liked him and thought he would be good to you, and you seemed to be more into him than anyone else you had ever introduced us to."

Ethan added, "Your outburst tonight explains a lot, but you're completely wrong. All men aren't the same. Maybe Marc is as guilty as you believe him to be, but that doesn't mean the next man you meet will be the same. You have to know for sure and the only way to do that is to confront Marc and ask for the reason he was in Susan's room."

"Put it to him," Ed said, "And demand an explanation. Then, at least, you have a basis to make a reasonable judgment. Don't throw away possible happiness over something some guy said to you over fifteen years ago."

I was surprised by Ed's remark.

"This is all about that jerk you were in love with in college, isn't

70

it?"

I felt ashamed of myself, but I knew he was right, and I nodded my agreement.

Ethan looked at me and then Ed. His eyes said he needed an explanation. Ed gave it to him.

"The first, and to my recollection, the only man our little sister ever loved did her wrong, and it seems she has been carrying that scar around ever since."

"Catherine," Ethan said, "That had to be over fifteen years ago, and you've been running your life because some college kid let you down?"

After thinking about Ethan's comment, I had to agree. I nodded my head, and Ethan continued.

"You were all of eighteen years old, and some jerk disappointed you, and you decided all men are the same. Catherine, you're so much smarter than that!"

I had no argument to counter what my brothers were saying. The only answer I had for them was, "It hurt so much."

And the tears started again.

Ed said, "I know Sis, a broken heart has to be the worst pain of all. But, you can't let it end your life. There are good men out there, and you're entitled to one of those. Maybe Marc is a scoundrel, maybe he's one of the good ones. You can't write him off without finding out for sure."

Ethan added, "If he is one of the scoundrels, you move on. Sometimes you have to go through a lot of chaff to get to the wheat. You're a great gal, Catherine. There are loads of men who would love to have a chance to make you happy. You can have your pick. But, you have to be willing to give back, and that means you have to learn to trust."

The conversation went on until early in the morning. I loved my family, and I knew they loved me. I also knew they were trying to help me, but this I had to do on my own. I did have to confront Marc and get to the truth.

Beth insisted I stay the night. I agreed, but I knew first thing tomorrow morning I was going to see Marc and lay it all out on the line.

Chapter 14 – Dinner with the Carters

Saturday morning I got up early and called Marc's apartment. Voice mail. I tried his cell phone. Voice mail. I tried his office at Antonelli Systems and was told Marc was out of town for the day. I didn't want this to wait, but I didn't have much choice. Marc's secret out of town Saturdays usually meant he wouldn't be home until the wee hours Sunday morning.

Beth was concerned. I thanked her for last night.

"I intend to take the advice I received and put it to use. I would find out what Marc was doing in Susan's room, and make a decision on how it would affect our relationship. After last night, I feel stronger and more confident, and I'm sure I can get through this."

I knew I couldn't see Marc today, so I went back to my apartment and set about doing my weekend chores. I tried to concentrate on what I was doing, but my heart wasn't in it. I kept thinking about every possible reason for Marc to be in Susan's room, with her half naked. I couldn't come up with one that made sense. At least, one that would make me believe it wasn't what it looked like.

Around two in the afternoon, my phone rang for the umpteenth time. I kept checking the Caller ID, hoping that it was Marc, but it was always Ted. I appreciated his concern, but I wasn't in the mood for him today. This time, I didn't recognize the number; it was an out of state exchange, and I hoped it was Marc calling from wherever he was today. It was Mary Ellen Carter.

"Catherine, I hate to bother you, but we missed our flight home, and we can't get out until tomorrow morning. We're in a strange city and don't know anyone. Would you have dinner with us tonight?"

I didn't want a repeat of our lunch fiasco, and I wasn't in the mood for company, so I tried to come up with a plausible excuse that wouldn't offend them. Mary Ellen promised not to bring up the subject we had talked about yesterday at lunch. Then, Jim got on the phone.

"Who is Dillman's Brothers best customer?"

Of course, I had to admit it was his company.

"Does Dillman Brothers believe the customer was always right?"

Again I had to admit he was right.

"Good, we'll pick you up at seven." And he hung up the phone.

I guess I was having dinner with the Carters. When I thought about it, I figured it wouldn't be too bad. If I could manage to keep Mary Ellen for asking too many questions, it would fill up the time and keep me from thinking about what was going to happen when I faced Marc.

Seven o'clock, the door intercom buzzed. I told Jim I was on my way and headed for the elevator. The ride to the restaurant was filled with casual conversation, and my first surprise came when we pulled up in front of La Chez.

Mary Ellen apologized.

"I hope you don't mind. Being strangers in town, this was the only really fine restaurant we know of. Jim knows one of the owners."

I said, of course, I didn't mind, and after Jim handed the keys of his rental to the valet, we headed inside. We were seated immediately and didn't have to wait in the bar. We ordered drinks, and after they were served, the waiter came over and asked if we were ready to order. Jim looked at his wrist watch.

"We need a few more minutes, we're expecting another guest."

Before I had a chance to question that statement, I got my second surprise of the evening. Marc showed up and stood behind the empty chair at our table. He glanced at the Carters and turned toward me.

"Let me guess! We missed our flight. We can't get out until tomorrow. We don't know anyone in town. I'm your best customer, and the customer is always right... Is that about it?"

For the first time since Wednesday afternoon, I generated a real smile.

"Almost word for word."

Marc shook his head and sat down. When the waiter came over for his drink order, Mark told him, "Champagne. Taittinger Blanc d' Blanc if you have it. If not, whatever you have that's comparable. And four flutes."

Remembering his office said he would be out of town all day, and knowing these trips for Nick meant a very late night, I was curious as to how he managed to be here tonight.

"I thought you were working for Nick today?"

"What made you think that?

"I called your office, and they said you would be out of town all day."

"It's dangerous to assume, Catherine. I was in Tallahassee

holding hands with one of my better clients. One of their servers crashed and even though the backup switched it over in a microsecond, three of their customers were dropped out and had to log in again.

My systems are getting so good everyone expects them to be perfect. I reminded the client before Antonelli Systems, it would have taken hours for a tech to switch over to a backup server."

Marc seemed very pleased with himself and his company. Then he asked why I had called his office.

"I think we need to talk."

"We will, Catherine, but now was not the time."

I nodded my agreement just as the waiter brought the champagne. After the glasses were filled and the waiter left, Marc said, "Listen, guys, I appreciate what you are trying to do, and I'm sure Catherine does too. Yes, there is a problem between Catherine and me. I won't go into it in front of the company's best customer. In any case, it won't be settled tonight. Catherine and I will work it out in time, but it's not yet the right time. OK?"

That got nods and small smiles from both of the Carters, and Mary Ellen asked why the champagne. She wanted to know what we were celebrating. Marc picked up his flute.

"How about Jim's fifty million dollar order?"

Everyone approved and before we had a chance to take a sip. Marc added, "To good friends, good people, and a pleasant dinner."

We clinked our glasses and toasted each other.

Dinner was pleasant. The conversation was casual with just a hint of business. When the check came, Marc reached for it. Jim insisted it was his treat, and Marc told him it had to be on Dillman.

"Suddenly, they can afford it, and since we did mention your order, it's deductible."

That got giggles from all of us, and Jim relented. Marc asked Mary Ellen if she liked to dance.

"Only every chance I get, but that isn't too often lately.

"I know a sweet little piano bar that has a dance floor with pleasant music and friendly people. I'm sure you'll like it."

Jim said that it sounded great, but they had a six AM flight tomorrow. When Marc asked why so early, Jim replied, "When I changed the reservation this morning, that's all that was available."

Marc told them, "I might be able to fix that. What time do you have to be in San Antonio tomorrow?"

"If we're at the San Antonio Airport by ten PM Texas time that would be fine."

Marc took out his cell phone and dialed a number stored in his address book. He put the phone on the table and hit the speaker key. Mary Ellen asked why he did that.

"You did the same thing Thursday night when Jim called to tell us he was on his way."

"I think it's very impolite to have a private conversation when other people are at the table. This way, everyone could hear what was going on."

A pleasant female voice said, "Hi Marc, what can I do for you this evening?"

The Carters and I were surprised by Marc's answer.

"Pam baby, if I answered that, you'd slap my face!"

From the phone, we heard, "Oh, cut it out, you've had more than enough chances. You're all talk and no action."

"That's only because I'm afraid of your father. I know all about his Navy Seal Training."

From the phone again, "Coward! And besides, Grandpa told me about your lady. He said you picked a winner. When are we going to meet her?"

"As soon as I'm sure she wants me," Marc answered.

"OK, enough of the bull," the voice said, "What impossible task do you expect me to do for you tonight?"

"Pam baby, is that any way to treat me?"

"That's the only time you call me," the voice replied.

"Busted…Honey, I need two tickets Fort Lauderdale to San Antonio for tomorrow afternoon or evening. First Class if you can."

"Oh! I thought you wanted something difficult like two tickets from Fort Lauderdale to San Antonio for tomorrow. But, two round trip tickets to the moon and back, this is easy, no problem."

"Might that be sarcasm I detect in your voice?"

"Gee Marc, I didn't think you were smart enough to understand sarcasm!"

After more chit chat, Marc gave Pam Carter's name and the flight they had booked for tomorrow morning, the call ended with Pam's promise to call back in fifteen minutes.

Mary Ellen commented, "You seem very friendly with that travel agent, even intimate."

"Pam's not a travel agent. I've known her for over ten years. She runs the Corporate Travel Department for NAS Financial Group. Her father, Nick Amonti, is a personal friend of mine. We tease each other all the time. It's just fun."

Fifteen minutes later, Marc's phone buzzed. It was Pam, and she was very apologetic. No luck on a later flight out on Sunday. She suggested Marc call Anna Lee. Marc replied that was his next choice. After a few more intimate comments between them, Marc disconnected.

Another stored phone number and a very sweet, cheery voice, with a definite southern tone, said, "Hi, Mr. Marc. Why are you calling little ole me late on a Saturday night?"

Marc's answer started another, even more, intimate conversation.

"Just making sure you were home, Anna Lee, and not letting some local boy take advantage of my best gal."

"Oh, Mr. Marc, you're such a tease. You know no one could take your place."

"Just wanted to make sure Anna Lee."

Marc asked if one of the birds was available for a trip from Fort Lauderdale to San Antonio tomorrow afternoon or evening.

Anna Lee told him, "ONE is on a long haul, San Francisco to Atlanta, and won't be back home until midnight tomorrow, but 'TWO' is due into Jacksonville around two tomorrow afternoon. I could have it ready to go at FLX between five and six tomorrow evening. And it fit right in with the schedule because they're scheduled to overnight in Dallas for an early flight Monday morning."

Marc thanked her and asked her to call Pam and let her know it was covered. He gave her Carter's information and after some more very intimate interplay between them, Anna Lee said, "You know, Mr. Marc, if Uncle Nick heard you talk to me like that, he'd fix it so you walked funny."

"Ouch!" Marc replied, "You wouldn't do that to me, would you Anna Lee?"

"Never, Mr. Marc, you're so sweet to me and besides, I hear there's a lady that might make good use of your charms."

"Your Auntie has a big mouth," Marc said.

Anna Lee giggled.

"You know this family has no secrets, and you're family. When do I get to meet her? She must be something special to get you interested!"

"When the time is right," Marc told her and then thanked her and said goodbye with a few more intimate comments.

Marc put the phone away.

"A G5 will be waiting for you at Fort Lauderdale Executive Airport between five and six tomorrow evening."

He gave them instructions to the airport and told them there was a car rental agent there to handle his rental.

"Do I get to dance with your wife tonight?"

Mary Ellen answered instead.

"That's a definite yes."

I guess we were going to the 88's.

During Marc's conversations with Pam and Anna Lee, Mary Ellen was looking at me, and she seemed to have questions in her eyes. Before we left the table, Mary Ellen asked Marc, "Do you talk to all women like that?"

Marc seemed surprised by the question.

Mary Ellen explained, "You seemed very intimate with both of those ladies."

Marc finally understood.

"Only with women I know extremely well and who know me just as well. No one takes it seriously as flirting but I enjoy complimenting them, and I'm pretty sure they enjoy the attention. Anna Lee is the sweetest gal you'd ever meet. She's a Georgia Peach and still lives in a small town in South Georgia. She takes care of the Charter Service for NAS Financial Group and like all NAS senior employees, she's related to Nick."

Jim commented it must be nice to talk so freely with women without fear of being taken seriously.

Marc said you had to choose the women very carefully, and you must have a long standing history with them.

"And the comment about making you walk funny?" Jim asked.

"That's just a GRITS way of keeping me in my place."

Seeing the question on my face, Mary Ellen explained, "G.R.I.T.S., Girls Raised in the South!"

Since Jim wasn't familiar with Fort Lauderdale, Marc suggested I ride with the Carter's and show them where we were going. I was disappointed. I wanted a chance to talk to Marc alone, but I tried not to show it. During the trip, Jim asked Mary Ellen if she would mind if he spoke to other women the way Marc talked to Pam and Anna Lee. Mary Ellen didn't have a ready answer.

After a few moments of contemplation, she said, "There would have to be two considerations. First, like Marc said, they would have to be special women with a long history and the ability to understand what the underlying meaning was all about.

Second, they would have to know, for a fact, you only talk to them that way in front of me, it's not something you would do behind my back."

"Sounds reasonable," Jim replied:

Then, aiming her comment at me, "Catherine, remember that little show I put on in Marc's office yesterday. Jim knows it never would have happened if he wasn't in the room. That's why it was okay with him. And, because Jim was there, Marc took it for what it was and not anything more."

I nodded my understanding.

"Is it really possible for two people to be so much in love with each other their fidelity never has to be questioned?"

Chapter 15 – Highs and Lows

When we arrived at the 88's, it was as if nothing bad had ever happened between Marc and me. He was as charming and attentive as ever. As soon as we sat down, Annie came bouncing over. Looking at Jim, she gushed, "A new man! Hi, I'm Annie."

Jim was all smiles.

"Well howdy little lady, I'm Jimbo, and this is Mary Ellen."

"Do I detect Texas in that drawl?"

"Sure do, honey, born and bred."

Looking at Marc, Annie said, "Hurry up and tell them the rules, I have to try this one on for size!" And she was gone. The confusion on the Carter's faces was evident, and both Marc and I had to laugh.

Marc explained, "Annie is a sweet, outgoing girl who loves to dance. Everyone here loves her, and all the men enjoy dancing with her, but she restricts her encounters to dancing. This is the one place where she doesn't have to worry about being hit on. Almost everyone here is a regular, and they all know her and her attitude."

"Is that what she meant by the rules." Mary Ellen asked.

Marc explained the Amonti Rule and both of them thought it was a good policy. Mary Ellen suggested they get the first dance over with.

"I don't want to deprive you of the chance to dance with Annie."

Jim smiled and indicated he was looking forward to his turn on the dance floor with the lovely lady.

Marc asked me to dance, but he did it very formally, not as he usually did when we were here before. It wasn't really like I was his girlfriend, more like just an acquaintance. On the dance floor, I again said to Marc we had to talk. He agreed.

"Yes we do, but I'm not sure either of us is ready for a serious discussion. I think we need time to adjust to what happened before we try to deal with it."

It wasn't going to be easy to get the truth from Marc. He seemed to want to put it off. I didn't understand why. If he was being intimate with Susan, no excuse would be good enough. If it was a misunderstanding, why not get it out in the open now. I was confused and disheartened, but I was determined to make the best of the night.

We all did the round robin and danced with the people who knew us. Mary Ellen was thrilled at how well Marc danced. She told me how lucky I was to have such a great dance partner. I told her it wasn't an asset, it was a problem. That got me an odd look.

"Because he's so good, every girl here wants to dance with him, and if it weren't for the Amonti Rule, we'd probably never dance together. But, it's not all bad. The friends we usually come here with are also excellent, one, in particular, is much better than Marc, so, it's usually a wash. And then, there's always Billy."

Marc laughed and explained who Billy was. All in all, we were having a good time. Mary Ellen and Jim seemed to be enjoying themselves, and if it weren't for the problem between Marc and me, it would have been an utterly fantastic night. When I danced with Jim, he asked me if I was alright. I said I was fine, but he knew it wasn't true.

"Listen Catherine. I know my wife sticks her nose in where it doesn't belong, but this time, I agree with her. You're a great gal, honey, and I know Marc is a good man. That's why I took the deal when you were in San Antonio. I wasn't sure if you could deliver what you promised, but I knew you guys believed you could. You two are obviously in love with each other. I'm pretty sure whatever happened to cause this rift can be fixed. Don't give up on him. I think he's worth fighting for."

"I want to. But I'm not sure if he wants to."

"He definitely does, honey, I'd bet the ranch on it,"

"Two to one odds?"

"A hundred to one," Jim answered.

I really didn't want my laundry aired out in public, but Mary Ellen and Jim seemed to be so sincere. It was impossible to tell them to mind their own business. And Jim did appear to have a handle on a lot of things, maybe he was right. Maybe this can be fixed. But, not before I knew the truth, or, at least, Marc's version of it.

The rest of the night was fun. I was determined not to let anything spoil it for anyone. Jim and Mary Ellen were having a great time. It was obvious they didn't party often. Of course, they attended corporate banquets and such, just like we all did, but this was different. This was let your hair down, laid back fun with good friends. Everyone at the 88's liked them, and Jim's Texas drawl and down-home manner turned the ladies on.

Mary Ellen told Marc, "Since you're the one who brought us here, it would be your fault if my husband winds up with one of these young gals."

But she said it teasingly, and we all knew it was in fun.

Marc seemed more relaxed than he had been in days. The combination of the Carter's coming to town to sign the big deal and the trouble between us had taken a toll on him. I knew the tirade in my office yesterday morning wasn't like him, and I blamed it on myself. I should have been there to help him, not add to his problems. In the beginning, I did agree our personal relationship would never interfere with business. I had let him down, and maybe that was as bad as him letting me down in Nashville.

Trust has many faces!

On a trip to the ladies room, I ran into Annie. She asked me if everything was OK between Marc and me. I said we were fine, and she asked if I had noticed anything different about him. When I inquired as to what she meant, she said, "In all the time I've known him, this is the first time he's not one hundred percent into the party. He seemed to be more into himself tonight. I thought it might be trouble between you and Marc".

Not wanting to get any more people involved, I told her we were having a rough week at work, and we were all not ourselves.

"Jim is a new customer, and he just signed the biggest contract our company has ever seen, and we were here tonight to try and unwind from a very stress filled week.

"It's just temporary, and I'm sure Marc will be back to normal the next time you see him."

She seemed to buy it. Then she said some things that made me want to cry.

"Marc is very special to me, and I want you to know why. You know how Marc is. He's always concerned about his friends. He always asks me how I'm doing and how my family is. He seems to be sincerely interested, not like it was just a comment people say to each other. So, one night I told him about my mother.

"Momma has a chronic back problem. The doctors said surgery might possibly fix the problem, but it was just as likely to make it worse. The pain was awful, and the only relief she got was from monthly treatments at the pain clinic. The treatment allowed her to function with almost no pain and lead a near normal life.

"Daddy had a good job, but his company was changing their Medical Insurance. The new insurance was willing to pay for the

81

surgery, but they wouldn't continue to pay for the pain treatments. Neither my mother nor my father were prepared to take a chance on the surgery, but they didn't know what else to do. Because my mother was in so much pain without the treatments, Daddy decided to give up the job he loved and find one where the insurance would cover the procedures."

Annie looked out to the dance floor where Marc was dancing with Mary Ellen.

"When I told Marc about it, he hired my father as a consultant to Antonelli Systems and paid him one dollar a year. That allowed Daddy to keep his present job and also made him eligible for the Antonelli Systems Medical Plan. Daddy said it was the best plan on the market. My mother's treatments would be covered in full, and Daddy would never have to worry about medical bills again."

This was so typical of Marc.

"That sounds like something Marc would do. He really did care about people, especially real people like you, Annie."

That made Annie smile.

"That's not why I told you this story."

When I indicated I didn't understand, she told me the rest.

"You're a beautiful woman. You know how men are. They buy you dinner, and they think that entitles them to a roll in the hay with you. You owe them."

I knew exactly what she was saying, and I nodded my head in agreement.

"I was willing to do anything to thank Marc, anything. He told me what he wanted from me. He said what he needed was for me to smile when I danced with him. He said my smile was more than enough reward for him. He also made me promise never to mention this to anyone and to never be afraid to come to him if I have a problem."

The final part of Annie's story made me wonder if I ever really knew Marc Antonelli.

"I love that man, Catherine. Most of the girls here love him. He's so easy to love, but he seems to find it difficult to accept love from anyone. He's pleasant about it, and he flirts with all of us, but for some reason, he's not ready to accept real love. That's why we were all so happy when you showed up. For the first time since I met him, he seemed to be in love. It's so obvious how he feels about you. All of the girls noticed. We were all happy for him. That's why I was worried tonight. He doesn't seem himself."

I assured Annie all was well between us. No sense getting her involved in our problem. If it doesn't work out, it will be up to Marc to tell them why. I'll never come here again. This is his place. His special place.

Back at the table, the party continued. Mary Ellen and Jim were having a ball. Jim was getting a lot of attention from the regular gals and Mary Ellen danced almost every dance with one guy or another. When she got a chance to dance with Billy, she was thrilled.

"Wow! You don't dance with that man. You just let him take you away."

Having danced with Billy myself, I knew exactly what she meant. Jim made some comment about who she was going home with, and with sweetness and sincerity in her eyes, she said, "Don't you worry, Jimbo, the last dance will always be yours, honey."

If it wasn't for the tension between Marc and me, it would have been a perfect night.

When we left, Jim said, "I trust you'll see the lady home safely?"

"Absolutely," Marc replied.

As they walked to their rental, Mary Ellen had both of her hands on Jim's arm and her head resting on his shoulder. They were like two young lovers who had just found each other. Marc smiled as he watched them walk away.

"All in all, a pretty good night."

The drive to my apartment was in silence. I wanted to talk to Marc, but I didn't know how to start the conversation. He seemed content to let things stay the way they were. When he pulled up in front of my door, I couldn't let it go on any longer.

"Marc, we have to talk."

"I agree, Catherine, but I'm pretty sure this is not the right time."

"When is the right time?"

"I'm sure we'll both know when that time comes."

I was not about to let this man drive away without some explanation of why he was in Susan's room. I tried to keep my voice from revealing my true emotions.

"Don't you think I'm entitled to some kind of explanation as to what was happening?"

He didn't hesitate.

"Yes Catherine, I most certainly do believe you have a right to a full explanation as to why I was in Susan's room with her dressed like that."

And then silence. It was evident that's all he intended to say, but I was not going to be put off.

"Well? Am I going to get an explanation?"

Again, he didn't hesitate.

"The time to ask for an explanation was Wednesday afternoon, not the following Sunday morning."

That comment made me angry.

"Why should I have to ask? Why wasn't it your responsibility to tell me why you were there?"

"I tried Catherine. I chased you down the hall, and I knocked on your door for twenty minutes. I called your cell phone a dozen times. You didn't seem to be interested in an explanation. Your actions Wednesday night on the way home indicated you didn't want to talk to me."

"What did you expect? All the evidence pointed in a direction that hurt me deeply."

"What evidence?" He asked.

"Do I have to spell it out for you?"

"Yes, you do!"

"You didn't expect me back until five o'clock. No one had seen you since you got back from your conference. You didn't expect me to knock on Susan's door at four fifteen, and you had your favorite champagne delivered to her room. She was, at least, half naked. How much evidence do I need?"

"Well, I guess you have the explanation that satisfies you. You definitely have the evidence... But, since we're on the subject of evidence, let me tell you about some other evidence. That is if you're interested in real evidence."

"What is that supposed to mean?"

Again, he didn't hesitate, and this time, his answer was accusatory.

"Let me lay it out for you. You find your boyfriend in a bad situation. Instead of trying to get to the bottom of it, you decide to seek comfort with another man."

"Wait a minute," I shouted, "Don't try to turn this around and put it on me!"

"I'm not putting anything on you, Catherine. We were talking

84

about evidence, but it seems you're only interested in evidence that suits your purpose."

There was silence again.

"So, Ted was trying to help me get through the flight home, that's all it was."

"I thought we were talking about evidence."

"What evidence," I screamed in frustration.

"Are you interested?"

"Tell me what you're talking about," I answered angrily.

Again, very accusatory.

"As I was saying, you find your boyfriend in a bad situation. Instead of asking him what it was all about, you seek the comfort of another man. A man, by the way, who has been trying to get into your pants ever since you met him.

"You ignore everyone else in your party and have a romantic dinner with him alone in your room. You change your seats on the flight home so you two can sit together and be away from everyone else. You don't take the limo back to the office to pick up your car. You decide to ride with your new best friend, and not back to the office. You didn't go home that night because you are wearing clothes out of your suitcase. The next day, it's obvious neither your car nor his left the parking lot all night. You and your friend both show up for work late and at the same time."

Marc paused for just a second. Mostly I think to get a breath.

"Your friend spends practically the entire day in your office cooing you. That night you stop for a drink at a very expensive bar. You allow you newest best friend to fondle you in public. That gets you so hot you can't wait to leave and be alone. Again, your car never left the parking lot all night. How's that for evidence."

What could I say? He was absolutely right. Anyone hearing that would believe I had jumped into bed with Ted. But, no matter what Marc had done, I wasn't going to let him think that of me.

"I didn't sleep with Ted!" I said as firmly and with as much conviction as I could muster under the circumstances.

Marc's reply came as a complete shock to me.

"I know that, Catherine. I know you. I know your character. I know you so well I could probably tell you exactly what you did Wednesday and Thursday night."

I had nothing to say. Marc was right. The evidence was

overwhelming. How could he believe it wasn't true? There was a long silence and then.

"Let's see how close I come…You find me in Susan's room. You think the worst. That's the part I don't understand. You decide you don't want to know why I was there, another part I don't understand. You hide from everyone because you're embarrassed.

"Ted comes along and comforts you. He suggests you avoid everyone else, and he makes arrangements for dinner, the cab to the airport, the change of seats and the ride back to the office. You decide not to pick up your car because the rest of us will be right behind you and you still don't want to face anyone. You don't want to go home and be alone, and you can't go home with Ted, so what other choice do you have."

Again Marc paused just long enough to take a breath.

"My guess would be Elizabeth. I could see the closeness between you two when we visited. You stay the night and don't have anything to wear to work, so you take something from your suitcase you wore in Nashville. You and Elizabeth can't share clothes. You're late because you didn't have your car and you didn't make arrangements for a car service the night before. Ted is either late by coincidence, or he waited for you downstairs. Thursday, he talks you into going for a drink. Not the local places we frequent, too much chance of one or more of the team being there. So, it has to be somewhere else."

After another pause.

"Ted, Tim, and Artie all know I'm keeping Jim's wife company until he gets through with his meeting and they know where I'll be meeting her. Just another coincidence Ted takes you to that very place. He slips his hand under your skirt, knowing you'd never make a fuss in a place like that. You get pissed and tell him you want to leave. Out on the street, you cut him a new one, and not wanting to deal with him, you take a cab home…Am I close?"

I had nothing to say. From outside, the evidence indicated because I was angry with Marc I jumped in bed with Ted. Marc not only didn't believe that, but he also figured exactly what happened Wednesday night and Thursday. Why was it so easy for him to trust me and so hard for me to trust him?

I had to say something. I was so in love with this man. I wanted him to be honest with me. Maybe we could still find something together.

Finally finding my voice, "Do you really know me that well?"

Again his answer surprised me.

"Know you that well? No Catherine. No one can know anyone that well. But as well as I do know you, that's what I believe you did. I may be all wrong, but I don't think so. I trust your character, and that's what I believe your character would force you to do."

Silence again for a few minutes before he added.

"It comes down to trust, Catherine. Not only trust in someone else but confidence in your own ability to be able to judge other people."

Another minute of silence and then.

"Catherine, what you saw Wednesday must have been a shock and a disappointment. I don't expect you to find me in a hotel room with another woman and not have questions. But, you should have had enough faith in our relationship to stand there and ask me what I was doing there.

It's been three and a half days since that incident, and you still don't know why I was in that room. You still don't know if it was innocent or was I being bad. Don't you want to know the truth? Even if it is bad news."

He was right of course. I did have to know, either way. I can't spend the rest of my life wondering if I threw away something wonderful just because I was a coward.

"Tell me, please. I do want to know."

But, he wasn't finished with his lecture.

"You have to be careful with assumptions. Catherine. Earlier, you said you called my office, and they told you I was out of town. You assumed I was on a job for Nick. That was a fair assumption because you knew the other Saturdays I wasn't in my office I was out working for him. Even though your assumption was wrong, you had enough information to base it on. Wednesday, you assumed I was fooling around with Susan. That was an unfair assumption.

"Since the day we meet, I have never given you any reason to think I was a player and you know Susan. She's not the type who would go after a man involved in a relationship. Plus, she's your friend!"

And he still wasn't done.

"Thursday, you saw me at a bar with a charming woman. You thought I was with another woman for my own pleasure. You made another assumption based on very little information, and you were wrong again. What you should have done is come over to the table

87

and let me introduce you. Then, you would have known for sure."

When it finally seemed he was through I said, "Marc I really want to know. I have to know. Please tell me why you were in Susan's room Wednesday."

His answer was like a punch to the gut.

"No Catherine. As I said before, the time to ask that question was Wednesday not today. If you really need to know the truth, you'll have to find out for yourself."

"And just how do I do that?" I demanded.

"Catherine, there's more than enough information available, if you truly want to know the answer. If it's important enough to you, you'll find a way."

Why was he doing this? I couldn't understand his attitude. If it was so innocent, why doesn't he just tell me? What is he hiding? Now, more than the truth, I wanted to know why he was acting this way. I said, in the most unfriendly voice I could conjure up, "Why are you being such a hardass about this?"

When Marc and I first started talking, he turned in his seat to face me and kept his eyes locked on mine the entire time. Now, he turned forward and stared out the windshield. He took his time before answering, and it seemed as if he was trying to pick his words carefully.

"Catherine, I tell people my marriage broke up because my business put a terrible strain on the relationship. That's not exactly the truth. The real reason is my wife couldn't trust me. I swear to you I was completely faithful to that woman from the day I met her until long after we split up, but she couldn't bring herself to believe that.

"I wasn't the rich, outgoing guy I am today. I worked hard trying to get my business together and the strain of always being accused of things I wasn't guilty of got to be too much."

He paused. I think he was trying to decide just how far he was going to go with his explanation. After a very deep breath, "It's impossible to disprove a negative, Catherine. I can prove you've been unfaithful to me by catching you in the act. That's proof. But I can never prove you have been faithful. That's impossible. Maybe you're good at hiding your indiscretions. Maybe I just never caught you. No matter how faithful you are to me, I can never prove it. I can choose to believe it. I can judge your character and make a rational decision, but I can never prove beyond a shadow of a doubt you've been faithful."

Another pause, this time, accompanied by a sigh.

"My wife needed proof. Every time she accused me of something, I had to find a way to prove she was mistaken. The more times I showed her she was wrong, the more she was convinced she was right. I walked around on eggshells constantly. I had to be careful how I talked to women. I had to be careful how I looked at women. It was not a pleasant way to live. It finally cost us our relationship. The irony is my wife was a beautiful, sexy, sensual woman. She had men crazy over her, and I trusted her completely. She never understood how much I was in love with her, right up until the end."

Another pause as he turned back toward me, looking into my eyes;

"Catherine, I will never again be with a woman who cannot trust me, or, at least, give me the benefit of the doubt."

With that last comment, Marc got out of the car and walked around to open my door. There was no reason to prolong this. That last statement was as definite as it could be. It didn't matter anymore why he was in Susan's room, I had lost him.

Marc walked me to the door, waited until I had used my key to let myself in and left.

It's weird how some things affect you. After Marc left me at the building entrance, I went to my apartment and had the best night's sleep I've had since this all started. No tears, no thoughts about what was to be. I just climbed into bed and fell asleep.

Maybe it was because I didn't have any decisions to make any more. Marc had made the decision for me. He would never be with a woman who didn't trust him, and I had proven I didn't. It was out of my hands.

Marc was gone. Gone out of my life forever, I was sure.

Chapter 16 – The Day After

Sunday morning I got up early. I made myself some breakfast, something I hadn't done since coming home from Nashville. Over hot oatmeal. I thought about the past three days. I went over Marc's words last night and what I had heard from my siblings and Mary Ellen Carter. Could they all possibly be wrong and I was the only one that was right.

Where they just stupid for trusting their men or was I the crazy one. I had only had one man do me wrong in my life, and I based my entire relationship with men on one incident. I had never allowed a man to get close enough to me to do me wrong again. I had always thought it was the smart thing to do. I had never allowed myself to fall in love with a man.

But, that wasn't entirely accurate. I had fallen in love. I had allowed a man to get close to me. I was madly and totally in love with Marco Antonelli, and I couldn't just let that man walk out of my life forever. I had to find a way to show him how much I loved him. I had to find a way to change his mind about me. I wasn't his ex-wife. I wasn't like her. How could he put us in the same category?

The same way you put him in Bobby's category, stupid!

Was it that simple? I couldn't let him go like this. Maybe we couldn't be happy together, but I couldn't let him write me off like this. Not without a fight.

I threw the dishes in the sink and hurried to get dressed. This couldn't wait. I had to get to him before he entrenched himself in that statement he made this morning. I had to talk him out of that.

In Marc's apartment building, visitors had to be announced before you could get to the elevator. I had to hope Marc would let me in. He wasn't a mean man. He wouldn't tell the doorman to send me away. I had to try to see him today, now.

The doorman was very friendly.

"Mr. Antonelli isn't in Ms. Jensen. I'm pretty sure he's gone to the Dolphins, Jets game with some friends."

That sounded reasonable He was a New York sports fan, and the Jets came to town only once a year.

What do I do now?

I was heading back out to the garage, only half paying attention to what I was doing and I almost bumped into someone. Being jolted out of my stupor, I realized it was Danielle Palmer. She was dressed the same way as the last time I saw her here in Marc's apartment building. We were both startled, and she recovered first.

"Catherine! Good, Marc did get in touch with you."

Confused, I told her I didn't understand.

"Didn't you talk to Marc this morning?"

"I haven't seen him since he dropped me off at my place last night."

That brought a confused look to her face.

"I don't understand. Didn't Marc tell you he was going to the football game with the guys today?"

"No, we were with a important customer last night, and I guess he forgot to mention it. I just thought I'd drop by and wake him up."

"I heard. The Carter contract, fifty million. You must be very pleased. Marc said the part you played in that deal was the most crucial."

"He's just being nice. It really was a team effort."

"Well let's not stand here, the girls will be here shortly, and I have to shower."

"I still don't understand," I told her.

Her reply was delivered as she ushered me toward the elevator.

"When the boys go out to one of these sports things, the girls get together and gab. We call it the Sports Widows Club. The guys hate that name because they don't do this very often, but the Jets are in town, and you remember the hockey game nonsense. I asked Marc to call you this morning and invite you to join us. Now that you're here welcome aboard."

Now I was in a quandary. Marc didn't call, probably because he didn't want me to come here. If Danielle still wanted me here, that probably meant Marc hadn't told her about our breakup. I couldn't think of any excuse that would seem plausible to her, so I was stuck.

And, I wanted to know why these women would hold their Sports Widows Club meeting in Marc's apartment and why Danielle felt comfortable showering there.

I gathered up all my resolve and followed Danielle to the doorman's desk. With a cheery good morning, she informed him, "Ms. Geer, Patrick, and Combs will be arriving shortly. Send them right up without announcing them."

That got her an equally cheery,

"Sure thing, Ms. Palmer."

Then, we headed for the elevator, but Danielle was going the wrong way. The elevator was down the right corridor, and she was going left. Not sure of where she was going, I just followed along. There was an elevator at the end of this hall also. And, we didn't get off on the fifth floor as I did with Marc, we went to the tenth. Now, I was really confused.

Did she live here too?

Halfway down the hall to her apartment, she pulled her baseball cap off. Her hair had all been tucked under it, and when the cap came off, it was a tangled mess.

"What happened to your hair?"

Danielle answered very seriously.

"A woman's hair is a weapon that can be used against her. The boys like to keep it real, so they grab me by the hair sometimes, and it winds up in a tangled mess. I've got a great conditioner that will undo this in no time."

"What kind of gym do you go to?"

Danielle laughed.

"It's not a gym. I work out at least once a month with my security team. It's self-defense training. Being the wife of a very wealthy man has responsibilities, and being able to defend myself is one of them. It's either that or twenty-four/seven bodyguards. Like I said, they like to keep it real and sometimes they get very rough. I've come home with some beautiful bruises on occasion."

When we entered the apartment, it was a mirror image of Marc's place. The master bedroom was where the guest room should be, and the dining room and kitchen were in reverse. The only thing that was in the same place was the living room and the doors to the patio. Even the alcove Marc used as an office was on the wrong side.

Danielle told me, "I'm headed for the shower. If you hear a knock at the door, it will be the girls. You know Stacy and Angie, and if a beautiful blond shows up, that would be Cindy. Just introduce yourself, you'll like her."

The beautiful blond was the first to show up. She was surprised when I opened the door for her.

"You must be Cindy. I'm Catherine Jensen."

Cindy was all smiles.

"Well, I guess Marc holding out all these years waiting for the right gal to come along really paid off."

Even though it made me feel bad, I thanked her for the compliment just as there was another knock on the door. Angie and Stacey arrived together.

Angie immediately said, "Good, I'm glad Danielle managed to get you over here today. We all want to know how you did it."

If this meeting had taken place last Sunday, before we went to Nashville, I would be so happy to be a part of this group. They all seemed like very nice people, and they were open to accepting me just because I was Marc's choice. They all seemed to think I was pretty special, considering Marc rarely brought his dates to meet them. But, under the circumstances, I felt like a fraud.

Danielle came out of her bedroom looking like a million dollars. We all sat at the dining room table, and I was the main subject of discussion. I tried to deflect the questions about Marc and me and attempted to change the subject. I said I hadn't realized Danielle lived in the same building as Marc. Danielle said there was a story about that.

"First, we don't actually live in the same building. There are actually two separate buildings. The only things we share are the lobby and the garage. There are two different elevators and the buildings only connect in the lobby. If you want to go to Marc's apartment, you have to go down to the lobby and take the other elevator to his floor."

After signaling my understanding, she continued.

"Marc moved in here about ten years ago, right after his marriage broke up. I moved in about two years later when I got a promotion at Deltron. I guess because our hours were so different, we never crossed paths.

"If I had seen him in the lobby or garage, I'm sure I would have remembered that handsome man. I was single at the time."

That brought giggles from the other ladies, and the story continued.

"I actually didn't meet Marc until the day of my wedding. He was one of my husband's business partners, and he was invited to our wedding. I did take notice of him that day! He was sitting at the same table as Terry, Stacy, Cindy, Dan, Harry, Angie and Tony.

"Since this apartment was all we really needed, we decided to stay here after we were married. About two months after we returned from our honeymoon, we invited Marc to dinner here. When my husband gave Marc the address, Marc started to laugh and said he lived at the same address."

Still trying to keep the conversation away from Marc and me, I asked, "So, all these people were friends of your husbands before you were married."

"Both my husband and I brought our old friends into our relationship. Now we're all friends. Some of our friends, like Marc, are also my husband's business partners."

"I'm confused," I said, "I thought Nick Amonti was Marc's only business partner."

Danielle gave me a weird look.

"I don't understand what you're saying, Catherine."

I was trying to figure out a way to explain myself when Stacy burst out laughing. The other girls looked at her, and Danielle asked, "What struck you so funny?"

Stacy stood up.

"It's Jensen, isn't it?"

I nodded in confusion and Stacy in a very formal tone said, "Ms. Catherine Jensen, may I introduce you to Ms. Danielle Palmer…Amonti."

Now, everyone was laughing, except me. Danielle quieted everyone down.

"Don't feel bad Catherine; it's a very common mistake. I'm just surprised Marc never mentioned it."

"Marc always talked about you two as separate business people. He said you were good friends, but I guess he just took it for granted I knew. The first time your names came up was about the Dillman thing, and Marc and I weren't seeing each other than."

Then I got another story about why Danielle wasn't known as Mrs. Amonti. It had to do with Nick not wanting her professional career credited to the fact she was married to NAS Financial Group. They met when she was first putting together the Diesel/LNG thing, and they married right around the time she signed the Paterson contract. Nick wanted all the credit to go to her and not his money.

Stacy said, "Catherine, you've seen Danielle and Nick together. They flirt with each other all the time, like newlyweds. Didn't that make you wonder?"

I nodded.

"Oh Catherine," Danielle laughed, "You thought we were fooling around?"

My red face answered that question. That brought on more laughs. Danielle said when they go to an affair that's connected with NAS, Nick introduces her as my wife, Danielle. When they go to an affair for her company, she introduces him as my husband, Nick.

"I can't count the number of times he's been called Mr. Palmer."

She also told me about the flirting game they play on the other people at their table who don't know they're married to each other.

These were very nice people, and I was having a good time with them and at the same time feeling very guilty because I really wasn't one of them. I wasn't the girlfriend of her husband's friend.

During a lull in the conversation, Danielle took me into Nick's office and showed me some of the pictures that were hanging there. The ones of her wedding were beautiful. I said that surely must be a Stacy Geer Wedding Dress and Danielle said it was a gift from Stacy. She also pointed to a picture of the plane we had taken to Key West and Nashville. She pointed to the nose and asked if I had noticed that. In beautiful script was written *Danielle* and above that was a caricature of a very sexy lady in a cheesecake pose.

"No, I hadn't noticed. Is the girl above the name you?"

She smiled, nodded and told me that story also.

Then, she said very quietly, "Catherine, is everything alright between you and Marc?"

"Why do you ask?"

"I know Marc is working very hard at Dillman Brothers and with his own company to look after and some things he does for Nick his time with you must be limited. I was surprised when you told me you didn't know Marc was going to a football game with the guys today. Considering Sunday was the only full day you two could spend together, it wasn't likely he wouldn't tell you about it.

"Marc is a good friend and the girls really like you and thought you and Marc were a good match, so I'm concerned about you."

It was all I could do to hold the tears back. I shouldn't be here. This was a fraud. I had to tell her the truth.

"Danielle, I really don't belong here. This is not honest. I was invited because of my relationship with Marc. Well, the truth is there is no relationship, it's over."

"Stop right there. It's true we met you because of your relationship with Marc, but you were invited here because we like you. You seemed like a great girl and Stacy, Angie and I thought you'd fit in with our little group. Not all of my friends have husbands or boyfriends who have relations with my husband. As to your relationship with Marc, that's not my business, but knowing how he feels about you, I'm curious as to what happened between you two. I like Marc. I think he's a great guy, and I thought you two were perfect for each other. I'd really like to know what happened. Maybe I can help!"

"No one can help. Marc said he could never be with me."

"Catherine, I can't believe that Marc would ever say a thing like that to any woman. Please, tell me what happened. Let's go back inside. They all know Marc, maybe we can fix this. That is if you want to fix it."

That was it. I couldn't hold back any longer. The floodgates opened. Danielle handed me a box of tissues and gave me a hug.

"When you get it out of your system, come inside and talk to us."

It didn't take long. There weren't many tears left in me. I gathered myself together as much as possible and went back into the dining room. Four sets of eyes were on me. Stacy was the first to speak.

"You're among friends, Catherine, and some pretty smart ladies. Let us help!"

I nodded and sat down at the table. I didn't know what to say. I didn't know how to begin. Danielle finally broke the silence.

"Why did he say that?"

"There was an incident last Wednesday, and I tried to talk to him about it last night. That's when he said he would never be with someone like me."

"That's awfully harsh," Cindy said, "Especially coming from Marc. He's such a gentleman; I can't imagine him saying something like that to a woman."

Angie had a question.

"Catherine, is that what he said, exactly, or is that what you thought he meant?"

"His exact words were he would never be with a woman who didn't trust him."

"That's not the same thing," Danielle said, "And, under the circumstances, quite understandable. I didn't know Marc when he was married, but Nick did. The breakup was very hard on Marc.

"According to what Nick told me, Marc's wife was obsessed with the idea Marc was fooling around on her. Nick said it was so extreme Marc finally decided to end the marriage. He left her.

"Because of Nick's involvement in Marc's company at the time, Nick and Marc spent a lot of time together. Nick said he never knew Marc to fool around, and he was so busy he didn't have the time even if he had the desire. Marc's wife even accused Nick of being Marc's alibi when he supposedly stayed late at the office. She said Nick was covering for him.

"According to my husband, leaving his wife was the most traumatic thing Marc has even done. So it's very understandable Marc would be gun shy about a relationship with someone who didn't trust him."

"So, the question is," Cindy asked, "Why does Marc think you don't trust him?"

"Because, I don't...No, I mean I didn't...NO, I mean...I don't know what I'm saying, I'm so confused."

Danielle slid the box of tissues across the table to me, and everyone was quiet while I got it together. When I had settled down, Danielle said, "Let's back up a little. I know Marc about six years. He's never been serious with anyone until you came along. Why don't you tell us how you got together?"

That brought a thin smile to my face.

"I made a pass at him,"

"Crimady, am I the only one who did it the old fashioned way," Cindy cried!

That brought giggles from everyone and an explanation from each. Angie said she was working for a company that was a supplier to Harry's company. They had seen each other a number of times over business and one day Angie asked him if he'd like to take her to dinner. That was the start of their romantic relationship.

Stacy told me, "I had known Terry for years, but we had never dated. We had both been friends of Nick's before the NAS thing, and we were two of his first projects. I called Terry up one day and told him to pick me up at seven, he was taking me to dinner. He just said okay, and we've been inseparable ever since."

Danielle said, "I just told you the story of the girl on the nose of the airplane. That's the outfit I was wearing when I seduced Nick. I didn't want there to be any doubt as to what I had in mind."

Cindy added she feels like an outsider.

"I'm the only one of the group who waited for Dan to ask me out."

After the giggles died down, Danielle said Marc and I seemed so happy together the last time she saw us. She wanted me to tell them what happened to change everything. And I did.

I told them everything from Wednesday morning when Marc kissed me right up until I met Danielle in the lobby this morning. They listened attentively, and when I had finished my story, they all vouched for Marc's innocence. Danielle was the most adamant.

"In the six years I've known Marc, he never was a player. He was single, charming, handsome and wealthy. He could have had a dozen girls a day if he wanted. He could have had two or three at a time. But if that wasn't his style when he was free, why would he change now that he's found someone to fall in love with?"

"I don't know. I wish I could be sure. How can I be sure?"

"What's his name, Catherine?" Stacy asked.

"Whose name?"

"The guy who did you so wrong you can't trust any man."

Danielle added, "We've all had one, mine was Jack Reynolds. My second job after college. He was the most handsome and charming man I have ever laid eyes on, maybe even better looking than Marc. I came home early one afternoon and found him in bed with my best girlfriend. I didn't think I'd ever get over it, but I finally did and found the mostest man I have ever known."

"Bobby. I don't even remember his last name. It was my first semester at college."

"Catherine," Cindy wailed, "That had to be fifteen or twenty years ago, and you're still carrying it around? Haven't you met any good men between then and now?"

"I don't know. I've never hung around long enough to find out."

"Dump them before they had a chance to hurt you?" Angie asked.

I just shrugged my shoulders and nodded ashamedly.

"There are a lot of good men out there, Catherine," Stacy said, "and you happened to run into one of the best, and he's in love with you. I'd bet my entire fall line Marc wasn't doing anything wrong."

"Then why won't he tell me why he was in Susan's room?" I cried, "Why did he say he never could be with me?"

"He didn't say that Catherine," Danielle admonished.

"He said he couldn't be with anyone who couldn't trust him. I believe it was a challenge. I think he wants to know how important the truth is to you. How badly do you want to know the truth? Or, are you like his ex, and would rather be right?"

"I'd start with the girl," Angie suggested, "Talk to her first and follow up on what she tells you. Marc must believe there is enough information available for you to piece it together. Show him the truth is important to you."

"I've tried calling her. She won't pick up the phone, and she hasn't been to work since it happened."

Cindy handed me her cell phone.

"Use this. Maybe she'll pick it up if she doesn't recognize the number."

What did I have to lose? They all knew Marc. Maybe they were right. Maybe it was a challenge. I took out my cell phone, opened my address book and used Cindy's phone to make the call. I hit the speaker button so the girls could listen in. It was picked up on the fourth ring, and a sad voice said, "Hello."

I steeled myself as best as I could.

"Susan, it's Catherine."

There was a very long pause and then a broken voice, obviously in tears said, "Catherine, nothing happened. I swear to you Catherine, he wasn't in my room more than a minute. He just came by to tell me something."

My heart was breaking. If she was telling the truth, what anguish she must be going through.

"It's Okay, Susan, but we have to talk. We have to find out what's going on here."

"Catherine," she cried, "I'm your friend. Even if Marc wanted something, I'd never do that to you, and he didn't, I swear!"

"Okay, Susan. I want to come over and talk to you. As friends, Susan. Please, it's important."

I had to give her a reason to let me come over. This was not going to get settled over the phone.

"Susan, what did Marc have to tell you?"

"He said there was a glitch in the Carter specs, and he thought we could fix it before dinner."

That knocked me into next week. Unsure of what I heard.

"Susan, Marc said he found a glitch in the Carter contract?"

99

"Yes, Catherine. He said there was a small problem, and he thought we would be able to fix it before you got back from your seminar."

"Susan," I begged, "Please, we have to talk. There is something wrong here. Please let me come over. We have to get to the bottom of this. I think that it's crucial to the team."

"Okay," she finally relented.

"And, Susan," I added, "I want Tim and Artie to come too."

"No," she cried, "They think I did something terrible."

"No, they don't. Have you heard from either of them?"

"Tim called about a dozen times, and Artie calls almost every hour, but I haven't answered the phone."

"They're worried about you. And they want to help you. Please, Susan. Let's get to the bottom of this problem, one for all and all for one."

"Okay," she finally said without much conviction.

"Give me forty minutes," I told her and we broke the connection.

Stacy immediately said, "That girl is completely innocent, or she's one hell of an actress."

"Susan is too innocent to be that convincing. Whatever the reason Marc was in her room, she had no part in it."

"Catherine, that sounded like good news why the long face?" Danielle asked.

"Did you hear why Marc was in her room?"

"Yes. Something about the Carter deal."

"There was nothing wrong with the specs on that contract. If there was, I would have had to fix them Thursday before Carter signed the deal."

"What does that mean?" Cindy asked.

"I don't know. Maybe Marc was using that as an excuse to be in Susan's room. Or maybe he was told there was a problem with the specs. I was told there was a problem also, that's why I went to Susan's room."

I thanked the girls for allowing me to join them and for their help with my problem. We all exchanged phone numbers, and I promised to let them know what I found out. Danielle suggested I call her, and she would pass on the news to the others. We all hugged, and everyone wished me luck and told me to stay positive.

Before I started my car, I called Tim and Artie. Both of them were worried about Susan. She hadn't come to work Thursday or Friday, and they were concerned she would quit.

I got them both to agree to meet me at Susan's apartment, but only after I convinced them I was pretty sure she had done nothing wrong. Artie was particularly vocal in his support of her. I knew he was angry that she was in the middle of something he was sure wasn't her fault.

And now, I was sure too! Susan had no part in this, but it still didn't answer why Marc was there.

Chapter 17 – Susan's Story

Susan opened her apartment door and the moment I looked at her, there was no doubt she was completely innocent. She invited me in, much too formally for friends and asked if I'd like something to drink. I requested a cup of coffee, thinking it would give her something to do while we were going through the opening phase of our discussion. I started off directly and got right to the point.

"Susan, I'm absolutely sure there was nothing wrong going on between you and Marc. I'm sorry for the way I acted on Wednesday afternoon and the way I treated you on the plane Wednesday night. I'm sorry I didn't call you Thursday to straighten things out."

I also assured her no one of the team thought she had done anything wrong. Then I told her I believed what happened Wednesday wasn't just a misunderstanding

Susan brightened a little and asked me what I meant.

"I'm not sure of anything except you and Marc weren't doing anything wrong. But I think it's important we find out exactly why Marc and I ended up at your room at the same time, neither of us expecting the other."

She was confused, and I couldn't blame her. I was confused too. The only thing I knew for sure was there was a bad odor about this entire affair. I asked Susan to tell me everything she remembered about Wednesday, the entire day.

"We all had breakfast together in the morning. I didn't have a conference so I thought it would be a good use of my time to work on the Alden contract. Artie told me he was going to work on it after his conference, and I thought I'd get a head start on the specs. I went back to my room to work alone on the specs."

I knew it takes a lot of concentration to deal with the numbers, and Susan and I often lock ourselves away in our offices or in the Plan Room to be alone.

"I didn't want to sit around in my good clothes and I didn't have anything clean to lounge in, so I worked in my bra and panties, I wasn't expecting company.

"The only contact I had with anyone was two or three phone calls from Artie asking about certain numbers for the contract. I was pleased because I had done quite a lot of work on the specs and I was sure the next day, back at the office, you and I could finish it up.

"A little after four o'clock, there was a knock at my door. I looked through the peephole and saw it was Marc. I didn't want to keep the boss waiting, so I threw on a robe and opened the door."

I waited while Susan poured the coffee.

"Marc came in, and I went back into the room. Mark never went past the little foyer where the door to the hall and the bathroom door are.

"Marc seemed surprised that I was alone. He asked if I had seen Ted. I told him I hadn't seen anyone since breakfast. Marc said Ted had found a small glitch in the Carter specs, and he thought the three of us could fix it before you got back from your conference.

"Then he said it would be too crowded in my room, and suggested I get dressed and when Ted got there to come down to the Business Center. He said he, Tim and Artie had been working there, and it was very comfortable and convenient.

"I swear, Catherine, he was only there a minute or two, and he never actually came into the room."

"I know, Susan. Marc is uncomfortable being in a closed room with a female he doesn't have a personal relationship with. Then what?"

"Marc turned to leave, and when he opened the door, you, Ted and a waiter were standing there. I didn't understand why you ran away like that. Ted must have told you Marc was going to be there. Marc had his computer and the Carter Master Disc in his hand. What could you have thought?"

What indeed. How stupid of me. Didn't even take a minute to survey the situation. Just assumed the worst, on wrong information, just as Marc had said.

"When you and Ted didn't show up for dinner, changed your seats on the plane and didn't come back to the office, I guessed what you thought."

I apologized as sincerely as I could.

"I acted like a stupid school girl instead of trusting my friend and an honest an honorable man. Susan, I'm not making any excuses for my behavior, but I believe there is more to this than just a chance encounter between you, me and Marc in your room."

Susan wanted to know what I meant.

"I'm not sure, but I think we should talk to Tim and Artie. They might be able to add something to your story. I called them, and they're both on their way here.

"Susan I have to know you forgive me, and we're still friends."

"Of course, Catherine, I just wanted you to know I wouldn't do that to you."

"I know Susan. And I should have known Wednesday, I'm sorry!"

Then, we had coffee and waited for the boys. Tim was the first to arrive. He brought his wife Emily with him. She was a great gal, and I was glad she was there because I thought she could give an opinion from a disinterested parties' perspective.

I told Tim I needed the same thing from him I needed from Susan. He didn't have much to say.

"I attended a conference with Marc and Artie and afterward the three of us went to the Business Center. Artie and Marc were working on the Alden contract, and I was cleaning up the Presser contract. I took the Master Disc with me on the trip, and I worked on it whenever I had time. Around ten to four I went to my room to drop off my computer, and when I met you in the elevator, I was heading to the bar for a pre-dinner cocktail."

"Did you see Marc, Artie or Ted during the afternoon?"

"Marc and Artie were in the Business Center from the time we got back from the conference until a little before four o'clock."

"Were they there the entire time?"

"I went to the men's room once, and stopped at the coffee shop once, but that was somewhere between two and three o'clock. Marc left twice and came back ten minutes later with a container of coffee and Artie left once, probably for the men's room. Overall, the three of us were in the Business Center from a little after noon until almost four o'clock.

"Ted had been in and out of the Business Center all afternoon. He talked to the three of us about the progress we were making on the two contracts. Because of the split commissions and the team thing, we all took an interest in everyone else's contracts."

"Did Ted say anything about a problem with the Carter specs?"

"I heard Ted say something to Mark about a small problem with a contract, but I didn't hear which contract. I was just leaving, but Artie was still there and should be able to tell you exactly what was said."

I asked Susan if anyone had talked to her about the specs on the Carter contract.

"I haven't spoken to anyone from the team since I drove away from the company parking lot Wednesday night. Marc knew I was upset and suggested I not come back to work until Monday. He said it would be all straightened out by then. He's called me every day to ask if I was Okay."

While we were waiting for Artie to arrive, Tim asked me what this was all about. I was ashamed to tell him, but I thought it was important for everyone to know because I had a dreadful feeling about what was behind this. I was already pretty much convinced it wasn't just a misunderstanding.

So, I told Tim and Emily.

"Wednesday afternoon I had gone to Susan's room to help fix a small problem with the Carter specs and found Marc and Susan together in her room with a bottle of Marc's favorite champagne being delivered. I thought the worst and ran away. I was so upset I never gave Susan or Marc a chance to explain. I admit now I feel like a fool for what I thought, but I don't believe it was all that it seemed to be."

I was questioned as to what I meant.

"After we talk to Artie, I'll tell you what I'm thinking. But, no one had talked to me about the Cater specs either, and the Carter contract seemed to go off without a hitch on Friday."

I asked Susan if she knew who had sent the champagne to her room.

"The waiter didn't know. All he told me is it was ordered to be delivered between 4:05 and 4:15. I refused to let him leave it. He took it back."

When Artie arrived, he seemed to be more interested in how Susan was doing than the reason I had asked him to this meeting.

But, he did tell me what he was doing Wednesday afternoon after the conference. His story matched Tim's almost exactly, except there were slight differences as to when Tim, Marc and he left for the men's room, and coffee, and exactly when Ted was with them, but the inconsistencies were slight and unimportant. They could be attributed to the fact no one was looking at a watch and timing anything.

105

When I questioned Artie about the conversation between Ted and Marc, just before the three of them parted, I was sure I was right.

"Ted told Marc he had been going over the Carter contract one last time and he found a slight glitch in the specs. Ted said it didn't seem to be serious, and since Catherine wasn't due back until five, maybe Ted, Marc and Susan could fix it before you got back. Marc said he had the master disc in his room and Ted said he'd go to Susan's room and let her know what was happening and Marc should pick up the master disc and meet him there."

"That's why Marc was surprised Ted wasn't there," Susan said.

I nodded, and Artie went on.

"About ten or fifteen minutes after I got to my room I heard loud voices out in the corridor. I stuck my head out the door and saw Ted and Marc banging on your door. They were begging you to open the door so they could explain. They said it wasn't what it looked like. After a few minutes, Marc left and headed for the elevator."

So, that's why Marc didn't follow me to the bar. Ted had him convinced I was in my room. Do I need any more proof?

I thought about what I was going to tell these people.

I looked at the four faces staring at me.

"Why don't we order some pizza and then I'll tell you what I did Wednesday and then you can tell me if what I'm thinking sounds reasonable?"

Everyone agreed and while Susan ordered the pizza and Tim and Artie went to the store for beer, I used the time to call Danielle. I told her what I had heard so far, and what I was going to add.

She could hardly contain her rage. I told her the only thing I wasn't sure of was the champagne.

"What hotel were you at, what time was the champagne delivered and what was Susan's room number?

"Nick's security guys have associates all over, and maybe they could get some information for you."

While we nibbled on the pizza, I could see the relief on Susan's face. It was also evident Artie was happy Susan's virtue was intact.

Emily glanced at the two of them and shook her head. I nodded, knowing what she was thinking. Everyone was happy we were all friends again. I was sure when they heard my story, that attitude would change, and I wondered if I should tell them the truth. Was it worth it to get them involved? This was between Marc and me, and maybe I should leave them out of it.

As the pizza boxes were being cleared off the table and the last swigs of beer were being swallowed, Emily said, "I know what you're thinking, Catherine. This has come too far to stop now. I have a pretty good idea where this is going, and if you don't tell them, I will. They were all involved in some way, and they have a right to know."

All eyes were on me. I shrugged and nodded. This would not be easy.

"Okay. I'll tell you what I did Wednesday and let you draw your own conclusions. I'm sure you know Marc and I have been seeing each other. I know it's not a good policy for co-workers to get involved, but it happened, and it was pretty serious.

"Wednesday morning, Marc stopped by my room and kissed me goodbye before he headed off to his conference. I stayed in my room until it was time for me to leave for my seminar.

"I met Ted in the lobby, and he walked me to the bus stop. Just before I boarded the bus, they conference delegate announced one of our speakers had canceled, and our meeting would be cut short by an hour. I was about to send Marc a text with the news, but Ted said he'd be seeing Marc and he would pass it on to him. I accepted that and boarded the bus, never giving it another thought."

I paused long enough for everyone to understand the situation.

"When I got off the bus, back at the hotel at four o'clock, Ted was waiting for me. Surprised Marc wasn't there to greet me, I asked Ted if he had told Marc I would be back early.

"Ted said no one had seen Marc since he got off the bus at noon. He added he was probably out sightseeing or something, and since he didn't know I was getting back early, he probably wouldn't be back until five."

Artie looked confused.

"That can't be right. Ted was in and out of the Business Center all afternoon. He even talked to Marc."

Tim agreed with Artie, and I continued.

"Ted said as long as I wasn't going to see Marc until five o'clock, maybe I could do him a favor. He said he had found a small problem with the Carter specs. He didn't think it was a serious error and Susan, and I should be able to get it taken care of before Marc got back from wherever he was.

"Since I had nothing to do until Marc returned, I agreed to go to Susan's room with Ted and try to find the problem."

Another pause while I let my words sink in. By the expressions on the faces in front of me, I knew they were thinking along the same line I was.

"When we got to Susan's room, a waiter was knocking on the door. He was carrying a bottle of Marc's favorite champagne. When Marc opened the door, I was shocked. Foolishly, I thought the worst and ran back toward the elevator. That's when I ran into you, Tim."

There was no mistaking the looks on their faces now. The same idea was in their eyes that was in my head.

"A setup!" Artie screamed, "That bastard set Susan and Marc up to look like something was going on between them, and then set you up to see it?"

"That's the way it looks," Emily said, "Not much doubt about it."

Susan was having trouble grasping the concept. Tim just shook his head in disbelief, but Artie was livid.

"I can't believe he'd go that far. I know he's been after you for as long as I've worked at Dillman, and Marc got in his way. But, why would he involve a sweet, innocent girl like Susan in his plans? Doesn't he care about anyone?"

I saw Susan's expression go from disbelief to surprise. I guess no one had ever come to her defense like Artie had just done. Emily noticed also.

"Will you two cut it out? Everyone at Dillman knows you two are sweet on each other. When are you going to man up and ask this sweet young lady out?"

Susan blushed. Artie just looked at Emily. And then looking into Susan's eyes said sweetly, "Susan, would you have dinner with me tomorrow night?"

Susan, still blushing answered, "Yes, Artie, I would love to have dinner with you."

Emily smiled, all satisfied with herself.

"Every dark cloud has a silver lining somewhere in it."

That lightened the mood in the apartment, but only for a few moments.

Tim finally asked, "How are things between you and Marc?"

"Over!"

"That can't be," Susan cried, "We'll tell him the truth and then everything will be alright."

I shook my head.

"It's deeper than that, Susan. It has to do with trust and honor. Marc is an honorable man, and I didn't trust that. He can't deal with mistrust. He feels it's disloyal."

Emily offered, "Have a little faith in the man, Catherine. I'm sure he loves you, and would be willing to work something out."

"But, it would never again be the same. We could never go back to what we had."

"True," Emily said, "But, maybe you can go to an even better place. If you love him, Catherine, have faith and fight for him."

Before I had a chance to contemplate what Emily was saying,

Tim asked, "What do we do about Ted?"

"We kick his ass," Artie shouted. Still, steamed Ted had gotten Susan involved in his plot.

"No, no," I pleaded, "This is between Ted and me. You guys can't get involved. We all have to work together. We can't let this affect the team. It's too important. It's too important to Marc!"

Everyone was quiet. I hadn't thought about the ramifications of everyone finding out what had happened Wednesday.

"This can't break up the team. We've come so far. Marc put everything on the line for us, and we can't let it all go now. We can't make it so uncomfortable for Ted he'll quit. We can't afford to be short a salesman. We have to find a way around this."

Emily agreed with me.

"If you do what you'd like to do, it would affect all of you, including Marc and it's not fair to him. It's not right the innocent should suffer for the guilty."

I started to feel better when I saw small nods of agreement from my three teammates. While the three of them talked it over, Emily and I moved into Susan's living room.

I liked Emily. Tim always seemed to be in a good mood and once when I asked him about it, he said it was his wife's fault. He told me she made him so happy there wasn't time for him to be in a bad mood.

I thought about the talk I had with my brothers and what Mary Ellen Carter had said. Was it possible some men could be trusted and if so, how did you know which ones? I wanted another opinion.

"Do you trust Tim?"

The question surprised her.

"Completely!"

"How can you be so sure?"

Emily looked toward the kitchen. She couldn't see Tim because there was a wall in the way, but she could see him in a way. It was as if she could always see him.

"Catherine, men are funny creatures. They have this natural instinct to spread it around. It's in all of them, it's natural. But, they are also romantics. I believe what a man wants most is to be truly loved by a woman.

"I'm sure they all want to be thought of as supermen in bed, and good providers and handsome and strong and all that macho stuff, but I believe what they covet most is the honest love of a good woman."

Looking at her husband through the wall again.

"Men aren't as devious as women. I believe a woman could have an affair and keep it from her husband easier than a man could keep it from his wife. Men wear their honor, it's important to them, and if it gets tarnished, a loving wife will see it. Tim knows if he ever strayed, I'd know it. And, that man loves me too much to hurt me that deeply. And it's my responsibility to make sure he always loves me that much."

"But, how do you do that?"

"By giving him what he wants most? I never let him forget how much I love him, how much I appreciate him. I never take anything he does for granted. I show him appreciation for every little gesture of love he makes to me. I make sure he knows he has the one thing he desires most, my love."

Emily took one more look toward the kitchen.

"If Tim picks up a seventy-nine cent rose from the convenience store on the way home, I make a big deal of it. I let him know how happy he made me because he thought of me. Men are romantics. Let them know you appreciate that and it will never stop. Take it for granted and it will go away. They like to be rewarded, so reward them."

"Is it really that simple?"

"It's worked for me."

My cell buzzed. It was Danielle. What she had to say was the clincher. Before Emily and I went into the kitchen, she added, "What I know of Marc and from what I've seen of him, he's worth fighting for. Don't let him walk away over this."

"It's not my choice. He doesn't want anything to do with me."

"Then, you have to change his mind."

We went back to the kitchen, and I told the others what Danielle had found out.

"The waiter had a couple of reasons to remember the incident. The two good looking women, one wearing not much more than a short, thin robe.

"The fact that a two hundred dollar bottle of champagne was sent back to the bar, unopened. The twenty dollar tip the manager gave him after crediting the cost of the bottle back to the gentleman's credit card minus a ten percent service charge.

"Ted ordered the most expensive bottle of champagne they had, with specific instructions for it to be delivered between 4:05 and 4:15. It was only a coincidence it happened to be the Tattinger."

I knew it would be difficult for all of us, but I made the others promise to forget everything they heard today. For Marc's sake, if for no other reason

"We all have to work with Ted, and this cannot get in the way."

I told them what Marc had said to me the night I suggested I wanted a relationship with him.

"Personal business stops at the lobby door."

They all promised, but we all knew it wouldn't be easy. We left amid hugs and kisses. Susan and I had special hugs for each other, and Artie stayed behind for a while.

I felt the four of us were closer than ever before! We would be okay.

Now I had to find a way to deal with Marc.

Chapter 18 – Surprise and Revelation

Monday morning I was determined to talk to Marc. I didn't know what I was going to say to him. I wasn't sure if I should tell him everything I knew. I just wanted him to know I cared enough to find out the truth and how sorry I was I didn't have more faith in him. Marc was in his office when I arrived, but Ted was waiting for me at the door to my office, and I had to deal with him.

"Catherine, we have to talk."

I answered in as neutral a tone as I could.

"Yes we do, Ted, but not here and not now."

"It can't wait. I really didn't know, I swear."

"Know what Ted?"

"That you were really in love with him."

I was torn between wanting to talk to Marc as soon as possible and hearing what Ted had to say. My decision was made for me when Sara buzzed my intercom and announced the entire team was to be in Marc's office right now. Ted and I walked over to Marc's office where we were joined by the rest of the team, including Sara.

Meeting in Marc's office was very unusual. Team meetings were always held in the conference room where the recording equipment was so we could refer to the transcripts later if necessary. Marc indicated this wouldn't take too long. He had a difficult time getting started. He got up from his chair, pushed it in and stood behind it. He seemed to be stalling.

"About six months ago, I did something that runs completely against my business principles. It was also against my better judgment, but selfishly, I did it anyway. There are reasons I run my business by a strict code of conduct, and abandoning this particular principle has come back to bite me. But, I'm a big boy, and I will deal with it."

Marc paused, again seeming unsure about what he was going to say next.

"My primary concern is my error in judgment may affect the performance of this team. We have come so far in eight months. We have exceeded every expectation. We are far ahead of the goal set for us by the people upstairs. Big things are happening, and tomorrow I will tell you about them. We accomplished all of this because you bought into the team concept. One for all and all for one. I cannot begin to tell you how proud I am of all of you."

Again he paused, this time looking down at his hands. This pause was longer. Finally, when he lifted his head, he scanned the faces in front of him.

"It's obvious to all of you there was an incident last Wednesday afternoon in Nashville. Those of you who know some of the details don't know as much as you think. Those of you who don't know the details have no reason to know. I take full responsibility for what happened and for the effect it's had on this team. I apologize to all of you."

Now his voice took on a firmer more commanding tone.

"Ladies and gentleman, we cannot let this affect the operation of this team. We must continue to drive forward together. We cannot exclude anyone or hold bad feelings toward anyone. What we do here affects all of us and, therefore, must include all of us. You are all friends. This has worked because you trusted each other. That has to continue. If there is a problem with me or another team member, straighten it out. If you think you know something, talk to someone about it.

"There is no denying what happened Wednesday was serious and is having a serious effect on this operation. I beg you all. Don't let my error in judgment spoil what you all have worked so hard for. In a little less than four months, I will be gone. There will be someone else in this office. To continue the work we have started, whoever that is will need the same level of commitment you have given me. Please, let's spend the next four months getting this team back to where it should be. Thank you!"

And, the meeting was over. Marc asked Ted, Tim, and Artie to stay behind and he dismissed the rest of us.

He took the entire blame on himself. He must know what actually happened. Why would he do that, just to save the team spirit, or was it because that is exactly what an honorable man would do?

I went back to my office hoping the meeting with Ted, Tim and Artie didn't last too long. I had to get Marc alone, if just long enough to tell him I did care enough to find out the truth.

Susan came into my office. She had tears in her eyes.

"We can't let him take the blame for this."

"Forget it, Susan. That's the only way it can be. It's the only way he will allow it to be. His error in judgment was getting personally involved with an employee, and it has come back to hurt us, all of us. It's the only honorable thing he feels he can do, and we have to allow him to do it."

"But," she started to say.

"Susan, he's a good man. He has to do this his way. We have to let him know we are on his side. We have to put this behind us no matter how difficult it is. Ted is a member of this team. An important member. We have to find a way to deal with this. I have to."

"Catherine, he's ruined your life. He's taken your love away from you. I don't care how much you admire Marc, how can you do this?"

I had to think about that for a moment, and the answer was simple.

"Because I love him, and this is what he wants me to do!"

Thirty minutes later, Sara buzzed me and announced there was a Mr. Ronald Brown on the phone. The news couldn't have come at a better time.

Ronnie was my best friend in the entire world. We had met in college and had remained friends even though we lived three thousand miles apart. As much as I loved and confided in my sister, Elizabeth, there was no one I could talk to as freely as I could to Ronnie. Our relationship had taken many turns over the years, but Ronnie had always remained my rock, my shoulder to cry on, my sunshine on a gloomy day, and just the thing I needed now. I could not only tell him everything that happened, but I could also tell him how I felt. Ronnie would understand.

Ronnie called this morning to say he was in town for the day and could I squeeze him in for dinner tonight. It was a joke because he knew I would cancel an audience with the Pope to have dinner with him. We made arrangements to meet at my apartment after work, and my day suddenly got brighter.

About eleven-forty five, Ted appeared at my door and again said we have to talk. I told him I did want to speak to him, but the office wasn't the place. I said, "Let's go out to lunch."

Just then, Marc came by, "Ready Ted?"

Ted shrugged his shoulders and left with Marc. Great, I thought.

I'd love to be a fly on the wall during that lunch.

114

An hour and a half later, Ted came back alone. He walked into my office and opened the blinds on my glass partition which had been closed since I got to work Thursday morning.

"Enough of this," he said.

He walked over and sat down in one of the chairs on the other side of my desk.

"Quite a man, you're Mr. Antonelli."

"He's not my Mr. Antonelli. Not anymore."

"Don't kid yourself. That man is totally in love with you."

"Maybe so, Ted, but he's not my Mr. Antonelli anymore, thanks to you, and I guess me also."

"Catherine, I will never be able to convince you how sorry I am. I would take it all back if I could. I had no idea. Until Thursday, outside La Chez, I didn't realize you were in love with him, and until this morning I had no idea how much he was in love with you."

"Ted," I scolded, "Everyone knew about us, how could you not know?"

"I swear, Catherine, I thought it was just an office fling. The man is handsome, charming and rich. According to the people we've had dinner with, in the ten years since his divorce, he's never had a steady girlfriend. I thought he was just dating you as a diversion while he was here. I had no idea you two were serious. Catherine, please, believe me, I cannot tell you how sorry I am I did this to you and got Susan involved."

With that comment, Ted walked over to the door that separated Susan's office from mine. He knocked gently, opened the door and asked Susan to join us. Susan came into my office looking very unsure. I nodded to her, and she sat down across from Ted. With what I perceived as sincere contrition on his face, he apologized to Susan for getting her involved in his plot.

He begged our pardon over and over, saying he knew neither of us would ever forgive him.

I didn't want to hear any more apologies, but I had to ask.

"Why, Ted?"

"Does it really matter?"

"Right now, it's the only thing that matters."

Ted proceeded to tell us a story that was so outrages it had to be true. Even a scoundrel like Ted couldn't make this up.

"I didn't plan any of this. I just forgot to tell Marc you were getting off early. Around three thirty, I saw the guys getting ready to finish up and head for their rooms. Thinking Marc would be looking forward to seeing you, I remembered you were coming back an hour early. The entire thing was just a stupid thought I had in the couple of minutes it took me to walk across the Business Center. I thought if I could get you angry at Marc I would have a chance with you."

When I reminded Ted in all the years before Marc arrived, I hadn't had any interest in him, he said his attitude had changed.

"I admit when you first came to work at Dillman, you were just another skirt I was chasing, probably the prettiest and classiest one, but just another potential conquest. The more you resisted, the more I was interested. When you started working for the Sales Department on the spec packages, I gained a lot of respect for you. I wanted to get to know you better, personally, not just sexually. You must have noticed the change in the way I treated you."

I had to admit it was true, but I told him I attributed that to a change in tactics.

"When Marc came along, it was easy to see why you would agree to a relationship with him, after turning me down all these years. I thought he would move on after a while, and you would be free again. I didn't think a guy like him would stay with one girl for any extended period of time. When the relationship continued, I got desperate.

"This entire thing Wednesday was just a spur of the moment idea, and after I started it, I changed my mind. Remember, I tried to lead you away from Susan's room, but Marc opened the door before I had a chance. I panicked.

"I knew I had to keep you away from Marc and the rest of the team so you didn't find out what I had done before I figured out a way to tell you myself. After you dressed me down Thursday outside of La Chez, I realized you were serious about Marc, and I had to try to fix it. I tried calling you all weekend, but you wouldn't answer my calls."

Ted looked as if he was going to cry, but I had no sympathy for him.

"Well, I must say, your plan worked, but only half way. You did manage to break up Marc and me, but you can stop thinking about the other part. That was never going to happen under any circumstances."

I already knew the answer to my next question, but I had to ask.

116

"What was that all about Thursday evening?"

"When we were in San Antonio, Jim Carter and I were in his office while you and Marc were talking to the Production Manager. Jim showed me a picture of his wife. It was obvious she was a knockout. Then last Thursday afternoon, when we were in Marc's office going over the details of the contract Marc and Jim were going to discuss at dinner, Jim called. You know how Marc is always putting his phone calls on speaker, we all heard Jim ask Marc to keep his wife company at La Chez until he got there.

"I thought if you saw Marc with another beautiful woman, it would keep you away from him long enough for me to figure out what to do, and that move I made on you was just to get Marc annoyed enough he wouldn't try to explain what happened in Nashville. It was pure panic on my part. I had to keep the two of you apart until I got a chance to fix things."

Ted had been talking so fast, trying to get it all out, he finally had to pause for breath.

"When we left the restaurant, and you screamed at me and took a cab home, I finally realized you were in love with that guy. I tried to think of a way to undo what I had done. I attempted to call you and explain everything. I wanted to make it right.

"I don't blame you for hating me, but Marc was right this morning. We can't let what I did ruin what we have been working toward for the past eight months. We have to find a way to get past this."

I didn't want to hear any more. It was evident he meant what he said, but that wasn't going to change anything. I couldn't forgive him, but I knew I couldn't be the cause of the team falling apart. I would do what was necessary to keep that from happening.

"As far as business is concerned, nothing will change. I will treat you just as I have before, but other than business, Ted, I don't want to talk to you, or have anything to do with you".

Ted nodded his head.

"I understand completely. I'll stay out of your way as much as possible."

When Ted left my office, Susan and I had a serious talk.

"I'll do what I told Ted because I don't want to hurt Marc any more than I have already."

Susan tried to tell me it wasn't my fault, but after Marc's comments Saturday night in his car, I knew I had to take part of the blame. All I had to do was have a little faith in him, and this would have ended at twenty after four on Wednesday afternoon.

Marc didn't return to the office and talking to him would have to wait at least one more day. At five o'clock I left to get ready for my dinner date. At least I had something nice to look forward to. Seven o'clock on the button, my intercom buzzed. I told Ronnie I'd be right down.

As soon as he saw me, Ronnie wrapped his arms around me and kissed me. It was a warm and friendly kiss and brought back the memory of the very first time we kissed. It was exactly like this, warm and friendly.

I had to remind myself to stop calling him Ronnie. He hated that nickname, and I didn't want to spoil my relationship with him over a stupid name.

One ruined relationship was enough for me right now.

Chapter 19 – Dinner with Ron

When I first met Ron in my freshman year at college, I was already in love with Bobby. Ron and I became buddies. Bobby was on the varsity football team and with practice, meetings, games, and classes, we didn't have a lot of time together, and Ron filled the void. Ron was in the Computer Science Program, and I was in Accounting. Ron was what today you might call a computer nerd. Bobby didn't mind my relationship with Ron because we both knew Ron was gay.

After I resigned myself to the Bobby situation, I started dating again. I had no trouble finding dates, I was pretty popular on campus, but most of my dates were just that, dates. Ron never dated, at least not publically. We remained buddies. We talked, and I told him stories about my dates, and we generally had a good time together. Ron was the only guy I knew who would never make a pass at me.

I didn't sleep around, but I did have some relationships during my college years, and I had gone to bed with some men in the three years between Bobby and graduation.

Halfway throughout the junior year, Ron won an award for some binary code thing he had developed. It was quite prestigious and after that, Ron became more outgoing and started hanging around with other students. Just before the end that year, I ran into Ron and a gorgeous girl on the Quad. They were holding hands and the surprise on my face must have been evident, because Ron laughed. Later that week, I met Ron alone and asked him about the girl he was with. Ron laughed again.

"Catherine Jensen. I am not now nor have I ever been gay."

"But I've never seen you with a girl before."

"You've never seen me with a man, either."

"I don't understand. Why didn't you say something?"

"When we first met, you were with Bobby. I knew because you both thought I was gay Bobby would let us hang out together. After you dumped him, I didn't know how to tell you. I didn't think you'd like me that way, and I didn't want to lose you."

"But, you never dated. All your spare time was with me."

"The code took up all of my time. I didn't have time for anything else. You were my oasis in the desert. You kept me sane, and because of your accounting classes, I could talk to you about numbers. It was a perfect relationship."

And then he said something that made me realize just how good our friendship was.

"I may not be in love with you, Catherine, but I do love you, and I always thought you loved me."

With or without benefits, Ron Brown was my best friend. He was right. I did love him, but not in a romantic way. Our strange relationship continued until we graduated. I was heartbroken when Ron moved to San Francisco, but the opportunity with a software company out there was too good for him to turn down.

We kept in contact, and whenever he was in Florida for business, he always made time to see me, but we never did become intimate. It would have ruined our perfect friendship.

He was just what I needed right now. I intended to tell Ron everything. How Marc and I got together, how I felt about him, what happened last Wednesday, the conversation between Marc and me in his car Saturday night, my meeting with the girls on Sunday morning and with the team Sunday afternoon and Ted's story today.

But, I didn't want my story to be interrupted, so in the car on the way to the restaurant, we talked about him. I knew Ron had left his job and started his own software company. It was a struggle, but getting better all the time.

"My guys developed a new piece of software that is going to be great, once we get the bugs worked out of it."

"Ron, my boss runs a systems company, and he might be interested in new software."

"This is security software and anyone who has a system connected to the internet, and that means everyone who owned a computer, would be interested."

We arrived at the restaurant, a nice, classy place. Our table wasn't ready, so Ron and I decided to wait in the bar. As we entered the bar area, it was as if it had been planned by Ted, I spotted Marc, standing at the bar talking to a blonde who was seated with her back to us.

Marc didn't see us enter, but remembering my lesson from Thursday night, I was determined not to make the same mistake again.

Grabbing Ron by the arm, I told him we had to say hello to someone I knew. As we approached, Marc looked in our direction and spotted us. The blond, seeing the expression on Marc's face change, turned around to see what he was looking at. A beautiful, sweet voice shouted, "Catherine, what a pleasant surprise."

I introduced Ron to Marc and Cindy, and Marc said, "I didn't realize you two new each other."

"You have to keep up, Marc. Catherine and I met at the Sports Widow's Club meeting yesterday. Danielle introduced us."

"Sports Widow's Club?" Marc barked, "The way you girls act, you'd think we did this all the time."

"Now don't get your panties in a wad. We know you guys aren't the typical sports nuts, but we still miss you when you do go to a game without us."

That brought a smile from Marc, and he included Ron in the conversation.

"My friends are all married, and when the guys go to a game, the girls get together to gossip about us."

That earned Marc a punch on the arm from Cindy.

Marc asked Ron what he did and when Ron told him his company developed security software, Marc was interested.

"My company is in complete systems. Got anything I might be interested in?"

"The new program we've developed is a giant leap forward, but it's still in beta testing."

"How long before the bugs are worked out?"

"If I had some financing, it would be a lot sooner."

"Catherine, you ought to introduce him to Nick. This sounds exactly like the kind of operation NAS would be interested in."

Ron looked at me, surprised.

"You know Nick Amonti of NAS Financial Group?"

"Slightly."

"Well enough to be invited to his wife's Sports Widow's Club," Marc announced.

As they continued discussing the financial issues, another man joined our group. He gave Cindy a kiss, and she responded with, "Hi baby!"

Cindy introduced her husband Dan, and after the standard small talk, Dan asked Cindy, "Well, has this guy finally convinced you to leave me and run off with him?"

Cindy brightened.

"Honey, you know he only talks like that in front of you. He's afraid if he ever said those things to me in private, I might take him up on it. And then he wouldn't know what to do with me."

The three of them laughed, and I knew what Cindy said was true. Just like with Angie, at the hockey game, Marc never hesitated to flirt with all the married women he knew, but only in front of their husbands. I think it's his way of being complimentary, without being taken seriously.

When their table was ready, Dan asked if we would join them. I didn't want to, but I couldn't think of a good reason not to. Ron came to my rescue.

"Love to Dan, but I'm only in town for the day, and Catherine and I have a lot to catch up on. Maybe another time."

That seemed to satisfy everyone, and as they moved toward their table, Marc told them to go ahead, and he'd join them in a moment. He took a business card out of his pocket and wrote something on the back. He held the card up so Ron could read what he had written.

"Her name is Janice Alvarez, and that's her cell number. She's Nick Amonti's daughter and she's the one who does the legwork for the company. I'll let her know you'll be calling. She'll ask a lot of questions, and if she likes the answers, you'll get your financing. It sounds like you have the type of operation they'd be interested in.

"The other name is my Operations Manager. Let him know how the beta testing is going. He might be able to offer you a few of our systems to help with that. When it's ready, I'd be very interested. We sell complete systems, and security is always a major concern."

Ron thanked Marc and said he would call both people as soon as he returned to his office. But, Marc had more to add.

"Ron, if NAS decides to finance you, you may not like the deal they offer you. Don't turn it down until you read the entire agreement, especially the options. I signed the same deal, and I've never regretted it.

"They are a fair, honest and honorable outfit. They'll treat you fairly. If you have any questions, give me a call, and we'll talk. I can give you the names of at least a dozen people who took that deal and never looked back."

With that, Marc shook Ron's hand and said it was a pleasure meeting him. He held my hand for a second and said smiling, "Not too late, Ms. Jensen, we have an important meeting tomorrow morning."

And he left to join his friends.

Ron and I continued with small talk until our table was ready. He commented on how nice my friends were.

"Everyone Marc has introduced me to is super friendly."

When we were finally seated, and our dinner ordered, Ron said, "Okay beautiful, what's going on. That guy is more than your boss and your friend... Give!"

And I did. I told him everything, including how foolish I felt, how much I loved Marc and after what Marc had said Saturday night in his car, how hopeless it was. I managed to get through the entire story without shedding one tear, but it wasn't easy.

Ron listened quietly and attentively.

"Why Catherine? From everything you told me, he's a good, honest man. Why were you so quick to judge him like that? Why didn't you, at least, ask him why he was there?"

"You know why. You of all people should know!"

It took Ron a minute to understand what I was saying.

"Jeez, Catherine, that was over fifteen years ago. Are you telling me after all these years, you haven't found one man who was worthy of your trust?"

This time, my answered angered him.

"I never let any man get close enough to me to ever hurt me like that again."

Ron tried to hide his anger, but he wasn't successful.

"Catherine, you're an intelligent person. How could you allow a jerk like Bobby dictate the remainder of your life? You're smarter than that."

"You know how much he hurt me."

"That was then, and this is now. That was Bobby, and this is Marc. I can't believe you can't tell the difference. You were eighteen years old, now you're thirty-three. You were a freshman college student, now you're a junior corporate executive. Everything in your life is different except your opinion of men. Which one of us is crazy here?"

I hadn't expected this reaction from Ron, but it fit right in with everyone else I had talked to. My siblings, Mary Ellen Carter, Danielle and the other ladies all seemed to indicate I was wrong not to trust Marc.

I had tried to protect myself from this kind of hurt all these years, and now that it had come, it was my own fault.

"I want to trust Marc, but now I would never get the opportunity. Marc is through with me. He made it very evident Saturday night."

Ron said he wasn't so sure.

"I could tell by the way Marc looked at you, he's in love with you, and I'm pretty sure he's looking for a way to make it right between you. Why else would he offer your friend so much help with his business?"

"That's just the way Marc is. He was a struggling businessman, and someone helped him, and now it was payback. Marc would have done that even if you weren't my best friend."

We continued to talk throughout dinner and just about the time the check was presented, Cindy stopped by our table.

"I hope you've had enough time to catch up. We're headed over to the 88's, and we'd love to have you join us!"

Ron immediately accepted, and Cindy asked if I knew where it was. I indicated I did, and she left with a wave and a, "See you there!"

When she was gone, I asked why Ron accepted so quickly. He didn't even know what the 88's was.

"The more you face Marc, the quicker you could come to an understanding. It won't help if you kept avoiding him."

"You have it backward. I've been trying to talk to Marc, but he's been avoiding me."

I told Ron about all the time Marc had been absent from the office this week. I also told him about going to his place Sunday morning and running into Danielle.

"Marc was the one doing the avoiding."

Ron didn't believe that was true.

"That man is in love with you. If he is avoiding you, it's because he doesn't know what to say to make you believe in him."

Maybe Ron was right, but would I ever get the chance to undo all the damaged I've caused. Could I ever trust any man to the degree that Marc needs? Could any woman trust a man that much?

Chapter 20 – Disappointment

The 88's was unusually quiet. I had never been there on a Monday night. Ron and I arrived right behind Dan and Cindy. They were seated at a table and waved us over to join them. Marc wasn't with them. Cindy gave me a sympathetic look, knowing I was disappointed.

"Marc said he had an early day tomorrow and decided to skip this."

Annie immediately came bouncing over. Looking at my date, she gave me an inquisitive look.

"Ron is an old college friend in town on business," I told her.

That seemed to pacify her curiosity, and she directed me to tell him about the rules and get it over with. I had to laugh in spite of my mood. She turned to Dan and Cindy and motioned for them to get on the dance floor. Annie was impatient tonight. I explained the Amonti rule to Ron, and he immediately got up to dance with me. I made a comment he was awfully anxious to get that out of the way, and he laughed.

"Wouldn't be right to keep such a charming and lovely lady waiting."

"Of course, you're referring to Annie."

Ron smiled and led me onto the dance floor. In spite of everything, I managed to enjoy the night. Dan was as nice as Marc's other friends. We were told how he and Cindy got together and how if it wasn't for Nick dancing with Cindy at his wedding they might never have gotten married. Cindy told us about Danielle's disastrous breakup with a guy when she first came to work in Fort Lauderdale and how Dan had helped her through it. They both seemed to have very special feelings for Nick and Danielle.

I told them that happened to me also, and Ron was the one who got me through it, and we had remained friends all these years, even though we lived over three thousand miles apart. When I headed for the ladies room, Cindy joined me.

"How's it was going with Marc?"

I told her we hadn't had time to talk, and I thought Marc was avoiding me.

"I don't believe that's true. Marc said something big was going on at Dillman, and he was right in the middle of it. He had been spending most of his time with the senior executives. I don't know the details, but it was going to shake everyone up."

I wondered if he was trying to get out of his contract so he didn't have to deal with me, or Ted. He still had about four months left on his contract, but because of how good we had done, they might be willing to let him go early.

We didn't stay too long, it was a weeknight, and the three of us had to work in the morning while Ron had a plane to catch. We all danced a few more times and then said goodnight. The ride back to my apartment was almost in complete silence. Ron seemed to have a lot on his mind.

"Do you think Marc was serious about calling NAS Financial Group?"

"I'm sure he was. That's how Marc got his company going, and it seems Nick has done the same thing for a number of small businesses."

"How does a man who was worth that kind of money act?"

"If you didn't know who Nick Amonti was, you'd never guess. He's just a regular guy. A very nice regular guy."

When Ron walked me to my door, I was sad. I didn't want him to go. I got a warm and friendly kiss. Ron always kissed me full on the lips. A closed mouth kiss, not romantic, but definitely intimate. It started when I thought he was gay and even after I found out he wasn't, it continued. I felt safe with Ron.

When we broke apart, I said, "Stay with me tonight!"

"I was hoping you'd ask. I never checked into a hotel, and all my stuff is in the car."

My couch wasn't convertible, and it was too short for Ron's five-eleven frame. Ron and I shared a bed that night, and that's all we shared. It wasn't the first time we had shared a bed, never naked and never for anything other than sleep. I always felt safe and secure when Ron was with me. I slept soundly and the next morning, I got very domestic and made breakfast for the two of us. While chomping down bacon and eggs, Ron asked, "What are you going to do about him?"

I didn't have an answer. It wasn't my decision to make. I shrugged my shoulders and sighed.

I got another warm and friendly kiss when we parted at my front door. Me, off to the office and Ron to the airport. I would miss him.

Now I had to deal with my life!

Chapter 21 – The Plan – Phase Two

When I got to the office, Marc was missing again. There was a message that there would be a team meeting in the conference room at eleven o'clock. Everyone was to be there, including Gino, Rich and Angelo, the Production, Procurement and Shipping Managers, Sara, the teams Administrative Assistant and Ben, the VP of Procurement and Production.

I saw Marc get off the elevator at ten forty-five. I got myself together and went to his office. I wanted to go to him and tell him how sorry I was, but I knew it wouldn't be enough. My only chance was to explain why I ran away Wednesday and try to get him to understand it wasn't him I didn't trust. But, he had gone directly to the conference room, and there were other people already there. When he saw me walk in, he summoned me over. He moved us away from the conference table.

"Catherine, the fellow you were with last night, seems like a good guy."

"He is! The best. He's been my best friend for over fifteen years."

"Catherine, I meant what I said to him last night. His operation is exactly what Nick likes to invest in. Don't allow him to ignore the opportunity. If Janice believes he's sincere, and his company has potential, NAS will definitely back him. And, if his security software is as good as he claims, I would definitely be interested."

"He'll call me when he gets back to San Francisco. I'll make sure he understands what you said and your motives."

Marc smiled and moved to the head of the table. He was just about to call the meeting to order when the phone rang. It surprised everyone. There were strict rules that there were no calls while the team was in a meeting. Marc believed it interrupted the flow of the meeting. Because Sara was attending the meeting, one of the clerical staff was at her desk and probably didn't know the rules. Sara immediately jumped up to intercept the call.

Marc put up his hand to stop her and picked up the phone himself. His conversation was strange, but understandable because it was one sided.

"Antonelli," he said into the phone, "Yes, I remember…What about…Impossible, I'm in the middle of a crucial meeting."

There was a very long pause while the person on the other end of the phone did all the talking. Marc looked at the clock on the wall.

"Where...Okay, give me about thirty minutes."

Marc hung up the phone.

"I'm very sorry people, but this seems to be important. We'll pick this up at two o'clock. But while I'm gone, look this over."

Marc picked up a rolled up drawing from the credenza behind him, put it on the table and unrolled it. It was a floor plan of office space.

"Gino, you know about this part, so while I'm gone, why don't you explain it to the rest of the team." And he left the meeting.

Gino flattened out the drawing, put some weights on the edges to keep it flat and said, "We're moving!"

We all gathered around the drawing as Gino continued telling us what was happening.

"We have no need to be near the Executive Staff or the Clerical Staff, and we're about to outgrow the room we have here. So, we're moving. Client Analysis, Design, Specifications along with Production, Procurement, and Shipping, will occupy an entire floor of office space in the new plant. That should be more than two and a half times more space than we have here."

After we looked over the plans, we broke for lunch. Tim and Artie asked me to have lunch with them, and I asked if Ted could join us. When they hesitated, I said, "Marc told us we couldn't allow anything to affect the team. This would be a good start at getting us back together."

They agreed reluctantly and the four of us, along with Susan went to lunch together. It was tense at first, but the talk about the big, upcoming move helped lighten things up. It was an impressive undertaking, and we knew it was because of us, and Marc's plan.

Back in my office, I watched the elevator lobby, waiting for Marc to return. He came in around one forty. As soon as he passed my office door, I got up and walked to his office. He was alone, and he seemed surprised when I walked in.

"Marc, we have to talk."

"Business?"

I shook my head.

"I know Catherine, we have a lot to discuss, but this is not the place, and twenty minutes is not nearly enough time. I promise we will talk."

"Tonight?" I asked hopefully.

"I have an important appointment. But, it will be soon, I promise."

Marc asked me to find Susan and Sara and bring them to the conference room.

"I want to talk to the original team before the meeting starts."

When we arrived, Marc, Ted, Tim and Artie were already there. We sat at the conference table, the three men on one side and the three females opposite them.

Marc took his usual place at the head of the table. There were only a couple of minutes before the others would arrive. Marc stood up,

"Are we okay guys?"

Tim, Artie, and Sara nodded almost immediately. Marc looked at Susan.

Okay, Susan?"

Susan looked at me and then nodded.

"Catherine?" Marc asked.

I wanted to let him know I wasn't going to disrupt the team. I knew how worried he must be about the spirit of the team and how necessary that was to his plan.

As sincerely as I could, I said, "Yes Marc, I think we'll be fine."

Marc looked at Ted. Ted looked down at his hands, then at Susan and me. I nodded to him, and Susan did the same.

"I think that's the answer you're looking for," Ted said.

"Guys, we have come so far, so fast even I have a difficult time believing it. It's all due to you six people and the all for one and one for all spirit you shared. Bigger and better things are on the way, and I want you all to be a part of it."

Just then, the others started drifting into the room, and our private meeting was over. Every member of the team was there, and one other face we all knew. When everyone was settled, Marc started his presentation.

"As you all know, my contract with Dillman Brothers expires in one hundred days. I told you when I first started here over eight months ago there would be no option for renewal. That's still true. Sometime within the next sixty days, you will meet the new Vice President of Client Analysis.

"I'm not sure who that will be. I've given my suggestions to the people upstairs, and it's being considered. I hope you give him or her the same effort you have given me. No one could ask for more.

"As nice as our offices are, we have outgrown them. Within the next thirty to forty days, we will be moving over to the offices at the new plant. The space is being prepared for us as we speak."

Marc indicated the floor plan that was still on the table.

"It has been decided we should all be housed under one roof, so to speak. So, as of Monday morning, Ben will be appointed Senior Vice President of the new Client Services Division. We will all be under this new division. We will all answer directly to Ben. He knows what we do here, and I'm sure he will carry on the team spirit that has gotten us to this place."

Again, he gave us a minute to contemplate what he had said.

"As most of you know, Jose, the supervisor of the Design Department is retiring at the end of this week. I expect all of you to attend his retirement party. I have suggested a replacement, and the boys upstairs agree. This change and the others I am about to mention will be announced at the company banquet in less than two months. But, I convinced the bosses you deserve a heads up on what's about to happen, so here it is!

"The new manager of the Client Analysis Department will be positioned at vice president level. I was given the title of Senior Vice President because the Dillman brothers thought I needed the clout to get the job done. As of Monday, I will assume the temporary position of Vice President of Client Analysis. Also, Gino, Rich and Angelo will be promoted to VPs of Production, Procurement and Shipping respectively."

That brought a round of applause from the group. Gino, Richard, and Angelo were elated. We couldn't have done it without these three departments, and we were smart enough to know it. Marc waited for things to quiet down, and indicated the newcomer to the group.

"It has been decided, again on my suggestion that Jennifer take over the Design Department when Jose retires. That position will be elevated to director level."

The room suddenly got quiet. Marc noticed the change in mood.

"Susan, we all know you were in line for that position, but you're too critical to specifications. I couldn't think of anyone to replace you if I moved you back to design.

"But, it's not all bad news. You will take over the department and be elevated to Director of Specifications."

This time, the room got ghostly quiet. Marc had just given my job to Susan. Where exactly does that leave me?

Please Marc; don't transfer me out of the department. I'll make peace with Ted, I'll be good!

This time, Marc ignored the change in mood.

"Questions, Comments?" Marc asked.

The room was quiet. All eyes were on me. Finally, Ted spoke up.

"Marc where does that leave Catherine?"

Marc sighed and looked at me.

"Catherine, I wanted to talk to you privately before the meeting, but that lunch engagement was necessary. When you were teaching me about the spec packages, I realized how much you loved working with the numbers. And, I can't think of anyone that is better at that then you are. But, in my position, I have to decide what's best for the company and not what any individual employee would want."

I wasn't going to make this any harder on Marc then it had to be.

"I understand Marc!"

He nodded at me and continued.

"The Design Department and the Spec Department are too important to allow them to flounder without proper supervision and guidance.

The cooperation and coordination between these two departments is so important I decided they had to be combined, and there is no one in this company that understands the workings of these two departments better than you do.

"So Catherine, it has been decided the new Design and Specifications Department would be headed by you. To ensure you get the proper co-operation from Client Analysis, Procurement, Production, and Shipping, it has also been decided the position should be at VP level."

The applause from the others was sincere. I was stunned. I couldn't have been more stunned if Marc had fired me. Why? How could he do this with the way things were between us? I guess he really did mean it when he told me business was business, and there was no room for personal feelings.

When the room had quieted down, Marc continued to address me.

"Catherine, I know how much you love what you do here, but this new position is vital. Susan and Jennifer will report directly to you."

All I could do was nod my head. Then, Marc turned the floor over to Ben. He gave a very short speech. He praised Marc and the team for what we had accomplished, congratulated everyone on their promotions and said he expected great things from us.

Before Ben left the conference room he told us, "All of these appointments and promotions would be announced at the company banquet. Please keep it as quiet as possible until then."

After that bit of news, Ben and Marc left us to congratulate each other.

We didn't get out of the conference room until close to quitting time. I noticed Marc was still in his office, and I went in. I didn't know what to say to him, so I just stood there. Marc saw my discomfort.

"I'm sorry Catherine. There is no one with your knowledge of specs and design and with your administrative skills. I knew right from the beginning these two departments were the keystone to the entire operation, and I needed someone I could trust there."

Then with a big smile, he added, "It won't be all bad. You can always look over Susan's shoulder and kibitz. And, you can always demand she allow you to play with the numbers! You will be her boss!"

I had to smile at that. I knew Marc felt bad about taking me out of the spec department and making me an administrator. I did love working with the numbers. But, I knew he was right. Business was business, and this had nothing to do with us.

Marc said goodnight and left the office. I closed up my office and headed for the parking lot. I was surprised to see Ron waiting for me.

"I couldn't go back to California and leave you like this. We have more to talk about."

I was sure Ron had no idea how happy I was he was there with me. My smile should have given him some idea of how much his presence meant to me. He suggested we go to a quiet place where we could have a few drinks, then dinner and talk. It sounded perfect.

I wanted to tell him what had happened at the meeting today, and also pass on to him what Marc had said about Ron calling NAS Financial Group.

Chapter 22 – Dinner with Ron II

"Burgers and beer okay? I found a nice quiet place where we can talk in private."

I told him anything was fine, just having him here with me was all I needed. Then I told him what Marc had said about calling NAS.

"Marc sounds like a good guy. I have heard about Nick Amonti and had been contemplating trying to get some financing from him.

"According to the word on the street, Amonti won a lottery worth about thirty million dollars. He started a capital investment company with his kids as partners and employees and turned that thirty million into close to a billion in a very short time. The word is he did it without ever cheating anyone, or being greedy. He seems to be a man of his word and could be trusted."

I also told Ron about the meeting and the short talk we had in his office afterward. Ron just shook his head.

"It's probably the first time in history a senior executive apologized for promoting someone to a vice president position."

"It's because he knows me so well. He knows I'd rather be a clerk working on the specs. I didn't want to be a vice president."

"If Marc knows that, why did he promote you?"

"As far as Marc is concerned, personal feelings have no place in business. He feels he needs me in this position for the benefit of the company. Remember what Marc said when I told him I hadn't gone to bed with Ted? He knows me so well. And I don't know him at all!"

Just as we pulled up in front of a pub, downtown, Ron said, "Maybe it's about time you got to know him. Maybe that will help you believe in him."

Inside, Ron led me to a booth along the back wall. It was an old-fashioned wooden booth, but they had put cushioned pads on the seats to make them more comfortable. The backs of the benches were very high, and when you sat down in the booth, it was almost as if you were in your own private little room. It was perfect for intimate conversations. Ron ordered two beers, and the real conversation began.

"What do you intend to do about Marc?"

"I don't know! I love him. I want him to love me, but I don't know how to get him back, and even if I do, I don't know if I can keep him."

"Why not?"

"Marc lives by a code, a set of rules, and one of those rules is he won't be with a woman who doesn't trust him. I told you about his marriage."

"Why don't you trust him?"

"You know why. You were there. And even if I did, I could never prove it to him."

"Why couldn't you prove it to him?

Remembering Marc's statements in the car, Saturday night I said, "Because you can't prove a negative. Even if I did learn to trust him, I could never prove to him I did."

"I don't understand."

I tried to recall Marc's words.

"Ron, I can prove I don't trust you just by questioning everything you do. But there is no way I can prove I do trust you. Even if I didn't question what you did, it could be I just don't want to have a fight, or I really don't want to know the truth. There is no way I can prove to you I do trust you."

On mulled that over for a minute.

"I think you're wrong. By questioning me, you're saying I do want to trust you, I do want to believe what you did was not bad, so please tell me the truth."

"What's the use? It's what Marc thinks that counts and he knows I didn't trust him, and that's enough for him."

"Maybe. Tell me Catherine, when you do talk to him, what are you going to say?"

"I'm going to tell him how sorry I am."

"That's it?" Ron growled, "How about telling him why. How about the truth. Tell him the whole story. That you've lived the past fifteen years of your life based on what some idiot said to you."

"Oh, Ron, how is that going to help?"

"At least, he'll understand it's not him. At least, he'll know you want to trust him. At least, he'll know you want to try."

There was at least five minutes of silence between us.

136

"Catherine, if Marc was here right now, do you think you can be honest with him? Do you think you can tell him everything you feel? Could you tell him everything that bothers you? Could you really open up to him?"

I'd like the opportunity to try."

"If you had a chance would you really try?"

I had no answer for him. Ron looked at me and sighed.

"You said he knows you so well but does he really? He knows your character. He knows how you guard your virtue. He knows many things about you, but does he know what you fear?

Does he know what makes you hurt? Are you ready to trust him enough to let him know those things? Would you open up to him completely and not only tell him how you feel about him, but how you feel about love. Would you allow yourself to be vulnerable to him?"

I didn't know how to answer that. Could anyone open themselves up to another person that much?

"Catherine, do you love me?"

"You know I do."

"Do you trust me?"

"It's not the same thing. You're my best friend, not my boyfriend, not my lover."

"But, do you believe I would never do anything to hurt you?"

"Yes Ron, I know you never could do anything to hurt me."

"You're right Catherine. I would never do anything to hurt you even though I know how."

Ron took a swig of his beer as I tried to understand what he was saying.

"Catherine, I know what you fear. I know where you are vulnerable. I know so much about what you feel inside, that I can take you apart emotionally. Does Marc know that much about you?"

I had no answer. I reached for my own beer as I tried to understand what Ron was saying.

"Catherine, trusting Marc is more than believing he will always be faithful to you. You also have to trust that his love for you is so strong that he will never hurt you. You have to be willing to tell him how and why you hurt. You have to be ready to make yourself vulnerable to him and trust that he won't use it against you. If you truly love this man, you have to be willing to give all of yourself to him."

We sat quietly for a few minutes. I tried to understand and wondered if I was capable of doing that with any man. I knew he was right about us. I did trust Ron that way, but I never looked at Ron as I did other men. He was my buddy. He wasn't like any other man in my life.

Ron finished his beer and sighed.

"I have something to tell you," he said very solemnly, "I had lunch with Marc Antonelli this afternoon."

To say I was stunned would be a lie. I was shocked into total incredulity. How could my best friend do this to me?

"That was you who called during the meeting this morning?"

I got a nod in response.

"Ron, how could you?" I cried.

"Catherine, I was there when Bobby did that to you. I remember how hurt you were, how unhappy. But in all the time I've known you; I have never seen you as unhappy as you were last night. The disappointment I saw when we got to that club and you found out Marc wasn't coming was something I had never seen in you before. I couldn't go back to California and leave you like that. I had to do something, and the only thing I could think of was to find out how he felt about you."

"Oh, Ron!" is all I could say.

But Ron wasn't done.

"Catherine, that man is in love with you. He's as unhappy as you are. He's a brilliant man, Catherine. He knows how to put things in order. He knows how to get things done. But he hasn't the faintest idea what to do about you. He's completely lost."

That only made me feel worse. Not only had I lost him, but I had also made him suffer. I wanted to cry, but I managed to hold the tears back. Or, maybe there just weren't any tears left.

Ron had to lean out of the booth to summon the waiter. He made a circular motion over the bottles to indicate he wanted two more beers. When the waiter returned, he brought three beers instead. I looked up and was surprised to see it was Marc standing there. Ron grabbed one of the beers.

"I'll be at the bar."

Marc stopped him.

"No, stay, please. You know Catherine better than anyone. Maybe you can help us."

Ron looked at me, and I nodded, "Please!"

Marc slid into the seat opposite me, and Ron sat down beside me. There was no conversation for a while, until Marc said, "Tough week."

I didn't know if it was a question or a statement, probably both. All I could do was nod my agreement. Marc never took his eyes off mine.

"Catherine, I have to know what I have done to make you distrust me so easily. Is it the way I flirt with other women. It doesn't mean anything. They all know I'm not serious, but I can stop if it displeases you. What has brought us to this place?"

"No, Marc," I finally had the courage to answer, "It's nothing you've done. It's the unknown that frightens me."

"If there's something you want to know Catherine, just ask me. I have no secrets. That's all that would have been necessary Wednesday. I would have told you why I was there, and even if you didn't believe me, you could have checked it out."

"I know why you were there. You were right. If I wanted to know the truth, I had to find out for myself, and I did. I know you were set up, and I walked right into it. I'm so sorry."

Marc seemed to accept the fact I had taken the trouble to find out the truth on my own. But, he still wanted to know why I distrusted him and why I wouldn't let him explain.

"I can understand it was a shock when I opened the door, and you saw Susan and me in the room, and Susan dressed that way, but when I came to your room, why didn't you allow me to explain."

"I wasn't in my room. I met Tim in the elevator, and I asked him to buy me a drink. When you and Ted were knocking on my door, I was in the hotel bar with Tim."

139

"I don't understand. You and Ted got in the elevator together, and when I got to your room, Ted was knocking on your door, trying to explain."

"Tim got on the elevator two floors down, and when we got to my floor, I didn't want to deal with Ted, so I got back on the elevator with Tim."

Marc shook his head.

"I guess that's the last piece of the puzzle I didn't know."

We were talking at least, and I didn't want it to stop. But I had questions of my own I needed answers to and the first one was critical

"Marc, what would you have thought if the positions were reversed? What if you went to my room and Ted opened the door, and I was in the room half dressed?"

He thought that over before he answered.

"I can't tell you what I would have thought at the moment. It's impossible to prophesize about something that hasn't happened, but I can tell you what I would have done. That I'm sure of."

I waited for his answer, and it only made me feel worse.

"I would have asked you what was going on and expected an answer. Then I would have drawn a conclusion based on what I saw, what I know about you and what you had to say. If I didn't like the conclusion, we would have a discussion about it, a very serious discussion."

"And what would that be like?"

"Again, impossible to say, because it hasn't happened. Would I be angry you were there? It depends on why. Catherine, there's more than one way to cheat on your lover."

Marc paused. He was picking his words carefully.

"I know Ted has been after you since long before I arrived on the scene. I have seen the way you act with him, and I'm sure he knows it's impossible. That's why he was desperate enough to pull this stunt. In the scenario you mentioned, I probably would think it was innocent, or Ted walked in on you when you weren't prepared for company. That's the same reason I was sure you hadn't slept with Ted, Wednesday or Thursday nights, in spite of what happened at La Chez."

It got worse and worse. How could this man have so much faith in me, and I have no faith in him. But, I had to know where this faith came from.

140

"Mary Ellen told me what you said to her when she saw what Ted did. How could you be so sure of me?"

"Remember Saturday night when we talked about assumptions?

I nodded.

"I don't know, Catherine. Not for sure. But I've gotten to know you. I'm pretty sure I know your character. I know you're not likely to jump into bed with a guy like Ted under any circumstances, and I am doubly sure you wouldn't do it because you were angry with me.

"It's an assumption on my part, based on what I know about you. I have no proof, I could be all wrong about you, but it's the best information I have."

"So, it's all based on trust," I said.

"Not only confidence in you. It has something to do with trusting you and something to do with how much I trust my own judgments and something to do with the way you act. You heard what Dan said about my wooing Cindy, and you heard what she said about it.

"She knows it's not a big deal because I never do that unless Dan is present, and if I have a woman in my life, I wouldn't do it if she wasn't present. The way you present yourself tells a lot about you. I've been around you for over eight months. I've seen how you act under different circumstances. I've made an assessment about you based on many factors.

"Catherine, I may be all wrong about you. Unless I find you in bed with someone, I'll never know for sure. But based on what I know about you and what I've observed, I had to make a judgment. And, that judgment is you're not very free with your virtue, and you are most likely not prone to fool around when you have someone special in your life."

And after a pause, he said, "Then, there's the other thing."

"What other thing?"

"Nick Amonti swears you can read a person's character in their eyes, and Danielle said if Nick ever did anything to hurt her, she would see it in his eyes. Considering they are the most in love couple that I have ever met, they may have something there. I've never seen any kind of deceit in your eyes. That's why I am so anxious to know what I have done to make you distrust me. What prompted your judgment of me?"

Ron spoke for the first time since Marc sat down.

"Tell him, Catherine. Tell him the whole thing. If you want this man, open up to him. It's the only way."

The only way or not, I had to tell him the truth, even if it meant I would lose him. If my trust in him was so important and I couldn't give him that trust, then I would only be hurting him. I thought about how to say it.

"It's not you Marc. I have never been able to trust any man."

"Why?"

"It's your only chance Catherine, do it," Ron prompted.

"Marc in my freshman year of college, I fell madly in love with a football player. He was a junior, and I thought I was going to spend the rest of my life with him. One day, my afternoon class was canceled. I knew football practice was just about over, so I ran all the way over to the practice field to tell Bobby we could spend the entire afternoon together."

I brought up the image of what I saw.

"When I got there, I didn't see him. One of the other players made a pass at me. I told him Bobby would beat the hell out of him if he found out. The other guy laughed and said he didn't think so because Bobby was under the grandstands doing one of the cheerleaders. I didn't believe him, and he told me to check for myself.

"More to prove him wrong than any other reason, I went behind the stands. I found Bobby with his pants around his ankles and one of the cheerleaders half naked. I got hysterical, cried and carried on."

Marc shook his head.

"You don't trust me because some snot nosed college kid cheated on you?"

"It's not only you, Marc. I've always been afraid it would happen again, so I've never let any man get close enough to me to hurt me like that again. You were the exception. I've never allowed myself to love any man until you came into my life, and when I saw you in Susan's room, all that hurt came back."

Marc's reaction surprised me. He was more emotional than I had ever seen him. He seemed sad.

"Do you think you are the only woman a man has cheated on? That had to be what between fifteen and twenty years ago. Are you telling me you have never had a serious relationship with a man in all that time?"

I just nodded.

"Why, Catherine," he pleaded, "You're an intelligent woman. How could you let some college kid do that to you?"

"It's what he said. He told me to grow up. He said that's the way all men are, and I had better get used to the idea!"

Marc's got quiet and thoughtful.

"Catherine, you catch your boyfriend with his pants down. To justify his actions he tells you that's how all men are and you accept that as a world shattering revelation? Some not dry behind the ears college kid? You're much too smart for that!"

I had no answer. The way Marc put it, it sounded silly, even stupid, and maybe it was.

"Maybe you're right. But ever since that day, I believed it was true. I believed all men were like that, and I've never been proven wrong."

"You never will be proven wrong, Catherine. Because, as I said before, you can't prove a negative. You can prove your man is unfaithful, but you can never prove he is. And besides, your boyfriend was right, that is how men are!"

I couldn't believe what Marc had just said, and I could feel Ron tense up at his words. But before he had a chance to say anything, Marc explained that statement.

"It's true, Catherine, that's how all men are at seventeen, eighteen, nineteen years old. As soon as we realize it's more fun to fondle a girl's breast then it is to pull her pigtails, we only have one thing in mind."

He paused for a moment and looked to Ron for agreement. Getting no response, he continued.

"But, must of us, outgrow that phase... No," he corrected, "We don't exactly outgrow it, it's more that we run into a particular girl and realize making love is so much better than just plain sex. And, it doesn't have to be the till death do us part kind of love, it just has to be a caring relationship. For some men, like Ted, it takes longer, for some it happens early in life. I learned that when I met my ex-wife. I was twenty, and I found out being loved by the woman you love is better than anything else in the universe. If it wasn't for the fact she couldn't trust me, we'd probably still be together today, and I'd still be faithful!"

I didn't know what to say to him. It all sounded so logical, but Marc was so smooth, was it just a line. How would I ever know? As if he were reading my thoughts, he said, "Catherine, you'll never know for sure. You have to take the information you have and make a judgment. And, you have to have enough faith in yourself to trust that judgment. It's not only belief in a man, but it's also confidence in your own ability to make a reasonable judgment."

Not knowing what else to say, I asked,

"Where does that leave us?"

He didn't answer right away. I could tell once again, he was choosing his words carefully.

"I'm sorry Catherine. I'm as wrong as you are. You're an intelligent woman, and you allowed emotion to dictate your life. I consider myself an intelligent man and I did the same thing. Maybe emotional scars take longer to heal than physical ones. Maybe some never heal. But we have to learn to live with them.

"We're both equally wrong here. You're making me responsible for what that jerk did to you all those years ago, and I'm making you responsible for what happened between my ex-wife and me. That's unfair to both of us and very unfair to our relationship. We both have a lot of thinking to do."

After some more thought.

"Catherine, I'm not going anywhere. I don't have someone waiting as a backup in case we don't work this out. The only thing left for us is to continue to talk. We're not where we were last Tuesday, but there's no reason we can't get back there, or even to a better place. But, we have to talk.

"I'm not asking for blind faith. I don't expect you to totally trust everything I say and do. What I need from you is the benefit of the doubt until you have a chance to figure out what all the information you have means. If you want to know something, ask me. It's that simple."

Does he mean that? Can I ask him about things that bother me? I had to know.

"Marc, will you tell me what you do on Saturdays?"

That question surprised him. He hesitated before he answered.

"I've told you what I do. I either work at my office, trying to catch up, or I'm working for one of Nick's companies. Last Saturday I was in Tallahassee, with a client of Antonelli Systems. You've been to my office. You've seen how much I have to do."

I needed an answer. It was important, not only because I wanted to know about the parties he seemed to be at on some Saturday nights, but I needed to know he would indeed answer anything I questioned, without getting angry, So, I pushed.

"You never told me what you do for Nick."

Again, he looked surprised.

"Catherine, forgive me. Between Dillman Brothers, my company, the work I do for Nick and our relationship, I've had a pretty full plate. I thought you knew."

"Will you tell me now?"

After another thoughtful pause, he said, "No...I'll do better!"

With that statement, he took out his cell phone, called a number from his address book, hit the speaker button and placed the phone on the table between us. After three rings, a very sexy voice answered.

"Hi good looking, what did I do right to earn a call from you in the middle of the week?"

Marc was his usual flirty self and told her he couldn't wait until Saturday to talk to her. That made her laugh, and her comments indicated she accepted it as all in good fun.

Then she got serious.

"Don't you dare tell me you're going to cancel? If that's your intention mister, I'll cut off a piece of your anatomy that would make you very unhappy."

Marc grimaced.

"That's the second time in a week a woman threatened my manhood."

The voice on the phone asked what he had done to earn such a threat and who had made it.

"It was Anna Lee," Marc told her.

"What did you do to that sweet Georgia gal to warrant such a threat?"

"I was just being my sweet, lovable self."

The voice laughed. Then Marc got serious.

"Marcie, I'm bringing a guest with me on Saturday."

There was silence on the other end.

"Marcie, are you still there?"

Marcie's answer made Marc laugh.

"We must have a bad connection. It sounded like you said you were bringing a guest this Saturday."

"That's what I did say,"

More silence from the other end of the phone.

"Someone special?"

"Very special."

"This I have to see. I've always been curious as to what it takes for you to consider a gal special!"

"You'll have to stay curious until Saturday."

"OK, honey, I'll make the arrangements. See you Saturday;" and the call ended.

Looking into my eyes again, Marc said, "Okay? All you have to do is ask me. Saturday, you'll understand what I do for Nick."

Then, "The burgers here are great. They use fresh meat, not frozen patties and the fries are fresh cut."

We all ordered burgers and fries, and the conversation switched to small talk. Marc and Ron talked about their businesses, and Marc reminded Ron about calling NAS and Marc's Operations Manager. It turned out to be a pleasant evening, even though I still wasn't sure where Marc and I stood.

When we left, Marc asked Ron if he had made arrangements for a hotel for the night.

"Ron can stay at my place." I offered.

Marc didn't seem to have any problem with that.

"Good! Having a good friend around is probably just what you need right now."

We separated, and Ron and I headed for my apartment. We talked late into the night. Ron trying to convince me Marc and I would get together again, and Marc was definitely a man who could be trusted.

I hoped he was right.

Chapter 23 – A Second Chance

Wednesday morning, I showed Ron how to lock up the apartment, and I left for work. I got another warm and friendly kiss before I left. Ron would be on his way to San Francisco before I got home.

Back at work, I settled into my office, hoping my concentration would be improved. Marc knocked on my glass partition on his way to his office. I got a smile and a wave. Ten minutes later, he was back on the elevator. I wouldn't see him the rest of the day. After contemplating the events of the past two days, I made a decision. I went Ted's office. He didn't seem too busy, so I walked in and sat down across from his desk. I had to do this.

"Ted, I love Marc. I think he is a good and honest man. I do not want to hurt him in any way. For the sake of the team, I propose we put the events of the past week behind us. I can't allow my personal feelings to get in the way of us working together as easily as we have in the past."

Ted was surprised by my comment. He was as contrite as a man could be, and he tried to apologize for his actions last Wednesday and Thursday. I stopped him in mid thought.

"It's over Ted. We can't change it. It happened, and it's done. I just want everything between us to go back to normal, for the team's sake, for Marc's sake."

"OK, Catherine, I will do whatever it takes to make sure this doesn't affect the team, but what about Susan and Artie?"

"I'll talk to them. I'll find a way to fix it."

Ted agreed and just before I left his office, he said, "You're quite a woman, Catherine."

My next task was Susan. It wasn't as difficult to convince her as I expected.

"Catherine, all I care about is how this has affected you. This entire affair had given Artie the incentive to tell me how he felt about me. Overall, I considered myself way ahead on the deal. If you could forgive and forget, then I will too. I'll talk to Artie. I'm sure he'll agree."

We decided to have lunch together, and when she walked into my office around noon, she suggested we invite Ted. I smiled, thinking it would show everyone else all was well between the three of us. So, Susan, Ted and I went to lunch together at the Pub. The conversation was guarded at first but eventually loosened up.

That afternoon, Danielle called. She had called me every day since Sunday. I told her of the meeting I had with Marc and Ron last night. She seemed sure it was a good sign. Danielle was convinced Marc was in love with me, and she was also sure he would do everything in his power to make it right between us. Her words made me feel better. I also told her I was going with Marc on Saturday.

"I've been trying to convince Marc these things wouldn't be so boring if he brought a date with him, but Marc's attitude was business is business. When Nick does one of these things, I usually go with him, and we would fly in the night before and stay until Sunday evening. That makes it less strenuous and gives us a chance to visit whatever city we're in."

Danielle didn't volunteer any information about what Marc was going to do for Nick on Saturday, and I didn't ask. I'd know soon enough.

Thursday, I got another wave, and a smile as Marc headed up to the Executive floor. I was back in the work routine. My administrative duties wouldn't kick in until we move to the new offices. Thursday afternoon, around four thirty, Marc stopped in my office. He seemed unsure about what he was going to say to me.

"Catherine, about Saturday."

"Don't cancel! Please don't cancel."

"I should have mentioned this sooner, but my mind has been entirely occupied with other things."

"What is it, Marc?"

"It's going to be a very long day. I'll have to pick you up at six AM, and we won't get back until around three or four Sunday morning."

"That is a long day."

"That's not all. You can dress casually when I pick you up, but you'll have to bring something with you for a business lunch, a cocktail party, and a formal banquet, along with makeup, shoes and anything else you need. We'll be using one of Nick's aircraft so you can leave your dresses and gown in a garment bag. They can be hung up while we're on board."

"Marc, why couldn't we leave Friday night or stay over or come back on Sunday. Why does it have to be all in one day?"

After thinking about it for a moment, he said, "Because, with everything that has been going on, I haven't been thinking clearly."

With that, he took out his cell phone, dialed a stored number, and hit the speaker button. A sweet southern voice I recognized answered,

"Hi Mr. Mark, what can I do for you today!"

After a few flirty remarks, he asked Anna Lee how he was getting to Memphis on Saturday. Anna Lee replied Karen was taking him. Marc asked if she was available Friday evening or Sunday afternoon. After checking her schedule, Anna Lee said Karen would be available in Jacksonville from two o'clock Friday afternoon until seven o'clock Tuesday morning.

"Can you have Karen standing by at FLX Friday evening at five o'clock and I'll need her to bring me back sometime Sunday afternoon or evening. There'll be two of us for the flights."

After a few more flirty remarks, he said goodbye and disconnected. His next call brought that same sexy voice I had heard on Tuesday evening.

"Hi good looking. Two calls in the same week. Are you trying to spoil me?"

After some more flirty interplay between them, Marc asked if she would set us up for an arrival Friday night and a departure Sunday afternoon.

"I wondered why you stopped coming in the night before and insisted on leaving right after the banquet for the past six months. Why the change?"

Marc looked into my eyes.

"Because, Marcie my love, the reason I wanted to be in Fort Lauderdale Friday night and all day Sunday, is coming with me this time!"

After a slight pause, Marcie said, "Marc, I'm so happy for you. You deserve a special woman in your life."

I didn't know if Marc's answer was reassuring to me or not.

"Don't break out the champagne just yet, Marcie, I still have a lot of work to do before I can make that claim."

After some pleasantries, the less flirty kind, this time, the call was disconnected.

"Thanks, Catherine. I don't know why I didn't think of that. I can only blame it on how many things I'm trying to juggle at the same time. Even though this will be mostly business, we will have some time for us, and I think that is important right now."

"See how good I can be for you. I'm going to fix it so you can't survive without me."

That brought out a big smile from Marc.

"I can live with that."

Marc then reminded me what I would have to bring with me, and now, that included a dress for dinner in Memphis Friday night and something casual for Sunday. He also suggested I make plans to leave the office early so I would be ready to leave my apartment by four fifteen, at the latest. He said with his schedule, he might not see me until he picked me up tomorrow night.

I told him I had promised to stop by Danielle's apartment after work tonight, but after that, I would go home and pack. I thought my comment about stopping at Danielle's required some explanation, but Marc didn't want to hear it.

"Danielle chooses her own friends. Whether you and I make it or not, has no bearing on your friendship with those ladies. They're not friendly toward you because of me. They like you, and think you will fit in with their group."

With that, he was gone with one more of his great smiles aimed in my direction. I was beginning to have some hope maybe we could get back together and make it work.

As promised, I stopped at Danielle's apartment on the way home. The doorman was the same one who was on duty the times I stayed at Marc's place.

"Go right on up, Ms. Jensen, Ms. Palmer is expecting you."

I thanked him with a smile and headed for the elevator. When Danielle opened the door, I was greeted with a warm hug. Stacy was there. Danielle informed me that Cindy and Angie were on their way. Nick was also there.

There was casual small talk until the other two ladies arrived and then Danielle told Nick to disappear. This was to be ladies only. When Nick was settled in his office, the inquisition began. I brought them all up to date, and they all seemed to think Marc and I were on our way back together. I told them I still had misgivings.

"I'm still not sure I can entirely trust any man to the degree Marc needs."

Angie told me to give it time.

"Keep your eyes open and question everything that doesn't seem right. Don't accuse, just question in an: "I need to know way.""

The other girls agreed. They said the more I questioned, and the more I got answers that indicated there was nothing wrong, the easier it would become to trust Marc.

Then I told them Marc had agreed to leave Friday and return Sunday. I said because it was going to be such a hectic day, with a business lunch, a cocktail party, and a banquet, we wouldn't have any time to ourselves if we left and returned Saturday. Danielle looked confused.

"The only thing Marc has to do for Nick is attend a banquet. I have no idea what the other events were for."

Danielle asked Nick if he knew what the lunch and cocktail party were about. Nick wasn't sure either.

"I know when Marc was in a city where his company has a client, he often stopped by to visit. It probably has to do with Antonelli Systems business. That's why, even though the banquet usually wasn't until eight o'clock in the evening, Marc often left Florida around six Saturday morning. It wasn't always like that. Marc used to leave Friday night and return Sunday, but that stopped about six months ago."

Six months ago. Right around the time Marc and I got together. I remember his conversation he had with Marcie this afternoon,

"I'm bringing the reason with me."

Marc was leaving Fort Lauderdale at six o'clock on Saturday mornings and coming back around three o'clock Sunday mornings just so he could spend Friday nights and Sundays with me. That's why he was always so tired on Sunday. Both the long Saturdays he spent at his office and the long Saturdays when he worked for Nick were so we could be together.

The man apparently wanted to be with me, and I'm sure he loves me, but is that enough to keep him faithful to me. What was it Marc had said? I not only had to trust him, but I also had to have faith in my own judgment.

Everything I had seen that made Marc look bad, Danielle in his apartment building, Marc in Susan's room, Marc and Mary Ellen at La Chez turned out to be just the opposite of what I feared. And Saturday, I would find out about the Saturday night parties Marc called me from.

What is wrong with you, Catherine Jensen? Use your head girl. Everyone thinks you're so smart. Are you?

Danielle broke into my thoughts, "What are you wearing Saturday?"

"I haven't given it too much thought. I have a few gowns I bought for the company banquets, and I have one or two nice cocktail dresses. I'll put something together when I get home tonight."

Stacy looked at me and ordered, "Standup."

I did, and she looked me over as if she were sizing me up. Then she nodded at Danielle. They both took me by the hand and led me into Danielle's bedroom. Danielle closed the bedroom door and opened her closet door.

"Now I know what a kid in a candy shop feels like," I said in awe.

I had never seen such a collection of beautiful clothes in my entire life. Even the fanciest boutiques I have been to didn't have a collection like this. Nick Amonti might lead a simple life, not in accordance with his wealth, but it was obvious he spared no expense where his wife was concerned.

"First," Danielle said, "Dinner tomorrow night in Memphis."

Danielle and Stacy started going through the dresses in the closet and choose a simple scooped necked red dress with a hemline that stopped at mid-thigh. I was instructed to try it on, and then I was paraded in front of Cindy and Angie. Receiving their approval, I was ushered back into the bedroom where I tried on some the prettiest dresses I had ever laid eyes on. All, Stacy Geer Designs. The four ladies agreed on the red dress for dinner with Marc, Friday night. A powder blue simple 'A' line dress for the business lunch and a gold cocktail dress that fit me like it was painted on.

The first gown they picked for the banquet was absolutely stunning. I couldn't believe anyone could look that good, especially me. The back was cut all the way down to the waist. There was nothing to keep the dress from falling off the shoulders, and the front was cut in a v that ran almost all the way to my navel. I couldn't take my eyes off the mirror. I asked how do you keep the dress from falling off, and they both laughed. Danielle took a roll of double stick tape from a drawer in the closet.

"You tape the dress to your shoulders and chest."

Stacy added, "Amazing what we women will do to look sexy for our men."

This time, I was not only paraded past the girls, but Danielle wanted Nick's opinion also. Nick asked what the occasion was, and when we told him it was for the banquet Saturday night, he said no. Danielle was surprised.

"If we were going this Saturday instead of Marc would you wear that gown?

Danielle looked at me.

"No, I wouldn't. We'll find something else."

Back in the bedroom, Danielle apologized to me. She said while she was trying to make me dazzle for Marc, she lost sight of what they were dressing me for.

Then she asked, "Don't you have a company party coming up soon?"

"Yes, the annual company banquet. It's in two months."

"Formal?"

"Yes, they're always formal."

"Good. You can save this gown for that affair. We'll find something else for Saturday."

After trying on three or four more gowns, Stacy and Danielle settled on a beautiful white strapless gown with a long slit along the left leg. It too was stunning, but not nearly as daring as the first one. This time, Nick approved. Before we went back into the bedroom so I could put my own clothes back on, Nick said, "Catherine, I hope I didn't hurt your feelings. You looked terrific in the gown, but..."

I interrupted him.

"I understand Nick. As Marc's date, I'll be representing your company, and I must do that with dignity. I have no problem with what you said. I wouldn't want to do anything that didn't seem proper."

That brought out a smile from Nick, and I got a kiss on the cheek.

"Catherine, I know the past eight months have been very hard on Marc. I don't know if Marc told you, but he took the job with Dillman Brothers as a favor to me. Between that and trying to keep a handle on his own company, he's been under a lot of pressure. I would have liked to take these banquet responsibilities away from him, but most of these things are scheduled almost a year in advance, and clients aren't happy when we make changes to the original contract. Things should settle down for him when he's finished at Dillman. Hang in there till then, will you. I'd hate to be responsible for messing this up for Marc."

I smiled and told Nick I was giving it my best, and that seemed to satisfy him.

When I was dressed, and the four of us were back together again, I protested about wearing such beautiful and expensive clothes out of Danielle's closet. They were all Stacy Geer Designs, and the gown and cocktail dress were Stacy Geer Design Originals. That meant one of a kind. I told Danielle I couldn't allow her to let me borrow such expensive clothes.

"I would die if anything happened to one of them. What if I spilled something on that beautiful gown? It must be worth ten or twenty thousand dollars." I whined.

Stacy laughed, "Closer to five hundred dollars."

I was about to protest, but she raised her hand.

"Catherine, the material, and labor that went into that dress cost about five hundred dollars. The rest is the name, and I owe a good part of that to Mr. Amonti."

Danielle said, "You're not borrowing them, Catherine, they're yours."

Before I could digest what she had said and answer her, Cindy added, "Don't worry about it, Catherine. We all have clothes from Stacy's collection. Stacy has always been very generous to us with her talent."

Again, before I could say anything, Stacy said I'd be doing her a favor.

"Catherine, it's advertising. Dressing beautiful women like you in my clothes is like having a live, walking billboard. A woman sees how great you look, realizes you're wearing one on my designs, and she attributes your beauty to my dress. She wants to be that beautiful too, so she wants one of my dresses."

I finally was allowed to say something but to no avail. I was going home with five beautiful Stacy Geer Design dresses, and they were mine to keep.

I had a good family and nice friends, but I had never met people like this group. No wonder Marc liked them so much. He said good people like to hang together, and these were very good people. And, Marc was one of them. And, as unbelievable as it seemed, they believed I was too.

If I could get Marc back, my life would be perfect! Or am I just fooling myself?

Chapter 24 – Flight to Memphis

Just as he had said, I didn't see Marc on Friday. Five o'clock, my doorbell rang. I asked Marc to come up and help with my luggage. I had just one carry on bag, but I also had four dresses, each snuggled away in their own garment bags Danielle had given me. I was surprised to see a limo waiting when we reached the street. Noticing my surprise, Marc said, "Nothing but the best for an Amonti employee."

That made me giggle. I couldn't picture Marc as being anyone's employee. Marc introduced me to Thomas, our driver. Thomas placed my carry on in the front passenger seat, with Marc's and the garment bags were carefully laid flat in the trunk, on top of Marc's. The same one I saw hanging on the door the morning he said he was going to Miami for Nick.

On the ride to the airport, Marc explained that the limo belonged to NAS Financial Group, and Thomas was a company employee. He also told me Thomas was a member of Nick's Security Team. Remembering what Danielle had said about her workouts with the security team, and how quickly they found out about the champagne in Nashville, I had questions. Marc had the answers.

"People as wealthy as Nick have twenty-four/seven bodyguards for themselves and their families. Nick thought that was a burden, so instead, he put together this security team, mainly ex-Navy Seals and police officers and they set up a system to keep everyone safe. Each member of Nick's family has a unique cell phone and certain pieces of jewelry with panic buttons. If pressed, the team would know one of them was in trouble and could track exactly where they were. Since the team had good relations with every police force in Florida, they could have a police car on the scene in minutes. When any member of the family traveled out of Florida, they made arrangements with a local security company to keep an eye out for a panic signal.

Also, every member of Nick's family takes classes with the security team. They are a combination of self-defense and situational awareness training. That's why Danielle was dressed the way she was when you ran into her.

They are very serious, and they treat her and the other family members pretty rough. They try to make it real, so in case something does happen, they will react without thinking."

Being rich wasn't always what other people believed.

"I've taken classes with Nick's security team, and I work out with them monthly. I can take care of myself in most situations, but I'd never want to go up against Nick, who was trained by the Navy Seals and I'd think long and hard before I tried mixing it up with Danielle.

The guys on the security team say she was the most dedicated student they had. Because she didn't want Nick to worry about her when they weren't together, she took her training very seriously."

When we reached the airport, we pulled up next to a different plane than the one Marc, and I had taken to Key West, and the team had flown to Nashville. But, this one also had NAS painted on the tail in big red letters. Two men greeted us, and Marc introduced them as out flight crew. One went aboard, and the other took our luggage from Thomas and brought it onto the aircraft.

Seeing two men surprised me. I asked Marc who Karen was. Marc smiled and pointed to the nose of the airplane. In beautiful script was written the name *Karen*. Marc explained the other plane was Nick's and he named it after Danielle. This one belonged to Nick's son and was named after Nick's daughter-in-law. He tried to tell me the difference between a BBJ and a G5 but didn't mean much to me. They were both beautiful and comfortable, and this really was the way to fly.

The seats were arranged unusually for an airplane. Some faced forward as in a normal plane. There were two couches which were situated sideways along the walls and a couple where the seats faced each other, one facing forward and one facing aft, with a table between them, much like a small table at a restaurant. Marc chose one of these for us. He said he wanted to look at me during the flight, and it did make it convenient for us to talk.

I loved to fly, and everything about the experience excited me, from the moment the engines were started until they were shut down at our destination. Mark seemed very blasé about it all. When I told him how excited I was, he said, "The next time we fly in *Danielle*, I'll send you up front, and you can sit with the pilots and watch them do their thing."

That really excited me. He reminded me both Nick and Danielle were pilots and were both certified to fly the BBJ. Then the conversation turned to us.

"How are we doing?"

I thought very carefully before I answered.

"I love you Marc, and I want what we had before, but I'm not sure you will ever feel the same way about me ever again."

"I love you, Catherine, and I know you're not my ex-wife. I know it's not fair to put that on you. I'm trying to deal with that, believe me. I don't want to lose you. But, I'm not some, 'do every broad I can college kid', and you can't put that on me."

"I know that Marc, and I'm working on it. This trip should help. It's one of the things that bothered me, but I was too afraid to ask you about."

"Why? Why were you afraid to talk to me about it?"

"Because I was afraid I wouldn't like the answer."

Marc was thoughtful for a moment.

"I tried to explain something to my wife, but she never understood. Maybe you will. Let's take two different scenarios. First, you love a man and trust him completely, and one day you find out he was unfaithful. Or, you love a man and mistrust him. You're always trying to catch him doing something wrong, and one day you find out he's been unfaithful. In which of those cases would it hurt more?"

I didn't have to think about it.

"If you love someone, and they are unfaithful, it always hurts."

"OK," Marc went on, "Let's say you love a man and trust him completely, and he's always faithful. Or, you love a man and mistrust him, and it turns out he has always been faithful. Which one of those couples will be happier together."

The message was clear. If your lover was unfaithful, it would hurt just as much whether you trusted him or not, but if he was faithful, you'd never be truly happy unless you believed he was. Every time I had doubts about Marc, it turned out I was wrong. How many incidents would it take before I trusted him?

It really was simple. If Marc was unfaithful to me, it would hurt just as much whether I trusted him or not. If he remained faithful, and I didn't trust him, I would never experience true happiness with him. Logically, it made sense, but emotion is not logic, and although talking helped me to understand the logic, it wouldn't be enough to deal with the emotion. I had to make a decision about Marc.

Could I trust this man's character as much as he seemed to trust mine?

Marc seemed to trust me so completely. How far did that trust go? A thought came to me.

"Marc, how do you feel about my relationship with Ron?"

157

"Considering he delayed his flight home and demanded I have lunch with him, I'd say you have a very good friend. We can never have enough of those."

"Doesn't it bother you he stayed at my apartment Tuesday night? He also stayed with me Monday night."

Marc was surprised by my question.

"Are you suggesting there is something I should be concerned about?"

"No," I said quickly, "But, you know we've been friends for over fifteen years, don't you wonder if we've ever been lovers?"

Marc didn't hesitate.

"Catherine, remember the night you told me I should look closer to work?"

I nodded. That's the night it all started between Marc and me.

"Any man you've ever been with before that night is not a concern to me. From that night forward is all I'm interested in. If you and Ron had an affair before I came along, I have no problem with your friendship. If you've gotten together since that night, then we have a serious issue."

"But, you know how close we are, and you know he spent two nights at my apartment, how can you be so sure?"

"I'm not sure. I can never be sure. I can only use the information I have to make a judgment, and as I've said before, I don't see you as that kind of girl. I don't believe you would jump into bed with a man while you were in a relationship with another man. It doesn't fit my conception of who you are. And, as close as Ron is to you, I'm sure he feels that way as well.

"Catherine, I've told you this is all my judgment. It's all I have to go on. I've been with you for about eight months. I've listened to you, I've observed you, and I've made love to you. I see you as a woman who is not very loose with her virtue. I see you as an open and honest person. I have to use what I know about you in every decision I make about you. It's all I have."

The remainder of the flight we talked about what we were going to do in Memphis. A car would be waiting for us at the airport and take us to a hotel where we would change and then on to dinner. Tomorrow, we had lunch with one of Marc's clients at noon and then a cocktail party at four. Then, back to the hotel to change and a formal banquet at eight thirty. A pretty full day.

"Years ago, I was in a city for one of these engagements and my company was installing one of our systems in that same city. I stopped by to see how my guys were doing. The client was so impressed the president of the company had stopped by to check on the progress of the installation, I decided when Nick sends me to a city where Antonelli Systems has a client, I would try to arrange a lunch date with that person.

"The cocktail party was added this trip by the client we're having lunch with. When I contacted him to let him know I'd be in Memphis, he asked him why I hadn't been in my office for months. I told him about my consulting work for Dillman, and the client said an associate of his could be in the market for the type of work that Dillman does. The client arranged this cocktail party to introduce me to this man and a few others that might be interested in Antonelli Systems. It's going to be business all day, but we will have some free time on Sunday before we fly back to Florida."

When we landed in Memphis, a Town Car was waiting to take us to the Grand Hyatt. There, we were brought to a large, beautiful two bedroom suite. Marc had my luggage put in one bedroom and his in the other. After the bellman left, Marc looked around the suite.

"Only the best for an Amonti employee. I usually have a one bedroom suite, but since you're with me, Marcie ordered a two bedroom unit so we don't have to fight over the bathroom while we were getting dressed tomorrow."

Then he told me to get ready for dinner. I wore the beautiful red dress Danielle had given me, and when I emerged from my bedroom, it was clear Marc was pleased.

"Catherine, I'm going to have to work very hard to remember I'm here on business."

I took the arm he offered me and we went to dinner. At the restaurant, our conversation was about Marc and me, but not about the problem we were having or the trust issue. It was as if Nashville had never happened.

It was nice, and I started to have hope maybe this could work. We returned to the hotel immediately after dinner, Marc saying we had a very busy day tomorrow and a good night's sleep was in order. I hesitated before going into my room. Marc noticed.

"I'm sure I don't have to tell you how much I want to make love to you tonight. But, I think we need more time before we declare this problem solved."

He was right. I said goodnight and left him standing in the living room. I had a decent night's sleep. I slept, but not soundly.

Everything that had passed between Marc and me from the first day he was introduced to the team kept invading my dreams.

When I got out of bed in the morning, I was sure of only one thing. I was not going to allow this man to walk out of my life without one hell of a fight. I was in love with him, and I wanted to spend the rest of my life with him.

Chapter 25 – The Saturday Mystery

When I walked into the living room Saturday morning, Marc was dressed in a pair of casual slacks and a tee shirt. He smiled when he saw me and asked if bacon and eggs would do for breakfast. Thirty minutes later, when the Room Service Waiter rolled the cart into the suite, it was more like a mini feast than simple bacon and eggs. We ate in semi-silence, but I could tell Marc was in a good mood.

After breakfast, Marc went back to his bedroom to shower and get ready for our business lunch. I was about to do the same when there was a knock on the suite door. Thinking it was the waiter, back to fetch the breakfast cart. I opened the door and was greeted by a short, middle-aged, rather portly lady. She seemed surprised to see me, but recovered quickly and in that same sexy voice I had heard on the phone, said, "Hi, I'm Marcie!"

"I'm Catherine," I smiled at her.

"And, where is that handsome hunk of manhood you seem to have captivated so completely?"

I indicated Marc's room, "Taking a shower."

"Good, it will give us time to get acquainted."

Marcie had tons of questions, and I didn't mind answering them. Where we met, how we got together, etc.? When I told her I was the one who had made a pass at Marc, she was thrilled. I had tons of questions of my own, but I didn't have to ask.

"I work for Nick Amonti. I'm the Booking Agent and advance person and make all the arrangements for these affairs. I usually come into the city the night before to make sure everything is set up."

She didn't mention exactly what Marc did for Nick, but she did say he had been involved for years, and this was the first time in the past six months he had decided to make a weekend out of it.

"When he called and asked me to set this up for Friday to Sunday, I asked him why the change. He said the reason he stayed in Florida Friday nights and wanted to be back on Sundays was coming with him. I guess he meant you, honey, and I must say, I can understand his reasoning."

Just then, Marc emerged from the bedroom. Marcie spotted him and shouted, "Get over here and give mama a kiss good looking."

Marc hurried over and wrapped his arms around Marcie.

161

"This is the real love of my life, Catherine. If it wasn't for that husband of hers, we would have run away together years ago."

Marcie pushed him away and admonished, "Not in front of your lady, honey."

That comment warranted a laugh from all three of us.

Then, tilting her head in my direction, she said, "So, this is the lady you have been rushing home to be with. Is she as good as she looks?"

"Better," Marc answered.

Looking at me, she said, "Honey, I hope you brought something stunning for tonight. I can guarantee there will be at least a dozen women trying to snatch this hunk away from you."

"Only a Stacy Geer Original," I said smugly.

Marcie looked me over.

"Honey, on you a Stacy Geer gown would look spectacular!"

Marc surprised at my comment said, "I think Ms. Danielle Palmer and I need to have a talk."

"And why is that?

"She never seemed to be the matchmaker type."

"Trust me, Marc, it's all for you. The girls know you'll never find anyone better than me, and they just want to make sure you don't blow it."

Marcie laughed.

"If she's in with that group of ladies, you'd better behave yourself. They're very protective of their own."

That brought another round of giggles and Marc said I should get ready while Marcie and he went over the day's schedule.

While I was taking a shower, I thought back to the scene with Marcie when Marc walked out of his room. Typical Marc.

Marcie was not what I'd consider competition. I had no idea what Anna Lee or Pam looked like. I knew how pretty Cindy Patrick was, but Angie was at least thirty years older than Marc. He didn't seem to have any preference as to who he flirted with. He even flirted with my sister Beth.

"The only reason I hang around with Catherine is so I'll get invited here for one of your dinners. You're the real love of my life, Beth."

The comment didn't upset Sam, but it made my sister beam. It was probably just like Marc said. Just his way of being complimentary. But he did say he would stop if I asked him to. Would he? I could ask him. That would be a real test of how sincere he is.

When I came out of the bedroom in my blue business dress, I got an approving look from Marc and a whistle from Marcie.

Marc smiled.

"You should have seen her last night. I was worried some of these Tennessee boys were going to kidnap her!"

We all left the suite together and downstairs, the Town Car was waiting to take Marc and me to lunch. Marcie said she'd see us tonight at the banquet and left in her own rental.

On the way to the restaurant, I thought again about Marc's flirting ways. Did it bother me? Should I ask him to stop? But what if he just stopped doing it in front of me. What would that accomplish?

Lunch was at a very nice restaurant, and Marc introduced me to his client and his client's IT manager. The client, Anton, was a man in his sixties, very pleasant and friendly. The other man, Jonathan, was about forty and very good looking.

The conversation centered on the systems Marc's company had installed for them and how they were working. I was getting a lot of attention from Jonathan and Marc didn't seem to notice. The two hours we spent with them were pleasant, and Anton seemed pleased Marc had taken the trouble to meet with him when Marc was in town.

Back at the hotel, it was a mad dash to get ready for the Cocktail Party. This time, when I emerged from the bedroom in my gold cocktail dress, Marc stood frozen, just looking at me. I twirled around, giving him the full three hundred and sixty-degree view, and when I faced him again, he said, "Wow, wait until Jonathan sees you in that outfit!"

"Jonathon," I said surprised, "What made you bring his name up?"

"Do you think I didn't notice the rush he was putting on you? Did he ask you for a date?"

"We're leaving tomorrow, how could he ask me for a date?"

"He didn't tell you he'll be in Ft Lauderdale next month for a week-long seminar?"

"No, he never mentioned it."

"Maybe that's why he asked Anton if he could come to the cocktail party this afternoon. He wasn't interested in attending until after he met you!"

"Do I detect jealousy, Mr. Antonelli?"

Marc expression turned serious. He took me by the hand and led me back into my bedroom. He had me stand in front of the full-length mirror.

"Take a good look, Catherine."

Not knowing where he was going with this, I did as he asked.

"Pretty hot, wouldn't you say? A beautiful, tall, blue eyed blond, a figure most women would envy with great legs. Catherine, you are the kind of woman that will have every man we meet today at your heels. Every one of them will want to get to know you.

"And the ones that are lucky enough to talk to you will find out along with that beauty you possess intelligence, charm, grace, sensuality, elegance and so much more. All of that in one beautiful package. In your lifetime, you will meet all kinds of men, young ones, old ones, handsome ones, not so good looking ones, gentlemen and scoundrels.

They will all want to get close to you. Their egos will make them want to believe they can have a woman like you. Some of these men will be boring or crass, and you won't be able to get away from them fast enough. Some will be polite, respectful, good company and you will enjoy your time with them."

Marc looked at my reflection in the mirror.

"And, sometimes...you will be tempted to move the relationship further. Maybe just a quiet dinner or a stroll around the park. But, every once in a while, the temptation to go even further will surface. It happens to everyone. As much in love as we are, as faithful as we are, there is the grass is always greener syndrome just waiting for us to make a slip. It's human nature to want to know what's on the other side of the fence. Maybe we wouldn't want to live there, but we'd all like to sample what's over there."

I thought he was through, but he continued.

"Believe me, Catherine, the temptation will come. And, probably when you least expect it, when you're least prepared to fight it. That is what I have to deal with! I have to face the reality that other men desire you, and there will be some that feel they can have you. And I have to face the possibility that you may be tempted."

"Being in a meaningful relationship with a woman like you can drive a man crazy. The only way I can keep my sanity is to believe in you. Believe in us. I have to trust my opinion of you.

I have to have faith in my own ability to judge your character, your personality, the love you have for me. And if the time ever comes when I see something or hear something that might make me doubt that judgment, I have to face it, face you and ask for an explanation."

Again, I thought he was finished, but he had more.

"No matter how long we are together, I will never know for sure you have been faithful to me. I've mentioned before jumping into bed with someone is not the only way to be unfaithful. Fidelity to one person is a mindset. It is knowing in your heart, you are faithful and letting everyone around you know there is only one man in your life. One man, you want attention from. One man, you have an emotional attachment to. One man, you are willing to share intimacy with."

A longer pause this time.

"To answer your question, I will never be jealous when a man shows an interest in you. No! I have faith in you, I have faith in us. I can deal with all the Jonathans that come along, as long as I believe your desire is to stay faithful to me!"

Marc glanced at his watch and said we had to go. He gave me a kiss. Just a gentle peck, not a romantic or intimate kiss, and just before turning to leave my bedroom he had one more thing to say.

"I do love you Catherine Jensen, and I promise as long as we are together I will always be faithful to you! But, that's all I can offer you, my promise. I will never be able to prove it! And I will never know for sure that you have been faithful to me."

I gathered myself together and followed Marc into the living room. He offered me his arm and we headed for the door. Not another word was said. But I made a decision. I would not ask Marc to stop flirting with women he knew well. I did trust that he would never embarrass me by flirting for real with someone in front of me. I did trust him that much. One small step.

The longest journey starts with the first step. I took that step.

Outside, the car was waiting to take us to the cocktail party. On the way, Marc told me he would be meeting a couple of people who might have an interest in his systems. But the main reason for the cocktail party was that Anton wanted to introduce him to someone who might be interested in doing business with Dillman Brothers. Marc thought I could play a vital role in that meeting. We arrived at the hotel and just before we entered the ballroom, Marc stopped and looked at me.

"Did I tell you how dazzling you look?"

My smile was my answer, but I had something extra to add.

"If you think I look good now, just wait until you see me tonight!"

"If you can possibly look any better than this, it's a good thing Jonathan won't be at the banquet."

Then he added, "Do I have something to be worried about?"

Knowing Marc was teasing, I said, "Well if he didn't live so far away..."

"Don't forget, he'll be in Ft Lauderdale next month for a week-long seminar!"

That was the end of the conversation. We entered the small banquet room, and Anton immediately grabbed Marc and took him away to introduce him to some potential customers. I wasn't left alone, Jonathan was there to keep me company.

I had to control myself in order to avoid laughing. Just as Marc had said, Jonathon was good company. He probably was the type of man I would be willing to date if it wasn't for my relationship with Marc, such as it was. When Anton and Marc returned, they had another man with them.

"Eric, this is the lady I was telling you about. Catherine Jensen, meet Eric Tellerman. Eric might be interested in doing some business with Dillman Brothers."

Anton and Jonathon excused themselves and Marc, Eric and I had a very productive conversation. It seems Eric had heard about our deal with Carter Aviation and how close our tolerances were. He was more than interested in giving us a chance to win his business. Marc promised that one of our Senior Client Analysts would be in touch with him on Monday morning to set up a convenient time to negotiate a contract. When Eric asked if I would be back in Memphis to work the numbers for him, Marc told him, "Vice Presidents usually don't make field trips. It will be Susan, and she is almost as pretty as Catherine is."

That made me blush.

Before we left, Marc thanked Anton for arranging the cocktail party and told him we had made some very promising contacts. While they were talking, Jonathan said he would be in Ft Lauderdale next month and would I mind if he called me. As politely as I could, I told Jonathon, "I appreciate the offer but I'm in a relationship and it's beginning to turn serious."

He said he understood but indicated he was very disappointed.

On the car ride back to our hotel, Marc asked if Jonathon had asked me out. I relayed our conversation, and Marc said Jonathon was a good guy, and maybe the three of us could get together when he was in town. I smiled and asked if Marc was trying to get rid of me.

"I don't care how many men wanted to be with you, as long as they understood you are not available for anything more than a casual friendship."

Back at the hotel, I took my time getting ready for the banquet. I understood why Marc was always so tired after one of these trips. We had flown in last night and would sleep here in the hotel tonight, but I knew I would be worn out after this night was over. Marc had done this all in the same day just so he could spend Friday night and Sunday with me. If I ever had any doubt about how much he loved me, I didn't have anymore. Now, all I had to do was defeat this fear I had.

When I had tried this gown in Danielle's bedroom, the girls suggested I wear my hair up. I had very fine long hair, below my shoulders, and I always wore it down and natural. I spent a good deal of time getting it just right, and when I thought I was ready, I took a very long look at myself in the mirror. I wanted to see what Marc would see. Thinking it wasn't going to get any better, I walked into the living room.

Marc was in his tuxedo, all except the jacket and when he saw me, I knew he was pleased. Again, I did the three hundred and sixty-degree twirl and waited for his comment. It was better than I had hoped for.

"I've always thought Stacy's clothes were beautiful. But, on you, that gown is spectacular. Catherine, you are a beautiful woman, but in a very soft way. You always appear soft and feminine. But, tonight, you've brought out your elegant side, your sophisticated side. Tonight, Catherine Jensen, you are royalty. And, I, My Lady am your humble servant!"

The more he talked, the faster my heart raced, the weaker my legs felt, the more my head was spinning. I would gladly spend the rest of my life trying to please this man. And, I was absolutely sure I could succeed.

Marc put on his Jacket, brushed himself off, straightened his tie and with a gentlemanly bow, said, "Am I presentable enough to be your escort tonight, Your Highness?"

"Absolutely, My Lord. Tonight and every night if it pleases you!"

"That it does," he said sweetly, "It pleases me very much!"

Downstairs, I was expecting the same Town Car that had been assigned to us since we arrived last night. But instead, a white stretch limo was waiting for us. Noting the surprised look on my face, Marc said, "Royalty demands a White Coach if she's going to the ball, and I guarantee this one won't turn into a pumpkin at midnight

"I hope My Lady is wearing comfortable shoes tonight. I have a strong feeling she will be doing a lot of dancing."

And then he added sweetly, "And I pray she remembers who's taking her home!"

"Always," I responded as he squeezed my hand.

Thinking back to Marc's comments this afternoon, in front of the mirror, I asked,

"Marc, how do you do it?"

"Do what?"

I wanted to choose my words carefully, but I needed an answer.

"You are an incredibly handsome man. Your personable, respectful, well mannered, a great dancer...."

Marc interrupted me.

"I love the platitudes, but is there a question in there?"

"A very serious question." How do you let women know you're not available, and how do you resist the temptation?"

Marc gave that some thought before he answered.

"You have to understand. For ten years, I didn't have to resist the temptation, I was single and unattached. Since you've been in my life, there hasn't been any temptation...so far.

"But, there have been times when I have been with women I shouldn't get involved with for various reasons. It's really very simple. I never put myself in a situation where something that shouldn't happen could happen."

"I don't understand."

"Remember when I told you the security team treats Danielle roughly so if she's ever in a situation she'll react without taking the time to think about it. This is basically the same thing. There are rules I follow with women whether I'm interested in them or not. This way, it's a habit, and I don't have to think about what my feelings are toward the particular woman I am with."

After giving it some thought, he explained.

"Unless I have a long standing relationship with a women, and we both know what that relationship is, I will never be alone with a women in a closed room. There will always be at least one other person with us. When I was in Susan's room in Nashville, and I realized Ted wasn't there, I never moved into the room. I stayed in the foyer, told her to meet me in the Business Center and left. I had no interest in Susan, and I was sure she wasn't about to make a pass at me, but it's important to follow the rules at all times.

"Usually, if I have a casual or business relationship with a woman, I try to do lunch instead of dinner. Much safer environment, dinner is more intimate. If it has to be dinner for some reason, I pick a very casual restaurant. Nothing romantic or intimate. I monitor how much I drink so I don't get too loose. I don't allow the conversation to get too personal. The restaurants I took you to before the night we got involved were all very casual, remember."

Marc checked his watch.

"That night when you asked me why I wasn't married, if I was in a relationship, I would have answered that question in a way that would have prevented you from moving it further along in the direction it took that night.

"As far as letting people know I'm not available, it's basically the same. I only flirt with women who know I'm teasing. Again, a long-standing relationship. When I dance, I'm very careful how close I hold her and how intimate the dance is. I avoid intimate conversations entirely. I usually find a way to indicate I'm not interested before she has a chance to indicate she is, and I do it in a way that doesn't suggest I thought she was.

"It's not complicated if that's what you really want to do. Put yourself in the other person's place and try to judge what kinds of signs you're transmitting."

The conversation ended when we reached the hotel where the banquet was being held. Inside the ballroom, we were told our contact was waiting for us. Marcie looked lovely in her gown, and she introduced me to her husband. After looking me over, head to toe, she commented how lucky Marc was to fall in love with such a beautiful woman.

She gave Marc a list of who we were going to be seated with, names and positions in the company. She assured him everything was in place and told me to have fun. She also said, "Sometimes these things could be very boring, but I'm sure since you're here with him Marc would finally enjoy it."

But I did notice that Marc didn't flirt with Marcie as he had done this morning and on the phone.

My next surprise came when we were seated. Our seats were at the dais, next to the CEO of the company that was throwing the party and his wife. I still didn't know what Marc was doing here. What did NAS Financial Group have to do with this company, and why did they have to be represented here tonight. We were introduced to everyone at the dais, and when that was done, Marc excused us and led me on to the dance floor.

"Might as well get this out of the way and let the other guys have a chance with you."

Dinner was standard banquet fare, and Marc was right about my shoes. I did dance almost every dance, never with the same man twice, and only one additional time with Marc. He only danced about half as often as I did. If the music didn't stop while the food was being served, I wouldn't have sat down all night.

After dessert, the Master of Ceremonies moved to the podium and introduced the CEO. After a short speech about sales, profit margins, new products, etc., the MC introduced the COO, who gave out awards for Executive of the Year, Salesman of the Year, etc. Then the CFO talked about this year's Bonus Plan and how it would be distributed. All standard business banquet stuff, I had been to a number of these and knew the plot well. Then, as the MC was introducing the next speaker, Marc leaned over to me and whispered in my ear, "Now, you're going to find out what I do with my secret Saturday nights."

Just as Marc finished his statement, I heard the MC say, "Ladies and gentleman, our featured speaker this evening: Mr. Marco Antonelli of Antonelli Systems, Inc."

Marc winked at me, rose from his seat to polite applause and made his way over to the podium. He took the list Marcie had handed him out of his pocket and began by thanking all of the executives for inviting him this evening. He then made some comments about how nice it was to visit Memphis again.

He was about to start his speech, which was in a binder already on the podium, probably thanks to Marcie, when he stopped and looked out over his audience. When he started to speak, he wasn't referring to his speech.

"Ladies and gentleman! The speech I am about to deliver tonight is not my own. It was first given by a friend of mine who was very much in love with his wife. I had the pleasure of hearing it for the first time about five years ago and asked him if I could include it in my repertoire. I think it is a very important concept for us who toil in the corporate world and over the past five years I have given this talk dozens of times.

But, until recently, when someone very special came into my life, I didn't realize how very important this concept was. So, for the very first time, I am talking about things I not only believe in but will endeavor to follow from now on."

And with that remark, Marc began his speech on the importance of not allowing the corporate world take you away from the people who love you. It was about separating your work life from your personal life, and not letting your job destroy your family.

It was very impressive, but it wasn't dry and boring as these things usually were. Marc interspersed stories and jokes throughout the speech and seemed to have his audience captivated by his every word. I listened closely to what he was saying, and as I watched the people out in front of me, I could see they were paying attention too.

His jokes and humorous stories had everyone laughing, and he never hesitated to tell a joke on himself. He included two stories about us, one true and one pure fabrication and I had to laugh at both of them. One story had the audience in stitches.

It was about a couple who were crazy in love with each other but had never brought their feelings into the open. It revolved around a pair of ladies' panties that supposedly belonged to the woman's sister. When Marc got to the punch line, he was twirling a pair of ladies panties on the end of his finger, and when he said, "Just ask your sister," the audience went wild.

Marc went on to tell his audience, "They did finally profess their love for each other that night, and one month later they were engaged. They are extremely happy together even though they are both high powered executives for two different companies. They put aside time at home to share their work problems and vent when necessary, but when that time is over, it's all about them and their relationship."

Marc's speech lasted about forty-five minutes. In the closing, he said, "I know we can all do this. I've seen it in action, not only the couple I mentioned but with other couples I know. A stressful corporate job doesn't have to mean an unfulfilling personal relationship. I promise you people here tonight and my lady, it will not happen to me."

This time, the applause was not polite. It was genuine. They really enjoyed Marc's speech. Marc sat down next to me, and the CEO moved to the podium. He thanked Marc for such an inspiring talk.

Marc looked at me and winked, "Watch this."

Marc got up and moved back over to the podium. The CEO was surprised. Marc excused himself for the interruption and said he had one more story to tell. His stories had the audience in such a good mood, they were eager for one more.

The CEO yielded the podium and Marc, still smiling said, "Remember that couple I told you about? Well, as much in love as they were, for various reasons, they weren't sure if a romantic relationship between the two of them would work, so they decided to take some time to think about it. They made arrangement to have dinner together a month later. They had no contact with each other for the entire month, and when they met, at a restaurant in Texas, neither was sure of the outcome.

"But, once he looked into his lady's eyes, he proposed, right there in the restaurant. It must have been very romantic. She immediately accepted, and they spent a very romantic night together and watched the sunrise, snuggled in each other's arms. The following day, they drove to the lady's sister's house to break the good news."

Marc, now with a great big smile continued.

"Our hero pulls into the driveway and gets out of the car. His lady waits for him to walk around and open her door. Instead, he reopened his door, stuck his head in the car and said, "Honey, now that we're officially engaged, do you think I should give your sister her panties back?""

That brought the house down. Marc gave his audience a wave and returned to his seat with a big smile plastered all over his face.

"Always leave them laughing. I can't remember who first said that but it sounded good, so I try to follow that advice."

The rest of the evening was a semi-climax. Marc was definitely the hit of the night. We managed two more dances together, and of course, the last dance. All the senior executives thanked Marc for his speech. They all indicated he was the best feature speaker they've ever had. Marcie told Marc she always loved to hear him speak, but tonight he was really on.

"I should have had the good sense to bring Catherine with me sooner. It really did make a difference. If I was on tonight, it was because I was trying to show off for her."

Chapter 26 – After the Banquet

On the ride back to our hotel, we were both quiet. All I could think about was the possibilities of life with this man. I knew he loved me, but I also knew it would be tough to undo the damage that was done by both of us. My suspicious nature because of Bobby and Marc's fear of always looking over his shoulder because of his ex-wife.

Back in the suite, we both disappeared into our individual bedrooms to change. I had brought a beautiful peignoir set for tonight, not too sexy, but very feminine. When I returned to the living room, Marc was in casual slacks and a tee shirt. He was opening a bottle of champagne.

"What are we celebrating?"

"Hopefully, a new beginning."

I curled up on the couch. Marc brought me a glass of champagne and settled himself in one of the club chairs. We toasted our new beginning.

"Are we OK, Marc?"

His reply was thoughtful.

"That's a question we both have to answer. I don't think we're there yet, but we are making progress, don't you agree?"

I nodded my agreement and had another question for him.

"What you said in the car about avoiding temptation and being unavailable, is it really that simple?"

"Simple? No, it's not simple at all. Allowing yourself to be tempted is simple and easy. Avoiding situations that may cause you to be tempted takes a lot of thought and practice. It has to become routine. You have to be aware of your situation at all times, and avoid anything that could lead you astray."

After pausing to gather his thoughts.

"Remember the night this relationship between us started?"

"I'll never forget it."

"I'm pretty sure when you suggested we finish the work at the restaurant, you had no thought of starting a romantic relationship with me. We were just two business associates talking business over dinner. Do you agree?"

"Yes. I did think you were a very respectful, handsome, and considerate man, and I did fantasize about an affair with you, but I never expected it to happen. It was just day dreaming. You were way out of my league."

Marc smiled.

"Do you remember how quickly things changed? Just one little question and within a couple of minutes we were dating. Neither of us went to that restaurant prepared for what happened. We both had taboos about interoffice dating. I was your boss, a definite no-no for both of us. I did like you, and I thought about what it would be like to be involved with you in a personal way, but it never was going to happen, at least until after I left Dillman. Neither of us had too much to drink. Neither of us was seriously thinking about a relationship between us. Yet in the space of a couple of minutes, we became a couple. It happens that quickly."

When I didn't say anything, Marc went on.

"I was so sure it couldn't happen between us I forgot about my own rules. When you asked me why I wasn't married, I should have gently steered the conversation in a different direction. I should have given you the impression there was someone special in my life, and I wasn't available. Instead, because I wasn't vigilant, I fell into the trap. Also, I allowed it because I knew we were both single and available. That puts a different light on the situation. If I did have someone in my life, that personal conversation never would have happened."

"But, if you're in love with someone, why should you have to worry? Why should you be tempted? "

"Because, you never know what form temptation will take. You never know what can change your perception of the person you are with. A look, a word or an intimate conversation about things you shouldn't be talking about. And, you never know what the other person has in mind. What you see as innocent, he may think is a come-on. It's very complicated, and temptation is tough to overcome. So, the easiest thing to do is never be in a situation where temptation can turn into action. We can't always avoid the temptation. We can't always account for what the other person has in mind, but we can control the opportunity for action.

"There are some very devious people out there. We can't always tell what they have in mind. Do you believe Ted is the only man who would go to such lengths to accomplish his goal? Or, that there are women who might be just as devious? Avoid the opportunity, and you avoid doing something you never intended to do."

After a few moments of silence.

"Catherine you are a intelligent woman. You know how to take care of yourself, and I know you don't spread your virtue around easily. But, can you honestly tell me you never were with a man who you had no intentions of having sex with, and during the course of the date, something happened, and you wound being much more intimate with him than you intended?"

That last statement brought me to attention. He was right, and it had happened on more than one occasion. It wasn't that I couldn't go to bed with these men, or that I shouldn't. I was single and not in a relationship at the time, it was just they didn't turn me on that way, or I suspected they were in a relationship, and I had decided it wasn't going to happen. But it did, and I willing allowed it to happen. Maybe Marc was right. Avoid situations that could lead to action, unless you were willing to deal with what could happen.

We were silent for a while. All sorts of thoughts were going around in my head. I loved this man. I wanted to spend my life with him. I wanted to be faithful to him, and if he gave me a chance, I would be. And, more and more I felt he would be faithful to me. I had to convince him I knew that. But, I had one other question.

"Marc, why didn't you flirt with Marcie tonight? Was it because her husband was with her?"

Marc seemed surprised. He took a minute before he answered.

"I see my flirtatious nature bothers you. Not a problem. It stops now, okay."

"No, it's not okay."

That surprised him even more.

"Marc, I am in love with you. The man you are. I don't want to change you. I don't want you to adjust your personality to suit me."

"I'm lost, Catherine."

"You said I could ask you anything."

"That's true, you can ask anything, and I will give you an honest answer."

"But if asking you a question makes you believe that I don't like something or I don't trust you, then I'll be afraid to ask you anything.
"

Marc got up and poured us each another glass of champagne. When he came back to the living room, he was smiling.

"Okay, Catherine. I will take every question as a search for information and I won't act on it unless you ask me to."

"Marc, I've already decided that your flirting doesn't bother me. I know it's all in fun and only with women you know very well. I have no problem with that, but I would be terribly hurt if I found out you were flirting with some woman behind my back."

"Catherine Jensen. I not only love you, but I also respect you. I respect you as a woman and a person. That will never happen. Even if for some reason we were on the verge of breaking up, I would never embarrass you that way."

Before I could answer, he added.

"But once again, all I can give you is my word. I will never be able to prove it."

"Your word is all I need."

That made him happy. We sat quietly for a few minutes. I was trying to think of a way to bring up the question again. It didn't bother me. Not in a trust way, but I wanted to know. Before I could think of a way to ask the question without sounding unsure of myself, he answered it. Well, not exactly, he made me answer it.

"You know the answer to that question, Catherine. You should know better than most."

I tried to think about what he had said. And he was right. I knew the answer.

"Business is business!"

"Yes, Catherine. Tonight was business. Marcie was giving me relevant information. Who we were sitting with. The correct order of people I should thank for inviting us. Which speech was waiting for me on the podium. No time for fooling around. Marcie's husband has no problem with our teasing each other. This was business."

I uncurled myself from the couch, walked over to him and sat on his lap.

I kissed him gently, looked right into his eyes, "Make love to me!"

We stood up, I took his hand and tried to lead him to my bedroom. He resisted. I turned to face him. He pulled me toward him and kissed me passionately.

"I've been making love to you for the past week."

Then, he lifted me up in his arms and carried me into my bedroom. It was gentle and tender. I could feel the emotion pouring out of him. This man loved me. I have never felt love like this before. I tried to let him know just how much he meant to me. I would do anything to please him, to show him how much I loved him. And I wanted him to know that.

The next thing I remember was something was nibbling on my ear. I opened my eyes and turned around to see Marc smiling down at me.

"What time is it?"

"After ten, breakfast will be here in thirty minutes."

"Not enough time for an encore," I pouted.

"There's always after breakfast," he said sincerely.

That was enough to get me up and moving. I took a quick shower and instead of getting dressed, I put on the same peignoir I had worn last night just so he wouldn't forget that last statement.

Breakfast was another mini feast, and we ate in silence. And after the night's sleep we had, the 'After Breakfast' was wonderful. It also resulted in a nap, and it was three o'clock before we finally climbed out of bed. There was just enough time for us to shower, dress and pack.

The ride to the airport was in silence, with us holding hands in the backseat of the car. On board *Karen*, we took the same seats we had occupied on the flight to Memphis. For a while, we just looked into each other's eyes.

Finally, he said, "What do you see?

"The man I am totally and completely in love with."

"But, can that man make you happy today and tomorrow? Can that man be true to you? Can that man put you first in his life? Can he make you his one and only love?"

"And, can you make him happy today and tomorrow? Can you be true to him? Can you put him first in your life? Can you be sure he will always be your one and only love?"

Before I had a chance to answer, Marc said, "I don't need you to answer those questions, Catherine, but, you do have to answer them… for yourself."

We were silent for a very long time. We were already in our descent before he spoke again.

"Catherine Jensen, I am totally and completely in love with you. I can envision spending the rest of my life with you. I know you are not my ex. I know you are not like her. I can promise you I will always remain faithful to you and no other woman will ever think I am available to her.

"But, Catherine, that's all I can offer you. My promise. I have no way to prove to you what I say is the truth."

And, that was what it was all about. I knew this man loved me. I knew this man wanted to be with me. I knew I could have him. But, I could never be truly happy with him until I could honestly answer those questions.

Would he be faithful to me and would I be faithful to him.

The real question was, could we?

Chapter 27 – Home Again

Thomas picked us up at FLX and drove us to my apartment. I asked Marc how we were doing. He said he thought we had made a lot of progress, but he felt we weren't quite there yet. I asked him what it would take to get us all the way there. He said only I had the answer to that question.

He saw me to the door and waited until I was inside and then he left with Thomas. It was going to be a very long night. I thought about his last statement. I felt, in my heart, it was true. Marc was in love with me, I was sure of that. He intended to be faithful to me forever. I was sure of that too. I knew I wanted to be faithful to him. The question, could we, went both ways. I was sure I would be true to Marc, but could I satisfy his need that every other man I met knew that was true? I knew I could. At least I was pretty sure I could. But, maybe Marc was right about temptation. Was the answer to avoid situations where temptation was possible? But, how did you know?

He was right about our first date too. I had no intentions of having a relationship with him when we left the office that Friday night. What made me say the things I said? What made me do that?

Could it happen that fast and that easily with anyone? Do you have to avoid situations even with people you know?

We didn't get to see much of each other all that week. Saturday, Marc was entrenched in his office as usual. We did spend Sunday together, but it was evident Marc was worn out. I convinced him we should just stay in and relax. It was nice having him around my apartment. No plans, just spending time together. We didn't talk much about us. Everything that could be said had been said. Marc did say he was thinking about another team get together.

"The others seemed to help with the togetherness, and now that we have so many new members on the team, maybe we need a chance to party together."

I thought it was an excellent idea. Everyone at Dillman knew about our little gatherings and a party with all the new members would help bring them into the team mentality. We spent a good part of the day planning. It wasn't strenuous, and it turned out to be fun.

There were seventeen members on the team now, not counting the assistants the other VP's and Sara were going to hire shortly. With spouses and dates, that came to thirty-two people for the party. Marc's original idea was dinner and then something where the team could let down and be informal. I asked Marc if it had to be on a weekend.

"Not necessarily, but I don't want anyone to be worried about being late for work the next day."

An idea was swirling around in my head, but I couldn't put it all together. The part about work the next day was a road block. Marc noticing me deep in thought asked what was going on. I told him my idea, and he loved it. But that roadblock was still there.

We shelved the discussion, and I started preparing dinner. The only time Marc had a real home cooked meals was when he visited his sisters, my family or at Nick and Danielle's apartment. Danielle, it was reported, was an excellent cook. He ate out most days. I wanted to make sure he enjoyed dinner tonight, so I went all out. He tried to help, but I banned him from the kitchen.

"If I'm to prove how indispensable I am to you, I have to show you what you'll be missing if you dumped me."

"You've already accomplished that task, Catherine."

When dinner was ready, I called Marc from the living room. When I didn't get an answer, I went in search of him. He was asleep on the couch. I didn't have the heart to wake him, but he must have sensed my presence because he opened his eyes and smiled.

"That's what I'd like to see every time I wake up."

He was very apologetic about falling asleep, and I assured him it was not only alright, but it made me feel good he was comfortable enough with me to do that. Dinner with Marc in my apartment was cozy and intimate. I had visions of doing this over and over again. I could really enjoy taking care of this man.

After dinner, I allowed him to help me with the dishes. Not much of a chore put them in the dishwasher and press a button. I had done all the pots and pans earlier. Then we lounged around and watched some television. Marc seemed relaxed and content. When it was time to go, he gave me a kiss.

"I had a wonderful time today, Catherine, a really wonderful time."

That earned him a kiss, and I was snuggled in his arms.

"What do I owe you for that great dinner?"

I looked at my bedroom door. Marc followed my gaze and threw up his hands.

"Oh, alright, if you must."

I was about to answer him but was interrupted by a long, passionate kiss. And then, I was in his arms and being carried into my bedroom. Now, I was twice as glad he had taken a nap earlier.

Monday morning, Marc took his time. I made breakfast for the two of us and asked him if he was going to work in the casual clothes he was wearing. Marc said he'd call Sara and tell her he'd be late and then go home and change. He didn't want to leave me any earlier than absolutely necessary.

At the office, it was just like the previous week. We were so busy Marc, and I didn't see each other much, but he did manage to wave and smile at me at least once a day. Marc stayed late at work almost every night, and we only managed to have dinner together once that week. Before we knew it, it was Saturday and Marc was back in his own office trying to catch up.

Around twelve o'clock, Marc called. He asked me if I had any plans for tonight.

"Marc, I haven't had plans for a Saturday night since we got together."

"Why don't you go over to my apartment? I'll have the doorman let you in. I'll be home around eleven. And, why don't you bring something to wear to work on Monday?"

I agreed immediately. I packed a bag as quickly as I could. On the way over to his place, I stopped and did some shopping. I knew he had the necessary pots, pans, and utensils there, probably never used, but I didn't know what kind of food stuff was available, so I bought everything I thought I would need. I also picked up a couple of bottles of wine and some very sweet desserts.

When Marc came home, I had dinner ready. I made sure it wasn't too heavy. I knew he would be tired and wouldn't want to eat much. But, he acted like it was a feast. I knew he was pleased, and that pleased me. We didn't make love that night.

No, that's wrong, we didn't have sex that night. But Marc fell asleep with his arms wrapped around me and it was as close to making love as he was capable of, and it more than satisfied me. Sunday, I let him sleep late. It paid big benefits later.

When he was done with his shower, I had a lovely brunch all ready for him. Just as last Sunday, we lounged around the apartment until dinner time. This time, I made the same roast he had complimented Elizabeth on when we had dinner at her house.

"I can't tell the difference between your roast and Beth's,"

I informed him our mother had made both of us pay attention in the kitchen.

"Even though you two intend to spend your days in some office, you better learn how to feed your man," she had told us over and over.

"Smart lady! Now I know where your smarts come from."

Sunday night, we made love in his bed.

The following week was just as hectic as the previous two. On Wednesday, Marc made an announcement.

"We will be moving to our new quarters in three weeks. That Monday, we need to come in early and pack everything in boxes that will be supplied by the movers. Since it's a major move, we won't have any offices to work in on Tuesday, so we'll have the day off. And, since we have the day off, I've planned a team outing for Monday night. After we've packed up our offices, you can go home and change for dinner and dancing."

And he added, "The dancing part was Catherine's idea."

Then Marc informed me he had a speaking engagement in Norfolk, Virginia the weekend before that. I was not sure if I was invited, and I didn't want to ask. He apologized for not letting me know sooner.

"I'll have Marcie fax you a copy of my upcoming schedule, so you wouldn't be caught by surprise."

I still wasn't sure if I was invited, until he asked, "Are you going to wear the same gown you wore in Memphis?"

"If it pleases My Lord."

Marc's smile was my answer. Then he told me he didn't have any clients in the Norfolk area, so this would be the banquet only.

"We can fly in late Saturday morning and leave when we wake up on Sunday."

It sounded fantastic.

Friday, I went straight home from work, packed a bag and spent the entire weekend at Marc's place. Saturday, Marc was in his office as usual, so I packed a box lunch and drove over there to surprise him. Just before I entered his parking lot, I had a thought.

Do I really have the right to drop in on him unannounced? Am I taking too much liberty?

I sat in my car for ten minutes trying to make a decision.

"What are you afraid of Catherine? Afraid you'll catch him doing something wrong? Do you trust this man or not?"

I made up my mind and walked into the front door.

"Catherine Jensen for Marco Antonelli," I announced to the security guard.

After a brief phone call, he handed me a Visitors Pass and instructed me to sign in. Two minutes later a young man got off the elevator to escort me to Marc's offices. There was genuine surprise on Marc's face.

"And to what do I owe the pleasure of your company this afternoon?"

I held up the bag I was carrying.

"Lunch!"

I was rewarded with a great big smile. While I set out our mini lunch, Marc excused himself for a moment. When he came back into his office, he said, "Catherine, you couldn't have picked a better day. I really could use this break right now. It's been a hellish morning."

I couldn't have been more pleased. I asked him what was going on, and he told me all about the problems he was having with a new system they were getting ready to install for a client. I felt I was a real part of his life. I didn't have any knowledge of what he was talking about, but he was trying to involve me in what he did.

When he couldn't stall any longer and knew he had to go back to work, he called a young man into his office.

"Go with Tim. I'll say goodbye after you're done."

Not knowing what he meant, but not wanting to distract him from his business, I went with the young man. He took me into a small room and asked me to stand in front of a camera. I pouted.

"If I knew I was going to have my picture taken, I would have prepared."

The young man smiled.

"Ms. Jensen, don't you fret. You look mighty fine, ma'am!"

After the picture was taken and the young man had fiddled with some equipment, he handed me an ID Card.

"This will get you past the guard downstairs. You'll still have to sign in at night and on weekends, but you won't have to wait for someone to come down and escort you."

Well, I guess that answers that question.

Marc has just given you permission to walk in on him anytime I pleased. That has to count for something. When I was brought back to Marc, he was hunched over a conference table with a half dozen other men. They all looked worried.

"Marc, you seem busy, I'd better go."

Marc just nodded absentmindedly. Suddenly, he turned toward me.

"No, wait! You're a numbers person, maybe a fresh set of eyes will see something we missed."

I protested I didn't know anything about his business, and not much about computer systems, but Marc said it was just a formula, something like the ones we use at Dillman.

"We put a set of values into the computer, the computer does all the calculations, and we expect a certain value out. But we keep getting the wrong answer, and we can't seem to track down the problem."

The first question I had to ask, "If you know what the answer is, why do the calculation?"

"It's a test formula. We use a set series of values to ensure the programs and equipment were running correctly."

He handed me a chart and explained what the computer was doing. I asked him for a calculator and a copy of the formula, so I could track each part separately. Everyone in the room laughed.

"It would take you a month to run those numbers by hand. The computer does it in a couple of minutes."

I looked over the flow chart and started asking questions.

"Equipment OK? Right formula? Programs OK?"

To each question, I got the same answer.

"Checked and rechecked" Ran it on three different systems, the same result."

I looked over the flow charts, and only one thing made any sense.

"Don't you guys have a saying: Garbage in, garbage out?"

"True, Catherine. But those input specs come directly from the manufacturer."

"And what makes you think they're right?"

Marc looked at me with the weirdest expression. He turned back to the table and started leafing through papers. He picked up one and then another and put them down. Picked another one up and returned it to the pile, then picked it up again. I could see the wheels turning in his head as he did mental calculations. He slid the paper across the table to one of his guys.

"Check the output on this, all three units."

Two of the men ran out of the room with the spec sheet. Marc turned to the remaining people, "I told you she was as smart as she was beautiful."

"True on both accounts boss," one of the older men said, "But if she's so smart, what is she doing with you?"

Marc laughed and said he'd better get me out of there before I caught wise. Back in his office, I said to him, "Told you I was going to become so indispensable you wouldn't dare dump me,"

Marc's smile was all the reward I needed. While we waited for the test results, I showed Marc my new ID card and asked what that was about.

"It just means you won't have to wait for someone to come downstairs and escort you up here. You have access to my offices, twenty-four/ seven."

"Aren't you afraid I'll walk in at the wrong time?"

"There is no wrong time for you to surprise me with a visit, Catherine."

One of Marc's people came into the office and announced the specs were indeed off, by a factor of five. Marc told him to make the adjustments and run the programs. Marc turned his attention back to me.

"My reward for being involved with such an intelligent lady is I get to take the rest of the day off and take this Pretty Lady to a fabulous dinner and a trip to the 88's. It will take a couple of hours for the programs to run. Why don't you go home, pick out something sexy and meet me back at my apartment."

Then, he took an envelope from his desk drawer and handed it to me. It contained a key.

"This is my spare key to my apartment. On the way out this morning, I left word with Building Security you have unrestricted access. Now, you can surprise me at home too."

Marc had just told me I could walk in on him, unannounced, at any time, at work or at home.

What more proof could I want?

That evening we had dinner at Danielle's Kitchen, the most fabulous restaurant in Florida. I knew you had to make reservations weeks in advance there, and I was surprised. I was sure Marc hadn't anticipated having tonight off. The maite'd greeted Marc warmly and told him it has been too long since his last visit. The bartender and the staff also seemed to know Marc well. Naturally, I was curious. Marc didn't bother to explain, and I was sure he was gauging my reaction. Remembering the advice I had received from Danielle and the other gals, I decided to ask him why he was so well known here.

"Because I own a piece of this place."

I looked at him and then took a good look around the restaurant. It was the most beautiful, upscale dining room I had ever seen. The staff was impeccably dressed, and the service was top drawer. Marc told me the food was equally as fabulous as the décor and the service.

"Nick Amonti had been in the restaurant business before he made his money. He wanted to open a great restaurant here in Fort Lauderdale, and because he intended to name it after his wife, he wanted it to be perfect. He financed the entire project and enlisted some of his friends to help.

Terry Daniels supplied the kitchen equipment, I did the reservation, seating, back office computers and software. My friend, Tony Marchetti built the place, practically on his own, took him an entire year.

Cindy's husband Dan did the legal work, getting the permits and licenses and such and Stacey designed the uniforms.

As a reward for the fantastic job we did, Nick rewarded four of us with a piece of the project. Stacey refused to take a share because she felt she owed her entire career to Nick. We each own ten percent of the restaurant and Nick transferred the other sixty percent into Danielle's name. One of the perks of being an owner is I can get a table here without a reservation anytime I wished."

Dinner was fabulous, and when it was time to leave, Marc asked Andrei, the maitre'd for the key to the wine cellar. It wasn't really a cellar. There are no basements in south Florida, it was a separate room off the dining room. In addition to the racks and racks of red wine, it had a walk in cooler for the whites and a large space in the middle that could be used as a private dining room. After giving me the tour, Marc asked, "Do you think the gang would enjoy having our Team Morale Booster Dinner here?"

"Are you kidding?" I answered, "Dinner in a private wine cellar at the most fabulous restaurant in all of Florida? Who wouldn't want that?"

Marc smiled and said it could be arranged. I stayed with Marc that night and Sunday we again just lounged around his apartment.

I could get used to this!

Chapter 28 – Busy Time

The next week was very busy. Marc spent most of his time with Ben, the new SVP of Client Services, our new boss. We were all preparing for our move to the new offices and getting ready for what was probably going to be our last Team Morale Booster Party.

On a Monday, two weeks before the move, Marc had to go to Pittsburg to deal with one of Antonelli System's clients. He wouldn't be back until Tuesday afternoon. After I kissed him goodbye in his apartment, he left for the airport. I got ready and went to work. Ted was waiting for me when I arrived at the office. He seemed upset and unsure of himself. He followed me into my office and sat down opposite me at my desk.

"Catherine, are we friends, I mean, really friends?"

I had to think about that. We both were acting like nothing had ever happened. We were trying very hard to put Nashville behind us, but there was that lingering feeling of disappointment in him. And, I knew the original team still had doubts about Ted and if I would ever get over the hurt he had caused me.

Finally, I answered, "Yes Ted, I think we are friends, again."

Ted said he had to talk to someone, and I was the only one he could trust. I asked if it was business and he said it was personal, very personal. I reminded him the office was for business only and suggested we have lunch together. He eagerly agreed and went back to his own office.

Before I had a chance to settle in for the day's work, my phone rang. It was Jonathon from Memphis. He told me he was in town for the seminar he had told me about and asked if we could get together. I told him I had lunch plans for today, but I was free tomorrow. Jonathon said his lunch breaks were very short, and he wouldn't have time to travel across town to meet me. Instead, he suggested dinner tonight. I accepted and told him to pick me up at the office at six.

As soon as I hung up the phone, I realized I had made a big mistake. Marc would not be happy. But, I didn't want to call Jonathan back and cancel. I had to give this some thought. Just before Ted and I left for lunch, Jonathon called back. He said the seminar was ending later than he expected and could he pick me up at seven instead.

I asked him what restaurant we were going to.

"The hotel I'm staying at has a very nice restaurant upstairs, and I thought it would be nice and quiet there."

The only hotel in town I knew of that had a restaurant upstairs was the Hyatt on SE 17ᵗʰ Street, and that particular restaurant was very romantic. I told Jonathan I would meet him at his hotel, and I would call his room when I arrived. That seemed to please him.

When Ted came by my office to take me to lunch, he asked if we could go to a place where we wouldn't be disturbed. When I asked if he meant La Chez, he didn't think it was humorous. Whatever was bothering Ted, it was serious.

I took him to the Ice House, the burgers and beer place Ron had taken me to the night Marc joined us. The booths there would be quiet and private. Once we were settled and the food ordered, Ted began to tell me about his problem.

"Do you remember the girl I took to the last company banquet?"

I remembered her well, not Ted's regular fare. Constance was bright, poised, interesting and classy. The only thing this lady had in common with Ted's other dates was she was beautiful.

"I remember, Ted. Not your standard type of date. We were all surprised when you showed up with her."

Ted nodded.

"You're right. Connie is not like most of the girls I date. In fact, she has a lot in common with you. That's what attracted me to her. I've been taking her to the dinners we had with Marc's friends and with the new clients. Her class was what I thought everyone would expect from a man in my position."

"Good thinking Ted, but that is a very crass thing to do. It sounds like you're just using her."

"It is very crass, isn't it?"

I just nodded and asked him what was going on.

"I took Connie to a dinner Saturday night, with a new, important client and everything went really well. When I was taking her home, she told him she felt like a very expensive tuxedo. A special tuxedo I keep in the back of my closet and only wore when I wanted to impress someone. And if I didn't want more of a relationship than that with her, she was going to move on. The truth is she was right."

"It sounds like you really care for this girl, Ted, so what's the problem?"

What Ted said next was a revelation.

"Catherine, I've always believed men and women weren't meant to be monogamous. I believed everyone, men and women alike had multiple lovers, even if they were in a serious relationship. That's why I never got serious with any woman. No woman had ever screwed me, but it had happened to friends I knew, and men I knew who were in serious, intimate relationships, cheated on their women. If you didn't get serious, you couldn't get hurt."

What is he saying? How can he feel that way? Can a man be as frightened as I am? Can Marc's fear of not being trusted be as awful as my fear?

"Catherine, I'm not trying to make excuses for what I did in Nashville. I'll always regret that. But part of my justification was that I didn't believe a man like Marc could be faithful to one woman. And considering how little time you two spent together, I was pretty sure you had someone else also."

"Ted, our limited time together was circumstances."

"I know that now. Marc explained everything at that lunch we had together the Monday after Nashville. Catherine," he asked tentatively, "I now realize you are serious about Marc, probably thinking about spending the rest of your life with him. Do you really believe you will be faithful to him forever?"

Considering I was about to have dinner with a very good looking and personable man, who had shown a real interest in me, at a very romantic restaurant, in a little over six hours from now, while my lover was out of town, how do I answer that?

"Ted I don't know what's going to happen ten years from now, or ten days from now, or even ten minutes from now. The only thing I know is I want this man to love me, and I will do whatever is necessary to make sure he stays in love with me. I believe if I ever did cheat on Marc, I could never again be able to accept his love. And I'm not about to give that up."

"What do I do?" Ted asked.

"You start by telling her the truth. You tell her how you feel about her, but you're afraid of a real relationship. You tell her you want a real relationship with her, and you intend to do whatever it takes to be faithful to her, and you plan to make her so happy she wouldn't want to be unfaithful to you. It's a gamble, Ted, but the odds are on your side."

The conversation continued on the same plain for a while and then we headed back to the office. I made a few phone calls and went back to work. Around four o'clock, Marc called to say he missed me. I told him I was having dinner with Jonathon and would be home before eleven. I didn't get a good read on Marc's attitude about my news.

At five o'clock, I went home to get changed. It took a while for me to decide what I was going to wear. I was sure Marc wouldn't want me to dress down to discourage Jonathan, but I wasn't about to dress up either. I picked a pretty but conservative dress, redid my makeup and hair and headed for the Hyatt.

When I arrived, I used the house phone to call Jonathan's room. He said he wasn't quite ready and why didn't I come up while he finished up. I told him I'd be perfectly safe in the hotel bar, and that's where he should meet me. He sounded disappointed. When he arrived at the bar, it was evident he was unhappy, but, that's life!

Dinner was pleasant, and when we said goodnight I told Jonathan when Marc got back, I was sure he would want to have dinner with him before he goes back to Memphis. When I got home, I was very pleased with myself. But, Ted's story this afternoon kept reverberating around in my head.

A male version of Catherine Jensen. I didn't have as many boyfriends as Ted had girlfriends, but the theory was the same. Never get close enough to get hurt. Poor Ted!

Tuesday, I left work early, went to Marc's apartment and started preparing dinner. Marc's plane was due in around four, and he would be home before five. When he opened the apartment door, he was genuinely surprised. Taking a deep breath, he asked, "Another one of your mother's recipes?"

I nodded and gave him a welcome home kiss.

"A man could get used to this."

"That's the plan, Mr. Antonelli."

Marc asked if he had time for a shower. I told him the Lord of the Manor could dine at his convenience. After his shower, Marc helped me set the table. He casually asked how dinner went last night. I told him it was fun, and it filled up the time while he was away. He asked if Jonathan behaved himself.

"Of course, he did, what did you expect him to do, jump me in the restaurant?"

Marc's answer made me warm all over.

"The thought has crossed my mind on more than one occasion."

I knew Marc wanted details, but he wasn't going to ask, so I volunteered.

"I met Jonathan at his hotel, The Hyatt on SE 17th Street and we had dinner upstairs."

Marc and I had dined there, and he knew how romantic it was. I gave him a few minutes to think about that.

"Cindy thinks he's cute."

"When did Cindy meet him?"

I went over to him and put my arm around his neck and looked directly into his eyes.

"Marc, I have heard every word you have ever said to me, but more importantly, I understood them. Did you really think I would agree to have dinner in a romantic restaurant alone, with a man who has shown an interest in me? I asked Dan and Cindy to join us."

Again, Marc's answer was a kiss. Dinner was cozy. Marc told me about his trip.

"The problem you helped solve at the office on Saturday was the key to the entire system. We would have figured it out eventually, but your fresh pair of eyes opinion saved us weeks, maybe months of work."

"I keep telling you Marc, indispensable!"

"You already are, Catherine, and if you keep spoiling me like this, I'll make sure you never get away from me."

After dinner, I allowed Marc to help with the dishes, just to keep him close to me. Then we went into the living room to relax and enjoy each other's company. Marc sat on the couch, and I sat on his lap.

I told him about my lunch date with Ted. Marc thought he was probably sincere in what he told me.

"Do you remember when I told you all men are like that until someone special comes into their lives? Maybe Connie was the one."

I wanted to know if there was anything we could do to help Ted.

"The only thing is to treat Ted as a friend and treat Connie as if she's your friend's girl and not just his date."

That made sense. But, now that we were talking about relationships, I had a question of my own.

"Marc, Can I ask you something?"

"Anything."

This was not going to be easy, but I had to know.

"Why didn't you question me about my date with Jonathan?"

"What kind of questions?"

Again, I chose my words carefully.

"When you called me from Pittsburg, and I told you I was having dinner with Jonathon, why didn't you tell me I shouldn't do that? After all of your talks about avoiding situations and seeming available, it must have bothered you. And when you got home tonight, why didn't you ask what we did last night and why didn't you want to know what made me decide to have dinner with him alone when you were out of town?"

"You said Dan and Cindy were with you."

"But, you didn't know that when you called, and you didn't know that when you first got home. You specifically said, do lunch not dinner in a situation like that. You said it's so easy to appear available even when you're not. You said it was impossible to know what would bring on temptation. You must have wondered what went on between us. You must have been upset I ignored your rules. Why didn't you talk to me about it?"

Again, he was thoughtful before he answered.

"That question has many parts. Yes, when I called, and you told me you were having dinner with Jonathan, I was unhappy. But that was not a discussion for the phone. It had to wait until we were face to face.

"Then, when I walked in the door tonight and saw you here preparing dinner, I couldn't ruin your surprise and the work you put into it. If you didn't mention that Dan and Cindy were with you, we would have had a discussion, but not until after dinner.

"You looked so happy to see me, and you had gone to so much trouble to prepare that wonderful meal for me, I wasn't about to spoil it."

As always, everything he said made sense. But, I had more questions. I asked him about his rules.

"Do you really believe such strict rules are necessary, and if I don't agree, where does that leave us?"

"Excellent question. First, the only reason I told you about my rules, was because you asked me how I avoided temptation. If you believe for a minute I will never be tempted by another woman, or if you think some devious woman couldn't possibly maneuver me into a situation I shouldn't be in, you are not dealing with reality.

194

"During my marriage and the few short relationships I've had since, I decided it was better to avoid a situation than to try to resist it. I developed the rules I told you about to keep me out of trouble.

"Remember, I told you, fidelity has many faces. Not only do I want to avoid being in a situation with another woman, but I never want any other woman to think she has a chance with me."

Marc looked directly into my eyes.

"But, you have to understand, Catherine, they are my rules. Rules for me to live by. I would never demand, or even suggest you follow them.

"If you don't believe they're necessary, but followed them because that's what I wanted, then they would become restrictive, and you would eventually resent them, and that would definitely affect our relationship.

"I'm sure you have your own set of rules you follow. After being free to date anyone you wanted for fifteen to twenty years, I'm sure you know how to protect yourself. All I ask is you think about what you do, not in terms of whether I'd be upset or not, but how what you do would affect what we have together. You're such an honest person any indiscretion would weigh on you and you are such an open person it would be impossible for you to keep it from me."

Marc took a minute before he asked a question.

"What made you decide to invite Dan and Cindy? Was it because you thought it was a better idea not to have dinner alone with Jonathan, or was it because you thought I'd be angry if you did. That's a vital question you have to answer for yourself. And what would you have done if they weren't available."

I wanted to answer that as honestly as I could.

"After I agreed to dinner with Jonathan and hung up, I just thought I had made a mistake. I didn't think about why. I thought about calling him and canceling, but then I thought about Dan and Cindy. I told Cindy I had a dinner date with a man, you were out of town, and I didn't want to go alone. I had already had a backup plan if they weren't available. Susan would never have turned me down, but I thought Cindy and Dan were closer to Jonathan's age, and they would be better company."

I tried to judge his reaction and finally decided to tell him the rest.

"Jonathan called me during his lunch break this afternoon. He said he just wanted to thank me for a lovely evening. But, before he hung up, he asked me if I had a problem with him. When I asked him what he meant, he said he just wanted to know why I felt it necessary to be chaperoned last night."

Marc smiled, and before he had a chance to say anything, I continued.

"I was surprised by his question and thought about it before I answered. I told him I had never given it a thought. It was just since Marc and I got together, I've never had the desire to have dinner alone with any man but you. And, as I was saying that, I realized it was true."

It was a while before either of us spoke again. Then, what he said made me understand Marc's true feelings.

"Catherine, I've told you this before. You are a beautiful, sensuous, classy woman. You are intelligent, poised and elegant. You will attract the attention of men, and you will probably enjoy that attention. I can deal with that. I promise I have no problem with the attention you receive from other men.

"And, I can deal with the fact it makes you feel good. Everyone wants to feel attractive. I don't consider that a problem in any way. But, if you crave that attention, if you go out and seek that attention if you give an indication you want that attention from any man other than me, then we have a problem."

Marc looked directly into my eyes again.

"I don't see you like that. I think you enjoyed the attention you received from Jonathan in Memphis, but it wouldn't have upset you if he completely ignored you. I don't think you're the kind of woman that constantly needs reinforcement of her attraction to men. But, knowing you are the type of woman that will continually receive that attention, I have to accept that fact and believe it has no other meaning to you."

It was very obvious to me that faith in each other worked both ways. And after this discussion, I wanted to know why I agreed to dinner with Jonathan so quickly and why I changed my mind. I had a feeling the answer to those two questions was going to be crucial to my relationship with Marc.

Then I asked him if he thought I had anything to worry about with Jonathon.

"When I called his room to tell him I was there he suggested I come up while he got ready, and he sounded disappointed when I refused, and he really seemed disappointed when he found out Dan and Cindy were going to join us. He also said when I told him, in Memphis, I was in a relationship he didn't realize I meant you."

Then, Marc asked me if it was important that I knew how the evening would have gone if I hadn't invited Dan and Cindy? I thought about that and said I wasn't sure how to tell when I should take precautions.

Marc's answer was quick and to the point.

"Always as far as I'm concerned! It's the only way to be sure. But, as far as you're concerned, that's up to you. Remember, Catherine, it's not only what you might get involved in, what you might do, but how you are perceived. And, that's not always under your control.

"To some men, agreeing to a date when your guy is out of town is enough to make you look available to him. To others, it might take more than that. A simple thank you, a good night peck on the check might do it. When you agreed to dinner with me out of town and agreed to meet at his hotel, you gave an indication you might be available. When you showed up with another couple, you slammed the door in his face. No matter what his intentions were, you said no in advance."

Then, Marc took me by the hand and led me into his bedroom, and for the first time in our relationship, we made love in the middle of the week.

Thursday evening Marc and I had dinner with Jonathan. His attitude toward me seemed to be completely different, more respectful. Maybe Marc was right. I had slammed the door in his face. And that's the way it should be.

Saturday, Marc and I flew to Norfolk for Marc's speaking engagement. Before we left the hotel for the banquet, I had asked Marc if he intended to tell the story about your sister's panties. When he said he always told that story, I slid my hand into his jacket pocket and took out the panties he had secluded there. I flipped them across the room, and when I got an inquisitive look from Marc, I opened my purse and produced a pair of my black lace panties.

"Just so you remember mine are the only ladies panties you're allowed to touch."

Marc was as good as he was in Memphis and although his speech was on a different subject, he held the attention of the audience just as easily as he did the previous time. Of course, he interspersed his speech with jokes and stories, and the 'your sister's panties' story got the biggest laugh. And, just as he did in Memphis, he sat down after his speech and then got up again to tell them the other part of the story. Again, he brought the house down.

On the flight home, I asked Marc what was going to happen to us after he left Dillman. I reminded him he had less than ninety days left.

"We'll be like every other couple that only saw each other at night and on weekends. We really don't get to see each other much at work, because I'm was always running over to the new plant or meeting with someone. But when I'm was finished with Dillman, my Saturday's would be free."

I thought that was a fair compromise.

Chapter 29 – Marc's Last Team Party

We were moving to our new offices. Ben's office was double the size of the other vice president's offices. On one side of the large space would be a typical office setup. On the other side would be a small conference area where Ben could confer with clients and his staff.

Sara also managed to find the perfect receptionist. Caitlyn was mid-forties, pretty, but not gorgeous, friendly, patient and experienced. Our new offices would be guarded by a large marble Reception Desk in the elevator lobby, and Caitlyn was the perfect gatekeeper. Jennifer had five people in her department, but Susan hadn't yet found anyone willing to move over to Specs. Brian moved up to Senior Analyst, and Ted and Artie had found new replacements. That brought the team count to twenty-six. With spouses and dates, there would be forty-eight of us at the party.

Marc had arranged for dinner at a small ballroom at the Hyatt. The wine cellar at Danielle's Kitchen was too small for all of us, but Marc said we were going to have a mini party there with just the original team before he left Dillman Brothers. After dinner, we were all going to the 88's to dance. Monday was always slow there, and the owner had closed the club to all but a small group of regulars. It promised to be a fun night.

Marc suggested I bring what I intend to wear to the party over to his place this weekend. He said I could change there Monday afternoon after we were finished packing up our offices. He asked if I decided what I was going to wear and I told him I had a few nice choices I was considering. With a wicked grin, he asked if I would consider the red dress I wore to dinner on Friday night in Memphis.

I had considered that particular dress. I knew it dazzled him in Memphis, but I thought it might be a little too sexy for a company affair. Then I thought about the gown Danielle had given me to wear for the company banquet. That was even sexier.

"I'll bring it with me on Friday, and whether or not I wear it on Monday would depend on your behavior over the weekend."

That brought out a warm smile, and I knew in my heart Marc, and I were going to be together forever.

Monday, everyone was in the office early. Starting around two in the afternoon, as they finished their packing, they began to drift out and go home to change. We were all scheduled to meet in the lobby of the new plant at six o'clock.

Marc and I left around three thirty. I did wear the red dress I had worn in Memphis and Marc's approval was evident. We were quiet as he drove us back to the office. Everything that had to be said between us had been said. We were a couple in love, but how long we would remain a couple was a decision that couldn't be decided with more words. We needed a sign, something to prove to both of us we truly believed in each other.

The bus was just pulling into the parking lot as we arrived back at the office. Marc gathered everyone up and sent them out to board. On the way to the hotel, Marc took the driver's microphone and gave a short speech. He stressed the reason for this party was to bring the new members of the team into the fold.

"I expect you all to mingle and get to know each other. This team is now four times its original size, and the spirit of camaraderie and teamwork will be more important than ever. Other than that, the plan is to have fun, but easy on the booze."

Dinner was fun. The original team sat together, and Marc reminded us it was our job to make the newer members of the team feel like they belonged and contributed. Move around and talk to everyone he said. After dinner, we boarded the bus for the trip to the 88's.

Seven tables had been set up near the bandstand just for us. Marc had hired the weekend combo for the night. The regulars allowed in that night were all people Marc, and I knew well. It promised to be a fun night. Five tables were more than enough to handle our group, but Marc wanted seven, explaining the empty chairs at each table were so we could move around and sit with the newer people.

As soon as we were all seated, Annie came bouncing over. Looking over the crowd, she announced.

"Ok, I can deal with this!"

Then she told everyone about the Amonti Rule and added, "This was a very friendly place, and all of the men here tonight are gentleman and all of the ladies are ladies, so don't be afraid to dance with anyone. Alright everyone, let's get that first dance over with, we're here to party!" and she was gone.

Almost everyone got up to dance. As Marc and I headed for the dance floor, I noticed Ted and Constance were one of the few couples that didn't leave the table. After the first dance, we started moving around and changing partners. Some of the regulars came over and joined us. Of course, Marc's second dance was with Annie.

Later, when the band played a hold your partner and sway type song, Ted and Constance did move to the dance floor, and they held each other romantically. The party moved right along, and it was having the desired effect. We all changed seats, occasionally so we could mingle with everyone there. The new people seemed to feel like they fit in and I thought this was going to work out well.

I had intended to dance with Ted, as a further indicator all was well between us, but although Connie had danced with Marc, Tim and a couple of the club's regulars, Ted so far hadn't danced except that one time. I asked Bobby to play a meringue and grabbed Ted's hand,

"Let's go, Ted!"

Ted looked up at me.

"Catherine, I don't know how to dance."

I pulled him out of his seat.

"It's about time you learned," and I dragged him onto the dance floor.

The basic steps of the meringue aren't very hard to master, and it became evident Ted had rhythm. Learning to dance should come easily to him. He did very well, and the way we laughed and carried on, it had to be evident to everyone there all was well between us. When we got back to the table, I looked around, and when I spotted Annie and Billy dancing together, I pointed them out.

"Connie, see that guy dancing with Annie? Make sure you dance with him tonight. And, then bring him back here and tell him Ted needs dance lessons. Billy is the best teacher around."

Ted looked at me, wondering what I was doing.

"Ted, all women love to dance, and if you intend to stay with this lady, learning how to dance would be a good sign of your intentions."

Ted looked shocked, but Connie smiled.

"Thanks, Catherine. I was trying to think about how to bring that subject up."

Later, I grabbed Billy and brought him over to the table. He asked Connie to dance, and when they returned, I asked how it went. Connie's eyes shined.

"WOW!"

Billy was very used to the accolades he received from a new dance partner, smiled his gratitude and told Ted he gave dance lessons every Saturday and Sunday morning right here at the club. Ted glanced at me, not in a friendly manner, but after looking at the expression in Connie's eyes, he said, "We'll be there."

Connie smiled, I smiled and finally Ted smiled. Having completed my good deed for the day, I was about to leave them alone when I heard Ted say to Connie, "I did promise to do whatever it takes."

I didn't stay around to hear any more. It was turning out to be a super night. I found Marc by the piano. I asked Bobby to play something mellow, and I took Marc onto the dance floor. Marc congratulated me and when I inquired as to what for, he said, "That little spectacle you and Ted put on should put Nashville to bed once and for all."

"How do you know that was my intention?"

"My assumption is based on the best information I have available."

And then he laughed, long and hard.

He was teasing me, but it made me happy. Marc really did know me, and I was sure I was getting to know him just as well. After the dance, Marc said we had to mingle, and we went our separate ways to spend time with our new team members. All of the original team had heeded Marc's words and had been circulating among the new people. When I got back to the table that Connie and Ted had been sitting at, Connie was alone. Ted was over talking to Brian and two of the new Junior Analysts. Connie asked me if I had a minute to talk.

"Ted told me about your lunch date last week. I think it had a huge impact on his thinking, and if it does work out between the two of us, you would be responsible for a large part of it. Ted agreeing to dance lessons makes me believe he was serious. I feel better about our relationship than I ever have before."

"Connie, the advice I gave Ted came from my own experience. My thinking was exactly like Teds, and only now am I allowing myself to trust a man and my own judgment of him. I like Ted, and I admit I agree with Marc, if I had met Ted under different circumstances, I might have been interested in dating him. But now, I thought we could be good friends."

"Even after Nashville?" Connie said, "Ted told me if we were going to have a real relationship it had to start with complete honesty. He told me the entire story of his pursuit of you from the beginning and of everything he did in Nashville and the days after. He also told me about the meeting you had about the incident and the meeting he had with Marc about it. He said he thought you were so in love with Marc that for the sake of the team, you would try to deal with it."

Connie looked over at Ted talking to one of the new assistants.

"I responded to Ted's honesty by telling him things about my relationships I am not particularly proud of. I think the mutual confessions helped us start a new relationship. Dancing with Ted and bringing Billy over to talk Ted into dance lessons indicates your friendship was more than a show for the sake of the team."

"It's difficult not to like Ted, and I could understand how it was so easy for him to find all of those women to go out with him. We're not there yet, but I think Ted and I could still be good friends, and now that I had solved my own problems about trusting relationships I was sure Ted could too. I think you're just what Ted needs in his life. I'm rooting for you two to make it."

I also told her I would be available if she ever wanted to talk. Our conversation was interrupted by Ted.

"The two women who know me better than anyone else in the entire world. Trading war stories about me?"

"Ted, honey that's something only Catherine and I will ever know!"

That brought smiles from all three of us. I excused myself and looked around for someone I hadn't mingled with yet.

Before I had a chance to leave, Ted gave me a kiss on the check.

"Thanks, beautiful, I owe ya!"

"I'll keep it in the bank for a rainy day," I replied and then moved two tables over to talk to Caitlyn.

Everyone seemed to be having a good time. The new people seemed to be outgoing, and I thought they might fit right in with the rest of us.

Marc had been doing his best, going from table to table talking to everyone and Ben had been on the move all night also. I had danced with most of the new male members of the team and some of the female member's dates and husbands. Marc said involving the spouses and dates helped with the feeling of camaraderie. I was beginning to agree.

Every time I glanced in Marc's direction, I got a big smile. Just when I was about to leave Caitlyn and find another member I hadn't talked to yet, Susan passed by. She said she was going to make a pit stop, and I decided to join her. On our way to the ladies room, Susan remarked how well the party seemed to be going, and she also commented on my dance with Ted.

"Is it as good between you two as it seems?"

"It's getting better all the time. Things between Marc and me are going so well it's difficult to stay mad at Ted. In some ways, it may even have helped our relationship for the long term. And, it looks like Ted has finally found someone special. I hope it works out for him, she seems really nice."

Considering the 88's was just a Piano Bar, the place was very nice, clean and pleasant. The restrooms were large and done up nicely, and you had to pass through a foyer to get to them. The foyer was sort of an oasis away from the main room and was large and well appointed. Subdued lighting, pictures on the walls, carpet on the floor and benches along the walls, where you can rest, and maybe take your shoes off for a few moments.

Susan and I were leaving the ladies room and heading back through the foyer when Susan stopped dead in her tracks. I looked at her, and seeing the expression on her face, I glanced in the direction she was looking in.

No, no, no this can't be happening. It can't!

Chapter 30 - The Other Incident

There in the corner of the foyer was Annie, cuddled tightly in a man's arms and the man was...Marc! I wanted to run away screaming. I wanted to hide. I wanted to pretend I hadn't seen this.

"No Catherine, you can't! You have to know! Look him right in the eye, that's what Danielle had said!"

I motioned for Susan to go back to the others and I walked toward Annie and Marc. As I approached, he lifted his head and looked directly at me. The lighting wasn't all that good, and I couldn't see his eyes. As I got closer, I tried to see something there. Nothing! There was nothing there I could understand, but that was good, wasn't it? Because what I didn't see was...guilt.

"Faith, Catherine. You have to have faith or it will never work between you."

When I was close to them, I expected Marc to say something, but before I knew what I was doing, my mouth opened and three words came tumbling out.

"Can I help?"

Marc took a half step back from Annie. He lifted her chin with his hand so she could look into his eyes.

"Annie, talk to Catherine. Maybe she can help. She's the smartest lady I've ever met. And, she's good people, Annie. Talk to her, this can't go on any longer. It has to be settled."

Annie, through her tears, said, "I don't want to bother anyone else with my problems, it's not fair."

I took Annie's hand and made her look at me.

"That's what friends are for, Annie. We are friends, aren't we?"

Annie nodded and allowed me to lead her over to one of the benches in the foyer. I told Marc to scoot.

"This is ladies only!"

Marc turned to go, but before he left, he said, "Tell Annie about our first official date."

That gave me a hint as to what this was all about. I got Annie to focus on me and asked, "Billy?"

"Oh, Catherine," she cried, "I've done everything to tell him I like him, and I want more than to be his dance partner, but he just ignores everything I say to him."

I could feel the pain, and I understood what she must be going through. I tried to think of something to say to make it better. It was obvious Billy liked Annie. It was also obvious that Billy was very shy around women. I thought about what Marc said just before he left us alone. I understood what he was trying to tell me.

"Annie, we all know how shy Billy is. He has no problem asking a girl to dance because he knows he's so good they all want to dance with him. But when it comes to anything else, he doesn't know how to act with girls."

"That's why I've been dropping so many hints. I've been trying to let him know if he asked me out I would say yes."

I asked Annie if she knew how Marc and I got together. She said Marc had never told her about it.

"I was just so happy for him that he found someone special I never thought to ask."

I told her the entire story of the night I suggested Marc look closer to work. Annie couldn't believe what I was saying.

"You made a pass at him?" she said with more than a little surprise in her voice.

I nodded and told her if she really wants a chance with Billy she has to stop dropping hints and tell him exactly how she feels, straight out. Annie said she was afraid.

"What if he said no?"

"If he's going to say no tonight, he'll say no tomorrow, or next week, or next month. Wouldn't it be better to know for sure now, so if he does say no, you can stop tormenting yourself and get on with your life? How long do you intend to put your life on hold hoping Billy would finally get the hint?"

We sat there for a while, and when Annie had gotten control of herself, we went to the ladies room, put cold compresses on her eyes and redid her makeup. When we returned to the main room, Marc was talking to Ben.

I wanted Annie to take some time before talking to Billy, so I brought her over to our table and told Artie this lady needs a dance partner. Artie dutifully got up and took Annie onto the dance floor. Susan looked at me with a hundred questions in her eyes.

"All is well! All is wonderful!" I told her.

That seemed to satisfy her. It seemed Marc and Ben were having a serious conversation, so I continued to mingle. Almost an hour past before I finally got Marc alone, near the piano. He asked if Annie was OK. I told him she was better, but only time would make her OK. He nodded his agreement and thanked me for caring. I told him it was obvious he was in over his head, and I was happy to come to his rescue. That made him laugh.

"You seem to be of the opinion I couldn't handle the situation."

"And just what did you intend to do about it?"

"Probably the same thing you did. Tell her to stop whining and tell the man how she feels."

"Maybe, but what makes you think she'd take that kind of advice from a man?"

Marc thought about it and conceded I was probably right. He pointed to the dance floor. Annie and Billy were dancing together and seemed to be having a serious conversation.

Five minutes later, Annie came running over to us, threw her arms around Marc's neck and planted a killer kiss right on his lips. When she backed off, Marc said, "What was that for?"

Annie, all excited replied, "That's for getting involved with the greatest gal in the entire world."

"I don't deserve to get rewarded for that Annie. Catherine is the best thing that ever happened to me."

Annie was all giggles, and she wanted to get me alone to tell me what happened. Marc refused and said since he was a part of this, he was entitled to know the result. Annie and I looked at each other, and we both shrugged. So, Annie told us both what had happened.

"I did exactly what you said, Catherine. I told him I didn't want to be just another girl he danced with.

"I told him I liked him too much for that, and I wanted to get to know him away from the club. I said I wanted to find out if there could be a special relationship between us. And do you know what he said to me," she added, all excited.

Marc and I both shook our heads and Annie said, "He asked me if I wanted to learn how to boogie?"

I wasn't sure I had heard her right, and if so what that was supposed to mean, but Marc seemed to understand.

"Really! He asked if you wanted to learn how to boogie."

Annie nodded her head and smiled like a school girl on her very first date.

Marc had to explain.

"All of the girls have asked Billy to teach them how to boogie. He's told them all no. He said it's too complicated and would take too many weeks of instruction, and he didn't have the time because of his other dance classes."

Annie was nodding at Marc's explanation.

"Then he asked me if I would have dinner with him tomorrow night so we could talk."

Annie was so excited she was having trouble getting her words out.

"Then he asked me to sit with him."

When we managed to get Annie settled down, I suggested she bring Billy over and sit with us. He'd probably be more comfortable with us than he would be sitting with all the other regulars. Annie beamed and nodded. Then she was gone.

Marc turned to me,

"Does this mean Dillman Bros. can expect your resignation in the morning?"

Surprised at the comment, I asked him, "Why would I resign?"

He answered with a big smile,

"Well, since your new business is going so well, I thought you might want to pursue it full time."

Still not knowing what he meant, I gave him an inquisitive look.

"Your Match Making Business. Susan and Artie, Constance and Ted, Annie and Billy you are three for three so far."

That comment made me giggle. I looked into his eyes and I said as sincerely as I could, "If I go four for four, I promise I'll retire."

Looking right back into my eyes, he said just as sincerely, "In that case, Ms. Jensen, I'll start making arrangements for your retirement party."

Could it possibly get any better than this!

Chapter 31 – After the Party

We stayed until closing. Ben and Marc stood by the door of the bus as people boarded. They said something to everyone and were probably taking a head count to make sure no one got left behind. When we reached Dillman Bros, where everyone had left their cars, Ben and Marc again stood by the door and talked to everyone that got off the bus. I was standing next to Marc, and I realized they were making sure everyone was sober enough to drive home. Everyone passed muster, and when all had left, it was just Ben, his wife, Marc and me.

Marc asked, "What do you think, worth it?"

"Definitely," Ben answered, "And I'll make sure it continues."

After Ben and his wife left, Marc and I headed to his apartment. On the way, I asked what he and Ben meant.

"Ben is convinced these Morale Booster Parties were worth the expense, and he's agreed to keep them going. I'm also sure Ben was the man to lead the department. He believes in the team concept and will keep that going too. I also think Ben will become a real member of the team and not just the boss."

When we got to Marc's apartment, I headed for the bedroom to change. I had brought a special nightie for the occasion. Marc asked me if we could talk first. He poured us each a glass of wine and led me into the living room. I curled up on the couch, making sure I was showing more leg than a proper girl should. I knew Marc liked looking at my legs, and I also allowed him to see I was wearing stockings and not pantyhose. Since his comment when I wore my bikini in Nashville, I tried to dress to please and tease him. It did seem to be working. But, Marc was in a serious mood tonight. Once again, he appeared to take the time to choose his words carefully.

"Catherine, will you tell me what you thought when you saw Annie and me together in the foyer?"

Wow, you didn't expect this. How do you answer that?

Now, I had to choose my words carefully.

"Marc, I know for us to work, I have to be completely truthful with you. So, the answer to your question is when I first saw your arms wrapped around Annie like that, I thought, "Not again." But I remembered all the advice I had received about facing you and asking for an explanation, so I headed over to you to ask what was going on. But on the way over, I thought about the best information I had, and I made an assumption that Annie was in trouble, and you were trying to help her."

Marc thought that over.

"Will you tell me what information you had that led to that assumption?"

I had made my decision so quickly back at the club, I didn't really understand exactly what had created it. But thinking about it now, I had an answer.

"Marc, I know you love Annie, and I know Annie loves you, but I also know you are in love with me, and I know the difference. I also know you are an honorable man and would never turn down a friend in trouble. Annie told me she had made herself available to you, and you didn't take advantage of her then, so why now and why in front of our entire staff? Why would you embarrass me like that? It was so quick I didn't think it out in detail like this, but that's the only thing that made any sense. And, because I am in love with you, I wanted to help you do whatever it was you felt you had to do. That's why I asked you if I could help."

"But it was wrong," he said.

I didn't understand what he meant, but he was quick to explain.

"Everything you just said is right, including the fact I would never want to embarrass you like that. Annie knows I am not available. She may know that more than you do. Annie does love me in a way, and she wants me to be happy, and she knows my happiness lies with you, and she'd never do anything to spoil that. It was just a friendly embrace, with no romantic or sexual connotations. I was just trying to settle her down, but no one knew that except Annie, you and me.

"If someone else had seen us, what would they think? And, even though the three of us know it was innocent, our entire staff and all the regulars were in that club. We both know everyone who was there tonight, and if one of them saw us like that, it would be an embarrassment to you.

I'm sorry for not thinking about that. My only excuse is I was caught off guard, I'm sorry!"

Marc was absolutely right, but I didn't care. I had faced the fire and come through it. I had seen him in the arms of another woman, a woman I knew he loved and had faith in his love for me.

Maybe this was the sign I was searching for.

Then, I told Marc I had been thinking about the conversation we had the night he came home from Pittsburg.

"What I said to Jonathan the next day when he called was the truth. I had no desire to be alone with any other man under any circumstances. It was nice to have something to do while you were gone, and dinner was pleasant, but I was sure if Dan and Cindy weren't there I would have been very uncomfortable."

Marc asked me why I thought I would be uncomfortable.

"Because Jonathan invited me to come to his room, had reservations at a very romantic restaurant, his disappointment when I introduced Dan and Cindy and his question the next day I felt he didn't respect the relationship I have with you. And, I never want anyone to have any doubt about that.

"Marc. I am totally and completely in love with you. I don't need attention from any other man as long as I have yours, and I want the entire world to know I am not available to anyone else for anything more than a casual friendship. And that also means the next time Ron comes to town, he won't be staying at my apartment."

"I'm sure Ron knows that but it's not a problem, you can always stay with me."

And then, we made love. I'm not sure why it was so special tonight. Maybe it was because of what happened with Annie. Maybe it was because I understood how Marc thought and I agreed with him. Maybe it was because, for the first time in my life, I had complete faith in a man's love for me and mine for him. Whatever the reason, it was wonderful!

Life was beautiful!

But, it's always darkest before the dawn and brightest before the storm. And a storm was on the horizon that would take Marc down.

Chapter 32 – The Dark Days

It took us a week to get situated in our new offices, and none too soon. Artie and Susan had made the trip to Memphis as Marc promised and Eric had come to Dillman Bros. to work out a deal. The meeting was held in Ben's new office. Ben, Artie, the five vice presidents, and Eric were sitting around Bens conference table. The senior Mr. Dillman was also at the meeting, mostly as an observer. He wanted to see exactly how we were going to run this operation. This could be as big as the Carter Aviation deal, and everyone was excited.

Eric had brought the design sheets for the parts he wanted us to give him a quote on, and I had asked Susan and Jennifer to look them over and see if there was anything we couldn't handle. About an hour into the meeting, Ben told me to check with Susan and see if she had any problem with the design. I left the meeting and headed for Susan's office.

Ben had kept all of Marc's rules in place, and that meant no phone calls during a meeting, even cell phones had to be turned off. On the way to Susan's office, I looked at my phone and saw there had been five calls from Cindy in the last hour. That seemed serious, so I took the time to call her back. When she answered, it felt as if I had been hit in the chest with a two by four. The breath rushed out of my lungs, and I felt dizzy. I yelled at Susan to get Ted and follow me.

I ran down the hall and rushed back into Ben's office. Everyone looked at me as I ran over to Marc and held out my hand with the cell phone.

"Marc, you have to take this, it's Cindy," I said, almost out of breath.

Marc, seeing the expression on my face, grabbed the phone from my hand and moved over to the other side of Ben's office. I turned to everyone at the table.

"I'm sorry gentleman. Marc's best friend and mentor has been involved in a plane crash, and he's missing at sea."

Then remembering why Marc had taken this job, I told Mr. Dillman, "It's Nick Amonti."

Mr. Dillman nodded his understanding. Ben told Ted to take Marc's place and Susan to cover for me.

"Go with him Catherine. He's going to need you!"

I walked over to where Marc was talking to Cindy. When he was through, I told him I had explained everything to the group, and we were free to leave. He handed me the cell phone, took my hand and we headed for the elevator.

On the drive over to Danielle's apartment, Marc told me the story.

"Nick loved to fly, and he often ferried planes around South Florida for a friend of his that owned an air freight company. Yesterday afternoon on a flight from Freeport to Fort Lauderdale, the controllers lost contact with his plane. He is down, and the Coast Guard is conducting a full search."

"How do they know he crashed?"

"Based on the time he left Freeport and the amount of fuel on board, he couldn't still be in the air."

When we reached the lobby of the apartment complex, it was packed. News and TV people, well-wishers and the curious. Marc just waved at the doorman. He waved us through and reached for the phone to let them know we were on the way up. The door to Danielle's apartment was opened by a woman I didn't know. She threw her arms around Marc's neck and started to cry. When Marc got her to settle down, she looked at me.

"You must be Catherine. I'm sorry we couldn't meet under better circumstances."

"Marc hearing her words said, "I'm sorry. Catherine Jensen, this is Colleen Rogers, Danielle's sister."

Under the circumstances, it was very awkward. Neither of us knew exactly what to say. Glad to meet you seemed inappropriate at the moment.

Then Marc said, "This is the 'your sister's panties' lady."

Colleen gave him a weak smile and asked if he still told that story.

"Only every chance I get."

That seemed to relieve the tension a little. Marc asked Colleen how Danielle was holding up. Then, he asked about Lindsey, Joe, and Anna Lee.

"Lindsey's on her way, but Joe refused to allow Anna Lee to come to Florida. The G5 was going to drop Lindsey off and then take Joe to Georgia to be with Anna Lee."

Stacy came over and gave me a big hug.

"I'm glad you're here. Marc's going to need you if this turns out bad."

She hugged Marc and told him, "Everyone has been calling. It's been a madhouse here. The phone hasn't stopped ringing all day."

A wealthy man like Nick Amonti missing at sea was big news Marc went over to Dan and Terry and talked to them about a plan.

"Danielle doesn't need all the noise and excitement this will generate. Have you heard from Harry, Angie, and Nick's kids?"

Terry told him, "Harry and Angie are out of town but are on their way back. Janice was here last night, and Nick's son was here this morning. The other girls are on their way."

Marc said he had a plan to keep things quiet here at the apartment.

"I'll have Pam get set us a couple of banquet rooms at the Hyatt. Harry, Tony, me and Nick's kids can set up there, and you can send everyone over. I'll have all the phones calls coming into the apartment forwarded to the hotel. Then, if this lasts awhile, we can restrict the flow of people and calls to Danielle's apartment."

Dan and Terry agreed, and we prepared to leave. Just as we were getting ready to go, Danielle and Cindy came out of the bedroom. Danielle came over and wrapped her arms around me. Cindy gave Marc and me hugs and told me to keep an eye on Marc.

"He will try to hide it, but this will have a terrible effect on him if they don't find Nick alive."

I assured her I would be there for him. Marc took a key from his ring and handed it to Dan. Why don't you and Terry alternate? Lindsey and Colleen will be able to take care of Danielle. You can use my apartment to get away for a while. Dan agreed, and Marc and I left.

We went straight over to the Hyatt. I drove, and Marc spent the time on his cell with Pam, making the arrangements. NAS Financial Group did a lot of business with the Hyatt chain, and the arrangements would be everything we needed.

Then, I found out what true friendship meant. Marc called Tony Marchetti. Marc and Tony had been friends since grammar school. The conversation was very short.

"Tony, I need you to meet me at the Hyatt on SE 17th Street as soon as possible."

That was it. No explanation, no reason. Marc hung up and called his office to have them transfer the calls from Danielle's apartment to the Hyatt and bring over the necessary equipment to roll-over the incoming calls to six phones, plus computers and a database to keep a list if people who called. His last call was to NAS Security.

He was informed a Security Team was already at the apartment, and Marc asked for a team to be sent to the Hyatt to help keep order.

Ten minutes after we arrived at the Hyatt, Tony Marchetti walked in. Marc was busy with the hotel manager, so Tony asked me what was going on. I had met Tony a couple of times during my relationship with Marc. He was a sweet guy, and I knew he was Marc's best friend. I explained about Nick's plane being down, and Nick was missing. When Marc was done talking to the hotel manager, he told us what was being done for us.

"One of the banquet rooms was being set up for the press. Two suites were being set up to accommodate us and the Antonelli Systems team was already setting up the phone equipment."

Tony took charge of setting up the press room and Marc, and I went upstairs to set up the suites. One was to be used as the information center with the phones and the other for us to relax in between shifts. After almost nine months working with Marc, I was not surprised Marc had the entire operation going so quickly.

The afternoon of the second day, I convinced Marc to take a break. We drove over to his apartment for a shower and change of clothes. When we got to his apartment door, he remembered he had given his key to Dan and Terry. I produced the key he had given me at his office the Saturday I surprised him with lunch.

"I told you, indispensable!"

Marc reached toward me and wrapped his arms around me. He didn't say anything, just held me tight. I knew the anguish his was feeling, and it made me warm all over to know I was there for him. When he finally stepped back from the embrace, he just looked at me.

"I know, Marc. You don't have to say anything."

He took the key from my hand and unlocked the apartment door. We were greeted with a surprise. Stacy and Terry were sitting at the dining room table having a cup of coffee. I suggested Marc shower and change. He did as I suggested and I was left with Stacy and Terry. They looked miserable.

"We only have hours left before the Coast Guard calls off the search. They estimate a man under those conditions could only last three days, and we were fast approaching that limit."

"Does Marc know?"

"Marc knows how it works. The Coast Guard would remind all ships and planes in the area to keep an eye out, but the official search would soon be over."

Because I had been spending weekends at Marc's apartment, I had managed to stock his pantry and refrigerator. While Marc showered, Stacy and I prepared a fast dinner for us. Basic steak and potatoes, but it was better than the sandwiches we had been living on at the hotel. After that, we returned to the Hyatt so Marc and I could take our turn on the phones.

On the afternoon of the fifth day, while I was getting a cup of coffee for Marc he got a call from Dan. Marc banged his fist on the table, so hard everyone in the suite took notice. All eyes were on him, and realizing what he had done, he looked around and gave a thumbs-up sign.

Suddenly, as if we had been locked in a sealed room and a hole had finally been bored in, the tension seemed to ooze out of the suite. When he had disconnected from the call, he told us the news.

"No details, but they found him, and he's alive. He's on a Navy ship, and on his way to Norfolk."

The news of Nick's rescue brought the reporters back, and the phones were busy again. It would be at least another twenty-four to forty-eight hours before we could close up shop here. One of the calls Marc received was from Marcie. She said she didn't want to bring it up before, but Nick had a speaking engagement a week from Saturday in Louisville.

Marc asked if I was in the mood for a trip to Kentucky and then told Marcie he would take it. That night, we slept at Marc's apartment. When I again produced my key to open the door, Marc took me in his arms and again held me tight. But, this time, he did say something.

"Definitely indispensable and I'm smart enough to know it!"

The next day, Marc suggested I go back to work and inform everyone he would be back in a couple of days. He wanted to spend a day in his office to check up on his company and let everyone there know Nick was going to be OK.

When we first got the suite organized, Marc had insisted we keep a log of the incoming phone calls so everyone could be thanked afterward. After we closed up the suite, he went over the phone logs. It was just as he expected, basically Nick's and Danielle's families and friends, Marc's sisters, Nick's business partners and friends, and some of Danielle's clients, along with reporters and unknown well-wishers. Ben had designated Sara as the Dillman contact with us, and she kept everyone there informed. They all knew how important Nick and his friends had been to our success, and both Dillman brothers knew they were able to keep their new plant because of Nick.

Three names on the list Marc recognized, but he was surprised to see there. My sister Elizabeth and both of my brothers had called numerous times. When he showed me the three names, I told him I was so busy I didn't get the chance to keep them up to date on events, so they took it upon themselves to check in.

Marc commented, "Good people usually come from good families!"

When Marc called Elizabeth to thank her for her concern, she insisted we come to Sunday dinner. We hadn't been to dinner with either family since Nashville. The first Sunday we had open was the day after the Dillman Company Party, but Marc agreed. He promised we would be there.

Life was back to normal, at least as normal as it could be considering Marc was still committed to Dillman Brothers, his own business and a speaking engagement next weekend.

When I returned to work everyone was interested in Nick's condition. I found out Eric had signed a contract with Dillman for over forty-eight million dollars. It seems Memphis was a very fruitful trip.

I found out what Marc does on those mysterious weekends. We met a potential client that just gave us the second biggest order in the companies' history. And I met Jonathan, who forced me to think about the things Marc had talked to me about. Things like not appearing available and avoiding certain situations. The more I thought about Marc's rules, the more I was sure he was right.

Marc had less than sixty days left at Dillman Brothers. Then he could pay attention to his own business. Danielle and her two sisters flew to Pensacola where the Navy had transferred Nick to a civilian hospital.

Marc and I flew to Louisville on Saturday morning. On the way to the banquet, I asked if he was going to tell the 'your sister's panties' story. He said he always told it because it always got a big laugh. I reminded him when he introduced me to Colleen he mentioned she was the sister in the story. He said it was true. I asked him if that meant the story was about Danielle and Nick.

"Yes, it is. When things get back to normal over there, you should ask Danielle to tell you the story of how they got together. It's a beautiful story. It's so beautiful it will make you cry, and Danielle loves to tell it."

Then I asked him who Joe was and why he wouldn't allow Anna Lee to come to Florida.

"Lindsey is Danielle's older sister and Joe is her husband. Anna Lee's is their daughter. Nick had done something very special for Anna Lee and her son, and Anna Lee had a very special feeling for Nick. Joe thought if the situation didn't go well, Anna Lee was better away from the action. He went to Georgia to hold her hand. Like I told you before, good people usually come from good families!"

Marc was as good as the other times I had heard him speak, but this time, giving the speech about separating corporate life from family life seemed to have more meaning to him. It's as if Nick's experience had made him more aware of how fragile life and love could be.

Back at the hotel, we made love and slept late. Sunday we flew back to Florida in silence. Marc seemed to be deep in thought. The following Sunday we had dinner at Marc's sister's house. Everyone appeared to be happy that Nick was on the mend and Marc, and I were together again. Marc's older sister confided, "I was so disappointed when I heard there was trouble between you and Marc. You were the only woman since Marc split from his wife he paid any serious attention to. I hoped your relationship would be permanent."

So do I!

Chapter 33 – Annual Company Banquet

At the office, the week flew by and suddenly it was Saturday and time for the Dillman Brother's Corporate Banquet. I brought my gown over to Marc's apartment on Friday and stayed there that night. Saturday, Marc went to his office for a couple of hours but came home early. He didn't want to be late for the party.

When I came out of his bedroom wearing the gown Danielle had given me for the affair, Marc was speechless. I did my usual three hundred and sixty-degree twirl and waited for a comment. Finally, finding his voice, he said, "Catherine, you are ravishing. What have I done to deserve you?"

Then, he walked around me, very slowly.

"Are you sure that's not going to fall off?"

"Hope not!" I answered playfully.

"How?"

"It's a secret."

Marc smiled, and I knew he was pleased. The gown was very sexy, but not revealing. Everything that should be covered was covered. My back was naked to my waist, and the v cut in the front was cut practically to my navel, but not a hint of the breast was showing, and thanks to the double stick tape wouldn't show no matter how I moved or twisted. The slit along the leg was cut high enough that stocking were out of the question. This was a pantyhose night.

It was exactly the kind of thing Marc had described in Nashville. It was very sexy, but it left more to the imagination than it revealed. I had put my hair up the way I did in Memphis, and his reaction told me he loved it.

On the ride down in the elevator, I asked if we could stop by and show my outfit to Danielle. When she opened the door, it was obvious she was pleased. She brought me in to see Nick. He was still recuperating from his ordeal, but he got up when he saw me. He told Marc to take good care of me tonight and not let me out of his sight.

Marc said, "I'm considering calling NAS Security and requesting a four-man team to surround her all night."

Nick laughed and said, "But, who's going to watch them?"

That comment made everyone laugh. Of course, I loved the attention. Attention from my man and a trusted good friend. I knew everyone who saw us tonight would have no doubt who I belonged to and who's attention I craved.

In spite of Marc's insistence, we include the new team members in everything we do, tonight he arranged it so the original team sat together at one table. He explained this was probably the last time we would all be together. The other members of the new team were at tables adjacent to ours, and we still managed to convey a team spirit.

At these annual parties, the younger Dillman brother would walk around the hall while the band was on a break. He was known as the Grape, and he had a microphone, and an earpiece he claimed was connected to someone he called the Grapevine.

He would talk to different people and tell their secrets. Who was recently married, who was keeping company with whom, who's kid got accepted into a prestigious college.

He also used the opportunity to announce recent promotions. Since there had been so many promotions on our team recently, we expected a lot of attention from him tonight. It was a fun gag, and everyone enjoyed it.

During the first break, he came over to our area and talked to Gino, Rich, Angelo and Jennifer, letting everyone know they had all been promoted. He also mentioned that Gino and his wife were celebrating their tenth anniversary this coming week.

During the second and third break, he moved around to different tables, telling secrets he claimed the Grapevine was telling him. It was all fun, and everyone he talked about loved the attention.

During the next break, he wandered over to our table. He stopped behind Marc.

"Marc, you and I have to talk later. I want to know how you got so many beautiful and talented women to work for the Client Services Division.

I'd also like to know how you managed to get these five lovely ladies seated at your table tonight. But right now, I would much rather talk to these beautiful women."

The Grape put his hand to his ear as if someone was talking to him in his earpiece. He moved over to Constance. He took her hand, and she stood.

"Connie, according to the Grapevine, it seems you've managed to put a saddle on our resident bad boy. The question is do you think you can tame him?"

Connie smiled.

"I've got the saddle on Grape, but I haven't got it cinched up yet. And why would I want to tame him? I kind of like him the way he is!"

That got a laugh from everyone, and the Grape moved on. His next stop was Emily.

"Emily, you get more beautiful every year. I've always wanted to know how Tim manages to hold on to you."

Emily stood up.

"It's easy Grape. Tim is a good husband, a great father and he's really dynamite in bed!"

That brought a big laugh from the crowd. Sara was next, and after announcing her promotion, he said, "Sara, according to the Grapevine, you're not the only member of your family to get a promotion."

Sara was all smiles.

"That's right Grape, my husband was just promoted to Vice President of South East Marketing at Tyler and Tyler."

A round of applause followed that announcement. Susan was next, and after mentioning her promotion, he put his hand to his ear.

"You don't say. Anyone, we know? You're absolutely sure?"

Susan still standing next to Grape didn't know what was coming. Then the Grape made an announcement.

"Single gentleman of Dillman Brothers, I guess it is my duty to inform you all the beautiful and charming Susan Cunningham is no longer available."

Then turning to Susan, he asked, "Might we know who the lucky gentleman is who managed to capture your heart?"

Susan, blushing said, "I think I'll keep that bit of information to myself for now."

The Grape nodded his understanding, and as he moved toward me, he slapped Artie on the back and said, loud enough for all to hear.

"Way to go Artie!"

That resulted in another round of applause, and now both Susan and Artie were blushing.

When the Grape reached me, he put out his hand. I took it and rose to my feet. The Grape twirled me around once and said, "Catherine you are stunning tonight. That surely must be a Stacy Geer Gown you are wearing."

"Yes it is Grape, thank you for noticing."

Then, with a playful attitude, he said, "I know you have just been promoted to Vice President of Specifications and Designs, but I never realized vice presidents pay was that good."

I had to wait for the applause in recognition of my promotion to die down.

"Although I do appreciate the raise in pay, Grape, it isn't quite enough to allow me to buy a Stacy Geer gown. This was a gift."

The Grape smiled.

"Do we have an exclusive here tonight? Are you willing to tell us the name of the wealthy suitor who has lavished such a gift on you?"

With the biggest pout I could muster, I said, "Sorry to disappoint you, Grape, no such luck. This gown was a gift from the designer, Ms. Stacy Geer."

"Name Dropper," Grape said and after glancing around the table, he turned to Marc.

"Well, since there are no more beautiful ladies to talk to at this table, I guess I'm stuck with you Marc."

Marc stood up, and Grape asked him how he managed to get so many beautiful women at his table. Marc looked over his left shoulder and then his right as if he wanted to make sure no one was eavesdropping, and then leaning over to Grape as if it was a secret, he said, "Rank Has its Privileges."

Grape indicated he didn't understand.

"As the head of the department, I got to set the seating arrangements!"

That got a laugh from the crowd, and Grape said it was good to be the boss in a situation like that, and then he said more seriously.

"Speaking of rank, with all the promotions announced tonight in your department, how does it feel to be the only one that was demoted?"

Marc too got serious.

"Grape, I was always just the manager of the Client Analysis Department and the title of SVP was just a courtesy title. Now that they had the right man to head the Client Services Division I'm happy to step back to my original position at Dillman."

Grape put his hand to his ear, indicating the Grapevine was telling him something.

"Marc is it true you'll be leaving Dillman Brothers in less than two months?"

Marc stated it was true, and then the Grape asked if Marc had picked his replacement.

"Grape, it's not my province to select the next Vice President of Client Analysis. I know what this job requires, and I've made my recommendation to the board. They are considering it along with a few others. The announcement will be made when the board makes their decision."

Again, Grape put his hand to his ear. Talking to the fictitious person on the other end, he asked if it was definite. Was the Grapevine sure of his information? Then with a shrug of his shoulders, he said to Marc, "According to the Grapevine, the board had made their decision, and they have decided to go with your choice."

Marc looked toward the head table, and when the senior Mr. Dillman nodded, Marc smiled.

"In that case, it will be my pleasure to tell you who the new Vice President of Client Analysis will be."

Then taking two steps away from me, Marc stuck out his hand and said, "Congratulations Ted!"

Ted was stunned. I'm sure everyone at our table was surprised. I didn't know if he would be Marc's choice, but knowing how Marc thought, business is business, I understood his reasoning.

Ted got up from his seat to shake Marc's hand. I rose from my seat and applauded. Everyone else at our table followed and then everyone in the Client Services Division stood and applauded.

While Grape was congratulating Ted, Marc came back and sat down.

"I'm sorry Connie!"

Connie, not understanding his meaning, gave him an inquisitive look.

"I know the beginning of a relationship is critical, and I have just saddled your man with an enormous responsibility that will take some of his attention away from you and your relationship. Please, have patience. Give him some time to get settled in his new position. I think he is a good man, and worth waiting for."

Connie glanced at Ted, receiving congratulations from Mr. Dillman, Ben and the rest of the team.

"Marc, I think this is just what Ted needs. The responsibility and the acceptance from the others will settle him down, and he'll be a better man for the opportunity. I think it can only help us."

Marc smiled in response. When things quieted down, I went over to give Ted my best wishes. He seemed not quite ready to believe what just happened.

"Marc is right. You are the best man for the job and the entire team agreed with the decision."

And, truthfully he was the best man for the job. If they brought in a sales manager type from the outside like they had done with Marc, or promoted someone from a different department, it would have disturbed the entire flow of the team concept. Marc's decision was based on what was best for the department and the company. After a while, Ted leaned over and asked, "Marc, why?"

"It was the only choice I could make. It had to be someone who not only understood the team concept and what we do here, it had to be someone who totally believed in the one for all and all for one thing. No one on this team showed more involvement in the overall team concept than you did. You were always the first one to offer the others help, not only Tim and Artie but also Catherine, Jose, and Gino. It was obvious you understood and believed in what we were doing. But, the truth is I was sure it was you when we were working on the Carter Aviation deal."

We all were surprised at that comment. Everyone knew it was Marc who came up with the idea for the two thousand piece sample order. Ted said he didn't understand.

"Even though it was officially my client, it was you who set the entire thing up."

"Ted, when you're in charge, sometimes you have to go outside the norm. You have to take a chance. You have to put it on the line. A leader has to be ready to put himself at risk.

"It's not the second Carter order, it was the first. When you told me I was crazy for trusting Jim Carter, I told you to fill out the order, and I would sign it. When you put your signature on that two thousand piece order, I knew you were the man for the job. It was a done deal, that day."

That made everyone smile.

"Ted my remaining time here will be spent helping with the transition. As of Monday morning, you'll move into my office and assume your new position."

Then, after looking around the table, Marc told him, "They're all yours now Ted, take good care of them!"

The night continued, and as each member of the team thought about it, I was sure we all agreed Ted was the right choice. There had been some uneasiness around the office because we all knew Marc was leaving, and we weren't sure if his replacement would come in and change everything. Now that it was settled and we all knew Ted would carry on, we were all happy with the decision.

When the band took another break, Grape made another round of the hall and continued his commentary on any bit of information he had managed to collect from employees over the past month.

Just before the band was ready to start again, he made his way back over to our table. Holding his hand to his ear, he kept saying to the Grapevine he understood and that he'd ask him.

He made it seem like the Grapevine was pushing him to get an answer to a vital question. This time, he went directly to Marc. Marc stood up and asked Grape what the problem was. Grape was somewhat embarrassed.

"Marc, according to the Grapevine, you are very proficient at tripping the light fantastic."

Marc laughed at that.

"That's true, Grape, and I dance pretty good too!"

That got a laugh from the crowd. Grape asked Marc if he would demonstrate his skill. Marc said he would need a partner. Grape asked if he would do. Marc gave him a look that said more than it was meant to. That got another laugh. Grape looked around the hall, settled on our table.

"Catherine, would you mind?"

I rose from my seat, walked over to where Marc and Grape were standing.

"Of course not Grape. Anything for the greater glory of Dillman Brothers."

That got another laugh. Grape asked what type of music he wanted. Marc looked and me and inquired, "Waltz?"

I nodded my head, and Marc asked for 'The Loveliest Night of the Year.' I knew this was one of the favorite songs Marc and I danced too, and I had a feeling Marc had set this up. Grape backed away. Marc offered me his arm and we moved to the center of the dance floor. On the way there, Marc asked, "Up for a lift tonight?"

Marc and I had taken some lessons with Billy, mostly to bring me up to Marc's expertise and lifts were part of my training. Ordinarily, I would have agreed, but not tonight.

"Not if you want this dress to stay on."

Marc laughed.

"OK, we'll keep it simple. During the introduction, we'll curtsy and bow, and then I'll take your left hand and twirl you around twice, and when the verse starts, we'll be in hold."

Sounded simple enough, so I agreed. At the center of the dance floor, we faced each other. Marc signaled the band we were ready, and they started to play the intro. I curtsied, and Marc bowed. Then he stepped toward me, took my hand and twirled me around twice. When I faced him after the second turn, he wasn't in hold position.

The music had stopped. Marc was on his knee, and when I looked down at him he said, "Catherine Jensen will you marry me!"

My heart stopped for an instant and then started racing a thousand miles a second. My head was spinning, and my knees were weak. I opened my mouth to answer him, but no words came out. Finally, I nodded. I must have looked like a bobble head doll my head was going up and down so fast. Marc slipped a ring on my finger, stood up and kissed me gently.

Then he said, "Now let's dance!"

I found my voice enough to tell him my legs were so weak I couldn't possibly dance. Marc smiled that great smile.

"Nothing to it. The only thing you have to do is....trust me! I'll always be here for you."

I looked into his beautiful eyes and I knew. I did trust this man. I trusted him completely. Giving him a smile of my own, I said, "OK Marc, let's dance."

I don't remember the next few minutes. I must have gotten through the dance OK. I didn't wind up on the floor, I didn't have any crushed toes and no bruises on my shins. I didn't hear the music, or as I was told later, the loud applause from the other Dillman employees. I just let Marc carry me away to a place I had never been before.

When it was over, Marc kissed me again. This time, the kiss was long and passionate. Then, offering me his arm, we walked back over to our table.

We were immediately inundated with well-wishers. All the girls wanted to see the ring. I realized I had never looked at it myself. Holding up my hand, I saw it was perfect. Just like the other jewelry Marc had given me, it was expensive but not overdone. It fit my personality perfectly. I couldn't have picked a better symbol of our love myself. This man did know me that well.

Ted waited for things to quiet down before he came over to me. Smiling from ear to ear, he whispered, "Catherine, if there is one person who could possibly he happier then you two are, it's me."

I knew he meant it. I guess my engagement to Marc let him off the hook, at least in his own mind. And, I was so happy at this moment I wanted to let him off also. I quietly whispered back to him.

"Ted, all you really did was push up the timeframe. Marc and I would have had this problem further down the road. Because of you, we got it out in the open, and I believe we're both better for it. This time, I owe you."

Ted smiled and kissed me on the cheek.

"I'll keep it for a rainy day," he said.

I looked at Constance standing behind Ted and said, "I don't see too many of those in your future."

Ted, knowing I was looking at Connie, answered, "You might just be right about that!"

Both Dillman Brothers stopped by to congratulate Marc and offer me best wishes. The senior Mr. Dillman indicated he hoped Marc wasn't going to have me quit my job.

"Dillman Brothers needs you here."

Marc replied for me.

"Not to worry. I'll be out of a job in less than two months. Someone is going to have to support us!"

That got big laughs from everyone. After over ten months, everyone knew who Marc was, and he ran his own very profitable company.

The party broke up around one AM. Marc and I drove to his apartment in silence. Once there, Marc took me into the living room. He sat on one of the club chairs and pulled me down onto his lap. Marc was in a very good mood, and I've learned when his mood is like this, it excites his tease glands.

He told me he was thinking of a plan, and I was so happy, I would have gone along with anything he suggested. I knew some people were not going to be happy about his idea.

"We have dinner scheduled at Elizabeth's this afternoon, and I'd like to stop at my sister's first to announce our engagement."

That all suited me just fine. We talked for a while. He was acting like he didn't want this day to end. Finally, he took me into his bedroom. Instead of going into the bathroom and putting on a sexy nightie, I told Marc if he really wanted to know how I kept my dress on all night, this was his chance to discover my secret.

Marc undressed me very slowly, and then he took a warm washcloth and removed the adhesive from my skin. He was tender and gentle and afterward, I got to undress him, not quite as slowly. Then we made love. He was passionate and tender as always, but tonight had a special feeling. Every doubt I had ever had was gone. I loved this man completely, and I knew he loved me. I also knew I would always be faithful to him, and he would always be true to me.

The emotion we shared this night was total.

Chapter 34 – Family Dinner

Sunday, we got up early. Considering what took place in Marc's bed, I was amazed we could get up at all, but we had things to do. We were having dinner at my sister's house, with both of my brothers and before that, Marc wanted to stop and give his sisters the news of our engagement. It would be a very busy day. Marc reminded me of the plan he had described last night, and I was so giddy I again agreed. Before we left the apartment, I called my brother, Ed, and got him involved.

On the way down in the elevator, I asked Marc if we had a minute to stop by Nick and Danielle's. After checking his watch he agreed. Outside the apartment, I had Marc stand behind me as I stood directly in front of the door and rang the bell. When Danielle opened the door, I was standing with my left hand in front of my face, palm toward me. When she saw the ring, she squealed with delight. We were ushered into the apartment, and we both got gigantic hugs. Nick, still recuperating from his ordeal was in the living room and wanted to know what the screaming was about. I walked into the living room and walked over to Nick, waving my hand at him.

Nick immediately got off the couch and gave me a big hug, and then looking at Marc said, "I always knew you were too smart to let this one get away!"

"After seeing her in that gown last night, I figured I'd better tie her up before someone stole her away from me."

We didn't stay long, considering we had two other stops to make before we got to Elizabeth's house. The first stop was at the studio of the people who took pictures and videos of the banquet last night. Marc had made an arrangement for them to have a DVD ready for us of certain parts of the party. It was a short version, just including the part where Marc or I were involved, and, of course, his proposal and our dance. Marc told me, "With this, we could share the moment with our families."

Both of Marc's sisters were happy for us. They were very close to Marc and told me they were hoping he had enough sense to make our relationship permanent.

"Because of the change in Marc since he met you, we knew there was something special going on."

Marc was right about the DVD. It did seem to make everyone feel like a part of our engagement. We got hugs and kisses from both sisters, and the mood was so upbeat we had a difficult time tearing ourselves away. But my family was waiting.

When we reached Elizabeth's house, my brother Ed answered the door. He glanced at my left hand and smiled. I had taken my engagement ring off and placed it securely in the pocket of my sundress. I got a hug, and Marc and Ed shook hands. Everyone was glad to see we were together again. Elizabeth had prepared an excellent dinner for us, mostly because she knew Marc didn't get too many home cooked meals, and he had always sincerely complimented on her culinary skills.

We sat down at the table, and knowing everyone was curious just how Marc and I were doing. Marc let them know.

"We are solving our problem and things are looking better for us. Both Catherine and I want to thank everyone for helping us by talking to Catherine about the events in Nashville. You guys played a big part in our current situation."

Everyone took part in the conversation, all either saying they were so happy we solving the problem, or things like problem-solving is the key to a lasting relationship.

Halfway through the meal, while Marc was chewing on a piece of Elizabeth's roast, and complimenting her once again for being such an excellent cook. My brother Ed asked, "Marc since everything is going so well between you and my kid sister, don't you think it's time to pop the question?"

After putting another piece of meat in his mouth, Marc asked, "What question is that Ed?"

Everyone stopped eating, and the room got very quiet. That is everyone stopped eating except Marc, who kept chewing away as if he hadn't understood the meaning of Ed's question.

"You know the marriage question. Do you intend to marry Catherine?"

Marc looked up from his plate and stopped chewing. He looked at Ed, and then at me.

"Marriage? I hadn't considered that."

Marc put his folk down and looking off into space as if he were trying to make a decision.

"Catherine, would you consider marriage?"

Being thoroughly prepped by Marc on the way here, I too looked off into space too and replied.

"I really haven't given it any thought, Marc, but I guess we could discuss it."

While everyone else at the table just looked at Marc and me, Marc took on a very thoughtful look. After a few moments contemplation.

"I guess it would be more convenient. I mean, living together and all. We could see each other every night, and I do enjoy your cooking all most as much as Elizabeth's. And all of your clothes would be in the same place and that kind of thing."

The entire table was in a state of shock. This is not how marriage was discussed in this family. It was romantic and intimate, not like some business decision. I stole a glance at Ed, and he was trying very hard not to laugh. After a few minutes, Keith said, "Don't you think you two should discuss this in private?"

Marc looked around the table.

"No, you're all Catherine's family I see no reason not to discuss this. You might have some good ideas or suggestions."

Then looking back to me, "What do you think, Catherine, do you want to get married?"

I shrugged my shoulders.

"I guess we could. It probably does make sense. It would be more convenient and efficient."

That's when we reached the point where Elizabeth couldn't deal with us any longer.

"Catherine Jensen!" she yelled, "This is not the way you discuss marriage. You're talking about the rest of your life. This is not a business decision."

Then, turning to Marc.

"Catherine said you were so romantic, is this really the way you want to propose to my sister?"

Ed tried to back Elizabeth off, but she was not about to allow me to agree to marry this man like this. After a few more words about the sanctity of marriage, the beauty and meaningfulness of marriage, Marc told her, "I know what you're saying Beth, but you have to understand a man in my position has to consider everything."

Ed and Keith's wives were silent. Knowing both of my brothers were very romantic souls, I could imagine them thinking I was missing out on something wonderful. A romantic proposal in a romantic setting was called for, not a sensible discussion about convenience and efficiency.

Marc then brought up the necessity of a prenup.

"I can call my attorney after dinner and the papers could be ready first thing tomorrow morning. Would twenty percent of what I have now and forty percent of everything I made after we were married be sufficient?"

I acted as if I was giving it serious thought.

"I think thirty percent of what you have now and sixty percent later is more in line, because after all, I'll still be working and contributing."

After a couple of minutes of negotiation, during which I thought my entire family was going to have a simultaneous massive coronary, we agreed on twenty-five now and fifty after we were married.

"That was easy," Marc said, "I guess we are compatible. OK, after we stop at my attorney's office tomorrow morning, we can run over to the county courthouse and get the license. I guess, it would be simpler just to have the clerk marry us while we're there."

That was it. As I was about to tell Marc that sounded like a good idea, Elizabeth exploded.

"Catherine Jensen, you are not getting married in front of some court clerk tomorrow. You are going to have a formal wedding just like every other member of this family."

Then turning to Marc.

"You ought to be ashamed of yourself. How could you treat this so cavalierly? You're talking about my sister's wedding, not some business deal."

I was starting to think it was time to end this, but the reaction at the table only pushed Marc further. I glanced at Ed again, and he gave me a look that said relax. Marc threw up his hands in surrender at Elizabeth's tirade.

"OK, Beth! We'll have a formal wedding."

Then looking at me.

"I guess this means we're engaged. I'll send Sara out tomorrow morning to pick up an engagement ring for you."

That brought a storm of protests from everyone.

"An engagement ring is not something you send your secretary out to get. You either pick it out yourself or you take Catherine with you and pick it out together."

Feeling the wrath of my entire family, Marc looked at me and asked, "Would you trust me to pick out something?"

I put my hands in my lap and put on the ring Marc had given me last night. I looked around the table, and just as I had rehearsed in the car on the way over to Elizabeth's house, I said, "The jewelry you gave me for my birthday and Christmas was very tasteful. I think you can pick out something appropriate."

Then as I raised my left hand over the table, I added, "The ring you gave me last night is pretty nice."

It took a while before it all sunk in. One by one as they saw the beautiful engagement ring adorning my finger and they realized they had been had. Elizabeth looked at my hand and then looked at Marc.

"You ought to be horsewhipped. And you, young lady, ought to be spanked."

Marc smiled at her.

"Beth, if anyone is going to spank that sweet butt of hers, it's going to be me!"

Suddenly, Elizabeth threw her arms around Marc's neck. They were both seated at the table, and the sudden move almost knocked them both off their seats. They got to their feet, and Elizabeth hugged Marc so tightly I thought she was going to crack one of his ribs.

Sandra looked at her husband with fire in her eyes.

"You knew about this!"

Ed looked very sheepish.

"Sorry honey, I was sworn to secrecy under pain of severe torture."

Marc grabbed Sandra in a hug and told her it was his fault.

"I needed an ally that could be trusted."

Sandra smiled, and all was forgiven, at which point, Marc looked at his dinner plate longingly and asked, "Any roast left, Beth?"

We all sat down at the table again, and the questions started. Where, when, how, everyone wanted details.

Marc had draped his sports jacket over the back of his chair when we first sat down to dinner. He reached behind him, into his jacket pocket and produced the DVD.

"Recorded it all so she couldn't back out."

233

The mood around the dining room table couldn't have been more upbeat. Everyone was happy for us, but no one was as happy as I was.

After dinner, Marc gave Sam the DVD and asked him to set it up while Marc ran out to the car. By the time we were ready to watch the show, Marc had returned with a cooler containing four bottles of champagne, the Taittinger, of course. While he poured the wine, we watched the recording of last night's party.

It was a cut-down version and only showed the times when the Grape was talking to Marc and me. When we got to the part where Marc and I had moved to the center of the dance floor, I paid attention. I don't remember much after I came out of the two turns and found Marc down on his knee. I saw my head bobbing up and down, and I watched as Marc slipped the ring on my finger and then the kiss. And this time, I heard the shouts and applause from the Dillman employees.

The dance was beautiful. Marc led me around the floor, and I didn't miss a step, even those fancy parts Billy had taught us. I was completely under his control, and I liked that idea. Beth and my sisters-in-law had tears in their eyes, and each came over to give Marc another hug, telling me afterward I had a real romantic on my hands.

After a while, Marc asked Beth if she had prepared dessert. We all headed back to the dining room for strawberry shortcake and coffee. Tamping down the excitement was difficult.

After that Friday night when I poured out my fears and anxieties to my family, they had worried about Marc and me. This outcome was everything they had hoped for.

We stayed longer than we intended to. The celebration was too much fun to break up. On the drive to Marc's apartment, we were both very quiet. We did make love that night, but we didn't have sex.

I didn't think that was possible until I got involved with this man. When I woke Monday morning, I was cuddled against him with his arm around my shoulder, and I felt safe and secure.

I gingerly made my way out of bed, trying not to disturb Marc. After a shower, I dressed and got ready for work. I brought Marc a cup of coffee and woke him with a kiss.

His smile was my reward. While he showered and dressed, I made breakfast. Sitting across the table from each other, I didn't know what to say. Finally, Marc spoke.

"We have a lot to talk about now. How about dinner here tonight and then we can work this out."

He was right. This was not a fairy tale where they lived happily ever after. This was the real world, and we had a lot of decisions to make about our wedding and our life together. I agreed to his proposal, and we went to work.

Chapter 35 - Short Timer

I hardly saw Marc during the day, but everyone else on the team stopped by to share in my happiness and talk about what happened Saturday night. Now that the announcement of our promotions was official we all were busy moving into our new offices.

Susan took over my office, and I moved into a vice president's style office. Ted moved into Marc's office, and Marc took a small office that was reserved for one of one the additional Junior Analysts we would eventually need to hire. Marc had less than two months left on his contract, and he would spend that time helping Ted get involved with his new duties. From today on, it's was Ted's department.

Somewhere around midafternoon, Susan stopped by with a problem.

"With Jennifer's department being increased in size, it wouldn't be possible for me to take any of the design people into specs, and short of hiring recent engineering graduates; I won't be able to fill the empty vacant spaces in my department. Do you think it would be alright if I asked some of the people on the production floor to move into specs? They know what the specs were for, and they know how to use the information we supplied. They would be the easiest to teach."

After giving the idea some serious thought, I knew she was right. They would be the easiest to train, but Gino would not be happy. He would not be very willing to give up experienced people. I was pretty sure I could convince Ben this was a good idea, and, since we were all one team now, and it was one for all and all for one, I hoped we could get away with it.

But remembering what Marc said about cooperation and the need for the five vice presidents to work together I decided not to go to Ben. I would try to work this out with Gino. Susan and I went to Gino's office and presented her idea. As expected, Gino didn't like it.

"What does Ben think?

"I haven't talked to Ben, and if you turn us down, I wouldn't go over your head and try to convince him to overrule you."

That statement seemed to have an impact on Gino. I reminded him what Marc had said about the five department heads getting along, and that's the way I intended to run my department.

After a lengthy discussion, Gino agreed.

"I'll send the three people we decided to see you tomorrow and if they're OK with the transfer you and I will go to Ben together and get his approval."

We had a deal. As we were leaving his office, Gino called to me.

"Thanks for not going over my head."

"If this is to work, that's the way it has to be."

Maybe this vice president thing wouldn't be too hard after all. I left the office early and went to Marc's apartment to prepare dinner. I feared our planned discussion tonight would be on the heavy side, and I wanted to start it off with a great meal for him. When Marc arrived, I sent him to the shower and change into casual clothes, and I had the table set and everything ready when he came out of the bedroom.

During dinner, I told Marc about my talk with Gino. He didn't say much about it, but I could tell he was pleased with the way I had handled the situation. After dinner, I allowed him to help me with the dishwasher thing and then with a couple of glasses of very nice wine, we settled into the living room. Just before I curled up on the couch, I decided I needed to start writing things down. We had a lot of plans to make. Marc said there were blank pads in the bottom drawer of his file cabinet and pens and pencils in his desk. Marc noticed my hesitation.

"Catherine, there is nothing in my office you have to be afraid of. I have no secrets from you. In fact, it would be a good idea for you to go through my files so you get a sense of what my life is like. It might make it easier to deal with me when we're living together."

One more unlimited access into his life. This was going to work, I was absolutely sure.

When I had located pad and pen, I returned to the living room and started making a list: church, reception, bridesmaids, groomsmen, flowers, limousines and all the things that go into a proper wedding. As I was calling these things out, Marc interrupted me.

"There are more important things to discuss first."

At first, I didn't understand what he was saying, but then a thought occurred to me.

237

"You mean the prenup?"

Marc looked at me strangely.

"Catherine, there will be no prenup. If we do this, it will be till death do us part, so there's no need to make arrangements to cover a break-up. I wouldn't have asked you to marry me if I wasn't sure we would be together forever."

That made me feel good, but I was still unsure of what he wanted to talk about. I glanced at my list and knew there were probably a dozen things that I haven't thought of, but I knew he had something specific in mind. I gave Marc my 'what's that' look, and he responded with.

"Before we talk about the wedding, I think we should discuss the before and after. How are we going to handle the time before the wedding and what our life will be like after we are married? And then, there's the question of when."

"Any ideas?" I asked.

"How about this coming weekend?"

Before I had a chance to answer, he added.

"Catherine, I know brides think about a romantic wedding and all that, and I fully intend to give you everything you could ever hope for and more. But I want you to understand my primary focus here is to claim you as my wife."

That statement got me off the couch and into his lap. After a long, passionate but tender kiss, he said, "Now, let's talk about the before.

"I've lived in this apartment for over ten years, and I've always been very comfortable here. But, lately, my bed is awfully lonely when you're not in it! We really have to talk about what the living arrangements are going to be between now and the wedding."

That one, I had thought of. Maybe this coming weekend wasn't such a crazy idea after all.

I left the comfort of his lap and moved back to the couch. That generated a very disappointed look on his face, and I told him this was a very serious decision, and I couldn't afford to be distracted by being too physically close to him while I was trying to think. That brought out a wicked smile, but he agreed a serious discussion was in order.

"Moving in together before the wedding wouldn't go over very well with Beth or your brothers. How about a compromise. Friday, Saturday and Sunday night, it would be more convenient for you to stay here. When I'm finished at Dillman, my Saturdays will be free, and we could spend the entire weekend together, and it would be easier if we had to go on one of my speaking engagements. You would be home in your own apartment four days a week, and that should be enough to satisfy your family we weren't living together."

Then he added, "If I happened to drop over your place on Tuesday and Wednesday and I was too tired to go home, only on Monday and Thursday would we be apart."

Two nights a week sleeping apart from Marc was more than I wanted to deal with, but I knew he was right about my family. I agreed to his proposal, and we moved on.

Marc's next statement really got me thinking.

"Now, I think we should discuss the marriage," he said thoughtfully.

Chapter 36 – Marriage Plans

First, we talked about living conditions after the wedding.

"We have to decide where we're going to live, and how the household would be taken care of. Your apartment is too small for the two of us. Would you consider living here for a while until we got settled in our new life?

"And, as much as I love coming home to one of your fabulous meals, I don't think it fair to expect that on a regular basis, and although we could split the other chores, maybe we should talk about hiring a housekeeper to take care of things. We can continue to use the woman I have now, or find someone who could also cook.

"Next, remember the first time we had dinner together? I said you had a great future in the corporate world if you wanted it. After watching you work for the past eight months and what you told me about your meeting with Gino, I'm more convinced than ever that you can go as far as you want to. You have to decide how far you wish to go and how that fits in with our relationship. It also will have a bearing on whether or not you want children."

As usual, Marc had it all figured out in his efficient way.

"These decisions don't have to be made now, but we should start to think about them and be ready to talk about them. The important thing is we keep the communication between us open and honest. No secrets. It won't help our relationship if you wonder how I would feel about a decision you are thinking about. You have to know for sure what my feelings are, and that means we have to talk about it."

That gave me some things to think about. I was thinking wedding, not marriage. Marc was right. There was a lot to consider, and I vowed I would talk to Marc about everything. The next subject had never occurred to me at all.

"Catherine, I am an old fashioned Italian man. That's why I asked you to let me know you got home safely after our first dinner together. And, that means it is my responsibility to take care of and support my wife and our household. We have to talk about this, it's important to me."

It seems Marc has given our life together a lot of thought. Asking me to marry him was no spur of the moment decision. He must have been thinking about it for a while. I wanted to know just how long, and he did say I could ask him anything.

"Marc, how long have you been thinking about his?"

His reaction was a sorrowful frown.

"Since before Nashville," he said, "And when I thought I had lost you..."

That brought tears to my eyes. How could I ever have doubted this man? I was on his lap again, but this time, I just threw my arms around his neck and buried my face in his chest. Marc just held me for a while and told me not to cry.

"We have overcome a tremendous hurdle, and I have more faith in us than I ever had before. I am absolutely confident we're going to make it."

It took a while for me to get control of my emotions. When I had settled down, Marc said we only had one more thing to discuss tonight, and we would work on the rest tomorrow. I hated to do it, but I moved back over to the couch and waited for him to continue.

When he thought I was ready, he laid it out for me.

"Because it is mandatory I support us, we will have two separate accounts. One would be solely under your name and your control. The other would be a joint account we both would have access to. Everything you have now and everything you make would go into your account, and everything I make would go into the joint account. All of our expenses would come out of the joint account. By expenses, I mean everything. That includes your clothes, makeup, toiletries, everything and anything else that was normal everyday expenses."

I asked what I was supposed to do with the money in my account. He's answer was one more indication of what kind of man I had agreed to marry.

"I never want you to feel you are dependent on me. That account will serve many purposes. It's your safety net, so you don't always have to explain to me what you are spending money on. It will allow you to remain independent. You can use it for anything you want I will have no access to it.

"For example, let's say we buy Beth a nice Christmas gift, but you want to give her something special just from you, not us.

"Or, you want to help Ed pay for his son's college tuition. It would be easier getting him to accept the money if it came from your personal account, rather than our joint account. You will find uses for it, I'm sure. And, there's always the chance you would want to buy me a surprise birthday gift," He added with a smile.

Obviously, we didn't need my income to support us. I wondered just how much money Marc had and how much was going to be in the joint account. I know he said I could ask him anything, but did that include how much he was worth? I wanted to know. Not how much money he had, but if I was allowed to know how much.

"Marc, I know you said I would consider you rich. How rich are we talking about?"

Marc looked down at his hands, took in a very deep breath and let it out in one loud whoosh! He didn't answer. I thought I had gone too far.

"You don't have to answer that."

Marc lifted his head and looked across at me.

"Why wouldn't I answer that? There is nothing in my life you cannot know. That's why I told you to go through my files. Everything is in there. My hesitation is only because that is a difficult question to answer. It depends on so many things, and exactly what you mean by how rich are we. It all depends on the stock market, the housing market, the economy, and so many factors that vary from day to day. The standard for how much wealth you have is usually Net Worth, but that's a misleading number."

Marc struggled to put it into words.

"If I had to convert my assets into cash, it would depend on how long I had. If I needed all of the cash in thirty days, I could probably get thirty cents on the dollar if I had a year to raise the money, perhaps eighty cents on the dollar.

In addition to my Antonelli Systems stock, my portfolio contains stocks and bonds. That's handled by Danielle's brother-in-law. He's very good, and I suggest that's where you keep your account. Also, I have real estate holdings, commercial and domestic, rental properties and such.

Nick has also given me the opportunity to invest in small companies that Janice was sure would make it. I own ten percent of Danielle's Kitchen. I'm quite diversified."

After giving it some more thought.

"If you didn't have such a great relationship with Ron, I would have invested in him myself instead of sending him to Nick. It's just not a good idea to mix business and friendship like that. But, to answer your question, because I don't see any need to raise money in a hurry, I'll give you the Net Worth number. We have between four to five million dollars available to us as cash at any time. In addition, the other assets I mentioned give us a Net Worth of approximately one hundred million dollars."

I felt the pad slip out of my hands and fall onto the floor. I was powerless to stop it. It's funny how your mind operates. I thought Marc was worth four or five million dollars. Now, having been told that he is actually worth one hundred million dollars, and he definitely said us and not him, you would think I would have something profound to say. But, the only words that came out of my mouth were, "I'm going to need a bigger closet."

That resulted in a fit of laughter from Marc. I mean way down deep belly laughter. He shook so hard I was afraid he was going to rock himself right out of the chair and onto the floor. When he finally got control of himself, he looked at me and said sweetly, "I can do that for you!"

I had nothing else to say. My mind was trying to sort out everything I had heard tonight. After a minute, Marc got out of his chair, picked the pad up off the floor, took the pen out of my hand and placed both on the end table. Then he sat down next to me on the couch. He put his arm around my shoulder and pulled me close to him.

"There's nothing to be afraid of Catherine. You see how I live, nothing has to change. All this means is you never have to think about money. If you're in the mall and see a pair of five hundred dollar shoes you must have, you don't have to think about it. It means we dine at Danielle's Kitchen instead of The Olive Garden. We fly first class instead of a coach or use one of Nick's planes. It doesn't change who we are now. You'll get used to it."

I sat there with his arm wrapped around my shoulder and my head against his chest. I held his free hand in mine and tried to make sense of everything he said tonight. This man loves me and is determined to make me as happy as a woman could be. And just like Emily, I will do everything in my power to ensure he always feels that way.

After what seemed like an eternity, he helped me up and we moved into his bedroom, what soon would be our bedroom and we made love, both the emotional and physical kind. I emptied my head of everything we had talked about tonight and just reveled in his love.

This was going to work; I would make sure it did. And I honestly believed Marc would too.

Chapter 37 – Wedding Plans

In the morning, Marc said we should have a small engagement party.

"It will give your family and mine a chance to get to know each other."

I agreed it was a great idea. Unfortunately, small to Marc did not mean the same thing to me. In addition to my siblings and Marcs, we were inviting the entire original team from Dillman, the girls and their husbands, including Terry, who everyone considered a husband even though Stacy and Terry weren't married, Annie and some of the other regulars from the 88's. We would up with thirty-five people. Marc made the arrangements for Friday night. Dinner in a small banquet room at the Hyatt and then a trip to the 88's.

The rest of the week was busy at work. Marc stopped at his apartment and packed some clothes to leave at my apartment for the days he stayed over. I would bring more of my stuff to his place for the weekends. Marc decided since our Marriage Talk had been so heavy Monday night, maybe we should put off the Wedding Talk until the weekend. That suited me, and we spent the evenings just enjoying being together. But, it was very lonely Thursday night when Marc went home, and I had to sleep alone.

During the week, I had talked to Beth and my sister in laws about working and taking care of a man and the household. Although Beth didn't work, she did when she and Sal were first married. She was full of suggestions. Of course, they didn't take into account the fact my husband to be was very rich. But, I listened, and some of her ideas made sense. I also talk to the girls. They were all happy about our engagement, but I couldn't decide if they were happier for Marc or me. Not that it mattered. I had four very close new friends.

Friday, the engagement party turned out to be a blast. Both families got along, and that made me extremely happy. We partied late, and afterward, Marc said he was going to cut his day at his office short tomorrow. He would go in late and come home early. We had wedding plans to make.

Saturday, I made one of Elizabeth's special roasts. I knew Marc thoroughly enjoyed it. After dinner, we settled in the living room with my pad and pen and started to seriously plan our wedding and life together. Marc first went over the items we had discussed on Monday.

"As to your continuing to work, either at a job or a career and children, those weren't decisions we have to make right away. They could wait until we were settled in our new life, and got used to the idea of living together. But, we would have to think about them and talk if we had ideas or questions."

He asked me again if his apartment was good enough to start out married life in. That was an easy decision.

"It's more than we need. We can always move later if it becomes uncomfortable."

I did have objections to the money issues, but I knew Marc was set on being the sole support of us and my objections weren't worth the argument I was sure would follow if I voiced my concerns. I was sure I would find uses for the money that was in my individual account, and what I would spend out of the joint account wouldn't be excessive, so I gave in to that request. Once all that was out of the way, we talked about when.

"Catherine. I don't want to wait any longer than necessary. I know we have to satisfy your family this would be a formal and romantic wedding. I would prefer a church wedding, probably on a Sunday and a formal reception to follow. I want you to have the most romantic wedding possible, something you will remember forever, and I also want you to enjoy planning the wedding as much as possible.

Marc looked at me very seriously.

"One thing! You're not allowed to look at prices. I want the best of everything, and if you really love me, you'll spare no expense to make your wedding day the best day of your life."

How do you answer that statement? Just having him waiting for me at the foot of the aisle in the church would make it the best day of my life. But loving this man as I do and wanting to please him and knowing no matter how much we spend on the wedding, it wouldn't make a dent in his, (our), bank account, I planned on doing whatever was necessary to make him proud of our wedding day.

I was still having trouble with the 'our' bank account thing. Ever since the night Marc proposed, whenever he talked about money, it was always we, our, ours, never his. You might think this was the easiest part to get used to, but I was having a difficult time with the fact that he, *(we)*, were so rich.

"The sacrifices a girl has to make to satisfy her man. I guess I'll just have to learn to live with it!!!"

Bridesmaids were going to be a problem. I wanted both of my sisters-in-law and Marc's sisters. But, I also wanted Susan and Annie. That was already six, and I couldn't leave out the Sports Widows Club gals. I also couldn't decide which one of my brothers would walk me down the aisle and give me away. When I talked to Marc about these problems, he had an answer ready.

"When Nick's daughter got married, she had both Nick and her stepfather walk her down the aisle, one on each side of her. You could do the same thing with your brothers."

Problem solved. As far as the bridesmaids were concerned, he said the more, the merrier.

"I intend to commission Stacy to do all the gowns, and we'll pay for them. Unless you have something specific in mind, I'd like you to consider commissioning Stacy to do your wedding gown also."

That wasn't even worth thinking about. What girl wouldn't want a Stacy Geer wedding gown? Stacy only did wedding gowns under commission. They weren't a standard part of her collection. And that meant they were all one of a kind originals. I remembered seeing the picture of Danielle in her Stacy Geer Wedding Gown, and I couldn't desire anything more.

We continued talking late into the night, and one by one, decisions were made. The most important thing we didn't decide was the date.

"It has to be after I'm done with Dillman Brothers, but hopefully not too much after that. It also has to be during a time when I don't have a speech scheduled. Since they were scheduled so far in advance, it was tough to cancel. We need time for the wedding and honeymoon."

We circled possible periods when Marc would be free for three consecutive weeks. Since we were entering a slow period for the speeches, there were quite a few options available.

"Don't forget, I have a speech in San Antonio next weekend. I don't have any clients there, but it might be fun to invite Jim and Mary Ellen Carter to dinner Friday night. You'll have to leave work early that day so we could be in Texas by six o'clock."

I thought it was a terrific idea, and I made a note to myself to let Ben know I'd be leaving work early on Friday. Marc also said he would pick me up at my apartment Friday afternoon, and if I needed anything that was in his apartment, I should take it with me Monday morning. He showed me a color chart.

"I'm going to have the apartment painted, and I want you to pick out the colors."

We spent some time on that, and it made me feel good we had no trouble agreeing on a color scheme. Sunday we lounged around Marc's apartment again and filled in some of the details about the wedding. I wouldn't see Marc Monday night, and I wasn't looking forward to sleeping alone, but two nights a week was the best we thought we could get away with.

Monday night the girls got together at Cindy's apartment. I brought them up to date on the wedding plans so far. Stacy asked me if I had something specific in mind or would I trust her to come up with an appropriate design.

"I'm surprised Marc talked to you already. We just made the decisions over the weekend."

I had to explain what I meant. Stacy said she hadn't spoken to Marc.

"Do you think I'd allow you to get married in anything but one of my dresses?"

I was flattered, and when she said she would do all the gowns, but not under commission, they would be a wedding gift for Marc and me, I was speechless. I told her it was too much, considering the bridesmaid list was presently at ten. When I told them who I intended to have as bridesmaids, they all shook their heads. They said they were flattered I would consider them, but it wasn't necessary. I had to disagree.

"If it wasn't for your input on that Sunday morning, there might not be a wedding."

We argued about it for a while and finally came to a compromise. Stacy suggested, "Cindy, being the closest to your age could represent all of us. The sooner you get everyone in for measurements the easier it will be for me. Since you don't intend to see Marc Thursday, why don't you stop at the shop after work for your first fitting?"

That cut the list to seven. Marc was right. These were very good people, and I was one of them. Tuesday I told Marc about the meeting last night, and he didn't seem surprised.

"The more you hang out with them, the more you'll get used to it."

Wednesday flew by, and then it was Thursday. I stopped at Stacy's shop and got measured for my wedding gown. I made appointments for my bridesmaids to get their fittings and then I went home alone.

Friday, Marc picked me up at my apartment. Thomas carefully placed my garment bags in the trunk as always, and when we got to the airport, I found out we would be using the BBJ this trip.

Just as promised, Marc sent me to the flight deck, and I sat in the jump seat during the takeoff and climb to altitude. After that, I was told the flight would be boring, and they would call me back up front for the descent and landing. It was a blast.

Dinner with Mary Ellen and Jim was more fun than I expected. They were so happy we were engaged, and they seemed truly happy when Marc told them they were expected to attend the wedding. After dinner, they took us to a local spot they had found for dancing.

"After the night at the 88's, we decided we needed more time to enjoy each other."

It was a terrific evening.

Marc's speech on Saturday was on a subject I had never heard before, but he was as good as usual and captivated his audience. The 'your sister's panties' joke brought the laughs as always, and the follow up again brought the house down.

Sunday, we had brunch with Jim and Marry Ellen and then the flight home. Again, I got to watch the takeoff and landing from the cockpit. Sunday night, we went to my apartment.

"My place is probably full of paint odors," Marc explained.

It was a glorious weekend, and again I was lonely on Monday night.

Another week flew by and Friday I was anxious to be with Marc. I left work early and drove straight to his apartment. As usual, I had packed a bag with things I would leave at his place, and when I left Monday morning, it would be full of clothes he would need on the nights he stayed with me. Except for Mondays and Thursdays, my life was good and getting better. I was getting used to the vice president thing and felt I was pretty good at administration. Again, Marc proved to be right.

We were having dinner at Nick and Danielle's apartment, and Marc said he had two surprises for me. When I entered Marc's apartment Friday afternoon, it seemed strange.

It had been painted in the colors we had picked out, and the living room furniture had been rearranged. There was a very slight odor of paint still in the air, but it wasn't overbearing. I went immediately to the bedroom to shower and change. The bedroom too seemed strange. The new colors made it look entirely different, and I thought I'd have to change the drapes and bedspread to match.

After my shower, I grabbed clean panties and a bra from my overnight bag and went to the closet for Marc's favorite sun dress. No matter how many times I wore it, he always commented how much he liked it.

But, when I opened the closet door, it wasn't there. None of my clothes were there. Thinking the painters had to empty the closet to paint, I moved all the hangers trying to locate the clothes I had been bringing over here. I couldn't find anything that belonged to me. I checked the dresser drawers Marc had emptied for me, and they were empty. I couldn't understand what Marc had done with all of my clothes. I glanced around the bedroom trying to locate them, hoping he just forgot to put them back in the closet. That's when I spotted it!

On the far side of the bed, there was a door I had never noticed before. I had been in this room countless times and knew that this door had to be new. I went around the bed and gingerly open it.

A light came on automatically and there hanging in a brand new closet were my clothes. I looked around and realized this was just like the closet in Danielle's apartment. The night she and Stacy had taken me into her bedroom to try on those five beautiful dresses, I didn't realize her closet wasn't where Marc's closet was. It was on the other side of the room. Marc must have had this done over the past two weeks. That's why we couldn't come back here last Sunday night.

My clothes looked awfully lonely in that big space. In addition to hanging space for ten times more clothes than I had, there were shoe racks, drawers, and shelves. A full-length mirror hung on the far wall, and there was even a small bench in front of a lighted makeup mirror. I wondered where the room for this came from.

Moving back into the bedroom, I looked at the wall where the doorway had been cut and realized Marc's office was on the other side. Still wearing nothing but a bra and panties, I went into the living room and checked.

Marc's office was about a third of the size I remembered. Marc had given up the better part of his office to give me a closet all of my own. No wonder everything seemed strange when I came in.

Suddenly, I heard a door open. I looked toward the guest room, and a strange man, wearing nothing but a towel around his waist was coming into the living room. I screamed and ran back into the bedroom as fast as I could. I locked the bedroom door, not that the privacy lock could hold anyone at bay, and ran to the closet. Since none of my clothes were there, I grabbed one of Marc's shirts and covered myself as best as I could. I was looking around for something to block the door with when there was a knock on the bedroom door. From the other side of the door, I heard an unfamiliar voice.

"Ma'am, I'm sorry I frightened you. I didn't know anyone was here. Ma'am, are you alright?"

I ventured over to the door.

"Who are you and what are you doing here?"

"I'm Johnny Pierson, ma'am. I'm Anna Lee's son."

That name, I recognized. Anna Lee was Danielle's niece from Georgia, and I knew she had a seventeen-year-old son named Johnny. I opened the door a crack, just enough to peek out.

Standing about five feet away from the door was a young boy. I could forgive myself for thinking it was a full grown man, this kid was ripped and his blushing, extending all over his body, emphasized his muscle tone. And, wearing nothing but a towel around his waist, his finely toned body was fully on display.

"What are you doing here, Johnny?"

"Whenever Mamma and me are in town, I always stay in Mr. Marc's guest room."

Looking down to make sure Marc's shirt had me fully covered, I ventured out into the living room. Just as I was about to say something to Johnny, the apartment door opened, and Marc walked in with a pretty, petite girl who had country written all over her. Marc just looked at us. The girl screamed, "Johnny Pierson, go put some clothes on!"

Johnny gave her a, "Yes, ma'am." And ran back into the guest room.

Marc walked over to me and gave me an up and down look.

"I guess you've met Johnny?"

I nodded my head, and then he introduced me to Anna Lee.

"Whenever they are in Fort Lauderdale, Anna Lee stays with Danielle and Nick, and I let Johnny bunk here. It's either here or on Nick's couch."

"You could have warned me."

"They weren't expected in until six o'clock, but when the G5 got back from a charter run early, they rescheduled their trip."

Marc looked me up and down again.

"Is there a particular reason you're wearing my shirt?"

I looked at him with a smirk.

"You don't want to know."

Just then, Johnny came out of the guest room. He was wearing a pair of shorts and a tee shirt that did nothing to hide that toned body underneath. He walked over to us, and again tried to apologize. Marc looked at me and then at Johnny.

"This is what I come home to. My half naked fiancé and a naked man in my apartment."

I thought he was joking, but then turning to Johnny, he said, "Making out with my girl?"

Johnny turned cherry red, and Marc moved toward him. Without warning, Marc took a swing at Johnny. Luckily, those muscles were more than just for show. Johnny managed to duck away from Marc's fist and started backing up toward the middle of the living room.

Marc stalked him. He took another swing, and again Johnny avoided it. Then Johnny swung at Marc, but Marc backed away from the blow. I was so shocked at what was happening I couldn't move. I tried to tell them to stop, but no words would come out of my mouth. They circled each other, each looking for an opening. They both took swings at each other, but no blows landed.

Finally, I heard Anna Lee shout, "Johnny, you stop that foolishness right now!"

Johnny's head twitched slightly at the sound of his mother's voice, and that's all the opening Marc needed. He lunged at Johnny, wrapped his arms around the boy's waist and slammed him down onto the couch. Holding Johnny down with his left hand on Johnny's forehead, Marc used his right hand to…tickle him.

Johnny immediately started screaming, "No fair…no fair…no fair tickling!"

Marc back off and offered Johnny, his hand. When the boy was on his feet, Marc turned to Anna Lee.

"Anna Lee, you know better!"

Then Marc looked at me.

"Would you care to put some clothes on, or do you want to completely disrupt this boy's hormone balance."

I glared at Marc.

"I would if I could find them!"

Marc laughed.

"You said you needed a bigger closet!"

I ran over to Marc and threw my arms around him.

"I see I have to be careful what I say in front of you.

After a tender kiss, I went back into the bedroom to dress, Johnny and Anna Lee went to Danielle's apartment. When I came back into the living room, Marc was sitting on the arm of the club chair. Noticing I was wearing his favorite casual dress, he smiled.

Marc asked if Johnny frightened me. I told him the truth. Marc apologized.

"Anna Lee and Johnny were my other surprise, but I didn't expect them here so early. I thought I'd be home before they arrived."

I asked Marc about the staged fight, and his answer surprised me.

"It wasn't staged. All of Nick and Danielle's relatives trained with the security team, and taking a swing at Johnny like I did, helps to remind us trouble can come from anywhere at any time.

If I connected, it would be Johnny's fault and would be a good lesson to him."

Then I asked him why he scolded Anna Lee.

"When you're in a tough position, the last thing you need is a distraction. Anna Lee yelling at Johnny like that distracted him just long enough for me to take advantage.

Catherine, if I'm ever in a bad situation, you have one thing to think about and one thing only. Get to safety, any way you can. I can't give the situation the attention it deserves if I'm worried about you. Don't try to help me, don't cry, and don't scream. Just get away to safety."

Before I had a chance to say anything, Marc changed the subject.

"Good looking boy, isn't he?"

After thinking of Johnny wrapped in nothing but that towel, I had to smile as I nodded my head.

"Forget it, he's just seventeen years old.'

"That's legal in this state," I replied with a wicked grin.

That earned me a slap on the butt.

"Watch it, mister, you don't earn that right until after we're married."

"Then we'd better get on with it."

That earned him another long passionate kiss.

Marc changed, and we headed for Danielle's apartment. I asked Marc why he made the closet so big.

"Tony did it for me. I guarantee it's nicer than Danielle's. Tony was busy when Nick had her's done.

"You'll fill it faster than you realize. Rumor has it your friends have plans for a major shopping trip before the wedding."

When I tried to argue, Marc frowned.

"Catherine, remember all for one and one for all?"

I nodded, and he continued.

"That's us now. There will be no you or me, no his or hers. It's us, and since US is rich, you have to allow me to treat you the way it pleases me. I promise you will get used to it."

I knew he was right, but it would take a while and in the meantime, I would do whatever he asked.

Dinner with good friends as always was fun. Danielle was as good in the kitchen as I was told. Anna Lee was a sweetheart, and I could understand Marc's feelings for her.

She insisted on calling him Mr. Marc and me Miss Catherine. Johnny, in addition to being extremely good looking and in great shape was also very intelligent. His father had died in combat and had been awarded the Medal of Honor. That gave Johnny a free pass into whichever military academy he wanted. He already made up his mind it would be the Naval Academy, and he wanted to fly.

Nick told me,

"All three of Danielle's nephews had the bug, and they were all qualified pilots and were in the process of being certified to fly the BBJ."

How many times can I say it?

"Life was good!"

Chapter 38 – Picking a Date

Marc and I continued to plan the wedding and the possible dates we had circled on the calendar were adjusted. It wasn't easy to find the right date. It had to wait until after Marc was finished with Dillman Brothers, and we were both free enough to take three consecutive weeks off from work: one entire week before the wedding and two weeks for a honeymoon. It also had to be a three week period when Marc didn't have a speaking engagement.

We settled on seven bridesmaids. Marc wanted the bridesmaids and groomsmen to be couples, so they included Marc's brothers-in-law, Artie, Billy, and Dan Patrick. Since Elizabeth was going to be my Matron of Honor, and both of my brothers were going to walk me down the aisle, we picked Beth's husband Sal to escort one of my sisters-in-law. That left us one man short. I had an idea, but since it's was Marc's place to pick the groomsman, I didn't reveal it. But, we did have to ask the person he picked, so we talked about it. When the subject came up, Marc said, "I have someone in mind, but I want to get your opinion."

"Marc that's your decision, and I'll go along with anyone you chose."

"This is our wedding, and we both have to agree. Would you be comfortable if I picked someone like Jonathan from Memphis, or Anna Lee's son, Johnny? You seemed to be impressed by him, at least with his body!"

"I'm never going to live that down, am I?"

Marc gave me that silly grin he has when he's teasing me.

"Well, maybe if **one** of you had some clothes on?"

That earned him a punch on the arm, which earned me a hug and a sweet kiss.

"You would do that just to torment me, wouldn't you?" I said, only half-teasing.

Marc got serious and told me he was considering Ted. I said I had considered him, but I wanted it to be Marc's decision. Marc asked if I would have a problem with that, considering he would be escorting one of my sisters-in-law.

After about one seconds thought, I told him,

"Considering how everything turned out, I don't think either of my brothers would mind."

It was settled.

I got all of the girls over to Stacy's for measurements and fittings. Marc arranged for the guys to be fitted for new tuxedos, no rentals for this group. We had the church, the reception hall and were putting all the finishing touches on the affair.

One of the biggest items was the guest list. The only family I had was Elizabeth, Ed, and Ethan. Most of Marc's family lived in Italy. His two sisters were his only family here. Even counting their children, that totaled eighteen. The Sports Widows Club added eight more. Marc's old friends added another couple of dozen. When we added Marc's employees and the Client Services Division of Dillman Brothers, we were well over one hundred. I was shocked when the final list totaled between two hundred fifty and three hundred. Marc tried to explain.

"Some of my more important clients have to be invited. A couple of Dillman Brother's clients have to be also invited, people like Mary Ellen and Jim Carter and Eric, plus both Dillman Brothers and some of the Senior Staff."

This was going to be a much bigger affair than I had realized. Of course, Marc had no trouble paying for all this, but I was still a little overwhelmed by it all.

The honeymoon was on the agenda, and Marc asked if I had anyplace in mind. I had never given it any thought. Considering there would only be a little over four months between the proposal and the wedding, I had a lot on my mind.

"Whatever you decide will be okay with me."

"If you mean that, I'll make all of the arrangements, but I won't tell you anything about it until we actually get there."

After giving it some thought, I agreed. Knowing Marc, I knew it would be something wonderful.

Dinner was an issue we had to compromise on. I loved to cook for Marc, but he insisted he wouldn't enjoy it as much if I came home every night after work and slaved in the kitchen. So, we agreed I would prepare home cooked meals whenever I got home early, and the other days we would either eat out or do take-out. I also had been talking to Beth and my sisters-in-law about stretching meals out.

I was told if I doubled the size of the meal I intended to prepare, I could save half and just reheat it for a second meal. They all had tricks to make sure the quality of the meal wouldn't suffer. Marc contributed some ideas, and I also discovered my man wasn't a complete novice in the kitchen.

One Sunday morning, two weeks before Marc's contract with Dillman Brothers was up, I woke up to the odor of sautéed onions and garlic. When I made my way into the kitchen, I found Marc at the counter rolling meatballs. The odors coming from a gigantic pot and a couple of sauté pans on the stove were mouthwatering.

"What's going on?"

"You, lovely lady, are marrying an Italian, and I will take care of the sauce."

I looked at the size of the pot he was using.

"How many people do you intended to feed today."

"Have no fear, my dear, all will become clear."

Marc stopped what he was doing and giggled at his little rhyme. I had to giggle too.

"Why did you get up so early to start your masterpiece?"

"The sauce has to simmer for a while to meld all the individual flavors. While I'm busy in here, you could use the time to go through my file cabinet and get an idea of how our finances were set up. Write down any questions and any suggestions you might have."

I had no need to know details, but it seemed important to Marc I, at least, had an idea, so I did as he suggested. What I found was a varied list of investments. Most of the properties he owned were mortgaged. That seemed strange considering what his net worth was, so that went on my list. Each property file had pictures of the property along with the routine legal documents and a sheet disclosing year purchased, purchase price, mortgage amount, etc. but no ongoing expenses. All of his other files, including the portfolio Danielle's brother-in-law, handled were in similar condition, all original information but no continuous data. There were also Stock Certificates of the companies Marc had invested in, with the date of purchase, amount paid and the amount received when the options were executed.

Just like NAS Financial Group, some of the company stock Marc had invested in early on had been sold back at a profit, Marc continued to hold a small percentage in others, and some were sold back in their entirety.

Around two o'clock in the afternoon, Marc called me into the dining room. The table was set beautifully, with candles, a white linen table cloth, Sterling silverware and crystal glasses. The aroma coming from the kitchen all day was driving me crazy, and I couldn't wait to sample my future husband's culinary delight. And it was wonderful. Marc had made lasagna from what he said was a family recipe.

"I see I have to limit your time in the kitchen if I don't want to gain an additional thirty or forty pounds."

Crisp Italian bread and an excellent red wine complimented the meal perfectly. For dessert, he had Italian pastries and anisette coffee.

During that fabulous lunch, I managed to find the energy to ask Marc about what I found in his filing cabinet.

"A further indication of just how intelligent you are, Catherine. We actually own three companies. Besides Antonelli Systems, we also own Antonelli Management and Antonelli Investments.

"The management company takes care of the properties we own, pays the mortgages and bills, collects the rents, etc. The investment company takes care of the other companies we hold stock in.

"The reason all of our properties are mortgaged is because the return on our other investments is greater than the interest we pay on the mortgages."

Our conversation made me realize why Nick Amonti thought Marc was the man to help Dillman Brothers and why Dillman Brothers agreed. It seems my future husband has a great head for business. Marc also told me our three companies were the reason he had to spend so much time at his office on Saturdays. Although he had capable people to run things, he needed to stay informed about every facet of his three businesses, and until he was through with Dillman, Saturday was the only day he had to catch up.

I also didn't miss the 'we' own and 'our' properties in his answer.

We finished about half of what he had prepared.

"The remainder can be frozen and will make a quick meal on a day you don't want to fuss."

"What about that gigantic pot of sauce?"

Marc produced plastic containers from the pantry and filled them with that wonderful sauce.

"These are portion sized containers and with a pot of boiling water for the pasta, we could have a home cooked me in fifteen minutes."

There was enough for at least a dozen single serving meals. Between this and the suggestions I had gotten from my sister and sisters-in-law, I was sure we would not have to rely on take-out after we were married and I wouldn't have to be a slave in the kitchen. We would eat well even if I continued to work.

Afterward, we went into the living room to continue our wedding discussion. Before we got started, I asked Marc if he would consider allowing me to work for one of his companies.

"If you worked at my office, we could drive to and from work together, lunch together and see each other all day. That would be very nice, but before we talk about that, you have to decide if you want a job or a career."

I didn't understand what he was trying to say.

"Catherine, I already mentioned you had a great future in the corporate world if you wanted it. Everything you've shown me since that day has fortified my analysis of your capabilities. Even your questions today, about our businesses, indicate I am right about you. If you came to work for me, it would be just a job. I have a few positions you would be good at, and they even could entitle you to a title such as vice president. But, I don't have anything that would help you further your career."

After a moment of contemplation.

"Being Vice President of Specifications and Design is a step on the corporate ladder. You are capable of climbing to the very top of that ladder, but you have to decide if you want to make that climb. I can't help you with that. I will support whatever decision you make, and I will assist you in whatever way I can, but I cannot help you make that decision."

While Marc went to pour us some more of the excellent wine we had with lunch, I thought about what he had just said. He was right. I had to decide if I wanted a career or a job. In fact, my first decision was whether I wanted to work at all. Could I be happy as a stay at home housewife?

Luckily, Marc had already said this decision wasn't a front-burner issue. We could continue to talk about it, and I definitely would need his input. I wondered if he could make the decision for me, what he would choose.

Chapter 39 – Another Incident

When Marc returned with our wine, we talked about the wedding. We had almost everything settled, except the most important thing, the date.

"Are you having fun planning the wedding?"

"It's been hectic, but I'm having a ball."

"How did your shopping spree with the girls go?"

"That's plural, as in shopping sprees."

Marc had given me a Debit Card on his account and told me I couldn't outspend it. And, the girls were trying to prove him wrong, but we all knew it was impossible.

"You know what they're trying to do," I said.

Marc nodded his head.

"They're trying to make you shine for me, but what they don't know is you would shine if you were wearing a burlap sack."

That got me off the couch and onto his lap. I threw my legs over the arm of the chair and wrapped my arms around his neck.

"You really do love me, don't you? I mean really, really love me."

"I really, really, really do love you," he answered sincerely.

"Do you have any idea how much I love you?" I asked.

"I do," he replied, "And it's much more than I could ever hope for."

A sweet kiss and a lot of cuddling followed. When I finally got the courage to break away, I said, "Marc, I'm not a negative person, but I'm beginning to hate Mondays and Thursdays."

That brought out a serious look from Marc.

"I know what you mean."

"Good! In that case, I vote for the first Sunday we have circled on the calendar."

"That particular date is only four and a half months after our engagement."

"Another four and a half days is too long. I want to be Mrs. Catherine Antonelli. I would have married you the night you proposed if you had asked me."

"Believe me, Catherine, I thought about it. If it wasn't for your family…"

"Good, then it's settled. They'll just have to accept it!"

"Are you sure?"

"I'm surer of this than anything in my entire life."

And, it was done. I jumped off of his lap and went back to the couch. There was disappointment in his eyes.

"Now that we have a date, we have to finalize everything."

And in spite of his attempts to get me back in his lap, we settled down and started making arrangements for our wedding which now was only two and a half months away. But, later that night I made it up to him for jumping off of his lap so quickly!

Marc completed his contract with Dillman Brothers. The team had a farewell party for him in the Wine Cellar at Danielle's Kitchen, and we all had fun.

I asked Marc why he demanded a million dollars for the year he spent at Dillman.

"The SVP title and the salary were Nick's idea. The title was to give me the clout with everyone in the company I had to deal with and the salary was to impress the Dillman Brothers.

"Nick thought if they had to pay me that much money they would be more inclined to listen to my ideas. And, Nick was right. I don't believe they ever would have given in to the department name change, the new offices, and the original Carter Aviation deal if they weren't paying me that outrageous amount of money. It gave me an aura of believability."

We also talked more about his three companies and exactly how they operated. I spoke to him again about working for him.

"Catherine, once we're married, your name will go on the three corporations. That means you would be working for us, not me."

Marc regularly reminded me our marriage was just like the Client Analysis Department. One for all and all for one. It wouldn't be easy, but I knew I would get used to the idea. It's what my man wanted, and I would try hard to give it to him.

The wedding plans were coming along nicely. Nick had arranged to have me transported to the church in the same white carriage Danielle and Cindy used for their weddings. The church and hall were set. The dresses were completed and just awaited one final fitting a week before the wedding. Everything was in place except the honeymoon. Marc assured me he had it worked out, and he hoped I liked it, but he wasn't going to tell me anything about it.

Now that he was through with Dillman Brother, we did spend Saturdays together. Although, some of them were spent running around to florists, bakers, the church, and the banquet hall. It was crazy, but doing it together made it fun.

We stopped at the jewelers where Marc had gotten my engagement ring and picked out wedding bands. While Marc was doing the paperwork, I glanced at all of the engagement rings on display. The one I was wearing was the best of the lot. There were more expensive rings there, bigger stones and all, but the one Marc gave me fit my personality so perfectly I really did believe he knew me that well.

We kept to our schedule of weekends at his apartment, Tuesdays, and Wednesdays at mine, but Mondays and Thursdays were awful. I knew Marc felt the same, but as hard as I tried, I couldn't convince him to stay with me on those nights. We weren't fooling anyone, but Marc thought it showed respect for my family that at least we were trying to keep up the appearance. And, according to my brother Ed, he was right.

"The family has a lot of respect for your future husband. The charade about not living together is part of the reason because it was so important to Beth and the family."

During the two and a half months before the wedding, we spent time with our siblings and friends. Marc's friends were thrilled we were getting married. My friends thought I had made a great catch. Ron was pleased, not only about the wedding but how much credit Marc and I gave him for helping get us back together. It is hard to believe we almost broke up, and as each day passed, even harder to believe I hadn't trusted this man.

I had a lunch date with the Sports Widows Club gals, and I asked Susan to join us. They took to her immediately, even though she wasn't about to marry a multimillionaire.

Marc only had one speech engagement left before the wedding. It was in Kansas City, and he was as captivating as always. I thought I would be nervous as the date got closer, but all I felt was anticipation. There was no doubt I was doing the right thing. Being Mrs. Marco Antonelli was all I could think about. Life was good, and about to get better.

Two weeks before the wedding, we had to attend a Charity Ball. Tony's sister, Sidney, was in charge, and it was impossible for Marc to turn her down.

I dressed to please my man, in a new Stacy Geer gown, one I had purchased, and Marc's approval was apparent. The party was fun, but the only thing on my mind was the wedding. After the first dance with Marc, a gentleman I had once dated asked me to dance. I really didn't want to.

Jamey was not one of my better dates. He was one of the ones I had decided not to sleep with, but I did. Even after the talk Marc and I had about the subject, I still wasn't sure why I had. But, that was in the past, and I didn't want to make a fuss, so I agreed to dance with him.

During our turn on the dance floor, he started coming on to me. I told him I was engaged, and the wedding was in two weeks, but that didn't stop him. He suggested since the wedding was two weeks away, that meant I still had two weeks of freedom, and he was more than willing to help me get it out of my system.

I left him alone on the dance floor and returned to Marc. It must have been obvious how annoyed I was because Marc asked me if I was alright. Not wanting to start trouble, I made light of it and pretended nothing was wrong.

A while later, I decided to take a trip to the ladies room. I left the banquet hall and on my way to the restrooms, I ran into that same guy. Jamey apologized for his behavior and was trying to be polite

I said it was alright. He asked if he could kiss the bride, and thinking his contrition was real, I offered him my cheek. But, instead, he grabbed me, pulled me to him and kissed me on the lips. Caught off guard, it took a minute for me to regain my composure and attempt to pull away from him. I broke the lip lock, but I couldn't get out of his grasp. I told him to let me go, but he kept me pulled close to his him.

I heard a man's voice from behind me.

"The lady doesn't seem to want your attention, why don't you just let her go?"

Jamey's reply was mean and threatening.

"Back off, Bub, this is none of your business!"

The voice behind me answered.

"When a lady is in trouble, it's every man's business!"

I realized the voice behind me was Marc's.

Jamey laughed.

"If you had the chance to fuck her, you'd know this is no lady."

Marc spoke again.

"I know this young man, just seventeen years old. The last time I saw him, his mother yelled at him. I had to admonish her, and then tell my lady why."

"What the hell does that mean?" Jamey said.

Jamey had no idea what Marc was talking about, but I knew exactly what it meant. Marc was trying to tell me to get to safety and let him deal with the situation, but I couldn't break free from Jamey's hold on me. I could feel Marc was standing directly behind me now, and suddenly Jamey screamed and let me go. I backed away and moved back toward the doors that led to the ballroom. But instead of going in, I stood there and watched.

Marc had Jamey by two fingers, and he had those fingers pushed back so far it caused Jamey to fall to his knees. Marc had his back to me, and as I tried to hear what he was saying, the door behind Jamey opened, and two men walked out. They were friends of Jamey's, and they came to his aid.

Before they got too close, Marc said, "Any closer and I'll snap his wrist. Your friend was making a pass at my fiancée, and he wouldn't take no for an answer. If you two think, under the circumstances, he's worth fighting for, then we'll go around a few times, but I'll snap his wrist first to keep him out of the action."

The two men looked at each other and decided this was not a fight they wanted.

"Sorry, man. He can be an asshole sometimes. Let him go and we'll keep him out of trouble. No one has to get hurt."

Marc gave them a long look, dropped Jamey's hand and backed up a couple of steps. The two men ran to Jamey and helped him up. Jamey was screaming at Marc, calling him names, but his two friends led him away. One of them turned back toward Marc.

"Sorry man, and please apologize to your woman for us."

Marc just nodded and turned to enter the ballroom through the door I was standing by. I had never seen Marc angry, except the time when Jim Carter was waiting for me in Marc's office. But this was even worse.

When he was close enough to say something without shouting he said, "Need a trip to the ladies room, I'll escort you."

He put his arm around my waist and led me in that direction. I wanted to say something to him, but he pushed me through the door. It took some time for my heart to stop beating and control my breathing. When I had some semblance of normalcy, I walked back

263

out to the corridor. Marc was waiting by the door. His angry expression hadn't changed. I looked directly into his eyes.

"Are you angry with me?"

"No, Catherine, I'm not angry, I'm concerned."

He turned to face me.

"Catherine, didn't you understand what I said to him about Johnny?"

I nodded.

Marc shook his head.

"Then why didn't you go back into the ballroom where you would be safe?"

"There were three of them, I was worried about you."

"We have to talk, Catherine, but not here, not now. When we get back to the apartment, we'll talk."

Marc tried to lead me back into the ballroom, but I hesitated.

"Marc, what he said," I began.

"Not here, not now. Later, we'll talk."

Knowing Marc the way I do, I knew the conversation was over. Marc took out his cell phone and made a quick call. I didn't know who he called or what he said. I was tense the remainder of the night.

I was terrified of what he must be thinking, and only two weeks before our wedding, if there still was to be a wedding.

Marc tried to mask his feelings. We bid on a few auction items, but it was evident Marc was not really enjoying himself as much as he pretended. I couldn't wait for this night to be over so I could explain. Just before we left, Marc made another call.

When we exited the hotel, Thomas, and the stretch were waiting for us. There was another man with Thomas. I didn't know why Thomas was there. After we entered the limo, Thomas drove to the parking lot where Marc's car was parked. Marc gave the other man the keys to his car and Thomas drove us to Marc's apartment. Marc's car arrived right behind us, and the other man gave Marc his keys back. Then the other man and Thomas left.

Upstairs, I went directly to my closet to change. This was not a night for a sexy nightie. I picked out the pretty, feminine set I wore in Nashville. When I returned to the living room, Marc was sitting in his club chair with a glass of wine. He had the bottle and an empty glass on the coffee table and asked if I wanted some. I shook my head and curled up on the couch. I needed a clear head, Marc did not look happy.

"Catherine, I will never demand much of you, but there are three things I must have. First, I need you to love me. Second, I need you to have faith in me, and third, I need to feel you are safe."

I looked into his eyes and saw something I had never seen before fear. Was he afraid I had cheated on him? I knew Marc was having difficulty telling me what was bothering him, and I wasn't sure what he was afraid of, so I just sat and waited for him to let me know.

"I'm going to ask you to do something for me. And I don't want you to just say yes. I need you to mean it and take it very seriously."

He paused and looked for a reaction from me. I gave him my sincerest look and waited for him to continue.

"Tomorrow, I'm going to call Nick and ask him to sign you up for classes with the NAS Security Team. I want you to take those classes and take them seriously. I don't know what I would do if anything ever happened to you."

My heart started beating again, and I was able to breathe again. I looked into Marc's eyes and was sure it was fear I saw. Fear for my safety, not my fidelity.

I thought back to the day I met Danielle in the apartment lobby and the things she said to me about not wanting Nick to worry about her. Looking into Marc's eyes, I understood what she meant.

I had to reassure him. I had to let him know I would do what he asked. I had to let him know I would take this very seriously.

"Marc, I never want to give you moments worry about me. I will do what you ask, and I promise you, I will be the most dedicated student they ever had, even more dedicated than Danielle."

That seemed to satisfy him and lessen the tension, but I still had to explain Jamey and his comments. I decided to tell him everything.

"Marc, those comments Jamey made..."

Marc put up his hand to stop me. He came over to me and crouched down in front of me so our eyes were on the same level. When he spoke, his words were gentle.

"Catherine, I know in my heart since our relationship started you have been faithful to me. I've already told you anything that happened in your life before the night we went to the 88's for the first time is not related to our relationship. It's not a problem. You have to believe that."

I did. I did believe he meant what he had just said. I knew our relationship started that night. As far as Marc was concerned, my life began that night. But, I wanted no secrets from this man, and I wanted him to know no man had ever made me feel the way he does. I wanted him to understand he was like no other man I had ever met.

Once again, Marc showed how well he knows me.

"I said I don't have to know. I have no need to know. But, if you have a need to talk about anything, I will be here for you. And, no matter what you tell me, it will have no bearing on our relationship. I promise you my only concern is what happened since that first night and in our future."

I did tell him. I wanted to tell him. I wanted him to know what a fool I had been to allow this jerk to take advantage of me.

Marc was sympathetic. He said we all learn some lessons the hard way. He said the best thing to do was learn from the experience and move on.

After hearing my story, he also said he was sorry he hadn't broken the guy's wrist.

I also told Marc Jamey was the last man I was with before I met him, and it was one night more than three months before Marc came to work at Dillman. He asked me why there were no men in my life for five months.

"I decided if I couldn't find a real gentleman, I'd rather do without."

That brought out one of Marc's best smiles.

"I guess you were pretty happy when I showed up."

That made me smile for the first time since I danced with Jamey earlier this evening. If there was one thing I was absolutely sure of, this man loved me totally and would always be there for me.

What more could a girl want?

Chapter 40 – The Last Week

Our wedding was a week away. And it was going to be a very busy week, cumulating with the Rehearsal Dinner on Saturday evening.

Again, my idea and Marc's idea of a small intimate dinner didn't quite match. The wedding party included my sister Beth, who was to be my Matron of Honor and Tony Marchetti, who was Marc's boyhood friend and was to be Marc's Best Man, plus the seven Bridesmaids and seven Groomsmen. Of course, Tim and Emily and Sara and her husband were invited along with Nick and Danielle, Terry and Stacy and Angie and Harry. Jim and Mary Ellen Carter and Ron were in town for the wedding and were included. We had invited Jonathan, but he wasn't due into Fort Lauderdale until later that night.

During the five days, Nick was lost at sea, I found out Marc was very close to Danielle's two sister's and Nick's five children, and, of course, they were invited. The final total was forty-eight, including Marcie and her husband. Everyone who worked at Antonelli Systems was invited to the wedding, but thankfully not the rehearsal dinner.

Marc had reserved rooms at the Hyatt for everyone and had plans for a bus pick us all up and take us to the rehearsal and then back to the Hyatt for dinner. We would all spend the night there and then go to the church together tomorrow morning. All except Marc. After dinner, Marc was to go back to his apartment and Tony would pick him up there in the morning.

I had taken the entire week off from work, and I managed to fill the time with last minute chores, including my final fitting with Stacy. I did have time for lunch with Ron. I had to tell him I would never forget what he had done for Marc and me. Of course, he played down the part he played, but he did say something made that me extremely happy. Ron told me he had met someone special, and she was coming to Florida on Friday and would be his date for wedding festivities. I loved Ron and could only hope he had found the kind of love Marc and I shared.

Saturday morning I woke up in Marc's arms. The next time we shared a bed we would be Mr. and Mrs. Antonelli. The idea thrilled me and sent warm currents throughout my body. We had a light breakfast and then parted.

We both had last minute chores, and I wouldn't see Marc again until we met at the church for rehearsal. I waited for the movers to bring the remainder of my clothes and personal stuff over from my apartment. My furniture would go into storage until after the honeymoon.

My new closet was filling up with the items I bought on my shopping outings with the girls and my own things I had been bringing over from my apartment. My clothes ceased looking lonely in the big closet. It was filling up nicely. The very last thing I did before Thomas picked me up for the ride to the Hyatt, was pack for the honeymoon.

I wouldn't be back in this apartment for two weeks. I wrote a note to Marc and left it on the refrigerator door, where I was sure he would see it. It contained all of the feelings I had at that moment, and it turned out to be longer than I intended, but since he would be spending the night alone here, I wanted him to know I would be thinking about him and our future together.

I reached the hotel around two in the afternoon and spent the remainder of the time before we had to leave for the rehearsal with Beth, my sisters-in-law, and my future sisters-in-law. The girls from the Sports Widows Club stopped by, and Stacey dropped off my wedding gown. I hadn't seen Marc since breakfast.

At four, we headed for the church. Marc was waiting for me there, just as I knew he would be waiting for me tomorrow. I thought I would be nervous, but one look at Marc and I knew this was right. Rehearsal went smoothly and then we went back to the hotel for dinner.

Marc had hired a band, and between courses we danced. I only danced with Marc twice, the first and last dance. Nick was my second partner.

"Until you came along, I didn't think Marc would ever find someone. I'm sure Marc is glad he waited, and I'm glad he waited too. I'm sure you're the one to bring the happiness to Marc's life he deserves."

My next dance was with Ron. He had introduced me to his girlfriend, and we hit it off immediately. I thought Ron had a good chance of being happy with this woman and that made me happy. While we danced, Ron asked me if Marc would have any problem with our friendship continuing.

"Marc was entirely comfortable with our relationship, but we would not be sharing a bed anymore, dressed or not."

"How do you think Marc would feel if he knew about our relationship while we were in college?

I knew what he meant, and when I told him Marc did know about the strange relationship we had back then.

"I told Marc about every part of my life before he and I met. I don't want anything to turn up later he didn't know about in advance."

"What was his reaction?"

"As far as Marc is concerned, our life started the night we began dating and nothing before that matters."

"What about that guy Jamey?

Ron was my closest confidant, and I told him everything. When I told Ron about the incident at the charity ball and about our conversation afterward, he reminded me, "I still didn't believe it was just the strong drinks that Jamey ordered for you."

I usually drank margaritas, and when Jamey ordered Ajeno margaritas for me, I didn't realize that particular tequila had almost twice the alcohol content of the usual kind.

"Even the two strong drinks you had didn't account for your reaction. I've been with you when you had four or five drinks over a three-hour period and with the meal you ate that night you shouldn't have been as out of it as you were. I'm sure there was more involved."

"Please never mention that. Marc thinks I had too much to drink, and he told me to treat it as a learning experience. If Marc thought there were drugs involved, he'd want to go after Jamey and after talking to Nick Amonti's security guys, I don't want that to happen. Marc would probably wind up in a lot of trouble.

"They told me Marc was more than capable of putting down those three men at the charity ball without help. They said it was training, and Marc was very conscientious about his training. The only reason he had called Thomas and another security agent was because I was with him. If they were waiting for him in the parking lot, he didn't want me in danger.

"Marc made me promise to train with the NAS Security Team, and I intend to do that as soon as we return from our honeymoon."

That pleased my friend.

"You found yourself a good man, Catherine. Hang on to him, and take good care of him. I'm sure he'll take very good care of you."

That made my heart sing and earned Ron a kiss. Not the warm and friendly kind we were used to. Those were in the past, and I'm sure Ron agreed.

My next partner was Tony Marchetti. Marc had introduced me to Tony and his other childhood friends at various times during our relationship. Tony was Marc's best friend from grammar and high

school, and their relationship had endured even when they went to different colleges and choose different careers.

While Marc's interest had been in computers, Tony followed his father and became a finish carpenter. After Nick Amonti financed Marc's business, Marc introduced Tony to Nick, and he too became one of the NAS success stories.

Tony confided, "After Marc's previous marriage, I didn't think he would ever allow himself to get too close to another woman. You must really be a special kind of woman to break Marc out of the mindset he had developed about relationships. I know you're the perfect one to make Marc happy, and I know Marc will devote his entire life to your happiness. I'll always be there for Marc, and you can depend on me to always being there for you also."

I remembered the morning Cindy called about Nick's plane crash. On the drive to the Hyatt, Marc made a number of phone calls to set everything up. One of those calls was to Tony. It was a very short call.

All Marc said was, "I'm on my way to the Hyatt on SE 17th Street. Meet me there as soon as you can."

Tony was there less than thirty minutes later. If I had to measure Marc by the people who he considered his friends, he'd get a Triple 'A' rating. This was the man I was about to marry.

Dinner and dancing continued and just before dessert, Marc made a little speech.

"Thank you all for sharing this joyful occasion with us. We're here today thanks to the love and support of many people. Catherine and I will always be grateful to all of you who helped us through a very rough time in our relationship."

Tony toasted us.

"I know yours is a love that would last for all time. Catherine, thank you for bringing so much joy into my friend's life. Marc, waiting for the right woman to come along paid big dividends. I know you will treasure her always."

After dinner was over and the band took another break, Nick's girls were trying to get Nick and Terry to jam. Marc smiled, but I didn't know what they meant. When Danielle and her two sisters joined the chorus of pleas, Nick, and Terry shrugged, got up and moved over to the piano. There, they proceeded to create magic. They started slow, playing a boogie and then they started adding things and played faster and faster. It was as if they were trying to outdo each other.

I found out later, that was exactly what they were doing, that's what it meant to jam. Hearing them go at it, the bass player, the guitar player and the drummer from the band, went back on stage and joined them. Then it really became magical. The music coming from that stage was unlike anything I had ever heard, and Nick and Terry seemed to be holding their own against the professional musicians. It lasted for a while, but it couldn't go on forever, they were expending a lot of energy.

Terry nodded to the others, and they finished with a flourish. It was wonderful, and just the thing to wrap up this happy occasion. Nick and Terry high-fived each other, and they received congratulatory handshakes from the band members.

When things quieted down, Marc handed me an envelope. I gave him a 'what's this' look, and he said it was my wedding present. I couldn't imagine what he had gotten me. What could possibly fit in a plain white number ten envelope? He watched as I opened it and smiled at my surprise. Inside were certificates for the three companies Marc owned with my name listed as co-owner.

I guess the look on my face told Marc I loved his gift, but it also asked a question. He answered it before I asked.

"Catherine, I am totally yours. I not only offer you all my worldly possessions but all of my love. I promise to love you, care for you, protect you and be faithful to you."

In about twelve hours from now, I was going to marry a man who not only loved me completely but who knew me so well I would never have to ask him for anything. He would always have it there for me before I asked. Now I was glad I had left that note for him in the apartment. I wanted him to know he was always first in my heart and on my mind, even when we weren't together.

And, I suddenly hated the tradition that the groom couldn't see his bride before the wedding. I wanted to be with my man tonight, and tradition be damned. But as the party wound down, Marc dispatched me to my suite upstairs, and he headed for his, soon to be our, apartment. I had plenty of company and didn't have too much time to think about my loneliness. All of the girls at the party stopped by to give me a hug and tell me I was going to marry a good man.

Sleep didn't come quickly, and when it finally arrived it wasn't a very sound sleep.

I counted the minutes until it was time for me to put on my wedding dress.

Chapter 41 - The Wedding

Even though I didn't sleep well, I got out of bed the next morning full of life. I couldn't wait to get to the church and claim this man as my husband. The girls from the Sports Widows Club arrived first. They didn't stay, all except Stacey, who was there to make sure my dress was perfect. All of my bridesmaids stopped by and finally it was just Beth, Stacey and me.

To please my future husband, I wore stockings instead of pantyhose. Beth gave me my something old. It was the garter belt our mother had worn at her wedding. My something new was my beautiful Stacey Geer Original Wedding Dress.

Danielle had loaned me a beautiful set of jewelry, which consisted of a diamond necklace, matching diamond earrings and a matching diamond bracelet for my something borrowed. I couldn't imagine what the set was worth in dollars, but its real value was the friendship Danielle and I shared.

And my something blue was a frilly blue garter and instead of wearing it just above the knee as most brides, I wore this one right at the very top of my stockings. That earned a scowl from Beth and a giggle from Stacey, but, I knew Marc would appreciate the gesture.

I wore my hair down. I didn't want to be royalty today. I wanted to be a soft feminine woman for my man. Dressed, hair down and makeup complete, I took a look at myself in the full-length mirror. Just like in Memphis, I wanted to see what Marc would see. As much as Marc knew me, I was sure I knew him just as well, and the reflection staring back at me would please him, I was certain.

Just like Danielle's and Cindy's dresses, mine was three dresses in one. After the ceremony, Stacey would remove the train, and I would be wearing a ball gown. After Marc and I danced to The Loveliest Night of the Year, the skirt would come off, and I would be in my party dress. Stacey was amazing and there was no doubt her designs were worth every penny.

We met the rest of the bridal party in the hotel lobby. After hugs had been exchanged, everyone went outside to watch my grand exit from the hotel. My brother Ethan, who usually was the reserved one, looked as if he was ready to cry.

"Catherine, Marc is a very, very lucky man."

Ed and Ethan escorted me through the hotel exit, and we had to wait on the steps until the photographer and videographer were happy. There were pictures of the three of us, and then me alone. It took a while.

Then my brothers escorted me to my carriage. I had seen photos of the carriage in Danielle's and Cindy's apartments, but it was so much better in real life. Just before I stepped into the coach, Ed said, "I have a message for you from Marc. He told me to tell you this will not turn into a pumpkin at midnight."

Ed hadn't the faintest idea of what that meant, but I did. It was what Marc had said to me in Memphis when we left the hotel for his speaking engagement. I knew Marc was a romantic soul, but he managed to find a way to surprise and thrill me, again and again.

Once the four of us were settled in the carriage, the six white horses started pulling us toward the church. Ed opened a little door in the side wall of the coach and pressed a button and music came from outside the carriage. It was Beth Midler singing, and a gigantic smile lit up on my face as the four of us joined in the song, 'Going to the chapel and we're going to be married'. It was perfect.

Once we reached the church, everyone but the wedding party was ushered inside. My bridesmaids, Beth, and my two brothers were left in the vestibule. I knew the plan was for the groomsmen to escort Marc and Tony to the altar and then the procession would start. Our queue would be when the music changed from the organ to violins.

Marc had hired an orchestra with a half dozen violins to escort me down the aisle to him. My bridesmaids entered one at a time and after one final hug, Beth moved down the aisle. I was standing off to the side so I couldn't be seen from inside the church.

The doors were closed, and I stood behind them, flanked by Ed and Ethan. The doors didn't open until Beth had made it all the way down the aisle and was in position on the altar. When the violins started to play, the doors opened, and the three of us walked slowly down the aisle. I saw Beth standing on the altar, and directly opposite her were Marc and Tony.

When I had reached the halfway point, Marc left the altar and moved to the foot of the aisle to wait for me. It took all the strength I had to continue the slow walk to him. I wanted to run the rest of the way and fall into his arms.

When I finally reached him, the priest stepped down and said the required words. Marc was Catholic, and this was to be a strict formal Catholic wedding. After the introduction the priest asked, "Who gives this woman to be wed to this man?"

Ed and Ethan answered in unison.

"We do!"

And when I turned to each of them for a kiss, they both had tears in their eyes. My big bad brothers were mush melons, and I loved them for it. Ed placed my hand in Marc's, and we moved up to the altar.

The ceremony was formal, but Marc and I had both written our own vows. Neither of us had revealed to each other what we were going to say, but in different words, we both promised eternal love, fidelity, openness and honesty and of course, we promised each other the last dance. The exchange of the rings was beautiful with words Marc had written for us. And then it was time and when the priest said, "You may kiss you bride."

Marc looked into my eyes.

"Catherine, this is only the beginning. I promise to be there for you and protect and care for you."

And then he kissed me passionately.

The recessional was much quicker, and the line of people streaming out of the church to congratulate us seemed to last forever. I knew we had invited almost three hundred and fifty people to our wedding, but I never expected so many of them to show up at the church. When we finally were able to leave the receiving line, I was disappointed we headed for a white stretch limo instead of the beautiful carriage. Seeing my disappointment, Marc said the carriage would take hours to get all the way to Palm Beach to the Country Club where the reception was to be held. It made sense, and it was the only disappointment I would have this beautiful day.

Chapter 42 – The Reception

When we reached the country club, we were brought into a special room that had been set up for us. The only ones there besides the bridal party, their spouses and dates, were Ron and his girl Janette, Nick and Danielle, Stacey and Terry and Angie and Harry.

We stayed in that room until the cocktail hour was over and our guests were ushered into the main hall. I was glad for the rest. It had been a hectic day to this point, and knowing how Marc felt about his old country Italian manners, I was sure we would visit every table and say hello to every single person at the reception. It would be a very full afternoon.

Stacey removed the train of my dress, and we finally were ready to enter the hall. It took a while, and when Marc and I finally entered and walked to the center of the dance floor, the band played the beautiful song Marc and I loved to dance to. I was in heaven, and I was in the arms of my angel. The dance ended too soon, and we moved over to the head table. Tony stood and offered me a beautiful toast.

"Catherine, Marc and I have been best friends since childhood. On many occasions, I have asked him why he hadn't married and settled down. He told me he was waiting for the perfect woman to compliment his life. Since I've met you, I believe the wait was worth it. Seeing the happiness and joy you have brought to my friend, I believe he has found the perfect woman to make him complete."

Tony turned to Marc.

"Marc, I commend you for holding out and waiting for the perfect mate. You don't need my wishes for happiness. I know you two will always be happy together."

It was wonderful, and I could see the sincerity in Tony's eyes. He truly was happy for us. After that, we settled in for a very long afternoon.

As I suspected, Marc and I made the rounds and said hello to everyone that was there. We did manage to spend some time with family and friends, and we did manage to dance a couple of times. But, most of our dancing was with our guests.

Nick was first and the only thing he said to me was, "I'm sure you realize our little group is more than friends And, as the senior member of the group, I have the honor of welcoming you to our family."

I told him I had never met a nicer group of people, and I truly wanted to be part of this family.

Ron didn't say much either when we danced. He seemed happy and content, and I wasn't sure if his happiness was for me or because of Janette.

When I danced with Ted, I realized he had been taking his lessons seriously. Later, Connie told me he found out he really loved to dance and she thanked me again for pushing him into lessons.

I still had no idea about our honeymoon. I was sure Nick knew, and that meant Danielle knew, and that meant the other girls knew. I toyed with the idea of prying the information out of one of them but decided I didn't want to spoil Marc's surprise.

Because of Marc's wealth, we had put on the invitations instead of gifts to the bride and groom we would prefer a donation to Marc's favorite charity. I was sure St. Jude's Hospital would benefit from our wedding, and that added to my joy.

We cut the cake and did the bouquet and garter toss. The hem of my party dress stopped just above the knee, and when Marc reached for the garter, I just raised the hem a couple of inches.

Marc's hands were under my skirt and out of sight, and when he realized how high I had placed the garter his mouth formed a wicked grin. When I first thought of the idea to tease him like this, I didn't take into account the effect it would have on me. Marc's fingers sliding up my thigh were making me crazy with passion and when the fingers on the inside of my thigh went higher than they had to, I thought I would pass out from the excitement coursing through me. He just lingered there for a few seconds and then slipped the garter off my leg and tossed it over his shoulder.

Ted caught the garter and Susan caught the bouquet. Perfect, I thought. This was right up Ted's alley, but ignoring the cries of the other guests to go higher, Ted stopped just a few inches above Susan's knee. When he stood up, Susan gave him a kiss in gratitude. This was a new Ted, and I was sure Connie was the reason. When I got Ted alone, I told him I was proud of him. He said it was all Connie's fault.

"If I want to keep her interested, I know I have to clean up my act. The truth is, it's not as difficult as I would have thought."

But when I talked to Connie, she had a different perspective.

"The responsibility of his new position at Dillman Brothers and the talk Ted and you had at lunch has settled Ted down. He was becoming a complete man, respectful and caring. I think we have a great chance of a good life together."

I knew she was partly right, but I told her, "His new position and our talk had something to do with it, but I'm sure you're the principal reason for the change in Ted."

Her smile indicated she wished I was right. She was in love with Ted, and I hoped he didn't blow this chance.

When I got an opportunity to spend some time with Marc, he pointed to the dance floor. Annie and Billy had their arms wrapped around each other like a couple in love. I couldn't help but smile, and I told Marc, "I'm ready for my retirement party now!"

"When we get back from our honeymoon, I'll make arrangements."

"Let's keep it small."

"How small?

"How about just two people."

That made my man smile, and he nodded.

"What about Ron and Janette?

"I haven't had a chance to really get to know her, but from the short time I spent with her, I think she will be good for Ron. He seems happier than I've ever known him to be. You've talked to her, what do you think of her?"

"She's beautiful, intelligent and she has spunk, just like my wife."

That comment surprised me and hurt a bit. Why would he bring up his ex-wife, and why today, on our wedding day? I was more than a little confused until I realized he didn't say his ex-wife, he had said his wife. That was me!

I could get used to that.

The senior Mr. Dillman asked me if I had decided to continue in my present position.

"Marc and I discussed it and decided I wouldn't make a decision until we had settled into a routine. Marc didn't think it was a good time to make major decisions while all of this wedding stuff was going on. It would be at least a couple of months after we returned from our honeymoon before we even talked about it again and if I did decide to leave, I'll give you enough notice so you can find the right person to take over."

That seemed to please him.

I had given it some thought, and Marc and I had discussed it generally. I was enjoying my new position and a couple of incidents including the one talk Susan and I had with Gino made me start to believe I could be good at this. But, I agreed now was not the right time. I made Marc promise when we did talk about it, he wouldn't just say what he thought I wanted to hear, he would give me his honest opinion.

"You'll always have that."

And I knew I would.

We stayed at the reception longer than I expected. Considering we still had to return to the hotel to change and then leave for our honeymoon, I thought we'd already be on our way. But, Marc didn't seem to be in a hurry.

Finally, he asked if I was ready to leave. We danced once more to our favorite waltz and then ran out the door. The stretch was waiting for us and took us back to the hotel.

When we were in the suite I had left earlier that morning, Marc informed me we weren't leaving until tomorrow night.

"We can stay here tonight, sleep in tomorrow, have a late breakfast and then dinner before we board Nick's plane for our honeymoon. The travel arrangements are set for a late departure tomorrow night."

That was perfectly alright with me. It meant my new husband would make love to me earlier than I had anticipated. I could deal with that, especially after that little finger thingy he did while removing my garter. I still hadn't completely recovered from that.

I changed into my wedding nightie. It was a gift from Danielle. About five years ago, Stacey had decided to add sleepwear to her line, and as an anniversary present to Danielle, she named the new line, 'The Danielle Line of Stacey Geer Design.' The nightgown and peignoir were gorgeous. Not too revealing, but sexy as all hell.

Just as Marc had said about my bikini in Nashville, it left enough to the imagination. I knew he would be turned on. And, he was.

We made sweet, passionate love. The emotions that passed between us were stronger than ever before. I didn't think being married to Marc would make a difference, but I was wrong.

Having this man as my boyfriend was wonderful. When he became my fiancé, it was even better. But, nothing compared to tonight. It was if we were one.

Not husband and wife, but one entity.

Chapter 43 – The Honeymoon Delayed

Monday morning we did sleep late. Between the unfruitful sleep, I had Saturday night, the energy expended during the wedding and reception and our first night together as husband and wife, we definitely needed the sleep. Marc was already up and showered before I opened my eyes. He had a cup of coffee in my hand before I was fully awake. While I showered and dressed, he ordered breakfast. We sat around for a while, cuddled together on the couch. Marc told me he had a couple of reasons for the late departure tonight.

"Would you be very upset if I conducted a little business during dinner, before we left for the airport? "

I was surprised, but not unhappy. Even after he left Dillman Brothers, Marc had not been paying as much attention to his business as he should. He spent a lot of time with me preparing for our wedding. One business dinner on our honeymoon was not going to lessen the joy I felt at being his wife.

We spent the day at the beach, mostly just walking along the sand. We were dressed in casual clothes, not bathing suits, so we stopped at a nice little place for lunch. About three, we headed back to our suite to change for dinner and pack.

Thomas would be driving us to the airport directly from our dinner engagement. Marc asked me if I would wear the red dress I wore for dinner in Memphis. I couldn't refuse my husband's request on our honeymoon. Around five thirty, we packed our luggage in the stretch and Thomas drove us to the restaurant. It was the quiet place where Marc and I had taken me the first time we had dinner together.

We didn't have to wait for our table. I was surprised to see Nick, Danielle, Ron and Janette already there waiting for us. Marc said this was to be a business dinner. I didn't understand why our friends were there, but I didn't question anything.

Knowing Marc, I would know what was going on soon enough. After greetings and hugs, we ordered drinks and engaged in small talk about the wedding. When the waiter left our table with our dinner order, Marc said, "Catherine, I'm sorry to interrupt our honeymoon with business, but this couldn't wait until we returned."

"I really don't mind. Having dinner with friends was a pleasant way to spend part of it, but what has this got to do with business?"

Marc directed his answer toward Ron.

"Ron, my people have evaluated your software. They feel the beta testing should be completed before I return. I wanted to get this done before I left."

Ron didn't seem surprised by the news his software would be ready to market sooner than expected.

"The help your people gave me made that possible."

Then Nick joined the conversation.

"Ron, I'm sure Marc had told you why I do what I do. I'm rich enough to last four lifetimes. I don't need any more money. I just want to help people like you get a fair chance."

Ron acknowledged Nick's statement and Nick continued.

"I've invested a million dollars in your company. Our agreement gives you the right to buy back my shares at fifty percent of what the company is worth in two years. According to what Marc has told me, in two years, your company will be worth between five and ten million dollars. I don't need that much profit on our deal."

"I don't understand. I signed the agreement in good faith and if what Marc thinks is right, then you're is entitled to your profit."

"Legally, yes, but morally no. It doesn't feel right. I propose, canceling the original agreement and taking back the money I gave you. In its place, I will loan you one million dollars to buy back my shares. The term of the loan will be fair, and I will make a profit on the interest, but not two hundred to five hundred percent return on my investment. I'm making you this offer based on what Marc has told me about your software."

Ron was stunned. I was stunned. According to the way I understood what Nick had proposed, He was willing to give up two to five million dollars in profit for maybe a couple hundred thousand in interest payments.

It seems everything Marc had told me about Nick Amonti and how he felt about money was true. It was just a tool to invest in good people, and I knew Ron was good people. Ron was about to say something, but Nick interrupted him.

"You don't have to make the decision tonight. I know it's a lot to think about. Let's say ninety days."

Ron looked at Nick, then at Marc and then at me. I felt he wanted me to say something. I couldn't possibly know what to tell him. I looked at my husband of one day, looked deep into his eyes. I knew this was part of my wedding present. They were doing this for me.

Ron had a question.

"What if Marc is wrong about the value of the new software."

"In all the years I've known and been partners with Marc, he's never been wrong in his judgments. I have faith your new software would be as big a hit as Marc claimed."

We were all quiet for a while. I thought the conversation was over, but Marc had more to say.

"Ron, what I am about to propose to you has nothing to do with Nick's offer. That stands whether or not you accept my proposal."

Ron just nodded.

"I'm ready to purchase a one thousand user license for the new software with a three year guaranteed upgrade at one thousand dollars per user. But, I need a ninety day exclusive on the software."

"Marc I love the idea of selling one thousand pieces of my new product, but I'm not sure about an exclusive."

Marc had an answer ready.

"After ninety days, I will have a list of big name clients you can use in your marketing campaign, and that would also include endorsements by these clients. With these endorsements, Ron, you can double the price of the software right from the get go. You don't have to decide on this offer until the software is ready for market."

Again, it became quiet at our table. Ron finally asked if he could talk to me alone. I didn't know what I could say to him. I looked into Marc's eyes again, and he must have guessed what I was thinking. He knows me so well, he always seems to know what I'm thinking. He spoke to me softly. Not quietly, so no one else could hear, but softly,

"Remember the vows we exchanged yesterday?"

I nodded. I remembered every word.

"Use that as your guide."

Use our wedding vows as a guide? I knew he didn't mean fidelity, happiness, faith, and the last dance. No, he meant the parts were we pledged always to be open and honest with each other. Never hold anything back and trust. I smiled, and I knew exactly what to say.

"Ron, what I have to say I want to say in front of these people."

Ron nodded.

"I hardly know Nick Amonti, and I know nothing about how he runs his business. All I do know about him is what Marc has told me. I do know what Marc did at Dillman Brothers, but I have no insight into how he runs his own business. I'm not sure if he is a very astute businessman or just lucky. I also know nothing about your business."

I paused long enough to gather my thoughts.

"What I can tell you is the man I married is an honest and honorable man, and when he says his friend is also an honest and honorable man, I have to believe him. I don't know if the offers presented to you tonight will be good for you. I haven't the knowledge to make that decision. But knowing my husband as I do, I can honestly tell you these two men truly believe what they said is true."

Ron looked directly into my eyes for a long while before he spoke. He was looking for the truth in my eyes, and I tried to show it to him. Finally, he said one word.

"Deal!"

While the men talked details, the ladies decided to visit the little girls' room. Just before we headed back to the table, Janette said, "You really love him, don't you?"

Before I had a chance to answer she added, "Not your husband, I mean Ron."

Although the statement caught me off guard, I had an answer.

"For over eighteen years, that man has stood by me through everything. Marc and I may not be married if it wasn't for Ron interjecting himself into our problems. How could I not love him?"

Janette looked at Danielle and then back at me.

"I could see that. I could see you love him too much to hurt him just so your husbands could make more money. And I'm sure that's what Ron saw too."

Now I was sure. This was not just another girl Ron was dating. This one was special. I hoped Ron realized just how special.

After dinner, the two couples left for the 88's and Marc and I headed for the airport. We held hands in the back of the limo. I squeezed his hand.

"Thank you! I know that was more than just a business deal."

"I do owe him. Would we be on our way to our honeymoon if Ron hadn't poked his nose into our business?"

I didn't have anything else to say.

Chapter 44 – The Honeymoon

John and Jerry were waiting for us at the airport and helped with our luggage. Since I didn't know where we were going, I had packed for any circumstance. Once we were on board and settled in, the pilots went up front and closed the door. I was not going to watch the take-off from the flight deck tonight. I wanted to be with my husband.

I did notice the take-off roll down the runway was much longer than normal. Marc saw my concern.

"We're heavy with fuel tonight because it will be a long flight."

"What are we going to do with all that time?"

Marc looked toward the bedroom at the back of the aircraft.

"I thought we could share a new experience tonight. I've always wondered what it would be like to make love at forty thousand feet."

I had never had sex on an airplane, and if I understood Marc's comment correctly, neither had he. This would be a new experience for both of us, and I was looking forward to sharing this with him. I looked toward the door to the flight deck.

"They have very strict instructions not to open that door until we land."

That's all the incentive I needed. As soon as the seatbelt sign went off, I went into the bedroom and put on my wedding nightgown. When I returned to the main cabin, Marc had two glasses of champagne ready, and we drank slowly and intimately.

I had heard the term Mile High Club, but never gave it a thought. It wasn't something I ever intended to do. But on this beautiful airplane, in a private bedroom, with my new husband, it was delicious. I secretly hoped there would be many more long flights in our life together.

By the amount of sunlight streaming into the cabin, I estimated we arrived at our destination around mid-morning. When John came into the cabin to open the door and let down the stairs, a uniformed man came onboard. He talked to Jerry and John and then walked over to Marc and me.

"Passports."

Marc produced our passports and answered the man's questions in Italian. When the man was satisfied, we left Danielle and were driven to a beautiful villa in the hills with a great view of the bay. The only other people there were the husband and wife caretakers and their daughter.

"The older couple speaks little English and their daughter will translate for you when I'm not available."

If this was Marc's idea of a surprise honeymoon, he outdid himself. The villa was perfect, and we would be alone most of the time. I couldn't have been happier, or so I thought.

That evening we watched the sunset from the veranda and then made love. The next morning we were served breakfast in our room and then Marc took me for a stroll. He seemed to be familiar with the area. I found out jet lag is real and the remainder of the day, we spent at the pool, trying to get our bodies to catch up with the time change.

Thursday, after breakfast, Marc said we were going for a ride. Marc drove one of the cars that were parked at the villa and again, he seemed to be very familiar with the area and knew exactly where we were going. The route he took was along the coast, and it was a beautiful and exciting ride. After about three and a half hours, we arrived at a large farm. Marc parked in an area that had a dozen other cars there, and we walked around the house to the back yard and were immediately confronted by thirty to forty people. I looked at Marc for an explanation. Before he had a chance to answer, I heard a girl scream!

"MARCO!"

I looked in that direction, and a girl of about sixteen was running toward us. She didn't stop until she was close enough to jump on Marc and wrap herself around him, showering him with kisses. When he finally managed to peel her away, he introduced us.

"Sophia, this is Catherine, my wife! Catherine, meet my cousin Sophia."

Sophia looked me over and started talking to Marc in Italian. Marc stopped her.

"Catherine doesn't speak Italian, and I want you to be her translator while we're here. Promise me you won't leave her alone for a minute and tell her everything that is being said."

That seemed to please Sophia, probably because she knew she would be close to Marc as well as me. Then Marc took my hand.

"Come meet the rest of the Antonelli clan, your new family."

It was very obvious Marc was very close to these people. Sophia kept telling me everything that was being said to me and about me, no easy task with everyone talking at once. But, there was no doubt by the greeting I received they were pleased with Marc's choice of a wife. When things quieted down a little, Marc brought me over to meet his grandmother. Donna Antonelli was probably in her nineties, but she was still spry enough to give me a rib crushing hug. After looking me over, she told Marc, "You've done well, Marco."

Marc's family ranged in age from his grandmother all the way down to a one-year-old. The Antonelli men all had Marc's good looks, and the Antonelli women were very pretty, even the older ones. Sophia did a great job of keeping me informed on what was being said.

After we had a chance to say hello to everyone, Marc took me for a walk. We ascended a hill and stopped at a private cemetery. There were about two dozen headstones there. Marc told me who everyone was and how they were related to the family. The last grave we stopped at was Marc's parents.

"They would be proud I married so well."

I felt closer to Marc than ever before and I knew our life together would be wonderful.

When we returned to the house, we were ushered over to the tables set up in the backyard. There were three of them, long wooden tables arranged in a 'U' pattern. Marc and I were sat at the middle table, and the rest of the family took their places. I knew Italians loved to eat, and I knew of their hospitality, but I wasn't prepared for what was about to happen. The women disappeared into the house and one by one, each returned with a tray of food. The odors were driving me crazy even before they reached the table.

Marc was asked to say Grace, and Sophia told me what he was saying.

Along with the standard thanks for the food and the company of his family, and blessings on those who had passed on, he gave special thanks for bringing me into his life. That seemed to please Donna Antonelli. Before we started to eat, Marc leaned over to me.

"Catherine, go slow. Just taste everything."

I didn't understand what he was trying to tell me, until he added, "What you see here on the table is only the beginning."

And, he was right. For over four hours, the food continued to come out of the house. Course after course. Soup and fish and meat and pasta and salads and some things I had never seen before.

The wine was homemade, and I tried everything. It was all

wonderful, but when I asked Marc about some of the things I was eating, he said he'd tell me later. I was pretty sure I really didn't need to know. When the food finally stopped coming, big bowls of fruit and nuts were set on the table.

This was Marc's family, and he was so at home with them. Sophia never left my side the entire day. After the food, a couple of the men played what Marc called a 'squeeze box.' It was like an accordion, but it had buttons instead of keys. There was singing and dancing, although it wasn't any kind of dancing I was used to. If this was how I was to spend my honeymoon, I couldn't be happier.

Things quieted down around nine and by ten, we were back in the car and on our way back to the villa. Leaving these people was difficult.

"I usually visit at least once a year, and I'd like to continue that if it's alright with you."

It was more than alright. It would be mandatory. The ride home took only about an hour, and I asked Marc about that.

"We took the scenic coastal route north to Naples and the direct road back to the villa. Now that it was dark, the coast road wouldn't have the same appeal it had earlier."

Marc had said many times good people come from good families. Today proved he was right. Marc insisted we go to bed as soon as we arrived back at the villa. I thought it was because of all the driving and partying we had done. I was sure he had plans for our early bedtime.

And although he didn't disappoint me, his real reason he said was he had plans for tomorrow that would require us to get up early.

Friday morning, Marc told me we wouldn't be back at the villa until Monday. Not exactly sure where my husband was taking me, I over packed so I would be sure to have the right clothes for whatever he had in mind.

And what he did have in mind made me love him even more than I thought possible.

Chapter 45 - The Contessa

We took the coast road again, but this time, since the ocean was on my right and the sun on my left, I figured we were going south. Again, the drive took over three hours, but instead of ending at a farmhouse, we entered a city and stopped in front of a beautiful large house, what some might even call a mansion. Marc said we were in Calabria.

The door was opened by a very stately and refined woman, who upon seeing my husband, threw herself on him with the same abandon Sophia had done yesterday. After kisses and hugs had been exchanged, Marc turned his attention to me.

"Catherine, this beautiful lady is Contessa Philomena Maria Josephina De Constanza."

Then turning back to the Contessa.

"Grandmother, this beautiful and elegant lady is Catherine Antonelli, my wife!"

I got a long look from Grandma De Constanza and then she started talking to me in Italian and gesturing with her hands.

Realizing I didn't understand what she was saying, she looked to Marc for confirmation. Marc said I didn't speak Italian, but he was sure I would learn. That brought a smile from Grandma De Constanza.

"In that case, we will speak nothing but English this weekend."

And then she added, "That is until the farmers get here."

Marc shook his head at that comment, but he also smiled. We were brought out to the patio at the rear of the house where brunch was set up. The patio overlooked a large, beautiful lawn and garden. Workers were setting up tables and chairs for what looked like a big party. I wondered if it was to be in our honor considering the Contessa's comment about the farmers. Before we were finished with our brunch, people started to arrive. All of Marc's mother's family spoke English to varying degrees. Even the worst of them could be understood. The Contessa's rule of English only was strictly enforced by her in my presence.

Sophia and her family arrived, and I felt a little more comfortable with my translator close by. Marc's grandmother was very friendly toward me, and she was a gracious hostess. When we had a minute alone, she pointed toward Marc and Sophia.

"Sophia has had a crush on Marco since she was five years old. I'm happy to see you and Sophia are getting along so well. I always feared when Marco finally married Sophia wouldn't take it well, and she wouldn't be kind to his wife. But, it seems like Sophia approves of Marco's choice, and…so do I!"

More of the Antonelli family arrived, and the De Constanza family was there in abundance also. This was going to be a gigantic party, but the garden was large enough to hold everyone.

I noticed Marc's luggage was being brought in from the car and taken to the guest house at the other end of the garden. My luggage wasn't with his. I went over to Marc and commented on what I had seen, and he immediately went to the Contessa and started a very heated conversation in Italian. The few words he did speak in English didn't make me feel comfortable.

"I am on my honeymoon," which seemed to have no effect on his grandmother.

Then seeing I was close by, he grabbed my left hand and held it up, showing her my wedding and engagement rings. This too didn't seem to have any effect on the Contessa.

Finally, out of words, Marc took me by the hand and led me into the garden. He brought me over to a picturesque fountain and sat me down on the fountain wall. He paced for a few minutes, trying to get his thoughts together.

Finally, he stood in front of me.

"Catherine, do you love me?"

"I think that's pretty obvious."

"I want to tell you a story."

I could sense Marc was nervous.

"There were two families. One lived outside of Naples and had a farm that afforded them a pretty good living. The other lived in Calabria and ran an extremely successful business. These families had never met and knew nothing of each other.

"For reasons, no one could ever explain, both families decided their youngest child should go to America to complete their educations. There was no particular reason to send their child to America, but both families coincidentally made the same decision around the same time."

Marc started pacing in front of me as he continued his story.

"Air travel wasn't what it is today, and it was necessary to go to Rome for a flight to London and then on to New York. These two children, a boy of twenty-one and a girl of nineteen sat next to each other on the flight to London.

"When it was time to continue on to New York, the boy had their reservations changed so they would sit together for the Trans-Atlantic trip also. By the time they reached New York, they were inseparable.

"A year later, they flew back to Italy together to announce their intention to marry. At first, both families were unhappy with their decision. It would be as if a Georgia redneck was going to marry a girl from the Boston social set. But when the families saw how much in love these two were, they gave them their blessing. Because of this marriage, these two families became very close and started spending holidays together."

Marc continued to pace, but he kept his focus on me.

"The young couple were married right here in the church just a couple of blocks from this house. They returned to New York, and when their first child, a daughter, was born, they moved to Florida. The man became a successful businessman, and the young girl was a perfect wife. They had two additional children, and always came back to Italy for Christmas, Easter and other family occasions. The three children spent a lot of time here in Italy and were very close to both families. There were years when they spent the entire summer here."

Here, Marc paused as if bringing up a memory.

"One year, after the children spent almost the entire summer between the farm outside of Naples and the big house in Calabria, it was time to go back home to America and return to school. Their parents, anxious to see their children, after being away from them all summer, decided to fly over here and accompany them home. Instead of waiting for the scheduled flight from Rome to Naples, they decided to ask a friend of the family to fly them here in his small private plane. They never made it. All three people perished in the crash."

Marc stopped pacing and stood directly in front of me.

"As you can imagine, I am very close to these people. The thought of getting married without them present to witness the event was never a consideration. But the short amount of time between when we finally picked a date, and the wedding made it logistically impossible for me to make arrangements to get them all to Florida for our wedding. When you told me you would leave the honeymoon plans to me, I came up with this idea."

Now, Marc knelt down in front of me.

"So, Catherine Jensen Antonelli, would you do me the honor of marrying me in the little church here in Calabria where my parents were married, in front of my entire family?"

From the time Marc opened the door in Susan's room until I felt hope for us again, I had cried buckets. I didn't think I had any tears left in me, but now, the tears were flowing like rain. Marc wrapped his arms around me and held me close until I had enough control of myself to answer him.

"Marc, I can think of nothing that would make me happier than the opportunity to pledge my love, trust and fidelity to you in front of your family. I want them to know just how much I love you, and it is my wish to be a perfect wife to you."

Marc continued to hold me, and I could feel I had made my husband very happy. I hoped he understood just how much I wanted to do this, and how much it meant to me he wanted me to do this.

I was thrilled yesterday when he brought me to the farm and introduced me to his father's family. And today, when I realized we were meeting his mother's family my happiness was immeasurable.

I felt Marc was showing off. Showing me what great stock he had come from and showing his family what a good choice he had made for a wife.

Then, I found out about the disagreement between Marc and his grandmother.

"Catherine, there is one problem. The Contessa and Donna Antonelli have decided if we are to do this, we must respect the entire tradition."

"Exactly what does that mean?"

"What it means is we will not be together until the wedding unless we are chaperoned by at least three of the women from the family. We will not sleep together, we will not kiss each other, and we will not embrace each other."

"Is that really necessary?"

"No, it's not," Marc answered angrily.

"It's just a silly tradition my grandmothers want us to honor. I told them it was not right to keep a husband and wife apart, but they said if I truly wanted to honor my family, I would do this.

"You are expected to stay in the main house while I will use the guest house at the end of the garden. Sunday, we will spend our wedding night in the guest house, where my parents spent their wedding night.

"I told them I wouldn't do this. We'll go back to the villa and return early Sunday morning for the wedding."

I knew Marc wanted to spend as much time here with his family as possible. The Antonelli family was arriving from Naples, and the entire family would be here for the next three days. I couldn't let Marc leave and spend the rest of the week at the villa.

"Let me talk to them!" I suggested. Marc looked dubious at first but then agreed.

We approached the patio, where the Contessa and Donna Antonelli were waiting for us. I spotted Sophia and waved her over. Running up to us, I asked her if she knew what the grandmothers expected of Marc and me. She nodded her head.

"They are being very unfair. You are married only four days. They have no right to keep you apart."

I asked her to stay close and repeat everything I said so that Donna Antonelli understood. When we reached Marc's grandmother's, I chose my words carefully.

"Donna Antonelli, Contessa. Marco has just informed me of his plan for us to wed in the same church his parents were married in, with his entire family as a witness. I cannot find the words to express my joy that my husband would honor me in this way. I can think of no better way to honor him than to profess my love, devotion and fidelity to him in front of his family."

I paused a moment to gauge their reaction.

"I do not have to tell you what a good and honorable man Marco is. I am a very lucky woman he has chosen to devote his love to me, and I promise you I will devote myself to him."

I glanced at Marc before I continued.

"To honor my husband and his family, I agree to your request to be courted in the traditional way. Until I claim this man as my husband on Sunday, I will abide by your rules."

I let go of Marc's hand and took two steps away from him. The shock on the two old ladies faces was evident, but the expression on Marc's face would be etched in my mind forever. It was clear he was pleased with me. I looked directly into his eyes.

"After Sunday, no one will ever be able to keep me away from you."

Grandma Antonelli kissed me on both cheeks. The Contessa took me by the hand.

"Come, Catherine, let me show you to your room."

On the way to the grand staircase, I noticed my luggage, still sitting in the foyer. The Contessa instructed one of the servants to bring it to my room.

Upstairs, my luggage was being taken to one room, but the Contessa instructed the man to take it to another room instead. I was taken to a large, beautifully decorated room. It was definitely a feminine room.

"This was my daughter's room, Marco's mother. I'm sure she would be pleased if you would stay here until your wedding."

What could I say? How do you react to this? I thanked the Contessa and asked if I could make a request.

"Contessa, would it be okay if I asked Sophia to stay with me until Sunday?"

"That child has been in love with your husband since she was old enough to talk," the Contessa said, "I was surprised she took to you so quickly. I'm certain she would be thrilled with your request."

A maid came in and started to unpack my things. I wasn't used to such luxury. Suddenly I had thought.

"A dress," I cried, "I don't have a dress for the wedding."

The Contessa smiled and directed the maid to retrieve something from the other room. She came back with three garment bags, with the 'Stacy Geer Designs' logo printed on them.

"These arrived for you last week."

Last week? How long had Marc been planning this?

As much as I loved Stacy's clothes, I was sure this was not the type of wedding a Stacy Geer Wedding Dress would be appreciated.

But, I was wrong. When the maid unzipped the bags and removed the three dresses, they couldn't have been more perfect. The Contessa too seemed pleased with the choices, and I asked her to help me decide.

I tried on all three and modeled them for her approval. They were all Italian lace, ivory colored with a white silk lining. They were all form fitting, but not skin tight like the cocktail dress in Memphis, and all had wrist length sleeves.

The first had a choker collar and was cut below the knee, with the lining running all the way down.

The second has ankle length, but the lining stopped just below the knee.

The third was more daring. It was ankle length, with the lining running all the way down. The sleeves fit my arms snuggly but were unlined. My bare arms would show through the lace. The top of the sleeves stopped just below my shoulders, and the top was cut straight across from the upper part of one sleeve to the other. My shoulders would be bare.

I hesitated before I showed this one to the Contessa, but she knew there were three dresses, so I had no choice. When I came out of the dressing room, she looked me over, and then walked completely around me.

"I think this one," she announced, "It will make your husband proud."

I couldn't suppress my pleasure and threw my arms around the Contessa's neck. She was surprised at first, but relaxed and hugged me back.

"Catherine, only strangers, and some friends refer to me as Contessa. My grandchildren call me Nan."

It just keeps getting better and better!

Downstairs and out on the patio again, I couldn't wait to tell Marc about what happened in my bedroom, but I was interrupted by the arrival of additional guests. First, Marc's sisters, Amanda, and Angela arrived with their husbands and daughters. Then, my next surprise. Beth, Ed, Keith, and their families walked through the door.

And better, and better, and better!

By the time the greetings and hugs were done with, Marc had joined us. Knowing I had agreed to the grandmother's wishes, I knew I couldn't embrace Marc, but I promised myself I would make up for that on Sunday.

I took my family and with Sophia's help, introduced them to Marc's family. That took a while. Then Beth, my sisters-in-law and I sat down with the Contessa and Donna Antonelli. Marc's grandmothers were overjoyed my family had joined us for the wedding. And, as mothers and grandmothers do, they regaled us with stories about Marc's youth and his association with his cousin Dominic.

It seemed Marc and Dominic were always in competition with each other, but they were as close as brothers. Between the two of them, they managed to create enough mischief for ten boys. The Contessa told one story about a cherry pie she had prepared for some special friends.

"When my friends arrived, the pie had disappeared. I immediately suspected the two boys. That was their type of mischief. Both of them were very honest boys, and when I confronted them, Marc admitted he had taken the pie.

"When I questioned him as to what he had done with the pie, he said he ate it. I didn't think he had consumed the entire pie himself, and again when I questioned him, he admitted he had shared it with the pretty girl that lived on the next block. Both grandmothers laughed at the memory.

"He was only twelve or thirteen at the time, and I knew he would do well with the ladies when he grew up."

We talked for a while, with Sophia translating everything Donna Antonelli said for me and my sisters and our responses to her. I thought I was in Heaven. Could life get any better than this? I was married to a wonderful man. His family, who he was extremely close to, was accepting me without question. My family was there to help share my joy. Only one thing could make it perfect.

While Donna Antonelli and the Contessa continued to tell stories, Marc came over. I excused myself, and we sat quietly at a table in the garden.

"What are they talking about? Telling you all of my misadventures and the trouble I got into?"

"That's what grandmothers are for," I told him, "Tell me about the cherry pie."

Marc laughed. A deep down genuine laugh.

"It was around the time I decided I no longer wanted to pull a girl's pigtails."

I knew the rest of that line, and it made me giggle.

When Marc left me to introduce Ed, Keith and Sal to some newly arriving members of his family, I stayed behind at the table by myself. I wanted to contemplate the events of the past five days. I was hoping Marc, and I could return here often to be with these people.

A very good looking man approached my table. By his looks, he definitely was an Antonelli, but I didn't remember meeting him. He excused himself and asked if he might sit at my table. Good manners were an Antonelli trademark. I assured him it was okay, and he introduced himself as Dominic Antonelli.

He was as good looking as Marc and if this was the cousin Marc was always in competition with, I could imagine how that rivalry escalated when they were old enough to be interested in girls. I was sure they both could have their pick.

A few comments and compliments later, it became apparent he was putting a big rush on me. I was surprised. In spite of their rivalry, after all I had heard about Marc and Dominic from everyone, including Marc, I couldn't believe he would make a pass at his cousin's wife.

When he asked me if I was a friend or relative of the bride, I realized he didn't know who I was. My left hand had been in my lap, and he never saw my rings.

I was going to tell him, but I was intrigued, and I allowed him to continue. I was trying to find the most dramatic and fun way to let him know I was his cousin's brand new wife. When Dominic finally asked me if I was here alone, I never got a chance to answer.

Marc's sister Amanda came over to see her cousin, and I again witnessed the now familiar Antonelli family greeting. When they broke apart, Amanda said to her cousin, "Well Dominic, what do you think of Marc's bride?"

Dominic looked at her strangely, and seeing she was looking at me, he turned to me.

"You are Marco's wife?"

I raised my left hand up for him to see.

"Afraid so!"

Dominic was very embarrassed. He immediately started to apologize. It took a minute for Amanda to realize what was going on, and when she understood, she laughed.

"You didn't know Dominic?"

Dominic, trying to find a way out of his embarrassment shook his head.

"And you were making a pass at her?"

Dominic didn't have an answer. He just put his head down and tried to find a place to hide. Knowing Marc would want Dominic and me to be friends, I had to find a way to let him off the hook.

"It's alright, Amanda. Dominic was a perfect gentleman, and I was enjoying the attention too much to stop him. He really is very smooth!"

"That he is Catherine. It's in all the Antonelli men, but this one and your husband have more than their share."

That even made Dominic smile. Marc joined us and after greeting his cousin warmly, he looked at me. Turning back to

Dominic, he said in a very sure and commanding voice, "Top this!"

Dominic looked at me for a long moment.

"Beauty, elegance, grace, charm and our sense of humor: You have made it very difficult, cousin."

That made Marc beam, and Amanda started to explain about their ongoing rivalry. I told her I had gotten part of the story from Donna Antonelli and Nan, but I wanted to hear more.

Both men told of how they always tried to best each other, from the time they were little boys. Who could hit a baseball further, who could swim faster or ride a bike faster, who could date the prettiest girl, and when Dominic started to say, "Who would lose their ...," he was interrupted by Marc's elbow making contact with his rib cage.

Knowing what he was about to say, I couldn't leave it alone.

"Who would lose their virginity first?" I asked with a smile.

Now, both men were embarrassed, but Amanda and I loved it.

"Well," I insisted, "Who won?"

"Yes, tell us, I've always wanted to know!" Amanda added.

After looking at each other for courage, Dominic finally said, "Marco did, but he cheated."

I was just barely able to hold back the laughter, but I pushed even harder.

"How could Marco possibly cheat at that?"

Dominic's answer was delivered very seriously.

"He bribed her with half a cherry pie."

I completely lost it, and so did Amanda. When she had gained some control of herself, she said, "I've always wondered what that cherry pie business was about!"

And we both broke up again. Dominic noticed three of his aunts and a female cousin keeping guard about fifteen feet away from us.

"What's with the posse?"

Marc just shrugged. Amanda looked over at the women and then back at Marc.

"You didn't agree to that, did you?"

Mark shook his head, and when Amanda indicated she needed more of an answer, Marc looked at me. Amanda looked directly at me.

"You agreed to this?"

I just nodded. Amanda shook her head.

"Catherine, why?"

I gave her the only answer I could.

"This is Marc's family, and they have accepted me so easily. I wanted them to know how much respect I have for Marc and his family. I want to be one of them."

Amanda was about to say more but was interrupted as her sister Angela, Beth and my sisters-in-law joined us. Amanda immediately indicated the posse and told her sister what I had agreed to.

Angela laughed.

"That explains a lot. Let me tell you what else our new sister-in-law has accomplished today."

Marc, Dominic, and Amanda waited for her to explain.

"Sophia admitted she liked Catherine. She had told me she thought Catherine would be a good wife to Marco."

Everyone had worried the little girl that had a crush on my husband wouldn't like his new wife, but I had won her over.

"I really like Sophia, and I can see us getting along. I feel toward her as one might to a kid sister. I intended to ask Sophia to spend the next two nights with me in my room."

That brought up another issue. Angela announced to her sister.

"Guess which room Catherine is using?"

When Amanda didn't answer, Angela told her, "Nan put her in mom's room!"

That surprised both Marc and Amanda. Marc explained.

"The only two people who are allowed to use our mother's room are Amanda and Angela, and only when they were here without their husbands. Then, they use the guest house."

When I asked what that meant, Angela gave me the answer.

"What it means, Catherine, is you are not considered a woman who is married to her grandson. Nan thinks of you as a granddaughter who is married to one of the farmers. That is why she requested you refer to her as Nan instead of Contessa."

Amanda was surprised.

"I was married almost a year before my husband was allowed to call the Contessa Nan. It has to be earned."

"I still didn't understand what this all means.

"Catherine, it means you are one of us. You are family, our family."

I still wasn't sure what they meant.

"Didn't that didn't apply to Marc's first wife also?"

Dominic had the answer.

"No Catherine. Everyone liked Joanna. She was a fine woman, friendly, well mannered, polite and beautiful. The trouble between Marc and her never manifested itself around us. We were actually surprised when they broke up."

Angela added.

"It's true, Catherine. Everyone liked her, but she was never really into all of this family thing. As friendly as she was to all of us, she never really belonged. She was never a part of us."

Amanda finished.

"It is apparent to all of us you do belong. Not only you agreed to the traditional courtship, but it's also that you seem so comfortable with us. It's as if you were born to it. It doesn't appear to matter which side of the family you are with, the farmers or the aristocrats, you fit in!"

It took a minute for everything they said to sink in. I did feel like I belonged. It was like I was meant to be here with these people. And, I really did want to belong, for my husband and for myself. When I fully understood what was said, I felt my other idea would be alright also, but I wanted confirmation, just to be sure.

"Marc, I need your opinion. I'd like to ask Sophia to stand up with me on Sunday."

Marc immediately looked to Beth.

"Catherine and I have talked about it, and I think it's a fantastic idea."

Marc turned away from me and walked away, followed by his cousin Dominic. I looked to Amanda and Angela wondering if I had upset my husband. They both had beautiful smiles.

"Catherine, on top of everything else, you have just given your husband the most beautiful wedding present imaginable."

We all sat quietly for a while until Marc returned. He didn't say anything, but the look in his eyes was all I needed. Later that afternoon, I informed the Contessa and Donna Antonelli of my plan. They both were pleased. I wasn't going to ask Sophia until we were alone in our room that night.

I also asked the Contessa if she knew of a seamstress that could modify one of Stacy's dresses for Sophia. She said one of her maids could do it.

"I think the second one you tried on would suit her well."

And better and better and better…

Chapter 46 – The Party

The party started Friday morning and would last until Sunday night. My new family knew how to celebrate. I thought about Marc and me almost breaking up after Nashville and what my life would have been like if we hadn't found our way back. I knew everything I had now, and everything I was feeling was because I had learned to trust this man. This truly honest and honorable man. I was absolutely sure we would be happy together.

Marc and I were only together occasionally all day. And when we were, there were always three or four married women within ten to fifteen feet of us. Marc was allowed to hold my hand gently, but no other contact was allowed, and we couldn't talk in whispers. It wasn't easy, but I could deal with it for two days for the sake of my husband and his beautiful family, our family.

Around midafternoon, I was talking to the Contessa on the patio when Marc approached from the garden. He got my attention and asked me how I was doing.

"I'm wonderful. I'm on the greatest honeymoon a girl could ever dream of."

"Could it be better?"

I gestured around the garden where the family was gathered.

"What could possibly make this any better?"

"How about the other member of your family?"

Before I had a chance to think about what Marc had said, I heard a voice behind me.

"Hi beautiful,"

I spun around to face Ron and the girl he had brought to my wedding last Sunday. I was so excited I forgot who I was and where I was, and I threw my arms around his neck and kissed him.

Now, it was perfect.

I heard Marc say something in Italian, and I realized what I was doing.

I backed away from Ron.

"I'm sorry Marc, I forgot myself."

"It's alright, Catherine. I told the posse Ron was family, a cousin from the United States."

"When did I become a cousin?" Ron asked.

"It's either that or those four women are going to stone you to death," Marc told him.

"Hi, Cousin!" Ron shouted, and we all laughed.

Marc suggested I introduce Ron to the family, and I beckoned Sophia to join us. I did keep up the cousin pretense for the sake of decorum, but in fact, it wasn't a lie. Ron was family. Beth, Ed, and Keith were all familiar with Ron and our relationship and had always treated him like part of our family. They were almost as happy to see him as I was.

I questioned him about how he knew about the wedding on Sunday.

"When you and Marc left for the airport after dinner Monday night, Nick told me of Marc's plans and handed me two first class tickets, San Francisco to Naples, through New York's Kennedy Airport."

Ron also told me Nick and Danielle were very disappointed they couldn't be here.

"Nick's doctors advised against him taking such a long flight so soon after his ordeal."

That would be the only disappointment of the entire event. When I introduced them to Dominic, he gave me a wicked smile.

"Your cousin, you say! I too will be your cousin after Sunday. Can I look forward to such a greeting?"

"If you promise to behave yourself and act like a gentleman," I said in jest.

Very seriously, Dominic answered.

"Catherine, Antonelli men are always gentlemen."

I knew he meant what he said. It was a point of honor, and these people had honor in abundance. I smiled warmly, and I knew Dominic, and I would get along. As much as he and Marc competed with each other, they were two peas in a pod and loved and respected each other totally. I would be able to count on Dominic as if he was my own brother.

"I've heard that. And I've also heard Antonelli men never get involved with married women."

Dominic was surprised.

"Where did you hear that?"

"When I told Marco you made a pass at me, Marco said you

probably didn't know who I was. When I asked him how he was so sure and how was he so sure I wouldn't give into his handsome cousin, Marco told me Antonelli men don't pick flowers from another man's garden."

"It's true Catherine. It a tradition that has been passed down through generations and it is believed it has never been broken. And I will not be the first Antonelli to break it."

Then, taking Janette's left hand, Dominic kissed it.

"But I see no fence around this beautiful rose."

Janette blushed, but it was obvious she enjoyed the attention. Before Ron had a chance to protest, she withdrew her hand.

"That is a very tempting offer, Dominic, but I'm perfectly happy where I am planted right now."

Dominic made a sad face.

"It has not been a good day for a man's ego!"

Janette smiled at him.

"But, I'll keep your offer in mind in case my gardener doesn't build a fence for me by next planting season."

Ron blushed, and the three of us laughed.

We moved over to a table and joined Marc's sisters and my family. Marc stopped by for a few minutes, then he was off again. Ron commented for a newlywed he didn't seem to want to spend too much time with his wife. I started to explain, but Dominic interrupted me.

"It is a long story, a very romantic story my friend. Catherine, I'm sure Marco has told you the story of how his parents got together. Why don't you tell your friends?"

I relayed the story just as Marc had told it to me. When I had finished, it was quiet around the table. Dominic asked if that's all Marco told me.

I indicated it was.

"Didn't he tell you both families were against the marriage and how Marco's mother turned their objections around?"

"Marco did say something about that, but he didn't give me any details."

Dominic looked to Amanda and Angela for approval. Seeing them both nod, He told us the rest of the story.

"Both families were against their marriage. Aunt Regina, Marco's mother, was a pampered lady. She grew up here with servants attending her every need. Uncle Marco was raised on the farm in Naples. It was not seen as a suitable union.

"Marco's mother was the apple of her father's eye, and she also had a way with the Contessa. She knew, in time, they would give in to her just as they always had. It was our grandfather, Marco's father's father who was adamant and refused to give them his blessing.

Dominic again looked to his cousins for approval. They both nodded.

"The couple had driven from Calabria to the farm to talk to grandfather, but he would not discuss the matter. He refused to have any mention of it in his house. The people of Calabria are known for their stubbornness, but as I'm sure you already know, Catherine, There are no men more stubborn than Antonelli men. Grandfather had made his decision and the matter was settled.

"They couple spent the night at the farm. Aunt Regina in the house and Uncle Marco in the Bunk House where the workers stay during harvest. The next morning after breakfast, Grandfather went to the field to do his weeding. My uncle followed him to the barn to demand his reasons for denying his blessing.

"Grandfather, in a very reasonable tone explained to his son, that this woman was born into luxury and was sort after by every wealthy, eligible man in Italy. I am sure this woman loves you, my son, but you will not be able to give her what she needs. It is not a matter of wealth or luxury, it is a question of attention. This woman will require the attention of her own kind; sophisticated, educated, traveled people. A farmer's son will never be able to make her completely happy."

Dominic paused. He seemed to be getting emotional. Amanda and Angela also appeared to be getting glassy eyed.

"With that explanation, grandfather took his hoe and walked to the field to do his weeding. Aunt Regina, who had watched the exchange from the porch of the house, joined my uncle and was told what grandfather had said.

"After thinking about it for a moment, she kicked off her sandals, grabbed a hoe and in her pretty dress, followed grandfather into the field. She watched him for about ten minutes and then began to weed the adjacent row of plants. Grandfather had been a farmer all of his life and my aunt had never done a minutes manual labor in her entire life. There was no way she could keep up with the old man. But, she did. Mostly, because grandfather slowed down and allowed her to keep pace with him. They never said a word to each other.

"When it was time for the noon meal, grandfather headed back to the house. Aunt Regina followed. Her feet were cut and bruised from the stones in the field. Her legs were scratched from the barbed wires that held some of the plants in place. Her pretty dress was torn where she had caught it on a post nail. And her hands were blistered from the hoe handle."

Dominic glanced at his cousins once more before he continued. All three of them appeared solemn.

"While grandfather went to what you would call a mud room to clean up for lunch, Marco's mother disappeared into her room.

"When grandfather came to the table, Aunt Regina was already there, cleaned up as much as she could be under the circumstance, wearing another pretty dress and another pair of sandals. It was obvious she was uncomfortable. The cuts, bruises, scrapes, scratches, and blisters were painful. But she did not complain

"After the meal, grandfather sat on the front porch for his afternoon smoke. Aunt Regina helped grandmother with clearing away the table and straightening the kitchen. When she appeared on the porch, grandfather had just started back out to the field. Marco's mother kicked off her sandals, grabbed her hoe and began to follow him. He must have sensed her presence because he suddenly stopped and turned toward her. She didn't stop until she was standing directly in front of him.

"Grandfather looked into her eyes. He summoned his son to them and looked into his eyes. He took the hoe from Aunt Regina and handed it to my uncle."

Now Dominic was looking directly at me, and he definitely was teary eyed.

"Before he turned to go back to the field he said to his son, "No Antonelli woman has ever worked in the field, and your wife will not be the first." Marco's father followed grandfather into the field and together they continued to weed.

"Grandmother took Aunt Regina into the house and tended her wounds as best as she could. That night, at supper, again not a word was spoken. Afterward, Grandfather informed his son the three of them were to attend church the following morning. No questions were asked or explanations given."

Another pause, this time, to wipe away a tear.

"The next morning, Grandfather Antonelli, Marco's father and

305

mother attended six o'clock mass together. After church, they drove to Calabria. The Contessa was surprised when they showed up here. The four of them along with Aunt Regina's father sat on the patio where grandfather officially and formally asked permission for his son to court their daughter.

"Of course, the Contessa was against it, until grandfather explained what had happened the previous day at the farm. The Contessa looked at her daughter's blistered hands and cried. She could not say no to such love. Because they were scheduled to leave for America, the courtship lasted less than one week, and they were married in the same church Marco will wed you on Sunday."

When Dominic finished his story, Janette and I were both in tears. Amanda and Angela, having heard the story many times were still glassy eyed at hearing it again.

Dominic again looked to his cousins for confirmation, and again he received their approval.

"Catherine that is the spirit we see in you. That is why you have been accepted into this family so lovingly. The love and respect you have shown for Marco and his family is more than any of us expected. You are one of us now, and will always be."

Then, turning to Ron.

"You see, my friend, it was Catherine who agreed to the formal courting rules. Marco was against it. But, because Catherine has made the decision, my cousin endeavors to respect her decision and honor her wishes. Marco is keeping his distance from Catherine for that reason. Every time they are close, he wants to take her in his arms and embrace her. That would be disrespectful, and he is sacrificing his own desires to honor his woman."

Ron nodded his understanding. But, Dominic wasn't finished.

"My cousin has informed me you have played a vital and decisive role in the events that are to take place here."

Ron shook his head.

"It's nice of Marc to say that, but it's not true. They would have gotten together with or without me. Love like theirs could never be denied."

Ron was right, to a point. Marc and I would have gotten together again without Ron's help, I was sure of that. But there was more to it, and I wanted him to know. I reached across the table and took Ron's hand and looked directly into his eyes.

"Ron, I do believe nothing was going to keep Marc and me apart.

We would have found our way back to each other, maybe not as quickly, but definitely. But, we wouldn't be in the place we are in right now.

"You forced me to open my heart and tell Marc about my fears and misgivings. I never would have done that if you weren't sitting there pushing me. I trusted your judgment and it turned out to be right. That forced both Marc and me to open ourselves up to each other, and the resulting conversations have brought us here.

"We most probably would have gotten back together and maybe even married, but we would not share the love, trust and respect we have for each other if it wasn't for you. Because you have been a faithful and honest friend to me all these years I trusted what you were telling me to do and the result is a love affair I never imagined was possible."

Ron didn't have anything to say. Dominic finally broke the silence.

"Maybe not officially cousins, but definitely family!"

That made both Ron and I smile.

"That's how Marco feels," I said.

Suddenly I realized something. When I spoke to my family or Ron, I referred to my husband as Marc. When I was talking to his family, I referred to him as Marco. And, in truth, he was two different men.

One was the sophisticated cosmopolitan businessman, at home making million dollar deals and dealing with important and influential people. The other was a down home country boy who was just a simple farmer's son and who was as comfortable here among his own people as he was giving a speech at a banquet.

I was in love with both of these men, and even better both of these men were in love with me.

Could it get any better?

Chapter 47 – My Plan

I was still getting used to the jet lag and the last two weeks had been exhausting. Also, I still had things to do before the wedding. As much as I hated the idea, I decided I would have to break away from the festivities and get to my room.

I circulated around saying goodnight to as many as I could. When I found Sophia, I told her of my plan and asked her to find Marco and bring him over to the fountain.

As Marc approached, four of his aunts appeared out of nowhere. I wasn't surprised, it had been like that all day. Just as Marc reached my side, Sophia showed up with Ron and Janette in the toe. She introduced them to Marc's aunts and started a very animated conversation. She had positioned herself so Marc's aunts had to turn their backs to Marc and me.

Marc took my hand and led me to the side of the fountain out of view of his aunts. He wrapped his arms around me and planted a killer kiss on my lips. I didn't want the moment to end, but finally, I pulled back and peeked around the fountain to see if the posse had noticed.

"Don't worry, Catherine, We're not fooling anyone! They were young once too."

I fell back into Marc's arms and again we kissed passionately. Under the circumstances, it couldn't last too long, and as Marc brought me back around the fountain, Sophia came over to say goodnight to Marc. Ron and Janette walked away, and as Sophia and I headed for the house, I got a smile from Marc's aunts. My return smile was all the thanks they needed.

We stopped just long enough for me to ask the Contessa when the seamstress would be available. She replied she would send her right up to my room, and Sophia and I headed for the stairs. I asked,

"Do you mind leaving the party early?"

"No, I would rather spend the time with you."

I knew I was doing the right thing. There was a comfortable seating area in Marc's mother's bedroom, and that's where Sophia and I settled. I picked my word carefully.

"Sophia, you have met my family. I have two wonderful big brothers who will both walk me down the aisle on Sunday and give me away to Marco. I also have a wonderful big sister who has given me guidance and advice throughout my life and who stood up for me at my wedding in Florida. I am very lucky.

"But, I have never had a little sister. A younger sister that felt confident to confide in me and come to me for advice. I have always wanted a kid sister. Now that I have Marco, it is the only thing missing from my life. Sophia, would you be my kid sister?"

The reaction was more than I expected. More than I had hoped for. Sophia jumped out of her chair and threw herself on me. The hugs and kisses were so intense we both wound up on the floor. This caused us both to giggle like school girls. It was wonderful.

After we had gained some control of ourselves, Sophia said, "I only have brothers, and I've always wished for a sister, but you live so far away."

"Marco and I will come here often, and we'll talk to your parents about allowing you to come to Florida to stay with us when school was out."

That just broadened her smile. "I'll get you your own cell phone so we can talk all the time."

Her joy was evident and now, knowing how she felt, I was sure of what I was going to say to her next.

"Sophia, this also comes with responsibilities. I will need someone to be by my side on Sunday when Marco takes me as his bride. I need someone who loves him and respects him as I do. Will you be my Maid of Honor on Sunday and stand with me?"

This time, I was prepared for the onslaught, and since we were already on the floor, it didn't hurt. A knock at the door got us off the floor. It was Angela and Amanda. They had stopped by to help with the rest of my plan. When they looked at Sophia, they knew I had already told her I wanted her as my Maid of Honor. I went to the closet and took out the dress I wanted Sophia to wear on Sunday. My two sisters in law were impressed.

"Only a Stacy Geer Designs Original," I said.

While Sophia tried the dress on, I showed Amanda and Angela the other two dresses. They were a little dubious when I told them which I would wear on Sunday, but when I told them it was the Contessa's choice, they smiled. The maid arrived and set about pinning Sophia's dress. Seeing herself in the mirror thrilled her. The woman said it wouldn't require much, and it would be ready by late tomorrow morning. Now, the hard part.

309

I informed my three new sisters Marco, and I had again decided to write our own wedding vows, and I had an idea as to what I wanted to say.

"But, I'm not sure what I have in mind would be appropriate for the family. I need your opinion and help in getting it right."

They eagerly agreed. Then I told them the rest of my plan. That they weren't sure of at all but promised to help any way they could.

We were up late, and we had to sneak down to the den a couple of times to use the Contessa's computer. I wanted my vows to be typed out clearly, with large font that I could read through the tears I was sure I would be shedding after I heard Marc's vows.

When we finally called it quits, the party was still going on outside. I was sure it would last all night. I got sincere hugs from both of Marc's sisters and a promise to continue to help me with the vows as much as possible tomorrow.

I hadn't realized just how tired I was, and sleep came quickly in spite of my excitement. I slept late, and Sophia was up before me. When I finally opened my eyes, she had a pot of coffee waiting for me. We took our time dressing and reached the patio just in time for brunch. Marc was on the patio waiting for us.

"Don't tell me. Girl talk until the wee hours of the morning. Is this what I have to look forward to when Sophia comes to Florida?"

Sophia and I looked at each other, wondering how Marc knew of my plan to have Sophia visit us. I looked at the gleam in Marc's eye.

"This man knows me so well he knows every thought in my head, even before I do. I sometimes wonder if he really knows, or is he somehow putting those thoughts there."

Sophia giggled and asked Marc if it was OK to visit us.

"I've already talked to your parents. You'll be on the first plane the day school lets out."

That made us both happy. Marc said to me privately.

"We'll have to make sure Johnny isn't in town the same time Sophia is."

That made me giggle.

The rest of the day wasn't as hectic as the day before. I had already met everyone, and there were no more surprises. I spent a good part of the day with Amanda, Angela and Sophia going over my vows and exactly what the procedure would be tomorrow.

"You will walk to the church with the women of the family. You will walk down the aisle just as in Florida.

"The ceremony itself would basically be the same as both weddings would take place in a Catholic Church, but it will be conducted in Italian.

"The reception line would also be basically the same as it was in Florida except there was a strict pecking order as to how the guests would greet us after the ceremony."

I needed that part explained, and Amanda did.

"First, Sophia and Dominic. Then Donna Antonelli and the Contessa. Marc's father's family were next and then his mother's. After that my family and then friends."

I was told I didn't have to concern myself with this because it would all be arranged. My main concern was getting my vows right. I wanted them to be very special, and I wanted them to be proper.

Again, Marc and I were together for very short intervals. I knew Dominic's reasons for this were correct, and I knew if Marc didn't break down and embrace me, I would. One more day. I could do this. I circulated around as much as possible, but I spent most of the day with Amanda, Angela, and Sophia.

I did notice whenever I was alone, Dominic always made it his business to join me. I honestly believed this man, who was so close to my husband, didn't have any designs on me, but as the day went on, I began to feel uncomfortable.

The next time I was alone, sitting at one of the tables in the garden, Dominic joined me again. I gave him a semi warm greeting, and he seemed to sense something was wrong. Either I was not very good at hiding my feelings, or this man had the same uncanny ability to know what I was thinking as Marc did.

"Catherine, why do I suddenly make you uncomfortable?"

I tried to deny what he said was true, but Dominic didn't buy it.

"Would you like me to leave?"

I said no.

"If I stay you must tell me why my presence upsets you."

I didn't know what to say. Again, sensing my unease he took the lead.

"Catherine, if you are wondering why I choose to spend so much time alone with you, it is because Marco has requested me to do so."

Remembering a line I had heard a few months earlier, I asked, "Did he send the fox to guard the henhouse?"

As soon as the words left my mouth, I felt like a fool. I had to let him know I didn't mean that stupid remark, but before I got the chance, Marc joined us.

After seeing the looks on our faces, he said, "Catherine, remember the conversations we had in Memphis."

"Of course, I remember every word."

"That doesn't apply to Dominic."

How could he possibly know what I was thinking? Does he really know me that well?

I had to find out.

"Marc, how do you always know what I'm thinking?"

"Do you have to know all my secrets?"

"We did promise that to each other last Sunday, and I expect we'll make the same promise tomorrow."

"I guess we did say that. I don't know everything you are thinking. For instance, I didn't know you would agree with my grandmothers' idea of a traditional courtship. What I do know, you tell me with your eyes. You're such an open and honest person everything shows in your eyes.

"The way you looked at Sophia the past two days, I could see one or two visits a year wouldn't be enough for you. When I walked over here just now, I could see the concern in your eyes. It was easy to figure out you wanted to be close to Dominic, but you were afraid of seeming available."

"Catherine, if I ever felt you were available to me, it would not only break Marco's heart, it would also break mine. In the short time I've known you, I can say if I had met you first, I would have tried to make you my wife, not Marco's. But having pledged your love to this man, I can never hope to have you."

"Not even if I made myself available. Not even if Marco and I divorced."

"Not even then. You are Marco's wife, and I will never be more than a cousin. A very close and trusted cousin, I pray, but never more than that.

"My inappropriate advances the day we met would never have happened if you hadn't allowed me to believe you were alone. Marco is more than family to me. I would never do anything to hurt him, and now that I know you and know of your love for him, I would never do anything to hurt you."

"Dominic, I'm so sorry. I didn't mean to imply anything. I think all of this has been a whirlwind, and I'm not thinking straight. Please forgive me."

"Nothing to forgive, Catherine," he said sweetly.

Marc was ready to leave again, but I had another question.

"Why did you ask Dominic to babysit me?"

Marc used his hand in a sweeping motion to indicate the garden and all the people gathered there.

"You didn't expect any of this. You thought you were going to spend two weeks alone with your new husband. I believed you would fit in with my people. But, I never expected you to fit in so well so quickly and to accept all of this as easily as you have.

"I was afraid if you had too much time alone to think, you would worry about being accepted. I also knew agreeing to the traditional courtship rules would put as much of a strain on you as it does me. I didn't want you to have a moment's worry, so I didn't want you to have time alone to think about it. My cousin agreed to keep you occupied so you would not have a chance to worry."

Then, with one of his great smiles aimed at me, he was gone again before one of us broke the rules. I turned my attention back to Dominic and tried to apologize again.

He wouldn't allow it.

"Catherina, it pleases me you are careful not to allow another man think you might be available to him. It is impossible to know where one might find trouble, and the best way to avoid it is to avoid a situation that could lead to trouble."

"That's what Marco said in Memphis."

"It is true, cousin, not all men are as honorable as Marco."

"And you," I answered with a smile and got one in return.

As I watched my husband walk away, Dominic said, "I fear dear cousin I will find it necessary to keep the Fire Brigade alerted tomorrow night. The guest house is a fine old building, and I would hate to see it burned to the ground."

I turned my attention back to him.

"Is it that obvious?"

"Yes, Catherine. It is that obvious in both of you."

Sophia and Marc's sisters came over and suggested we put in some time on the vows. Dominic offered to help. I was all for that, I wanted them to be perfect.

We found a quiet corner of the garden and went to work. We managed to sneak away a couple of times during the day, and I was feeling better about what I wanted to say to Marc.

The rest of the day, I spent greeting new arrivals, talking to those I already met, hanging out with my family and getting to know Janette. The time I spent with her made me feel Ron may have found himself a prize. That just added to my happiness.

Around nine o'clock, I found Marc and told him I was ready for bed. I got one of his wicked grins as a reply, and I promised I would make it all up to him tomorrow night.

With a sad, little puppy dog expression, he replied, "I hope, my love, it will require more than one night."

There were too many people around the fountain to pull our little charade as we had done the previous evening. With a sigh and a shrug of his shoulders, Marc kissed my hand and told me to have sweet dreams, but only of him. As if I had a choice!

I gathered up Sophia, told Amanda and Angela we were headed for our room, said goodnight to my family, and we made our way upstairs.

Sophia's dress was hanging outside the closet when we got there, and I asked her to try it on. Before she emerged from the dressing room, Amanda and Angela had arrived.

When Sophia appeared, all three of us were pleased.. This was an emerging woman, and she was absolutely beautiful.

Sophia was embarrassed by our enthusiasm, and when we brought her over to the full-length mirror to see herself, she also was pleased with the image looking back at her.

The Contessa had an idea as to what we were doing, and she arranged for refreshments to be delivered. The four of us settled down and started going over my vows. I wanted them to be perfect. I wanted Marc to know exactly how I felt, but I also wanted them to be proper. I didn't wish to say anything that might be upsetting to Marc's family.

When I was sure every word was perfect, we again used the Contessa's computer to print out my vows in extra-large type. I was sure there would be tears tomorrow morning, and I wanted to be sure I could read and deliver every word.

With Amanda and Angela acting as my bridegroom, and Sophia standing at my side to whisper in my ear in case I flubbed a line, I practiced. When I was done, glassy eyes were evident on all of us.

Chapter 48 – The Wedding –Part II

Sunday morning Sophia and I were all giggles. My sister and sisters-in-law arrived just as I finished getting dressed, followed almost immediately be Marc's sisters. When Sophia came out of the dressing room, all eyes turned toward her. She was beautiful. Hair and makeup were done on both of us and just before we were ready to leave, the Contessa stopped by.

She brought a broach Marc's mother had worn at her wedding. After she had pinned it on, she stepped back and looked me over.

"Marco is going to be so proud," she said sweetly.

When we got downstairs, almost everyone was gone. About a dozen of Marc's aunts and female cousins were there to escort me to the church. It was a very formal procession, even though there were places we had to walk single file because the sidewalks were so narrow. Ed and Keith were waiting for me in front of the church. It wasn't the big beautiful cathedral type church Marc and I were married in last Sunday. This was a small, lovely neighborhood chapel. It felt perfect for the occasion.

After everyone was seated, Sophia walked down the aisle and took her place on the altar. Then, Ed and Keith escorted me to the front of the church.

There was no orchestra, no violins, not even an organ. It was so quiet the noise of a few late arrivals echoed throughout the church. When we neared the foot of the aisle, Marc stepped down to greet me. The priest asked, "Chi dà questa donna a sposare quest'uomo?

My brothers answered, "La sua famiglia dà questa donna a quest'uomo!"

Then Ed placed my hand in Marc's, and we stepped up onto the altar. I was surprised to see a microphone on the altar. This little church had a sound system and what Marc and I said to each other would be transmitted all over the church. This made me uneasy. Although I wanted everyone to know what I was saying to Marc, I wasn't sure I could do it so publicly.

The ceremony was very formal, and when it was time for our vows, we faced each other. Looking into my eyes, Marc recited his vows to me in Italian. When he was done, he paused and looked into my eyes.

"Catherine, I announced my pledge to you in Italian because I want everyone here to know what I have promised you today.

"When we got together over a year ago, I thought finally my life was complete. Then, when I almost lost you, I truly believed my life was over. It is your openness, your honesty, your love that has brought us to this place today. Never have I felt such love and devotion.

"I will spend the rest of my life trying to keep that love. I will work every day trying to earn that love. In order to deserve your love, here, as witnessed by my family, I pledge to you this day:

"My love, my honor, my trust, my respect, my fidelity. No one will ever love you as I do. You will always be first in my heart and in my life. No one will ever doubt my love for you nor will anyone question my faith in you, or my respect for the person you are.

"You are the only woman I will ever be available to and I will be available to you for whatever you require. I will hold your love in trust, and I will protect it as I protect you. I will be there when you need me. I will never forsake you. I will make it my life's ambition to make you feel safe, secure, wanted, needed and loved. With every beat of my heart, I will love you more.

"You are my love, my life, and now you will be my wife. And, until the day when my heart no longer beats, I pray I will always be the one you want to take you home from the dance."

Sophia handed me a hankie, and I did my best to wipe away the tears. I turned toward the altar to gather myself. Marc leaned over and whispered, "Take your time Catherine. We are in no hurry. We have the rest of our lives together."

It is amazing how his words could transform me. How easily he could transfer his strength to me. I was determined to do what I had planned, and after I wiped away the tears and blinked my eyes clear, I turned back to my husband.

I looked at Sophia. She had the sheets of paper in her hand with my vows to Marc. She looked at me expectantly. I smiled and nodded. She handed it to me.

With Sophia at my side ready to whisper in my ear in case I flubbed my lines, I looked directly into Marc's eyes.

"Marco Raphael Antonelli,"

Then looking at the paper in my hand.

"You are the man I have been waiting for my entire life. You are the answer to my dreams. Your love, honor, honesty and devotion have brought me to a place I have never been before.

"Now, as you claim me as your bride, I pledge to you I will be your wife, your woman, your mistress, your lover, your confidant, your assistant, your partner and your friend. I will always be there for you no matter what you might desire. I will be there to comfort you when you are sad: to share your joy when you are happy: to take care of you when you are sick: to help you when you are in need.

"To ensure I will always have your love and respect, I vow to you this day, in the sight of God and with both our families as witness, my eternal love, and fidelity. You will forever be the only man in my life, in my heart, in my dreams and desires. And no other man will ever think I might be available to anyone but you.

"No one can know the depth of my feelings for you, and I promise to devote my life to showing you how deeply my love for you is. I will always be open and honest with you. I will honor and respect you. You will never need more than I am willing to offer you.

"This I pledge to you this day as a sign of my love and respect for you.

"And until the last breath leaves my body and I rest with the others on the hill above the farm in Naples, Marco Raphael Antonelli will always have the last dance with me."

I felt Sophia squeeze my hand, and I knew I had done well. Thanks to Sophia, Amanda, Angela, Dominic and a liberal use of phonetic spelling, I had recited my entire pledge in Italian.

When I lifted my eyes from the paper to look at my husband, Dominic had his right hand on Marc's shoulder as if to steady him, and with his left hand, he was handing Marc a handkerchief with which to wipe away the tears that were streaming down my husband's cheeks.

Before I lost my resolve and my tears started again, I took the other sheet of paper from Sophia. But, I didn't need to look at it.

I had my vows memorized, and as I repeated them in English, I looked directly into Marc's eyes.

He had regained some control and the look on his face told me everything I needed to know. He took my hand, and we turned back toward the priest. I knew he was struggling as hard as I was, not to stop everything and jump into each other's arms.

We had agreed not to remove our weddings bands, so we both placed our left hands on the ring pillow for the blessing. We recited in unison;

"With this ring, I take you as my spouse and pledge to you my undying love and fidelity."

After a few more prayers and blessings, the priest pronounced us husband and wife. Marc took a step toward me, but before he kissed me, he whispered, "I must have done something right in my life because the Angels above have sent one of their own to be my wife."

Then he kissed me. It was a long passionate kiss. Much too long and much too passionate for where we were. But neither of us cared. When we finally broke apart, he gave me the greatest smile before we turned and started up the aisle.

The receiving line was outside on the steps of the church, and it was very formal in order. First, we were given a moment with Sophia and Dominic. Marc got a warm embrace from his cousin, and I got one from Sophia. Then, they traded places, and I got a more than cousinly embrace from Dominic. As he held me, he whispered, "You truly are an angel sent from heaven to make my cousin's life complete."

Dominic pressed something into my hand.

"When you two are alone, give this to my cousin."

I heard Sophia ask Marc if he would still love her.

"Always, Sophia. A man never forgets his very first love."

That made her smile, and she asked me if it was right if Marc still loved her. I gave her the only possible answer I could.

"Only if I am allowed to love you too."

That got me a beautiful smile in return, and Dominic and Sophia took their places beside Marc and me.

But first, Dominic shook Marc's hand and said, "Permesso, Signore?"

Marc nodded. Then Dominic kissed the back of my hand, looked into my eyes, nodded his head and said, very formally,

"Signora Antonelli."

Next came Donna Antonelli and the Contessa. They didn't say much to either Marc or me, but it was evident they were pleased. Marc's family was next in line.

The De Constanza men and women were all very complimentary, telling Marc what a beautiful woman I was and what a great wife I would be to him. The Antonelli woman were equally flattering, but the Antonelli men were very reserved and formal. Just as Dominic had done, as each passed us, they shook Marc's hand and said,

"Permesso, Signore?" and after Marc nodded, they each kissed the back of my hand, looked me in the eye, nodded and quietly said, "Signora Antonelli,"

And they moved on. It felt weird.

My family was next. Beth, Sandra, and Evelyn all still had tears in their eyes. Sam, Ed, and Ethan were glassy eyed. My nephews were very quiet and reserved.

Friends were last. Some people who Marc knew from the time he spent here offered congratulations and best wishes. Ron and Janette were next.

"Wow, you two really know how to get the tears flowing. There wasn't a dry eye in the house, including mine."

That got Ron an extra hug. He asked what was with the formality of some of the men. I wondered about that also. Ron said it seemed as if they were bestowing a title on me.

Marc was solemn.

"Not exactly. They were asking my permission to offer their allegiance to my bride. Signora Antonelli. It is a sign of acceptance.

"From this day forward, Catherine will forever be under the protection of every man in the Antonelli family. Just as I have previously pledged my protection to every Antonelli female."

Just as Marc finished his explanation, a very handsome couple came up to us. Marc seemed pleased to see them, but I didn't know who they were. The man, definitely Italian and very good looking embraced Marc and kissed my hand.

The woman, who was about my age and gorgeous, gave Marc more than a friendly hug, and then kissed him. When she finally let go of my husband he introduced them.

"Catherine, this is Joanna and Joe Andolenni."

The name sounded familiar, but I couldn't place it until the woman said, "The former Signora Marco Antonelli. I hope you don't mind we crashed your party."

They had been invited to our wedding in Florida and Marc was disappointed they didn't show up. I collected myself quickly and hoped I sounded sincere.

"We were disappointed you missed the wedding in Florida last week."

Her husband apologized.

"I'm sorry Signora. I had a business conference in California I couldn't get out of, but when Dominic told me about this ceremony, I thought it was a good time to visit my family."

Marc explained Joe had family outside of Rome. Dominic tapped Joanna on the shoulder, and she turned toward him and gave him the same embrace Marc had received. Then Joanna looked at my Maid of Honor.

"Is that Sophia?"

Sophia didn't know how to act. It was evident Joanna and Sophia knew each other well, but I got the feeling Sophia was uncomfortable acknowledging her. I smiled at Sophia and gave her a little head nod, and she embraced Marc's former wife.

"I haven't seen you in almost three years. What a beautiful young woman you have become."

Then I heard Marc ask, "When did you ladies get here?"

I turned to see Danielle, Stacy, and Cindy.

"We walked in just as Catherine was walking down the aisle. Just because my husband couldn't come didn't mean we had to miss this. Angie and Harry are out of town on a special anniversary vacation, and I didn't want to spoil their alone time, so I didn't tell them about this."

Marc and I got hugs, and Stacy and Joanna also embraced each other. They seemed to know each other well. I remembered Marc and Nick were good friends when Marc was married to Joanna, so it was natural they would know each other. Danielle and Nick didn't get together until about four years after Marc and Joanna split up. Joanna introduced Stacy to her husband.

"This is the woman responsible for all the money you spend on my dresses."

Stacy looked Joe over and gave Joanna a wolfish grin. Joanna smiled wickedly.

"What can I say? I have a thing for good looking Italian men."

Looking at Marc and Dominic, she added, "This one dumped me, and this on turned me down."

Turning to her husband and looking into his eyes, she said softly and very sincerely, "It turned out to be the best thing that ever happened to me."

Marc indicated everyone was waiting for us and said we had to go. The walk back was not like the procession to the church. This was more like a parade. We all walked down the center of the street, the sidewalks being so narrow. The men were singing and dancing as we made our way to the Contessa's house. When we arrived, the gates along the sides of the house had been opened, and the guests used them to enter the garden. Marc and I went into the house and up to my room.

Chapter 49 – After the Wedding

Once inside, Marc embraced me tenderly. He didn't say anything for a while, but I knew what he was feeling.

Finally, he took a step back and looked into my eyes.

"Catherine, I will never forget today. I will never forget this week. You have given your husband the greatest wedding present imaginable."

He wanted to say more, but I put my hands to his lips to silence him.

"All I want to hear from you is you know how much I am in love with you."

His smile was more than enough answer, but the words he chose were even better.

"Yes Catherine, I do know how much you love me, and I promise to spend the rest of my life trying to be worthy of that love."

We couldn't stay in the room for more than a few minutes. Guests were waiting. I noticed all of my things were gone. Marc said they had been moved to the guest house.

I handed Marc the Silver Dollar Dominic had slipped into my hand at the church. Marc smiled broadly, looked at me and nodded, but he didn't tell me what that Silver Dollar was supposed to symbolize.

Once downstairs and out into the garden, I saw a portable dance floor had been put down on the lawn, and there was an orchestra already in place. Marc led me over to the dance floor, and we danced to our favorite waltz. After the dance, I only saw my husband sporadically for the rest of the day, and never alone. We were busy dealing with our guests.

I spotted the girls sitting together and went over to sit with them for a while. Danielle, Stacy, and Cindy were with Beth and my sisters-in-law, along with Marc's sisters and Janette. They seemed to be getting along and that added to my happiness.

The main topic of conversation was how I had managed to learn my vows in Italian so quickly and why I had done that.

"I didn't want Marc's family to have any doubt as to how I felt about him,"

Stacy asked me what I thought of Joanna.

"From all I've heard from Marc and Dominic, she was a great woman, and if it wasn't for the jealousy thing, they probably still would be married."

"It was deeper than just jealousy of Marc," Stacy said, "Joanna was a nice person, and I always liked her, and we got along just fine. It was more a sense of insecurity she developed in childhood. When Marc left her, she moved back to New York to be with her family. Dominic lives in New York, and Marc asked him to keep an eye on her. Dominic finally persuaded her to seek professional help. I understand it changed her, and now she is finally happy."

As if she had a sixth sense and knew we were talking about her, Joanna stopped at the table and asked if we could talk.

I started to get up, but she stopped me.

"I know Stacy and Amanda and Angelia, and I assume the others are your family. We can talk in front of them."

We all squeezed a little closer together, and Joanna grabbed a chair from another table and sat next to me.

"Catherine, I am completely and hopelessly in love with my husband. He is honorable, honest, faithful, and everything I could want in a man, but the man you married today will always have a special place in my heart. I would like us to be friends!"

What could I say to that? Just as I was about to answer her, Marc was at the table.

"The two women who know all of my secrets shouldn't be allowed to share war stories."

Both Joanna and I smiled. She stood up, grabbed Marc's hand, "Dance with me, handsome!"

And off they went. I watched them float along the dance floor, and I knew she was right. She would always love him, and he would always love her. And, that was alright.

What Marc and I had was different, and their love for each other would never take anything away from us. And I was sure Joanna and I would be friends.

The party went on and on, long after Marc and I retreated to the Guest House. That night was magic. I don't know if it was what I had said to him in my vows or the fact I had learned to say it in Italian, but it had affected him in a very meaningful way. This was my man, and I was his lady, and nothing would ever come between us.

Dominic's prediction proved to be wrong. There was no need for the fire brigade that night. Although our lovemaking was passionate, it was also gentle and tender. Marc whispered in my ear, and although I didn't hear everything he said, I felt the meaning of his words.

Monday morning we had breakfast on the patio with our immediate family and friends. The girls were headed back to Florida and taking my family, Dominic and Marc's sisters with them.

Joanna and Joe were headed to Rome to spend some time with his family. Ron and Janette weren't ready to go home.

"The exclusive deal I have with Marc means I won't have much to do for a while, so I decided Janette and I would spend a couple of weeks in Italy as tourists."

We drove to the airport in Naples to see everyone off and then headed for the villa we had stayed in when we first arrived in Italy. Marc invited Ron and Janette to spend the day with us while they decided what they wanted to see while they were here. We had lunch by the pool and just lounged around. It had been a very busy four days, and we could all use a day off.

Marc said he and I were going to spend a couple of days at the farm, and I suggested Ron and Janette could stay here at the villa for a couple of days. After making the comment, I realized I didn't know if Marc had rented the villa for the remainder of the week.

"Marc, would it be alright if Janette and Ron stayed here?"

"Let me ask the owner."

He got up from his lounge and took a half dozen steps toward the villa. He stopped, turned, and walked back to me.

"Signora Antonelli, would it be OK if your friends stayed here for a couple of days?"

At first, I didn't understand what he was saying, and when I realized what he meant, I shouted, "This is yours?"

That got me a very stern look, and I corrected myself.

"Ours?"

That brought a smile from my husband.

"From the top of the hill to the road, and fence to fence. I bought it about five years ago. It's just about halfway between the farm and Calabria. I put your name on the deed last week."

My excitement was evident and made Marc happy.

"I've wanted to build a smaller villa on the top of the hill, just for two and use this one as a guest house, but I was waiting for the one I would share it with."

Janette asked what was on the other side of the hill, and Marc said he would show her. Ron glanced at them as they climbed the hill.

"Are you really as happy as you seem?"

My smile was my answer. Looking up the hill at Marc and Janette, I asked, "How about you? I've never seen you act this way toward any girl you've ever dated."

His smile was my answer. When Marc and Janette returned, Marc suggested, "You two can spend a couple of days here at the villa, and when you're ready, you can use one of the cars to drive to Rome, Florence, and Venice. There's a GPS in the car, and if you get tired of traveling, you could always come back and stay at the villa.

When you're ready to go home, you can leave the car at the farm, and one of my cousins will take you to the airport. Nick's daughter Pam can make all the arrangements for you."

Marc and I spent Tuesday and Wednesday at the farm and then took a shuttle flight to Venice. He wanted to take me for a romantic Gondola ride.

Anna Lee had *Danielle* meet us in Venice Friday night for the flight home. That meant another overnight flight and another chance to enjoy the benefits of making love at forty thousand feet.

Chapter 50 – Married Life

Saturday afternoon and Sunday we lounged around the apartment and Monday morning we were back at work, me to Dillman Bros and Marc to Antonelli Systems. Life began to take on some normalcy.

I called my sister and brothers to let them now we were home and had no choice but to accept an invitation to dinner on Sunday. I made arrangements to have a cell phone shipped to Sophia and set about sending out the Thank You cards. That was a chore.

We had received a list of people who had donated to St Jude's Hospital in our name, and our friends and associates had been very generous.

It was nice sharing a bed with Marc every night and not worrying about Mondays and Thursdays. Marc had a speaking engagement the second Saturday we were home. This one was in Boston, and we spent the weekend. Marc was as good as always, and we had a fun weekend.

I had dinner with the SWC girls, and all they wanted to talk about was the wedding in Italy. I also renewed my monthly girl's night out with Beth, Sandra, and Evelyn. The group grew to six when we invited Amanda and Angela to join us. The six of us became as close as real sisters.

Marc and I attempted to make out some kind of schedule. Holidays were going to be a problem for us. I had usually spent the holidays with Beth and my brothers, and Marc alternated between his sisters and his family in Italy. Now we had three places we wanted to be, and it was not going to be easy to decide where to go when.

We could alternate between my family and Marc's, and since we had all become so close, that meant we could spend the holidays altogether, just alternating whose house we were going to celebrate in. When we went to Italy, there was always the possibility of taking our Florida families with us.

True to his word, Marc had an airplane ticket in Sophia's hand the day school let out. I loved having her with us.

Married life started falling into a routine, as least as much of a routine life with Marc could be.

We did keep Marc's housekeeper on, and she did all of the heavy lifting. There wasn't much left for me to do and that left our weekends free to enjoy each other.

Marc and I left for work together each morning, and he always tried to get home around the same time I did. We ate at home most nights. The tips I had gotten from my sister and sisters-in-law plus Marc's great sauce meant we ate pretty well, and I didn't have to be a slave to the kitchen. Marc always helped with the cleanup.

I enjoyed my position at Dillman Brothers, and I found out I was pretty good at it. Business kept getting better under Teds' leadership, and everyone was happy. We kept adding new members to the team, but we took our time and picked people we felt would fit in. Ben did continue the Morale Booster parties, and they always seemed to have a positive effect on the team.

Marc and I hated being apart, but sleeping next to him every night and waking up with him every morning was wonderful.

Marc didn't mind my monthly sisters' night out or the SWC girls meeting on an irregular basis. I did take lessons in Italian, and when I became proficient enough, Marc decided to speak to me in Italian every time we were alone. He said it would help me understand the nuances and slang if I was exposed to it on a regular basis.

Amanda and Angela also spoke to me in Italian when we were together and, of course, my almost nightly phone calls from Sophia started taking place in Italian. Marc and Nick also talked to each other in Italian whenever Danielle wasn't around. I was learning, and Marc was proud of me. Of course, that made me happy.

Marc's comment about making sure Johnny wasn't in town when Sophia visited turned out to be a prediction. When the two of them met, the fireworks were like the fourth of July.

I told Sophia I had seen him first, and I had dib's and that make her blush. Suddenly, Johnny started spending more time with his Aunt Danielle, and his visits always seemed to coincide with Sophia's visits. If they didn't live so far apart, maybe something would have developed, but the distance was too great and when Johnny started at the Naval Academy, his time was very limited.

I had made a promise to Marc, and as soon as we returned from our honeymoon, I made an appointment with the NAS Security Team. My training started immediately and true to my word, I paid attention. Much of the training was Situational Awareness. Paying attention to what was normal meant knowing when something was out of place. Also, recognizing the possibility of dangerous situations and avoiding them.

I was given a new cell phone with a secret button. If I pressed that button, the NAS Security Team would know I was in trouble and exactly where I was. The physical part was just as Danielle had described. The boys held nothing back.

The theory was if they treated it as a real situation I would learn to act instinctively and not take the time to think. It was as rough as Danielle had said, but I was determined Marc would get good reports about me. I didn't want him to worry. I could still see the fear in his eyes the night we had the confrontation with Jamey.

I was happy and in love. I was totally in love with a man who I knew was totally in love with me. I did get used to being rich. I wasn't extravagant, but I never worried about money. I knew the well would never run dry. My gifts to my family were much more expensive then I was able to afford before, and I never hesitated if I wanted to buy a new dress or a pair of shoes, but overall, the money didn't have a big effect on me.

It was as Marc had said. We ate at better restaurants, stayed at the best hotels, traveled first class, but overall, we led a simple life. Family and friends were the most important things to us, besides our love for each other.

I did eventually ask Danielle how she and Nick got together. She told me the entire story one night over a couple glasses of wine. Marc was right. It was a beautiful story, and it did make me cry. I understood the way they felt about each other and why she referred to Nick as the mostest man she had ever met. I was sure the love Marc and I shared could equal it.

Marc and I both thought dinner with family and friends was a treat, and that was our main entertainment. We alternated between restaurants and dinners at home. When it was at our apartment, I went all out. Marc always lent a hand, and it was always a joy. Stacy wasn't much in the kitchen, but Danielle was an excellent cook and Cindy was pretty good too. Marc always enjoyed eating at Beth's, and all four of my sisters-in-law were very good.

What could I say? My life was as good as life could be.

Epilogue

Evelyn sighed as the maitre'd walked away after seating us. I leaned over to Sophia and whispered in Italian, "She's had a crush on that guy for years."

Sophia laughed, "I don't blame her. He's gorgeous."

I reminded her he was more than twice her age. She just gave me a wicked smile. I swear it was the same smile Marc gave me when he was being wicked.

"I didn't say I wanted to marry him!"

I couldn't help but smile. The others asked what we were jabbering about, and we both smiled. It was always fun when we sisters got together, especially when Sophia was in town. We had all grown so close it was if we had been sisters forever. Sophia and I had become extremely close, and she did become the kid sister I had always wanted.

Amanda asked me what our plans were for our anniversary. Marc and I would be celebrating our fifth.

"We both trying to get enough time off to spend a week at the villa. The small house on the top of the hill is almost complete, and we wanted to spend our anniversary there."

We alternated the restaurants we went to every month, and we had been to this one a few times, but this was the first time with Sophia. I told her this was the place where I saw Marco for the very first time. Beth, Sandra, and Evelyn looked at me.

"It was over six years ago. We were here for our regular night out, and I was telling you I was taking a break from men."

Sandra said she seems to remember something like that, but she doesn't remember Marc.

"As we were talking about my hiatus from men, the maitre'd sat a very good looking couple, and I thought the gentleman was the best looking man I had ever seen, and his date was gorgeous if a little young for him."

Evelyn looked surprised. She appeared to be bringing up a memory. Looking at me, she said, "That was Marc?"

And, after thinking about it a little longer, she added, "You're right, it was Marc!"

I couldn't help laughing.

"Leave it to you to remember a good looking man from six years ago."

Beth and Sandra laughed at my comment. They knew I was right. A good looking man never escaped Evelyn's sight or her memory.

"If he was with another woman, how did you meet him?" Sophia asked.

"A month later, Marco was introduced to us at my office. He had been hired by my company, and he was my new boss. That's how we met."

"What about the woman he was with that night?"

"Marc was having a business dinner with a client and the woman was someone who worked for him. She wasn't his date, she was one of his company's computer programmers."

While the girls talked about that night, I thought about the past six years. I still had no idea what possessed me to tell Marc I wanted a personal relationship with him. I had never been that forward with a man before.

I remembered Ted's set-up in Nashville and how Ron forced me to open myself up to Marc.

Our wedding was beautiful, but the honeymoon and the wedding in Italy where unforgettable. I was as happy as a woman could be, and it was all because of that man.

Dillman Brothers had more orders than they could handle, and the plant ran three shifts to keep up. Ted turned out to be a great VP of Sales, and we flourished under his leadership.

He and Connie married and seem happy together. I was surprised when they asked Marc and me to stand up for them. We couldn't refuse.

Artie and Susan also married as did Annie and Billy. Marc occasionally reminds me maybe matchmaking was my real calling.

I'm happy at Dillman Brothers. I learned to enjoy being VP of Specifications and Design and I am pretty good at it. I like being in the middle of decision making.

Marc's business continues to grow, as does his other investments. The money rolls in faster than we can spend it.

I did find uses for my personal account and it was nice having that freedom, even though I always made Marc aware of what I was doing.

My Italian is pretty good. I still don't get all the nuances and slang, but I practice with Sophia whenever she's in Florida and also during our almost nightly phone calls when she's at home. I'm good enough I don't need a translator when we're with Marc's family.

Between my job, Italian lessons, training with the NAS Security Team, and taking care of my man, my life is full. Full in a good way.

I never think about what my life would have been like if I hadn't met Marc. I know it couldn't have been as wonderful as life with him had turned out to be.

But, I do sometimes wonder what my life would have been like if I had allowed Nashville to keep us apart. If Ron didn't force me to open myself up to Marc, would I ever have trust in a man's love?

Marc had the Sliver Dollar Dominic had asked me to give him framed, and he hung it in his office. He did eventually tell me what the significance of that coin was. It was part of their ongoing competition with each other.

They had made a bet. The winner would get one dollar. The bet was who would marry the best woman, and even though Dominic hadn't married, he had conceded the win to Marc.

"Could it get any better than this?"

I knew it would!

331

From the Author

I hope you enjoyed this story. I really enjoyed writing it. If you did, please take a minute to write a review on your favorite retailer's website. Reviews are the lifeblood of new authors. They are the way other readers make decisions on what they will read. At this stage of my writing career, reviews are more important than sales.

If you did enjoy this story, I urge you to check out my other stories in this series. At present, there are five Romance Stories in the Danielle and Friends Series. The original story in the series is The Mostest Man. The next one, The Last Dance,

I am also working on the story of what Nick Amonti did for the government that earned him the $30,000,000 stake that started NAS Financial Group. It's a Terrorist Thriller, titled Eight Months in Hell.

And, a series based on one of the character in The Front Porch. This series will be titled: The Adventures of Riley. The first book in that series, Murder One, will be out in the fall of 2016.

If you have comments for me, please e-mail me at: NAS_Books@yahoo.com

Thank you for taking the time to read my stories. I hope you continue to check out my work.

Nick J Mercorella

Danielle and Friends Series

The Mostest Man - Available Now

The Last Dance – Available Now

The Front Porch – Available Now

The Lieutenant Commander – Available Late summer, 2016

The Cauldwell Incident – Available Fall, 2016

Other Works

Eight Months in Hell - Available 2017

Murder One – Available Fall, 2016

About the Author

Born and raised in Brooklyn, New York, I have had a very interesting if not profitable life. Married twice, divorced once, widowed once. Two wonderful children of my own and five more I inherited when I married for the second time.

I worked in management most of my life when I wasn't operating my own business. Had the opportunity to travel a great deal throughout our beautiful country, parts of Canada and Mexico and some of the islands of the Caribbean. I've visited 40 states and uncountable cities. Never been to Europe, Asia or Africa. Don't feel like I've missed much. Might like to visit Australia, though.

Coldest I've ever been was in Halifax, Nova Scotia in February. Hottest I've ever been was in Phoenix, Arizona in July. I've been in Salt Lake City in June when the sun didn't set until after nine o'clock at night. I've seen the Sierra Mountains from the observation car of a train. Sailed aboard a United Sates Nuclear powered aircraft carrier, twice. Never been in the military, but I respect all those who serve. Flown hundreds and hundreds of thousands of miles. Love to fly, but poor eyesight prevents me from qualifying for a pilot's license.

Now, I sit in Fort Lauderdale Florida thinking about love and writing Romance Novels. Not a bad way to spend my retirement years!